15/2/21

19/3/21

28/1/22

Please return/renew this item by the
last date shown to avoid a charge.
Books may also be renewed by phone
and Internet. May not be renewed if
required by another reader.

www.libraries.barnet.gov.uk

D1464532

LONDON BOROUGH OF BARNET

Published in paperback 2020
by Joffe Books, London
www.joffebooks.com

978-1-78931-174-7

Printed and bound in Great Britain by

Clays Ltd, Elcograf S.p.A.

MIX
Paper from
responsible sources
FSC® C018072
FSC
www.fsc.org

Dedicated to my dear friends Margaret and Alan Hughes, with love.

PROLOGUE

September 1993, Lincolnshire Fens.

The jogger ran steadily along the shadowy fen lanes, heading home. Across the darkening fields he could see the lights of his cottage. Just a few hundred yards and he would be passing the gates of Haines Farm, and then he was within striking distance of a hot shower and a long cool drink.

As he rounded a bend in the lane and came level with the farm gates, he slipped. A curse escaped his lips and he fought to keep from crashing down on the worn and pitted asphalt. Somehow he managed to regain his balance, and looking down to see what had caused him to break his stride, he saw a puddle of oil spreading out from the farm entrance.

Again he swore. His expensive running shoes were stained and splashed, probably ruined, he thought angrily. He looked across to the old farmhouse, and saw that a light burned in the kitchen. Still cursing, he decided to go home and change, then walk back and have a strong word with George Haines. Not only was he pissed off about his trainers, he knew that a few of the villagers took their dogs for a late walk down that lane, and most of them were wrinklies. A slip on tractor oil could mean a broken hip or wrist, or worse.

As he approached his cottage door, the security light blazed out with a blast of white halogen light. He glanced down ruefully at his feet, and froze.

He had expected to see black oil stains, but his trainers were stained with dark red smears. He tentatively touched the wet discolouration, and sniffed at his finger. His stomach roiled and a wave of nausea passed over him, then he turned tail and ran as fast as his tired legs would carry him, back to Haines Farm.

As the gates came into sight, he slowed his pace. Fear of what he might find flooded through him. He was a true "yellowbelly," a Lincolnshire-born country boy, and he'd seen some horrific accidents involving farm machinery. His mind played through a dozen scenarios of what may have happened. None of them were pleasant and they all involved copious quantities of blood.

To one side of the high double gates was a small access door. George Haines rarely locked it, and through it the young man found his way into the wide concrete area in front of the old farmhouse.

His presence activated the sensors on the security lights, and he instantly recognised the farmer by his fiery red hair and distinctive fluorescent jacket with the words *Haines Farm* stencilled across the back.

George lay on his stomach, his arms stretched forward in front of him and his fingers bent into claws. He was only a few feet from the gates and he looked as if he had been frozen in time as he desperately tried to crawl to the road.

The runner gasped. He looked up and saw the stationary tractor. Jesus! The man had run himself over! He'd seen that happen once before when a brake had failed and the colossus of a machine had lurched into its unsuspecting driver.

Yes! His legs, oh God, his legs! He clasped a hand to his mouth and fought back vomit. From the waist down, the farmer's clothing was black with blood.

'George?' The young man was no first-aider, but somehow he overcame his revulsion and felt the man's neck for a pulse. As he did, his fingers touched something slick and cold, and he snatched his hand away, falling back in disgust.

The lower part of George Haines' face had been tightly bound with wide clear adhesive tape. It was then that the runner realised that his neighbour had not met with an accident, but something far nastier.

He scrambled back through the gate and out onto the road, where crouching in the gutter, he pulled his mobile from his pocket and called the police.

* * *

The farmhouse was ablaze with lights. House lights, powerful police mobile lights, and blue flashing ones. Their shimmering rays danced across the darkened fenland and made the rural setting look uncanny.

'That's the chap who found him?' The older policeman pointed to the sweaty young man leaning against the side of a squad car. He was draped in a blanket and still wore the disbelieving, slack-mouthed expression that accompanies severe shock.

'Poor sod,' murmured his colleague, 'but at least he didn't go inside. One day he'll be very thankful for that.'

'Unlike us.' The detective inspector raised his eyebrows and gave his sergeant a resigned half-smile. He had hoped to reach the end of his service without seeing something like this again. He knew from experience that it would stay with him long into his dotage, and part of him felt cheated that he was to finish his career with such a harrowing investigation. 'Before we go in, tell me what the doctor said about this victim here.' He nodded towards the body that lay close to the inside of the gates.

The sergeant drew in a breath and repeated word for word what he had been told. His voice was a monotone, as if he were reading the information off, and the inspector knew that the officer was simply trying to keep his emotions at a distance. It didn't do to allow your feelings to interfere when you were dealing with a case like this.

A case like this. The inspector was pretty sure that other than him, no one in attendance had ever seen anything like this before. They were country coppers. They had their fair share of most kinds of crime, and maybe a little more than their fair share of fatal traffic collisions on the fast, straight roads, but deliberate, cold-blooded murder was not a common occurrence in the misty fens.

'The doc reckons that George Haines drove his tractor into the yard and switched off the engine. He climbed down from the cab, with his back to whoever attacked him. His assailant hit him across the back of the legs, just above the heel, with a heavy, bladed weapon, possibly an axe, but from the angle of the wounds, more likely a machete-style knife.'

The inspector had an immediate picture of the harvesters in the fields, wielding those wicked knives, slicing easily through the thick hard stems of cauliflowers and cabbages and placing them in the cups on the conveyor.

'Doc says it would have totally disabled him. The two blows severed both his Achilles tendons. They would have contracted up his legs like snapped roller blinds. He would have been in excruciating agony and unable do anything.'

They looked together at a long double-tracked bloody stain that led from the tractor to the gate. 'Except to drag himself away and bleed to death,' added the sergeant. He swallowed hard. 'And he couldn't cry for help, because our killer had wrapped packing tape around his mouth.'

'One thing was for sure, he crawled *away* from the house, so it's most likely that our victim knew his attacker had gone inside.'

The sergeant looked towards the farmhouse, then back to his boss. 'Time to check it out, I guess?'

The inspector nodded and they moved together towards the open front door.

They found Lydia Haines in the kitchen. It was warm, friendly and smelled of herbs, homemade bread, ground coffee and fresh blood.

When control had rung them, they had been warned that it had been a frenzied attack and to prepare themselves. The fact that they had been reminded about the counselling services available to them had spoken volumes. That was something that generally came after the event, not before it.

'Sweet Jesus! That gives "frenzied" a whole new meaning,' said the sergeant. The hollowness in his voice was not lost on his boss.

'Just try to take in the whole scene, son. Not just the victim. We need to know who and why, and we need to know quickly. We can't allow whoever did this to stay free for long.' He looked around and saw a white-faced uniformed officer standing in the doorway. 'You the local bobby, Constable?'

'Yes, sir, I took the call. First on the scene,' he paused, then added, 'For my sins.'

'You know these people?'

'Fairly well. George Haines' family have farmed this strip of the fens for donkey's years. And Lydia, his wife . . .' He glanced down at the bloodied body sprawled across the quarry-tiled floor and swallowed hard. 'She was a real community-spirited woman, into all the local stuff — WI, Guiding, church flowers. You know the type, sir, salt of the earth.'

'And not the kind of woman to get murdered,' whispered the sergeant.

'Is there a "kind?"' said the inspector slowly.

'I just meant some people are more likely to be victims than others, sir. And I don't put this lady into the "victim" bracket.'

'Because she's not a whore? Or a junkie?' He heaved a sigh. 'Right now, she's as much the perfect victim as I've ever seen. And someone out there would agree with me. Because someone saw fit to take considerable time to hack her to pieces. Someone really hated her.' He turned back to the local officer. 'Did they live alone?'

'No, sir, but thank God, their two children were being taken to the pictures by their aunt and uncle tonight. A birthday party outing for their cousin. Around ten kids went, including the two Haines boys.'

'By design, or just fortuitous?' murmured the inspector. 'Anyone else live here?'

'Two others, sir. The farm manager has a small cottage across the yard, and there's a woman who helps out with the children and the housework, like an au pair, I guess. She has a self-contained flatlet in a converted barn next to the garage. Neither is at home at present, but we've put out a call for them.'

'Names?'

'Ian Farrow is the manager. He's a divorcee, and the labourers on the farm reckon he keeps himself to himself. The au pair is a French woman called Françoise Thayer. Been here for two months, and again, she doesn't associate with the workers much.'

'Could they be having a relationship?'

'We did ask the men, but if they are, it's not common knowledge.'

'Well, one of them is the killer, or maybe both,' stated the inspector categorically.

The sergeant looked dubiously at his boss, but knew him well enough not to argue.

The inspector didn't speak immediately but looked around the room with narrowed eyes. The kitchen was of typical farmhouse design, modernised tastefully, keeping all the old features like the butler sink and the coal-fired range, but adding all the necessary labour-saving devices. 'Nothing has been stolen, so it's not a bungled burglary. And both of them knew their attacker. George was happy to turn his back and clamber down from his tractor cab, and Lydia had been pouring coffee.' He pointed first to the broken cafetière that lay close to her decimated body, then to two small coffee mugs that still sat on the pine table. 'According to the doctor, Lydia died first, so George was not yet home. As everyone else was out, she had to be making coffee for her killer. Everything says that she was completely relaxed, as relaxed as her husband had been when he returned.' He paused. 'But animals and humans have uncanny intuition about these things. They sense when something is wrong, but neither George nor Lydia sensed a threat. It was one of the two lodgers. I will stake my pension on it.'

With one last look at Lydia Haines, the inspector turned away. 'Let's allow the SOCOs to do their job, son. We have a killer to catch, and I'll guarantee that when we do, they will be the nastiest piece of work you'll ever meet.'

CHAPTER ONE

September 2015, Fenland Constabulary Headquarters, Saltern-Le-Fen, Lincolnshire.

DS Marie Evans knew that she should go home but the adrenalin still coursed through her body and kept her firmly anchored to her desk. Not that it was easy to concentrate, as her brain had decided to replay the crime scene on a continuous loop. If she closed her eyes for even a moment, Marie saw the dark blood pooling in the deep gaping wounds to the woman's ravaged body. It was as if the image had been seared into the skin inside her eyelids and a single blink was enough to bring it back.

Marie had been in the force long enough to have seen a lot of really bad stuff, but what she had seen that morning, in the remote house called Berrylands, out on the edge of the marshes, had been brutal in the extreme.

Her boss, DI Rowan Jackman, was still out at the scene. Marie smiled. He would be, wouldn't he? Jackman never left a crime scene until he knew that there was nothing left to uncover. It wasn't that he didn't trust forensics. He was like a human sponge, and he wouldn't walk away until he'd soaked up every last drop of information from the place.

Marie imagined him now, tall and straight-backed, in the midst of chaos but still managing to look as if he'd stepped off one of the pages of *Country Life* magazine. She saw his blue eyes narrowed, squinting in concentration as he tried to wring another piece of invisible information from the carnage in the kitchen of Berrylands. She wished she was still out there with him, but someone had to set up the action programme for the team and she had reluctantly volunteered for the job.

Marie glanced at the clock. Almost eleven. She yawned and logged out of her computer. She'd done all she could tonight. Her dilemma now was whether to go home, or drive back over the moonlit fen and join Jackman in the house of horrors.

One thing was for sure, she knew he'd still be there.

This vicious killing had hit him harder than usual, mainly because he'd known the victim. Not well, certainly not well enough to make his heading up the investigation a problem, but it still made it personal. It was never good to see a face you recognised when attending a sudden or suspicious death. It was as if the killer had touched you by proxy. Jackman hadn't said anything, but Marie had read it in his eyes.

Marie sat back in her chair and stared at the bulky stack of paper that she had produced in the last few hours. It was mainly background on the murdered woman, Alison Fleet, and her businessman husband, Bruce. She had been a well-known charity campaigner and he owned and managed the local Saltern brewery. They seemed to be the perfect couple, living a perfect life, without an enemy in the world. But Marie had discovered a long while ago that what you saw from the outside was rarely the truth. And even at this early stage in the investigation, she was uncovering a plethora of tiny anomalies in their "perfect" existence.

Marie looked across at the only other occupant left in the office and shook her head. 'Go home, Max. You look like shit.'

'Thanks, Sarge, I love you too.' DC Max Cohen grinned and ran a hand through his thick thatch of curly dark hair. He stretched and yawned. 'One more check to run, and I'll be off, okay?'

Marie nodded. 'As long as you do. Found anything that I should know about?'

'Nothing of gobsmacking interest, other than the fact that I don't think the purer than pure Mrs Fleet is quite as snowy as we first thought.' Max shuffled a pile of printouts and shook his head. 'I hope I'm wrong, but my guess is that if you burrow your way through all the good works and fundraising, you'll find that Saint Alison had a secret past. I'm sure there's more to her and her old man than people might think.' He looked up from his screen. 'How about you, Sarge?'

'Much the same, as it happens. Mystery after sweet mystery.' Marie grimaced at him, 'On the surface, everything in her garden seems to have been roses for the last ten years, but as I dig a little deeper, I smell manure!'

'Oh, lovely jubbly.' Max gave her a knowing grin.

Marie liked the young Cockney. Well, she did now. She liked the whole team. They were close, tight knit. They had to be, given the kind of work they undertook, but she had initially had something of a problem with Max, and it had nothing to do with his being an in-comer. Like most true fenlanders, she welcomed people from outside the county, knowing that some of the smaller marsh villages would have died without an injection of new life. No, it was simply that Max came over as a bit of a smart-arse, and he wasn't averse to voicing his opinions, especially when it meant getting one over on his younger colleague, DC Charlie Button. However, it hadn't taken her too long to work out that the bravado came from being the youngest of a large tribe of siblings from the East End of

London, and having had to stand his ground from a very early age. Plus, his parents had divorced when he was thirteen, which didn't exactly help with his attitude. And Marie had quickly noticed that even if Max chose to have a dig at Charlie, heaven help anyone else who tried it!

Now, a few years down the line, Marie knew that if you ever wanted someone to cover your back, choose Max Cohen. He did loyalty very well.

Marie pulled open her drawer and took out her keys. The call of the crime scene had been more alluring than her soft duvet. As she tidied her desk, she thought about what they had found, out in the sleepy rural village of Thatcher's Hurn.

She and Jackman, wearing protective suits, had warily entered the lovely old house, and tried to assimilate everything they saw. They had walked slowly and without speaking. The "golden hour" after the discovery of a crime was a vital period of time. It was the *only* time when the evidence was fresh, when the integrity of the scene had not been corrupted or contaminated, when what had occurred was still freshly emblazoned into the minds of witnesses. And to Marie, it was a time when something still hung around the site, something left over from the criminal's actions. To her it was like a slowly fading memory, where in those early moments, feelings, emotions and almost tangible shadows hung in the air at the crime scene before disappearing under the busy activity of forensic analysis. It was nothing spooky, it was simply an ability to read what she saw and understand what her intuition was telling her. And DI Jackman was the same, although he came at things from a totally different angle. Some thirteen years younger than her, he had travelled the academic route up the ladder. A degree in sociology from Cambridge gave him a clearer understanding of society and human behaviour than most, but his thoughts were based in theory, whereas hers were simply organic, the gut instinct of a beat bobby who'd become a detective sergeant.

Marie stared around the office. Right now her damned "organic" intuitive feelings were shouting at her that something was wrong about the way Alison Fleet had died in the kitchen at Berrylands. Marie had been overwhelmed by the impression that the whole thing had been stage-managed. Whatever had happened there just did not fit into any of the usual hypotheses. But what was it? She frowned. That was one good reason to get back out there and talk to Jackman.

'I'm going back out to Thatcher's Hurn,' she called across to Max. 'You get home and get some sleep.'

Max raised a hand in acknowledgement. 'Will do. This line of enquiry has dried up anyway. Night, Sarge.'

'Sorry, Sergeant Evans.' A civilian secretary was blocking Marie's exit, just as she was about to escape. 'The desk sergeant wants DI Jackman, but I can't find him anywhere and his phone is on voicemail.'

'He's out at the crime scene. Can I help?' Marie hoped the answer would be no, but the woman nodded quickly. 'I'm sure you can. Can you come downstairs right away?'

Marie's eyes narrowed and her tiredness magically lifted. 'What's happened?'

'The sergeant has someone in an interview room that he thinks may be of interest to DI Jackman.'

Marie beckoned to Max. 'Cancel my last words. With me, please.'

* * *

The uniformed sergeant looked pensive when Marie and Max hurried into the front office. His craggy face was etched even deeper with a mass of bewildered furrows.

'I could be wasting your time, DS Evans, but then again . . .' He stopped and rubbed hard on his chin. 'He could be just another fruitcake. God knows we get enough of them.'

'I sense another "but" coming on.'

'Yeah, well, this one has me puzzled.' He let out a loud exhalation of breath. 'Just when you think you can sum them up in a flash, someone like this comes along.' He frowned again. 'I think you'd better judge for yourself.'

He walked towards the row of interview rooms. 'He's in here, and the best of British.' The sergeant pushed the door open for them, then walked back towards the desk, shaking his head as he went.

The man was around twenty-five years old. He had thick, wavy, dirty-blond hair, pale staring eyes, and his clothes, far from suitable for the weather and the time of night, were soaking wet.

Marie looked at him with interest. He certainly didn't look like your usual druggie or petty criminal, and she saw intelligence behind that oddly disturbing stare.

'I'm Detective Sergeant Marie Evans, and this is Detective Constable Max Cohen. How can we help you?'

The young man gave a strange little laugh. It hovered in the stale air of the small, claustrophobic room, and sent a shiver down Marie's spine.

For a moment she thought he was not going to speak, then in a clear, strong voice he said, 'My name is Daniel Kinder and I murdered Alison Fleet.'

CHAPTER TWO

'What do *you* make of him?'

Jackman's voice was breaking up as he drove across the fen and back towards the station. The signal was often weak in that remote area.

'To be honest, sir, I haven't a clue.'

'I don't believe that for one moment,' echoed down the line. 'He must have made an impression on you.'

'Oh yes, he did that alright.' Marie felt again the shudder of apprehension when she'd heard Daniel Kinder give that strange laugh. 'It's just I don't know if he's barking mad, a time-waster, or . . .'

'Or a killer?'

'Mm, or a killer.' She hated to feel that way, but there it was. 'I decided to wait for you before I spoke to him anymore.'

'Have you arrested him?'

'Yes, sir, I had to. He's confessed to murder. And I've done the prelim stuff. I've searched him, seized his clothing and asked the doc to come in and see if he's fit to interview.' She paused. 'He's refused a brief, even though I urged him to have one, so I really need you here before I talk to him again.'

'Okay, I'll be with you in ten.' The line cut, and Marie was left with her confused thoughts.

* * *

'Before we go in, what do we know about this man?' Jackman straightened his tie, even though it was already perfectly centred in his crisply ironed collar.

Marie stared at her notebook, 'His name is Daniel Kinder, and . . .'

'Kinder?' Jackman asked, his eyes widening. 'Is he local?'

'Yes. He lives with his mother in one of those flashy houses out on—'

'I know, on Riverside Crescent,' he finished off grimly.

'You've had dealings with him, guv?'

'No, but I knew his father, Sam Kinder. He had some sort of business association with my family some years ago. He died a while back of some god-awful tropical disease. Bilharzia, I think.'

'I did think our man was too well-spoken to be some crackhead with a melting brain.'

'I can't speak for Daniel, of course, but his family were very well thought of. Sam Kinder was a rich man who almost singlehandedly brought water to hundreds of African villages. He worked with a Water Aid charity out there, that's where he got ill.' Jackman pulled a face. 'It was a cruel irony that he had to die of a waterborne disease.' He paused. 'I never met Ruby, that's his wife, but I seem to recall that they had just one son, although I don't think I ever knew his name.'

'Well, it seems that the mother is away trekking through Asia, trying to deal with her grief, and you're about to meet the only son. And I hope, sir, you're as baffled by him as I am.' She frowned. 'Because I'd hate to think I'm losing my knack for reading people.'

'Let's go see, shall we?' Jackman turned to enter the room, then stopped mid-stride. '*Daniel* Kinder? The name's familiar. Isn't he a journalist?'

'I haven't got that far, sir.'

'Well, if it is the same guy, he's pretty damned good.' He paused. 'But it can't be, can it? He's one of these up-and-coming young "voices" of the modern world.'

Marie shrugged then moved towards the door. 'Pass. But if that's the case, then his *"voice"* is now saying that he's just murdered someone.' She pulled open the door.

'After you, guv.'

They entered the interview room, and Jackman was immediately struck by the waves of nervous energy emanating from the young man in the paper suit. He waited while Marie unsealed a new tape and placed it in the recording machine, began the formal introductions and reiterated their suggestion that a solicitor be present. She looked hopefully at Kinder, but he shook his head and flatly refused representation.

Initially Jackman sat quietly and tried to appraise Daniel Kinder. The doctor had said that he was fit to be interviewed and in his opinion, an appropriate adult was not necessary. Jackman stared at Kinder and decided that he was not so sure. There was something about the young man that made tiny shocks run down his spine, like the notes on a scale.

He'd felt that way once before, when as a probationer he had been escorting a prisoner to a high-security psychiatric unit. There had been some kind of admin error that led to a delay, and Jackman had spent more time than he would have wished to with the "patient." He hadn't known how to communicate with the man or how to react to him. Although he'd never have admitted it to anyone, mental illness scared him.

Now he experienced a similar feeling, sitting in the interview room and looking at Kinder. Not that the man was threatening. He was outwardly calm, even if he was giving off more static than a high tension cable. It was his eyes that disturbed Jackman. The eyes told a very different story, one that was anything but calm.

'You say that you killed Alison Fleet? Perhaps you could explain how and why?' Jackman leaned forward. 'Actually, let's start with *where*, shall we?'

The man blinked rapidly then squinted, as if trying to recall it precisely. 'At her home in Thatcher's Hurn. A house called Berrylands.'

Nothing he couldn't have easily found out about, thought Jackman. The village had been featured on the five o'clock news, and the house name had not been withheld. 'And where in the house did you kill her?'

'The kitchen.' Daniel Kinder looked directly at him, an unspoken challenge in his clear enunciation.

Jackman kept his expression neutral, but he felt Marie, sitting close to his side, stiffen slightly. The site of the killing had not been released to the media. Then he considered the TV footage. Anyone with even the slightest knowledge of Berrylands could have worked that out from the positioning of the protective tents that the investigators had erected to keep the site from prying eyes.

'Okay, Daniel, so how did you kill her?'

'I stabbed her.'

'Why?' Jackman asked quickly.

For the first time the young man faltered. He gave a peculiar little shiver, moving his neck and head with a jerky movement, then very softly whispered, 'Because I have it in me.'

Jackman hadn't expected that particular answer. It should have been, "Because I hated her." Or, "Because I loved her and she cheated on me." "Because I was jealous." There was always a cause, something that triggered violent and unstoppable emotion.

'We all have it in us,' said Marie quietly, 'given certain circumstances. But very few commit murder. There is *always* a reason, Daniel, or a trigger. What was yours? What did Alison do to make you kill her?'

He drew in a long breath and said, 'It wasn't her. It could have been anyone. I was destined to kill at some point in my life. It just happened to be Alison Fleet.'

'What did you stab her with?' Jackman flung this back, trying to give the young man no time to think.

'A kitchen knife.'

For almost half an hour they questioned Kinder. Sometimes he answered immediately, at others he was vague or appeared confused, and then there were questions that he would not answer at all.

Jackman sat back, stared long and hard at Kinder, and confusion swept over him. 'Would you excuse us for a moment, please, Mr Kinder?' He pushed back his chair, stated for the sake of the tape that they were suspending the interview, and beckoned to Marie.

Outside, and a little way from the room, he leant back against the corridor wall and exhaled loudly. 'Okay, so he's got some of the details, but not enough by far.'

'Even *we* don't know what kind of knife was used yet, but she *was* stabbed.'

'Yes, but how many ways are there to kill someone? And I mean a bloody, violent death, not a premeditated furtive plan that involves hemlock or arsenic. You shoot them, beat them to death, drown them, strangle them or *stab* them, and what is the most likely in this country?'

'Stabbing.'

'Exactly.' He shook his head. 'He's guessing. He didn't do it.'

'But he's a far cry from your average time-waster, wouldn't you say?' Marie asked. 'And he's not your standard nutter either, if there is such a thing.'

'I agree completely.' Jackman sighed. 'But I really don't buy his story, and I'm not too sure how to tackle this.'

'Let's talk to him some more, sir. Throw in the fact you knew his father. Let's see if we can find the real Daniel and try to work out what he's up to.' Marie paused. 'He's giving off enough vibes to stun a charging tiger, and I want to know what is making an apparently bright, young, upwardly mobile journalist, suddenly decide that he's a murderer.'

'You have a point, as usual.' Jackman gave a chilly laugh, and together they walked back into the room.

'You are Sam Kinder's son, aren't you?' said Jackman, trying to keep his tone friendly. 'He was a colleague of my father. I was very sorry to hear about his death.'

Daniel drew his brow together, then relaxed. 'I'm his *adopted* son, Detective Inspector.' The words were said with gravity, as if they were meant to indicate something truly momentous. 'His death hit my adoptive mother and me very hard.'

Jackman nodded. 'A great loss, certainly to you his family, but to countless others as well. He was a really great man.'

It was Daniel's turn to nod. Then he thrust his head up and his jaw forward almost aggressively. 'What has this got to do with my murdering that woman? You do understand what I'm telling you, don't you?'

'I don't think you killed anyone, Daniel,' said Jackman without emotion.

Anger flared up in the pale eyes. 'I did! Why won't you believe me?'

Jackman decided to push a few buttons. 'Because you've told us nothing that you couldn't have easily found out. Especially someone in *your* line of work. You're a journalist, for heaven's sake! You have friends in the know. You hear whispers, you have contacts, you pay for little titbits of information.' He gave a slow shake of the head. 'No, Daniel. I don't know why you're doing this, but you're no killer.'

Without warning, Daniel Kinder jumped up and launched himself across the table, grabbing at Jackman's suit lapels. 'You have to believe me! Don't you understand? You have to!'

Marie calmly leant across and fixed Daniel's hands in an iron grip, and as Jackman had already moved swiftly back out of his reach, Daniel was left lying across the desk, sobbing that they must believe him.

'Okay, my friend, that's enough.' Marie slowly turned to Jackman and muttered, 'Methinks he fooled our duty doctor. We need a full medical assessment before we go any further.'

Jackman nodded and watched as Kinder was taken out of the room by two uniformed officers.

'Get the FMO to see to him!' Marie called to one of the men, above the noise that Daniel was making. 'And keep us posted on his status.'

Jackman watched the young man being half-carried, half-dragged down the corridor. 'Nothing more we can do tonight. I'm sure the doc will administer a sedative and he'll sleep until morning. Then we'll see what tomorrow brings.'

'I wonder if there's anyone we should notify?' asked Marie. 'Earlier he told me he had a girlfriend, but he wouldn't give her name. She's probably worried sick about him.'

'We'll send an officer round to his home on the off-chance that they live together. Other than that there's little we can do without his permission.' Jackman realised that his shoulders were aching. He stretched. 'Get home, Marie. Get some rest. This case is going to be far from straight-forward.'

'My thoughts precisely. See you in the morning, sir.'

Jackman watched her go, and as he often did, silently thanked the powers that be for a sergeant that he had managed to gel with. Marie Evans was a one off. She was almost as tall as he was, with rich chestnut hair that he was certain was natural, a sturdy frame and strong muscular arms and legs. He knew she spent a lot of time in the gym, keeping herself far fitter than a forty-five-year-old had any right to be. Her hair and her clearly defined and well-proportioned features always made Jackman think of a Pre-Raphaelite woman in racing leathers. Marie was also a highly skilled motorcyclist.

He smiled at her retreating figure, then shivered and allowed himself a worried sigh. An oppressive feeling swept over him and he suddenly knew that they were at the beginning of something titanic. This was not just the murder of one woman, although that was bad enough. It was the closest that he'd ever come to a premonition, and it wasn't a pleasant experience.

As he walked down the silent corridor he thought that this case had all the hallmarks of the worst kind of investigation. One where a mind truly *is* tangled and dark.

At the front desk he requested that an officer be sent round to the Kinder house, and prayed that whatever this case was about to throw at him, he would be up to it. He didn't have the years of experience under his belt that Marie did, and although he knew that he had the full backing of his team, he still had a lot to prove. No matter how dedicated he might be, and hell, he *was* dedicated, he was still a thirty-two-year-old fast-tracker from a privileged background. That was fine if you were chasing gold braid and pips on your shoulder, but Jackman aspired to something quite different. He just wanted to be a bloody good copper, and if he could earn the respect of his troops along the way, that would be perfect.

He smiled grimly as he returned to his office. He wondered what his team would think if they knew that his favourite pastime was thinking up exciting new places for top brass to stick their pips!

CHAPTER THREE

'Sorry to trouble you so late, miss, but might I ask if you know Daniel Kinder?'

The policeman was quite old, a rotund and pleasant-faced man who Skye Wynyard thought looked exactly like your archetypal 1960's British bobby.

Then the realisation that a policeman was standing on her doorstep after midnight and asking about Dan made her go ice cold. 'Yes, yes.' She stumbled over her words. 'Do you know where he is? Is he hurt? Is he alright?'

'He's quite safe, miss. May I come in and have a word with you? I'm PC Ray Hallowes.'

Skye stepped back. 'Yes, of course, please, do come in.' Words tumbled out. 'I'm Skye Wynyard. I'm Daniel's girlfriend. I'm staying here with him while his mother is abroad. What's happened to him?' The question was burning her throat. 'What happened?'

'He's at the police station, miss. He'll be staying with us for a while.'

'Is he drunk?' asked Skye incredulously. 'I mean, he doesn't drink very often, so if he'd had one too many, it may have affected him badly and . . .'

'He's not drunk, Miss Wynyard, but our inspector suspects that he is not very well.'

Skye shut up. Well, she would have to agree with that observation. For weeks now, Daniel had been far from himself. But what on earth had he done? She frowned and looked up at the policeman. 'Has he actually been arrested for something?'

'Yes, miss. But it was decided that he should be seen by our doctor. He's not . . . how can I put it? He's not acting rationally at present.'

'What has he been arrested for?' The words were leaden. Although she asked the question, Skye really did not want to know the answer.

'He's made certain claims, miss. Something that we'd like to talk to you about. You might be able to clear up a few questions for us.'

Skye pointed to a chair, then sat down on the sofa. 'What are these . . . claims?'

PC Hallowes lowered himself into the armchair and looked at her. 'He says that he has killed someone.'

Skye's hand flew to her mouth. Her first thought was that he'd been involved in a car crash, but his car was still parked on the drive. When Daniel had disappeared earlier, he had left his mobile, his wallet, his car keys, even his jacket. 'I don't understand. Do you mean an accident of some kind?'

'No, Miss Wynyard. He's confessing to murder, but as I said before, our officers are not convinced that he is in his right mind, so to speak.'

'Murder?' Skye felt a buzzing in her head and a sick dizziness. 'What on earth . . . ? Daniel?'

'I'm sorry. I've upset you. Can I get you a glass of water?' asked the policeman.

'No. It was just such a ridiculous thing to hear.' She shook her head. 'You don't know Daniel. He's the most caring, kind . . .' She shook her head even harder. 'He'd *never* hurt anyone.'

'So you've never heard him claim such a thing before? It does happen, you know. We get a lot of people come forward when there has been a murder, you'd be surprised.'

So, had there *been* a murder? Skye tried to think. Yes, of course there had. It had been on the news, a woman had been found dead out in a remote fen village. But what could Daniel have had to do with it? She looked at the police constable and frowned. 'Daniel isn't one of those people, I promise you. And I have no idea why he's said such a thing. It makes no sense.' She needed to talk to Daniel. 'Can I see him?'

'We'd like it if you came down to the station tomorrow to speak to the detectives in charge of the case, Miss Wynyard. I'm sure they would let you see him then.'

'I want to see him tonight, not tomorrow! I *have* to talk to him!'

'You can, but not tonight.' PC Hallowes' voice was soothing and he appeared completely unruffled at her outburst. 'You can see him in the morning. He's been given something to help him sleep. My visit is simply to allay any fears you might have about his whereabouts, and to ask for your help tomorrow.'

He smiled at her. Skye was reminded of a chubby, benign Father Christmas with a fractious child, and she wanted to hit him.

After the policeman had left, Skye checked the doors and windows and turned on the alarm. At least she knew now that Daniel wasn't coming home, so it seemed wise to secure the house, especially as the place belonged to Daniel's mother.

She looked around at the large, beautifully decorated rooms and felt uncomfortable.

It was a big house, and big houses were a magnet for burglars. Skye wished she could just run back to her cosy little flat, but there was Daniel's cat to think of. He loved it to pieces and she couldn't just leave it, and anyway that would mean having to come back in the morning to feed it, prior to going to the police station. And as her things were here, it made sense to stay.

Plus she was tired. Correction, she was exhausted. She should have felt relieved to know he was safe, but she was doubly distraught at knowing what Daniel had done. Confessing to a murder? What was he thinking?

Skye froze, as a realisation swept over her. For years Daniel had been unsuccessfully trying to trace his biological mother, and over a period of time his search had turned into a crusade. Now, as months passed without conclusion, he had become more and more obsessed and stressed. There *had* to be a connection.

Skye let out a painful sigh and energy drained from her. She felt as though her legs were made of lead and all she wanted to do was to sleep. With a supreme effort she dragged herself up and slowly mounted the wide staircase to their room.

As she climbed into the bed that she and Daniel shared, she wondered if the police would search the house. If they took his statement seriously, they would have to.

She pulled the duvet around her and began to worry. There were things here that Daniel wouldn't want to share, especially with the police. She eased the thick fluffy pillow under her neck and shut her eyes tightly. But what could she do?

As Skye fought back tears she felt a slight pressure on the duvet. Asti, Daniel's precious tortoiseshell cat, walked daintily up the bed and nestled into a tight ball against her chest. She placed an arm around the cat, and its warmth made her miss Daniel even more. Her fight against the tears was suddenly lost, and she hugged the cat until she finally fell into an exhausted sleep.

* * *

Daniel awoke around three in the morning, and saw himself curled up on the mattress in the cell. That was exactly how it felt, as if he were standing a little way away, observing his own sleeping body.

The drugs, whatever they had been, had made him feel weird, disconnected. But somehow he felt oddly peaceful — until he saw the blood.

While Daniel slept on, the silent watcher in the corner of the holding cell stared down at the blood dripping from his fingers and pooling around his feet. In one hand he held a knife, wicked and long-bladed. In the other there was a photograph, although the face depicted in it was now just an unrecognisable scarlet mess.

As the dark stain spread across the floor, it grew deeper. It began to cover his toes and creep up towards his ankles. He could feel the sticky fluid clinging to his skin.

He was going to drown in her blood!

With a scream, he dropped the knife and saw it disappear beneath the surface of the almost black blood.

Then he screamed again, and again, and again.

CHAPTER FOUR

The morning sunlight spreading across the fenland lit the fields with a green-gold glow that Marie felt belonged entirely to the few magical moments after sunrise. It was her favourite time of the day, and when she was driving the car, she always slowed down and turned off her radio, to allow the radiant silence to surround her. There was not a lot of peace in her life, so the little that she could acquire was always welcomed.

Today she was riding her beloved lime-green and spark-black Kawasaki Ninja, and it felt even better. You were out there, you had an added sense to complete the experience, and you needed to be a biker to understand about that enhanced sense of smell.

She could probably have told you exactly where she was, even if she had been blindfolded. The stretch that she was on now skirted organic fields that had been left untouched for a season, and the perfume that drifted across to her was a heady mix of clover and yarrow. There was something about riding in the fresh air that allowed you to breathe in the atmosphere of the land, to be part of it.

It would have been far quicker to ride straight through the town to get to work, but Marie always took her own personal ring road, a trip that circumnavigated Saltern-Le-Fen and brought her to the nick via the winding fen lanes. She loved the fens, loved the vast panoramic skyscapes, and the sometimes overpowering desolation of the marshland. It was a place that allowed to you to think clearly. Its sheer bleak beauty put everything into perspective. When the only thing you heard was the cry of an oyster-catcher, and the only thing that moved between the vista of clouds and the reedy water-world of the marsh was a leggy grey heron, you felt a rare peace.

As she drew closer to the town, she wondered what the day would bring. In her game there was never any way of knowing. She'd had a rotten night, her fitful bursts of sleep disturbed by thoughts of Daniel Kinder and the haunting feeling that there was something terribly wrong with him.

Even so, she was looking forward to seeing him again. He was so different from the usual scrotes that finished up in the interview rooms that his oddness was almost refreshing.

As the iron gates of the police station swung open, Marie felt a little shiver of excitement. The Alison Fleet murder, now given the random operational name of Nightjar, was already wearing a sinister cloak of mystery. It wasn't straightforward. It wasn't clear-cut. Nothing as yet followed a pattern, and as Marie parked her bike next to Jackman's 4x4, she wondered what they would find when they dug beneath the surface.

Saltern police station was housed in a rambling old Victorian building, once a prestigious grammar school, and before that an academy for the arts. Although its former glory was now heavily tarnished, and totally unappreciated by the steady stream of low life that passed through, it was still an awesome structure. In some parts polished banisters remained, along with stained glass windows and heavy wooden panelled hallways and corridors. Best of all, the huge high foyer with its ornately carved minstrel gallery, boasted a marble floor that, fortuitously for the police force, had been constructed using a chequered pattern of ebony-black and white tiles. This morning they sparkled from their overnight cleaning and Marie felt the familiarity of the old building wrap itself around her. This place was far more of a home to her than her small, neat estate house on the edge of town. And, she thought ruefully, she certainly spent one hell of a lot more time here.

Across the hall she could see Jackman hurrying towards her.

'Morning, guv. How's our self-confessed murderer this morning? Has he calmed down after his outburst in the interview room?'

Jackman thrust his hands deep into his pockets. 'He's in hospital.'

Marie's bright start to the day began to fade. 'Why?' she asked with a frown.

'He nearly brought the custody suite to a standstill last night. Scared the life out of the night shift. Screaming fit to . . .' He broke off and pulled a face.

'Kill?' Marie grinned. 'We are allowed to use that word, sir, even when referring to murderers, or alleged murderers.' They fell into step and headed for the lifts. 'So what happened?'

'The custody sergeant thinks it was a nightmare, but Kinder was in such a state they called the medical officer back in.' Jackman pushed the button for their floor. 'Apparently his blood pressure had rocketed, and considering the circumstances and his flaky condition, the FMO hedged his bets and had him taken to Saltern General for assessment.'

'So we can't interview him. Damn.'

'Well, the clock has stopped regarding the time that we can hold him, and his escorts have been warned not to talk to him about anything to do with the case, so I suggest in the meantime we get a bit of background on him, don't you?'

'Via the girlfriend, Skye Wynyard?'

'Absolutely, whatever kind of name *that* is. And she's due here, in,' Jackman glanced at his watch as the lift doors opened, 'twenty minutes.' He stood back and let her enter the lift.

'I'll just go and get out of my leathers, and I'll see you in the CID room, sir.'

* * *

When Jackman first set eyes on Skye, he decided that he had been wrong to assume that her parents had made a pretentious attempt to give their child an "original" name.

Skye suited her. Simple as that.

He watched her closely as Marie thanked her for coming in. Skye Wynyard had cornflower blue eyes and curly hair the colour of wet sand. And she was clearly worried sick over her boyfriend.

As Marie briefly explained what had happened during the night, the girl's curiously blue eyes widened even further. 'Hospital? Oh no! Can I see him?'

'I'm sorry, that's not possible. He's still under arrest.'

'But . . .' She fiddled anxiously with a thick bracelet. The dozens of tiny amethyst chips made an irritating chinking noise.

Jackman gave her what he hoped was a reassuring smile. 'As Sergeant Evans says, you can't see him yet, but we'll arrange a visit as soon as we know what is going on.'

Her face was full of concern, and Jackman knew that her nervousness had nothing to do with guilt and everything to do with finding herself in a situation that she didn't understand. The girl was bewildered. She flopped back resignedly in her chair.

Jackman continued to watch her. He liked to see what his professional instincts told him, then compare notes afterwards with Marie. Sometimes they agreed, but mostly he found himself backing off, cursing his purely academic surmises, and taking on board his sergeant's far more intuitive observations.

In Skye's face, Jackman saw honesty, worry, and what he took to be determination. He hoped it was determination to set things straight about Kinder.

'Do you believe that Daniel is capable of murder?' asked Marie bluntly.

'Not in a million years.' Skye's chin was thrust forward. 'He's a gentle, thoughtful, clever man, certainly not a killer.'

'And how long have you known him?'

'Around four years. We've been seeing each other seriously for two.'

'And where did you meet him?' asked Jackman.

'He came to the hospital where I work. I'm an occupational therapist at Saltern General,' she frowned, 'where he is now, I guess.' The frown disappeared. 'Daniel is an investigative journalist, and there had been a lot of bad press at the hospital. An MRSA outbreak and a big hoo-ha about poor staffing, you know the score with the NHS, but Daniel did an article about the unsung heroes. He took a very different slant on what goes on in general hospitals and saw it from the nurses' and the staff's perspective.' She looked at them almost shyly. 'When I read the piece in the paper, I was bowled over by his sensitivity, and yet the writing had real power. He didn't care that he was treading on the administration's toes and would probably get hauled over the coals. It read as if he believed every word, and when I got to know him better, I realised that he did.' She gave them a tired smile. 'It was funny, but on the day he first interviewed me, I knew instantly that we would become friends.' She turned her gaze to Marie. 'Just one of those moments, know what I mean?'

Marie nodded, and Jackman saw understanding and intense sadness in his sergeant's eyes. He sensed that she and her late husband Bill must have had a similar experience, and for a second he allowed his mind to ponder on where that magical point in time had taken place. Wherever it had been, Jackman was sure a motorcycle would have been involved. Bill Evans had been one of their finest motorbike cops and his love of racing had been the cause of his early demise. Jackman sniffed and brought his mind away from the past and back to the interview.

'So why, in your opinion, has this "gentle" man suddenly confessed to a brutal murder?' Marie was asking.

Skye drew in a deep, long breath. 'I don't know, but . . .' She stared at the desk before continuing. 'He takes his work very seriously. Perhaps things have got on top of him. He's had a lot on his mind recently.'

Jackman thought the explanation pretty lame, and was certain the woman knew far more than she'd divulged thus far. But he'd take it steadily. She could be very useful, so there was no point in alienating her on their first meeting. 'Personal things? Work-related things? Health issues? Can you be more specific?'

Again Skye Wynyard hesitated, and Marie leaned forward, her face closer to the girl. 'I can see how much you care for him, Skye, but if you really want to help him, you have to tell us everything you know. He's in serious trouble.'

Jackman took over, not waiting for a reply. 'Maybe more than you realise. Apart from wasting our time, even if he is not involved in Alison Fleet's death, he could be looking at a custodial sentence for obstructing the police in the execution of their duties. Perverting the course of justice? While we're dealing with Daniel, Skye, the real killer could be getting away with murder.'

The girl swallowed loudly, as if the gravity of Daniel's situation had finally hit home. Then she looked from Marie to Jackman and finally said, 'Could you come back to Daniel's house with me? There's something I think you ought to see.'

* * *

Half an hour later, Jackman and Marie were standing at the bottom of a narrow flight of stairs. Skye Wynyard was staring up towards the landing at a solid-looking door, a key clutched tightly in her hand. She was clearly having serious misgivings about inviting them to Daniel's house.

'Don't feel badly, Skye,' said Marie gently. 'We would have had to come here anyway. Daniel's confession is serious enough to warrant searching his home. It's so much better like this, honestly.'

'He trusts me, and now I feel I've betrayed him,' said Skye. 'Please, just try to understand that Daniel is . . .' Her voice trailed off, then realising that there was no going back, drew in a determined breath, gripped the key tighter and marched up the steep stairs, saying, 'You'd better see for yourself.'

Jackman stepped inside the long, attic room, and looked around.

It was nestled into a steeply angled roof with small boxy windows that jutted out. Dark stains on the walls beneath the dormers told him that they leaked when the wind blew the rain in from the east. He turned to look at the rest of the room and was unable to stop the gasp of shock that escaped his lips. He sensed rather than felt Marie tense beside him.

The only furniture in the room was a desk and a chair. The desk was worn, battered wood, covered in pale rings from ill-placed damp coffee mugs, and looked incongruous when you saw the state-of-the-art, touch-screen computer that sat on it. Dozens of boxes of copier paper, both new and used, were stacked unevenly in great piles across the floor, fighting for space with folders, files and carrier bags full of paperwork.

But none of this worried Jackman. It was the long wall that ran the length of the attic room that had shocked him. It was covered from floor to ceiling with press-cuttings, photographs, computer printouts and graffitied notes. And it wasn't just the volume of Daniel's research into his parentage that made Jackman shiver, it was the way it was displayed.

In the centre, at the hub of his weird wall-work, was a massively enlarged photograph of a woman. He recognised her immediately, as would most of the adult population of Great Britain.

It was a close-up of Françoise Thayer. Over twenty years ago, she had brutally and callously murdered her employers, George and Lydia Haines. Françoise Thayer, labelled by the media as the 'Blonde Butcher.' And just like that iconic police photograph of Myra Hindley, Françoise Thayer was also instantly recognisable, and equally as chilling. Hindley's eyes were shark-like — emotionless and dead, but Thayer's held a hint of dark amusement, and Jackman had always found that even more disturbing.

All the other pictures and paperwork radiated from the woman's evil smile, and below it, slightly apart, was a picture of Daniel Kinder. Beneath that, scrawled in giant, jagged black letters on the wall itself, were the words, *THE MURDERER'S SON.*

'I'm afraid that's what he believes.' Skye's voice was little more than a sigh. She shrugged, then looked beseechingly across at Jackman.

He eased his phone from his pocket. 'Sorry, Skye, but we need forensics in here, especially a photographer.'

'No! Please! This is not my house. It belongs to Daniel's mother and she's away.'

He could see her tears welling up, but before he could speak she was crying out. 'Oh God! I had no right to bring you here. No right at all.'

Marie moved quickly forward and placed an arm around the girl's shaking shoulder. 'Hey, don't worry. It's just part of the enquiry, and you've done the right thing showing us all this,' she said softly.

'Believe me,' added Jackman, 'as DS Evans said earlier, it's far better that you've invited us here. Now how about we go downstairs?' He closed his phone. 'We need you to explain exactly what this means. So we can try to understand.' He gave her what he hoped was an encouraging smile. 'Come on, let's go and sit down and you can tell us about Daniel.'

* * *

The whole thing seemed utterly surreal. They sat in the lounge and Skye felt that she should be offering light refreshments and making small talk with her guests. She needed to get her brain into gear, in order to make them understand what she knew about the real Daniel and his desperate wish to know the truth about his birth.

It took over half an hour, but at the end, she knew that she could do no more. She had silently prayed to whatever angels were around her and tried to make her speech succinct and her story credible. Maybe she had, because both officers seemed deep in thought.

'Is there the slightest chance that he's right?' The inspector looked at her with those infuriatingly sincere eyes. 'Could he be Françoise Thayer's child?'

'I've been helping Dan with his research. I've studied that woman for months but I've found absolutely no evidence, although . . .' Skye hated herself for saying what followed. 'The date of his birth does coincide with when Thayer had a child. A male child, but I can find no official registration.'

'And Thayer is dead, isn't she?'

Skye nodded. 'She died in prison, a year after her incarceration.'

'Murdered, as I recall,' added Sergeant Evans.

'They think it was a miracle that she lasted a year,' said Skye. 'Even the inmates thought she was the devil incarnate. And no one was ever charged.'

'Well, there's a surprise.' The sergeant threw the inspector a wry smile and they each raised an eyebrow.

Skye felt something like relief wash over her. For the first time since they had arrived, she thought that perhaps she had done the right thing after all. The two officers were certainly not what she had expected. For a start they had actually listened to her, and there seemed to be some kind of empathy going on between them. She wondered if they were an item. The woman was probably quite a bit older than the inspector, but that meant nothing these days. And the police force was well known for its "in-house" relationships. Daniel had written an article on the kind of jobs that were prone to produce unfaithfulness, and he had discovered that many police stations seemed to be hot-beds of illicit sexual liaisons. Not that that seemed quite accurate somehow for Jackman and Evans, even though he was good-looking in an "upper crust" kind of way. Skye decided that they were probably just a close and well-matched pair of working colleagues.

'Can you get hold of Daniel's mother?' the inspector was asking.

Skye pushed aside her thoughts about their personal lives and said, 'She's in Asia in some sort of retreat, but I don't know exactly where. Daniel doesn't either.'

'Maybe we can trace her through the embassies, or card transactions,' said Marie.

'I can tell you her last known destination, but it's rather vague.'

'What about a mobile phone?'

Skye shook her head. 'I'm afraid she took her husband's death very badly. She took off on what she called a healing spiritual journey. Cell phones aren't part of the package. The last I heard, even shoes had been discarded.'

'Risky,' muttered Evans. 'Don't they have snakes out there?'

Skye began to warm to the older woman. 'Oh yes, and poisonous ones at that, vipers, cobras, kraits . . .'

'Then let's hope her angels walk ahead of her.'

Skye looked intently at this policewoman. She had never heard a copper speak like that before. And it hadn't been sarcasm either. Skye believed in angels, and without thinking, touched the silver pendant that she always wore.

Daniel had bought it for her, and it was engraved with the words, "Protected by Angels."

'Yes, let's hope,' she echoed, then added, 'Will you be seeing Daniel? Would you tell him that . . .' she faltered. Tell him what, she wondered.

'We won't be seeing him, Skye. Not until the doctors have said that he is fit to be interviewed.' The sergeant's voice was soft, understanding. 'It's the law. We can only hold him for a certain amount of time without charging him, and when he entered hospital that clock stopped. If any of us talk to him about the case or anything relating to it, the clock starts again, and we can't stop it.'

Skye nodded, and part of her was almost glad. Until she'd seen Dan for herself, she didn't want to try to second-guess what on earth was happening in that mixed-up head of his. 'And what happens here? I'm worried about the fact that it's not my home, and policemen are going to be trampling all over it.'

'A forensic photographer will photograph the attic, then everything will be packed up and taken away as evidence. Considering the severity of the crime that Daniel has confessed to, the whole house will have to be searched, but we'll do everything we can to ensure that nothing is damaged and everything is replaced as it was, but . . .' The inspector pulled a face.

'I get the message,' said Skye. She wondered if Daniel had any idea of the mayhem that his ridiculous action had caused.

'Tell me, Skye,' asked Marie Evans. 'Regarding his journalism. Does Daniel work from home? Only I haven't seen an office.'

'No. He says he gets too distracted if he works here. He rents a small office in a friend's unit out on the industrial estate. The company is "Emerald Exotix," and his friend is called Mark Dunand. He imports exotic foliage from all around the world. I suppose you'll need to check that as well?'

The police officers stood up. 'If you could give us the address, Miss Wynyard, we would appreciate it. We will need to go there.'

Skye went to the kitchen and tore a sheet of paper off a memo pad. On it she wrote Mark Dunand's address and telephone number. 'I want to help Daniel, really I do,' she suddenly blurted out. 'He never killed that woman, I know it! I think his pain about his background has caused all this chaos.' She looked at them imploringly. 'When you do speak to him again, please try to see past what he tells you. Look at the actual evidence. Maybe you can convince him that he's terribly wrong about being a murderer's son.'

The inspector held out his hand. 'One thing we do really well, Miss Wynyard, is look at evidence. Believe me, we'll be taking everything to pieces, bit by bit, until we get to the truth.'

She nodded again and took his hand. The policeman's grip was firm and reassuring. 'The truth is all any of us wants, Inspector Jackman. And although it might be hard for you to believe, that's exactly what Daniel wants too.'

CHAPTER FIVE

Two nurses stared down at the sleeping figure of Daniel Kinder. Then one of them looked angrily at the uniformed constable who was stationed close to the bed.

'He's a hero, you know. Do you have to watch him like this?'

The officer, a man named Roger Lucas, chose not to get into an argument, and simply said, 'Sorry, miss. Orders are orders, and this man is under arrest.'

'There has to be some mistake,' said the other nurse, a chubby bottle-blonde with too much eye make-up. 'This man championed our cause a little while ago. He spent a lot of time with us. He's really nice. And,' she added almost aggressively, 'in our eyes he can do no wrong.'

'Then I'm sure he'll have nothing to worry about, but right now, we stay put.' Roger sat back on the chair next to the bed and grimaced. It felt quite strange. After all, it was usually the prisoner who was regarded with suspicion, not him.

As the nurses left, he glanced up at the glass window that separated him from his fellow escort, and his face darkened.

Outside the room, PC Zane Prewett lounged casually against the wall and talked to one of the other nurses. Roger wondered how long it would take for the girl to succumb to Zane's well-worn chat-up lines. He gave a disgusted snort and looked away. He hated working with Prewett, but today he'd had no option. His own crewmate was on leave and PC Kevin Stoner, Zane Prewett's long-suffering mate, had thrown yet another sickie. Not that Roger blamed him, poor sod. Working with that pig of a man must be hell. Roger liked Kevin, he was a good bloke, and for the life of him, he couldn't understand why he hadn't asked for a transfer away from Zane Prewett. Prewett, fellow police officer or not, was pure poison.

A different nurse entered the small room, and checked his prisoner's blood pressure.

'Excuse me, miss, but when will the doctor be seeing Mr Kinder again?' he asked politely, fully expecting another ear-bashing.

Surprisingly this woman smiled at him, and then shrugged. 'We're snowed under, so he's held up, but hopefully pretty soon.' She smiled again. 'Can I get you a coffee? I know you're not allowed to leave him and your mate seems rather involved with other things at present.'

'That would be great, if it's not too much trouble.'

She paused at the door, 'Let me guess? Milk and two sugars?'

Roger beamed back, and even though he usually took his coffee black with one sugar, said, 'Perfect.'

Her badge had said she was a staff nurse and her name was Kelly King, and although — unlike Zane Prewett — Roger was no womaniser, he couldn't ignore the fact that with her long fair hair caught back in a neat plait, she was very attractive.

He watched her go with a little sigh. A girl like that would not be unattached. If she wasn't married, then she'd be certain to have a string of admirers and he was no David Beckham.

He returned his gaze to his prisoner, who had begun to move restlessly on the bed.

Now this was a weird one alright.

Roger drew his brow together, puzzled. He'd read quite a few of Daniel Kinder's articles about local stuff, and one or two had been pretty thought-provoking. They were well-researched but with an edgy angle to them. He had always felt that Daniel should have been given a permanent slot in one of the big papers, a regular column. So why the sudden turnaround from competent journalist to sadistic killer?

Roger's first thought had been drugs. They were behind nearly all the irrational crimes that he'd ever come across. They could addle the finest brain and turn it into mush. And he was of the opinion that on the right cocktail of drugs, anyone could kill.

But then he'd heard that Daniel was clean. And if that was true, what then?

Roger looked at the good-looking young man who was mumbling incoherently in his sleep, and began to wonder whether it was all a hoax. Was it a scam? Had one of the big papers given him a chance at a once-in-a-lifetime scoop? Was Daniel Kinder some kind of undercover reporter investigating the police?

It was possible. There was a lot of bad feeling against the police right now. Two high profile cases about police corruption were hogging the headlines on an almost daily basis. His eyes narrowed. And if anyone was capable of getting under the skin and stirring things up, it was this man here. Maybe he should share his concerns with his skipper. Roger bit his lip. He hardly noticed Kelly King's alluring smile when she handed him his coffee.

* * *

Jackman sat in the passenger seat and glanced across at Marie Evans. 'You're unnervingly quiet.'

'I'm thinking about that attic room, sir.' She glanced at the rear mirror, then pulled into the fast lane. 'I sensed a real desperation in that place, didn't you?'

Jackman wondered if it had been desperation he had felt, or just mania. 'Even reading his articles, you know that Daniel has a passion for getting to the truth, and he'll find it no matter what the cost. Maybe his nature won't allow him to back off once he gets the bit between his teeth.'

'And maybe those teeth bit off more than they could chew when they started delving into his biological family tree.' She accelerated along the straight road towards the station. 'I think his inability to find answers is driving him nuts.'

'Nuts enough to kill?'

'I didn't say that,' Marie said seriously. 'But I'd say he's sliding into paranoia, wouldn't you? That stuff on the attic wall was mega-creepy.' She paused, then said, 'I know it was a while back, before you came into the force, but did you follow the trial of Terence Marcus Austin?'

'Up to a point,' said Jackman, trying to recall what he knew. 'He was the young man from Sheffield who murdered his whole family, wasn't he?'

'And several others. He was plagued by obsessive thoughts, and sadly no one saw the warning signs until he'd killed seven people — three children and four adults. If someone had looked at him earlier they would have seen all the classic symptoms of schizophrenia.' Marie indicated and slipped the car neatly back into the inside lane.

'He degenerated rapidly. In eighteen months he'd gone from university graduate to ruthless killer.'

'Are you suggesting that Daniel Kinder is a schizophrenic?'

'I've no idea, I'm not a shrink. But Terence Austin kept a diary, a notebook full of his thoughts, and I saw it.' Marie gave an involuntary shudder.

'You sound like you wish you hadn't.'

'Stuff of nightmares.' She pushed the window button, leaned out and flashed her identity card at the security camera on the entry gate to the police station car park. 'The worst thing was the way it went from perfectly normal comments and almost boyish doodles, to terrible graphic images and horrible scribblings about his unimaginably insane beliefs.' She drew in a breath. 'I don't know why, but as soon as I saw that attic wall, I thought of Terence Austin's notebook.'

Jackman released his seat belt and stepped out of the car. 'And yet, if you removed the two main pictures, it could have been one of those brain-storming techniques that supposedly aid problem-solving.'

Marie slammed her door and flicked the locking device. 'Or one of our own whiteboards. I know I'm probably being neurotic, but that was the impression I got, that something was escalating.'

'I don't doubt that you're right,' said Jackman, as they walked across to the main building. 'As soon as it's all been catalogued, we'll reconstruct that wall exactly as it was, and see what everyone else has to say about it.'

'Do you think we could get a psychologist to give us a professional opinion?'

'I'm going to talk to the super about it.' Jackman wasn't looking forward to that particular meeting. 'We need all the help we can get, budget or no budget.'

As soon as they were inside, a civilian approached them and said that the desk sergeant wanted a word.

'What now?' muttered Jackman.

The uniformed sergeant was a stocky man with a shock of prematurely white hair and a ruddy complexion. He beckoned them into the back office and closed the door.

'This may be nothing, but I thought you should be aware that there is considerable bad feeling being extended to our chaps down at the hospital.' He ran a beefy hand through his snowy thatch and shrugged. 'PC Roger Lewis has just rung in and said that they are being called "bad guys" because of Daniel Kinder's almost saintly reputation. His newspaper article, the one that turned them from an irresponsible shower of apathetic layabouts into sparkling angels, has given him a lot of fans in that neck of the woods.'

'Kind of to be expected then, isn't it?' said Jackman, sounding unimpressed.

'Fair enough, but PC Lewis actually rang me from the gent's toilet. There's a very high possibility that someone slipped a laxative into his coffee.'

Jackman's first thought was to laugh, and he noticed Marie trying to stifle a giggle, then he thought about it. Daniel Kinder could well be a sadistic killer, and his adoring nurses were compromising their security, just because he had supported their cause.

Sergeant Jim Masters waited until the penny dropped. 'It's alright. I've asked the super to have a strong word with the authorities at the hospital, and I've doubled the number of officers in attendance there. I'm aware that the hospital staff don't know exactly what Kinder has or might have done, but that sort of behaviour is not good enough.' He paused. 'But that's not what I wanted to tell you. PC Lewis has a theory.' He relayed the constable's idea that Kinder could be trying to get "inside" for an exclusive story.

'And he came up with that little gem while he was in the karzi? Nice work, in the circumstances. I'm impressed,' said Marie.

Jackman glanced across at his sergeant and saw doubt behind her smile. She was wondering the same thing as him. Could Kinder be *faking* it? And if he was, what the hell was he looking for in Saltern police station? What, or who was the object of his interest?

He thanked the sergeant and they walked slowly back to the wide staircase that led up to the second floor. Neither of them spoke. Then, as they reached the first landing Marie stopped, and gripping the polished wooden banister rail, slowly said, 'Roger Lewis is a good, solid copper. If he's right, this could be a serious problem for us.'

'Agreed. There's a very fine line between deranged and cunning. And if this is some clever scam to secure a story, what could be so important that it's worth risking getting banged up for?'

Marie shook her head. 'I can't begin to think. His career, his reputation, everything would go, *and*,' she paused, 'so would his relationship with Skye Wynyard, because I'm one hundred per cent certain that girl is worried sick over Daniel Kinder.'

Jackman pulled a face. 'She could still be worried sick if she knew that he was about to go after a scoop and was prepared to lose everything, including her, if he got it wrong.'

They walked the rest of the way to the CID room in silence.

* * *

Daniel Kinder saw the black uniform next to his bed and felt a surge of relief. He would have felt even better if there had been a metal grip around his wrist. It would have meant they were really taking him seriously. His mind wandered. He'd heard that PACE, the Police and Criminal Evidence Act of 1984, had turned everything around in favour of the criminals, so maybe they weren't allowed to cuff a suspect anymore.

He tried to focus on the policeman, but his eyelids felt as if they were made of concrete. He blinked, and everything in the room had changed. The policeman now stood close to the door, and a nurse was doing something with a needle and a cannula taped to the back of his hand. He wished that the woman was not a nurse. He wished she was Skye. She was all he wanted right now. No drugs, no fussing, no nothing, just his beautiful Skye. He blinked again, and the man was back beside his bed. What the hell had they given him? He was sleeping between blinks!

He groaned, and felt himself slipping away again . . .

* * *

Young Daniel looked around the unfamiliar room. It was plain, with stark white walls and the only furniture in it was two chairs. But what chairs! He sat in the huge soft leather armchair and wondered how much it must have cost. Hundreds of pounds, he guessed.

He could hear his parents talking softly to the man who was about to join him.

They stood just outside the room, but he could hear some of what they said, and he heard words like "anger", "unreasonable" and "cause for concern."

He had no idea why he was here. Things just seemed to happen to you when you were young, and no one ever explained why. He had seen his headmaster and his father talking, in what his mother would have called a "hugger-mugger" manner, sort of secretive and serious. But that was nothing new. The funny thing was that he rarely saw other parents in the headmaster's study. Sometimes Daniel felt that he was being watched, studied, assessed. When he'd mentioned it to his mother, she had laughed and told him not to be silly. In an expensive private school like his, every child was carefully monitored. It was part of the service.

The door clicked shut, and a nervous sick feeling crept into him. Why was this happening?

'Hi, Dan. I'm Conrad Young, and your mother and father want me to have a chat with you. Are you okay with that?' A tall man with thick brown hair and heavy dark-rimmed glasses flopped casually into the other chair.

The man's voice was deep and calming, and Dan's fears slipped away. 'Sure, although I don't know why I'm here.' He hoped he sounded grown up, even though he was not yet nine.

'I'm sure we'll find out as we go along, won't we?' He reached into a pocket in the side of his chair and removed a handset. 'Seen one of these before?' he asked pleasantly.

Dan looked up and realised that the room lights were fading and the wall opposite him was no longer white, but a soft golden yellow. As he looked it changed to orange, then to red. He watched the rainbow colours and said, 'That's really cool.'

'It's a light box. Helps you relax. Helps lots of things, actually.'

Dan breathed in and sank even further into the comforting thickly-padded leather seat. He'd like a room like this. Maybe his father . . . ? He started to think of ways to approach his dad, but the man was speaking again.

'So tell me, why did you hit your friend?'

Dan didn't feel so comfortable any more. So that's what it was all about. Lucas Rickard and his stupid Power Ranger.

'You hurt him, Daniel. Did you mean to?'

This was too ridiculous to be true! It was just some fight, over a toy that got broken. End of. He stared down at his hands. They had been folded calmly in his lap, and he saw that he was now digging his nails into his palms hard enough to make deep indentations.

'He said I broke his Power Ranger, but he did it himself. He hit me first. It was nothing, just a stupid fight.'

'You broke his arm.'

'He fell over! I just pushed him a bit to get him off me. He was yelling and screaming and I wanted him to stop.' He swallowed, and his voice dropped to a whisper. 'I only pushed him.'

'Okay, Daniel.' The man smiled at him, then looked away and stared at the wall as it changed from soft lilac to pink. 'You're right. Kids fight all the time.'

'I don't.'

'But you did that time, so what was different?'

Dan felt thoroughly miserable. He'd seen awful fights at school. The kids involved received a dressing-down and if it was really bad they were excluded for a while, but they didn't get sent to some weird clinic. He ignored the question and asked one of his own. 'Are you a doctor?'

'Yes, sort of.'

'Do you operate on people? Cut them open?'

The man smiled. 'I'm not a surgeon, so no, I don't get to do the gory bits.'

His smile was reassuring and Dan began to feel safe again.

'It's people's minds that I work with and children's minds in particular.'

Dan leant forward, his eyes wide. 'You're a shrink?'

'I study behaviour. What makes people act in a certain way.'

Dan flopped back. 'Then you're talking to the wrong person. You should have Lucas Rickard in here. *His* behaviour needs some serious attention.'

'Tell me about Lucas.'

'He's a bully and a liar. And he's *not* my friend.' Dan stared at the soft green wall as it slowly became the colour of the sea when they were on holiday. 'I have to play with him sometimes, because of something my dad calls "networking."' He frowned. 'His dad is always creeping around mine, trying to get my father to invite him to places, like stupid golf clubs and things. I know my father doesn't like him, but he's called an investor, and that apparently means I have to be nice to Lucas.'

'But Lucas makes you angry?'

'Injustice makes me angry,' Daniel said emphatically, with very adult certainty. 'He broke the toy and because he was scared of his father, he blamed me. Now *I'm* sitting here and *he* has a new Power Ranger. That's not fair, is it?'

'No it's not.' The man looked at him thoughtfully. 'Can you tell me exactly how Lucas finished up with a broken arm?'

'I told you, he fell.'

'Describe what happened.'

Daniel opened his mouth to begin, then closed it. Because he couldn't describe what had happened. And he couldn't lie either, that would make him no better than Lucas. 'I can't remember,' he said finally.

There had been a gap. A very small gap, but there it was. One minute Lucas had been pummelling him and yelling at him, then his "friend" had been sitting on the floor howling fit to kill and nursing a limp arm.

'I can't remember.'

* * *

Daniel heard himself speak the words, and saw the policeman's head jerk up.

'Ah, you're back with us.'

Daniel blinked, looked around the hospital room, and this time everything stayed where it was. 'I guess so.' His mouth felt as dry as chaff and his head throbbed like he had some super-hangover. At least they wouldn't interview him. He knew police procedures well enough. All he needed to do now was convince the doctor that he was fine, that his trip into police custody had simply overwhelmed him, and he'd be taken back to the station and locked up again. Thank God!

Daniel let out a long relieved sigh, and closed his eyes again.

CHAPTER SIX

'Panic attack, nothing more.'

Jackman stared suspiciously at Superintendent Crooke.

'And there's no use looking at me like that. The doctor said his blood pressure is now normal and declared him fit to interview. He'll be back with us in a couple of hours, and the clock starts again.' She glared at Jackman. 'So you guys need to get your fingers out, we don't want Operation Nightjar hanging around like a bad smell. He's one of two things, Jackman, a time-waster or a killer, and it's down to you to make up your minds which, and sharpish.'

Superintendent Ruth Crooke was a slim woman with pointed features, thin hair and a permanent expression of displeasure. She had a strange way of contorting her narrow lips when she was thinking, which made her look as if she were trying to swallow something unbelievably bitter. Marie had suggested it might be her name that had given her such an acerbic expression. It couldn't have been easy being a rookie police officer with a name like Crooke.

'And has he had a psychological assessment?'

'The A & E doctors have had the psych department take a look at him, and he's exhibiting no outward signs of any kind of mental disturbance.' Crooke exhaled noisily. 'So,' she looked pointedly at her watch, 'in a very short space of time, he'll be all yours. I suggest you go prepare your team and sort this out.'

'I was hoping that we could get a psychologist's opinion on the creepy montage that Kinder decorated his attic wall with, ma'am. Will the budget stretch that far?' Jackman gave her his best smile, and added, 'It would help to speed up the process.'

The woman's lips tightened until they almost disappeared. 'Inspector, the budget is barely covering toilet paper. And getting someone in from outside the police service costs mega-money.'

'Haven't we got anyone of our own?'

'There's no one I'd trust with something of this nature, and as the Fenland Constabulary doesn't warrant a police profiler, it could be difficult.' She looked at him, worry lines scratched across her weathered skin. 'I'll see what I can do, but no promises.'

Beneath the lines and the frowning countenance, Jackman remembered the fearless copper who had once loved nothing better than getting stuck in, no matter how dire the situation. Ruth Crooke had been a bright light, a tigress of a policewoman who had mounted the ladder with help from no one. Until she went one rung too high, and found to her horror that she had stepped out into thin air. Overnight her job description had changed from being a senior crime fighter to a desk-bound administrator. She no longer waded in to face off with the villains, now the only things she battled were targets, budgets, protocol, and agendas for senior management team sessions. Jackman knew she hated it all. He was one of the few who saw the sadness and bitterness concealed behind those tight lips.

'Much appreciated, ma'am. Thank you.'

* * *

Back in the CID room he found all three members of his team carefully working on a new whiteboard. They had set it up next to the existing one, which bore a smiling photograph and the victim's name, *Alison Fleet*.

'I got the photographer to fast-track the pictures of the attic wall, guv. As we won't be able to get the original material, we've used copy photos. We've isolated each item, enlarging it and printing it off.' Max looked pleased with himself.

'Excellent. That will save a lot of time. How's it going?'

Marie looked at their handiwork and raised an eyebrow. 'Well, I wouldn't hire him to do a make-over on my house. I think he was either high, pissed or—'

'Barking mad.' DC Charlie Button finished off the sentence for her.

Jackman smiled. Charlie was the youngest member of the team, a scruffy twenty-two-year-old with unruly hair and a spotty complexion. He looked more like a naughty schoolboy than a police officer, but the lad was willing. Willing and eager, and he occasionally had bursts of pure brilliance, which usually involved picking up on some blindingly obvious point that everyone else had missed completely.

Jackman turned to study the recreation of Daniel Kinder's visionary, schizoid artwork, and felt a chill. Even though they had lost the intense, deranged feeling of the old attic room, seeing the montage in this clinical setting made the hairs on the back of his neck rise up.

He stood there for some time deep in thought. Then he heard Charlie Button's voice breaking through the cacophony in his brain.

'*Can* killing be inherited, sir? I mean, even if he was that butcher woman's natural son, it wouldn't necessarily follow that he'd be a killer too, would it?'

Jackman tried to recall his college lectures. 'That's one for the experts, Charlie, although in Kinder's case I would be very surprised. As an adopted son, Daniel had a wonderful childhood, and a privileged upbringing. It's far more likely to be "like father, like son" in the instance of someone who had personally suffered at the hands of a brutal parent. I think it's much more about conditioning and desensitisation at an impressionable age than the predisposition to kill being a congenital thing.'

'And what if he simply *believed* that it was possible?' asked Marie. 'Sod all the rational thinking and the medical facts. If he believes it's true, then he could kill, couldn't he?'

'Yeah, mind over matter,' said Max emphatically. 'If the silly bugger's brainwashed himself into accepting that he has it in him to murder, then it's easy-peasy, isn't it?'

Jackman listened to them and nodded. 'Quite possible, but it's also possible that he is a very clever and devious man who has found an extraordinary way of getting into the heart of this police station.'

'But why?' asked Charlie.

'Because he's a bloody journalist,' growled Max. He turned to Jackman. 'Do you think there's something dirty going on within these walls, sir?'

'If there is, then I certainly don't know about it, but I think we should tread carefully with Daniel Kinder. Everything by the book, and meantime, keep our eyes and ears open. If Kinder has had a sniff of something unpleasant going on in Saltern-Le-Fen, then we need to get to the source of it before he does, okay?'

'Lovely,' grumbled Max. 'Not just a bleeding nutter and a poor dead woman, now we have to contend with an enemy within.'

'A *possible* enemy within, Max. We don't know, but it's a warning to be careful.' He drew in a breath. 'Now, have we got Kinder's computer from the attic yet?'

'Already with the techies, sir.' Max grinned. 'And I've made sure that Orac is dealing with it personally.'

'That's not her real name, is it? Please tell me it's not!' Jackman conjured up a picture of the tall, broad-shouldered IT chief with her white-blonde hair cut in a scary Mohican, and the oddest eyes he had ever seen. 'And what *is* it with those eyes?'

Max gave him a tolerant smile. 'The name? Well, you obviously don't like cult sci-fi, do you, sir? And the eyes — oh yeah!' His smile became mischievous. 'I'm reliably told they are mirror lenses. Makes the irises look like metal, like polished silver.'

Jackman was totally bemused. He wanted to ask why, but decided to protect his street-cred and instead gave a slightly bored shrug. 'Well, I *knew* they were contact lenses, of course. It was just that the name didn't seem to mean anything.'

'Orac was the supercomputer in *Blake's 7.*' Max looked at him hopefully, but since there was no response, continued. '1978 British sci-fi TV program. Orac was terse, short-tempered, talked down to humans, and its inventor gave it a massive ego. Starting to ring any bells?'

'I've never heard of it, but the description sounds vaguely familiar.'

'On the plus side, Orac was extremely valuable, could access limitless, critical information and could hack into any and every strategic master command computer.'

'Ah, well, now I *do* see the connection.'

'Good, because she'd like to see you later today. She reckons it's a basic system and she'll have stripped out anything interesting by close of play.'

'Wonderful. Can't wait.' In truth, Jackman found those eyes so fascinating and distracting that in any conversation with the IT Amazon, he was immediately on the back foot. There were very few people who could make him feel inadequate, but Orac was one of them, and she did it with bells on! Maybe he'd send Marie to pick up whatever info she'd sucked out of the unfortunate machine.

He looked at the clock. 'Right, Charlie, I'd like you to organise some uniforms and go visit that place where Kinder has an office. It's in the Fendyke Endeavour business park, a foliage importing company called Emerald Exotix. It's owned by a friend of Kinder's called Mark Dunand. Pick up anything relevant, stuff he's working on, contact details, and there should be another computer there, we'll need that too. Kinder will be back with us in an hour or so, so I'd like you all to collate what we've already got on him. Gather up everything we have, and the sergeant and I will go over it before we resume our interviews. The main thing we are looking for is a connection, no matter how tenuous, to link him to Alison Fleet. Quick as you can, guys. Like it or not, we're back on borrowed time.'

Jackman returned to his office, closed the door and for a moment relished the silence that enveloped him. The old building had afforded him a much grander office than his position as humble DI warranted, but all the rooms were big with high ceilings and long casement windows. It was how he had furnished it that made the difference.

Jackman liked to dress well, favouring well-cut suits, but his office was something else altogether. It might have belonged to Dickensian times. It was more like some elderly professor's library than the working domain of a modern young detective inspector.

One whole wall was shelved from floor to ceiling, and every inch was occupied by books. He had replaced the cheap metal-legged veneered desk provided by the constabulary with one of solid oak that he had picked up at a house-clearance auction. With its maroon leather inlaid surface, it suited the room perfectly. A green shaded banker's lamp sat on one corner of the desk, and instead of the usual official police passing out parade, the only framed picture was that of a powerful grey Anglo-Arabian event horse.

Jackman absentmindedly reached out and touched the photograph. 'Hello, my friend,' he whispered. This was his one true passion, apart from the police force. As a young man his precious Glory had carried him to win an assortment of cups, trophies and rosettes for eventing. When Glory had died, he had been inconsolable for months, and he still got a lump in his throat when he saw the video footage his mother had taken of the two of them in action.

At his home, in the tiny village of Cartoft, the walls were covered in photographs from his childhood, and in almost every one was an animal of some kind, mainly his beloved horses. Maybe it was a good thing that he had never married, for there would be no room for wedding photos. He smiled ruefully, because his mother would have disagreed. Strongly. Every letter she sent him — proper letters written with a fountain pen — she reminded him of his eligible bachelor status and how he should rectify that situation as soon as possible.

Marriage was most definitely not on Jackman's list of priorities. He liked things the way they were. He had a lovely home and, fortunately, a local couple to look after it while he spent long hours at work. Mill Corner had been a working windmill in the early nineteenth century. Now, although the sails were gone along with the "onion" cap, the tower still stood, and the attached buildings had been converted into a very comfortable house. He planned to use the outbuildings for stables, and when he finally retired he would once again have equine company.

A knock on the door broke into his reverie.

'The superintendent wants to see you, sir. She said to say that it's urgent.'

Jackman thanked the civilian, let out an exasperated sigh, and followed her out. A second summons into the super's domain so soon after the first could only mean trouble.

* * *

'Rowan. Come in and sit down.'

His heart sank. This was real trouble. Ruth Crooke using his first name was always a bad sign. She wasn't alone in her lair. Standing ramrod straight and wearing a face like a granite memorial, was Detective Chief Superintendent Wilson North.

'We've got a problem. I'm doing my best to keep it under wraps for the time being, but . . .' She drew in air and glanced anxiously across to the chief.

'Another woman's body has been found.'

'What?' Jackman was honestly shocked. 'Where?' A mass of contradictory thoughts gathered in his brain. Another murdered woman. Given that he was in custody, Daniel Kinder couldn't possibly be responsible.

He tried to keep his voice level. 'I'm assuming that we suspect murder, ma'am?'

'Yes, unless the victim managed to slit her own throat, after caving in the back of her skull.'

Jackman was pole-axed. He didn't need this right now, not with Kinder's imminent return and the time restraints on the interviews. 'You said her throat had been cut? Would that be in the same manner as Alison Fleet?'

'It seems that way, but we need you and the forensics team to get in there and take a look.'

'Well, at least we know it can't be Daniel Kinder.'

'Don't be so sure, Detective Inspector.' The chief's words hung like a guillotine blade over Jackman's head. 'We need the pathologist for the full facts, but it appears that she's been dead for a while.'

'A while?' Jackman gave a quick thought to the humid, warm weather and could almost smell the crime scene from where he stood.

'A while.'

As there was obviously going to be no way around this, Jackman decided he'd better get his head in order. 'Right, well, do we know who she is? Was she found in her own home?'

'The officer who discovered her could see nothing to help with identification without compromising the integrity of the scene. And she was found dumped in a derelict building that is awaiting demolition.' Ruth Crooke raised an eyebrow. 'That's how we've managed to keep everything quiet.' She paused. 'So far.'

'Okay, where is she?'

'On the road into Bracken Holme village, a mile or so before Frampton Shore. There's an old public house about half a mile out on the old London road. Been boarded up for months. Lost all its trade when the main dual carriage way was built. The wrecker's ball was due in next week.'

Jackman stood up. 'I'll take DC Cohen with me. That will leave DS Evans and DC Button free to begin the interviews with Kinder. Has the pathologist been notified?'

'He's en route from a court case in Lincoln. He'll meet you there. Now go!'

CHAPTER SEVEN

Jackman stared at what was left of the Drover's Arms. It had obviously never been picturesque. A bog-standard farm workers' pub, the sort that had no problem with its patrons wearing Wellington boots, even if half the farm-yard was still clinging to the soles.

They had been instructed to drive round to an area of hard-standing at the back of the derelict building. There were two police cars already there, discreetly parked behind an old store and invisible from the road. For once it seemed that the instruction to proceed "softly-softly" had been closely adhered to.

A woman constable hurried towards them, stopped, and beckoned them over to an open door in the rear of the dilapidated public house.

'She's through here, sir.'

Jackman heard the unsteadiness in her voice, and although the woman displayed no outward shock, he knew that she was shaken to the core. 'You found her?' he asked gently.

The WPC nodded. 'Had a shout about some kids car-rying a petrol can on the handlebars of a bike. A local saw them sneaking around the buildings here, and my partner and I came to check it out.' She shook her head. 'I wish that's all it had been, just a couple of kids messing about.'

Jackman looked around. Faded plastic flowers still hung limply from a mildewed hanging basket on a rusted wire chain. Advertisements for real ale, torn and almost unreadable, clung to the walls. Rubbish littered the entrance, and even from the outside there was a smell of damp and rotting vegetable matter.

'I don't think it ever had any Michelin stars, guv,' muttered Max, kicking at an orange net bag filled with festering blackened carrots.

'Probably not,' agreed Jackman.

'Even in its heyday it was the kind of pub where you wiped your feet on the way out,' added the WPC dourly. 'I've been to that many disturbances here over the years, I was glad to see it go. Thought that was the end of it.' She pulled a face. 'But here we are again.' She stepped inside. 'Take care, there's junk and filth everywhere.'

Not wrong there, thought Jackman as he sidestepped a pile of dog mess.

At the end of a long, narrow hallway they saw another uniformed figure.

'Sorry, sir, but I had to come up for air. The smell down there is something else.' The young officer was a pasty shade of yellow, and Jackman felt certain that he had recently been reacquainted with his lunch.

'Where is she?'

'In the beer cellar, sir. I'll show you.'

'Just tell us. No need to get another lungful if you don't need to.'

The policeman smiled gratefully. 'Go down the steps and turn left, sir. The barrel room is straight ahead and the victim is on the floor behind a stack of plastic crates.'

Jackman nodded to Max, and they began their descent of the steep stone stairs.

'Beer cellars are usually cold,' said Max hopefully. 'Maybe it won't be that bad.'

Jackman was a few steps ahead, and already the unmistakable stench was in his nostrils. 'Sorry to tell you this, my little Cockney friend, but you are very wrong.'

Max gagged as it hit him. 'So I am. Oh bugger! How I hate that smell!'

'I'd be very worried about you if you didn't.'

The cellar was far from cool. It was clammy and airless. Before they left, the owners had thrown everything of no value into the basement, and shut the door on it. Jackman saw broken chairs, tables and pictures. Stained cushions, filthy tea-towels and cardboard boxes littered the floor. All the barrels had been removed, no doubt by the brewery, but from the ceiling hung the lines and the "splines" that had carried the beer up to the bar. And then he saw the stack of blue plastic crates. They formed a welcome barrier between them and what they had come to see, but Jackman knew that he didn't have the time to hesitate.

'Okay, let's see what we've got.'

Together they approached the wall of crates, and tentatively looked round.

Jackman switched his brain to work mode, shut off his emotions, and simply logged what he saw.

Caucasian, fair hair, age difficult to determine, but from the rags that clung to her body, rags that had once been fashionable clothes, Jackman estimated the woman to be around twenty-five. She lay on her side, allowing him a view of the massive head injury, the torn throat and the shattered teeth. Sadly these weren't her only injuries. It took some doing to maintain work mode, but with an extra effort, he continued to make mental notes. The knife that had sliced into her throat had also inflicted dozens of other lacerations, and as he'd seen before with Alison Fleet, her clothing had been cut through, showing stripes of flesh beneath. He thought back to Alison and saw again her lightly tanned skin beneath the fine material of her blouse and skirt. Here there was only dark, putrid, decaying matter. Her feet were bare, the blackened toes nibbled by rodents, and Jackman didn't need a pathologist to tell him that this poor soul had been dead for a number of weeks. And that, he thought vaguely, puts Daniel Kinder squarely back in the frame.

Max had said nothing, and when Jackman turned to see if he was alright, he saw the young detective carefully making notes in his book. He looked up when he realised that he was being watched, and asked, 'Is it the same killer, do you think, guv?'

Jackman stepped away from the body. 'In my opinion, yes. We'll have to wait and see whether the pathologist agrees.'

'But not for long,' added Max in a whisper. 'Speak of the devil, sir.'

Jackman turned around and saw another figure carefully making his way down the steps and carrying a bulky bag.

'I hope you two are protecting my evidence?'

Jackman forced a smile. Try as he might, he had found it impossible to warm to the man. Dr Arthur Jacobs had a strangeness about him that Jackman could not fathom. In his experience most pathologists were odd. Some were extremely unsettling, and a few downright scary, but Jacobs possessed a detached stony coldness that matched some of the occupants of his mortuary. If Jackman had been asked for one word to sum the man up, he would have answered, *spiritless*.

'We've touched nothing, Dr Jacobs. And neither shall we.' He fought to maintain the smile. 'But I'm going to ask two questions of you, if I may?' He paused for a split second and as the pathologist opened his mouth to speak, he added, 'Oh, and don't worry, neither refer to the dreaded time of death.'

Jacobs allowed his bushy grey eyebrows to settle and said, 'Good job too.'

'I need to know if there is any identification on her, and as you also dealt with the body of Alison Fleet, sir, I'm anxious to find out if we are dealing with another victim of the same murderer.'

'That shouldn't be too difficult to ascertain, although I'm saying nothing official, understand?'

'Perfectly.'

He and Max waited patiently while the man moved carefully behind the screen of plastic crates. They heard several grunts and murmured words as the man worked, then after what seemed an eternity Jacobs stood up and looked at them grimly.

'First, there is nothing on her to help you identify her, and don't bank on help from dental records either. Our killer has pretty well decimated her jaw and teeth. And in answer to your second question, in truth I can't be certain, but there are several similarities to the previous death, and probably too many to ignore.' He drew in a long breath, seemingly immune to the terrible smell of death that hung in every corner of the cellar, and said, 'I suspect that my findings will show the killer to be the same person who murdered the Fleet woman.' His thick eyebrows drew together. 'But until you receive my preliminary report, assume nothing. Is that clear?'

'Crystal, thank you. I look forward to reading it,' Jackman replied icily, and tilted his head towards the stairs. 'Come, Max. We've got a lot of work to do.' He thanked the man again and hurried up the stairs, wondering whether he was escaping the crime scene or the pathologist.

'You don't like him, do you, boss?' Max looked at him shrewdly as they stepped into blessed fresh air.

'He's good at his job, and that's what matters,' answered Jackman.

Max sniffed. 'Fair enough, but if I snuff it unexpected-like, ship me over the county boundary. I don't like the thought of being on one of his dissecting tables.'

'Pardon me?'

'Oh, I don't mean he's a perv! He's . . . well, he's . . .' Max screwed up his face, trying to find the right words. 'I get the idea that he does his post-mortems with about as much compassion and consideration as he'd fillet a fish. He's a cold one, that's all.'

'Glacial,' agreed Jackman. 'But maybe that's how he copes. He's one of the few men we work with that I know absolutely nothing about.'

'No one does. And it's not for want of trying. Me and Charlie thought we'd do a little background research, but other than a string of letters after his name, we found naff all.'

Oddly enough, my father doesn't know of him either, thought Jackman. And that really was odd. His father had an address book of friends, family, colleagues, business associates, and assorted ancillary rank and file with almost as many entries as the Yellow Pages. Hugo Jackman was a past master at "collecting" people, because you never knew when one of them might come in handy.

'What did you make of that poor woman, sir?' said Max suddenly. 'Apart from being cut to ribbons, that is.'

Jackman puffed out his cheeks. 'Phew. Hard to tell really when a body is in that condition. It's difficult to see beyond the decomposition and the injuries, but I'd say she was mid-twenties, most likely British, and not on the breadline.'

'Mm, I agree, especially about being fairly well off. She had a T-shirt under her top, and I'm sure it was a designer label. I think I recognised a pretty pricey logo underneath all the staining.' He kicked at a piece of loose asphalt. 'Do we have a serial killer here in Saltern, sir?'

Jackman swallowed. That was something no copper wanted on their patch.

There would always be killers, in the same way that there would always be talented artists, child prodigies, concert pianists, left-handers and people who could fart *Rule*

Britannia! It was one of the varied talents humankind had developed. One man had the ability to dive from a ten metre board and enter the water with barely a ripple, and another could take a life, with as little fuss. But the serial killer, that most feared and heinous of beasts, was something else altogether.

'It's far too soon to start thinking like that. For all we know, the killer could have had a deep-rooted personal grudge against both the dead women. There are a dozen different scenarios that we could apply to what has happened, Max, and none of them involve serial killings.' He tried to look stern, but deep down he was wondering exactly the same thing.

After a few words with the uniformed officers, they hurried back to the car. The superintendent would be champing at the bit for an update, and they needed to tackle the mountain of work that this new find had thrown their way.

Max drove, and after a mile or so Jackman realised that there was none of the non-stop chatter that usually accompanied their journeys. He glanced across, and was shocked to see a tear squeezing itself from the corner of Max's eye.

He touched Max's arm. 'Want me to drive?'

'I'm okay, sir.' He rubbed his jacket cuff roughly across his eyes. 'But how can someone do that?' He swallowed noisily. 'I mean, it's inhuman! To take some lovely young woman, some girl, well, she was little more than a kid really, and do that to her.' He shook his head as if to rid himself of something that clung to it. 'It's just horrible. How is someone capable of a thing like that? Why do they do it, boss?'

'If I knew that, I'd be a rich man.' Jackman exhaled. 'There's no simple answer, I'm afraid. From what our case files tell us, I can only guess that some of them live in a fantasy world, disconnected from reality, where violent crime is all part of some horrible psycho-sexual game that they need to play out. Some seem to simply *like* inflicting hurt on people. And others think that they are perfectly justified in killing, for whatever reason their twisted mind has come up with.'

Max murmured his assent and returned to concentrating on the road ahead. After a while, he sighed. 'I just can't look at their faces.'

Jackman recalled the detective staring intently at his notebook, recording the details of the woman's clothing. 'I can understand that.'

'Is there something wrong with me, boss? All the others seem to cope. Some of them even manage to joke about it.'

Jackman shook his head. 'It's what we said about Jacobs, Max. Everyone finds their own way to cope with bad situations. Black humour is high on the mechanism list, but others find it heartless, offensive even. It depends on your personality.'

'You won't tell the others, guv? About me blubbering.'

'It's the last thing I'd do.' Jackman meant it, although he knew that no one on his team would think any the less of Max for shedding a tear for a dead girl. In fact he was pretty sure that Marie would find it endearing. 'Oh, and it's not a sign of weakness, Max, it's compassion for others. Without that, you'd be a crap copper.'

* * *

Jackman talked to the pathologist. Marie sat across the table from Daniel Kinder, alongside Charlie Button.

Kinder was very calm, maybe a little too calm. Marie wondered if he was still suffering the effects of the sedative.

As they had on every previous occasion, she recommended he use the services of a brief, but once again he refused, so she continued. 'We have received the results of fingerprinting taken at the scene where you profess to have committed a murder.' Marie paused, staring at the impassive face opposite her. 'There is nothing in the report to place you at the scene, Daniel.'

'I was obviously very careful.' He sounded unemotional.

You, my son, are a very different animal to the one I met in here last night, thought Marie. She narrowed her eyes. Until Jackman had assessed the situation out in Bracken Holme, they had decided not to mention to Kinder that another woman had been found. Marie was still certain that he hadn't killed anyone, and that news of another body would come as a complete surprise to him, but now was not the time to present him with that particular nugget of information. Even now she heard Jackman's warning to be careful, that Kinder might just be playing a dangerous game.

'What do you want from all this, Daniel?'

There was confusion in his staring eyes, then he asked, 'What do you mean?'

'Well, you've come to us, you've set the scene, you must have a finale in mind.'

'It's not a game.'

'Isn't it?' Marie matched his stare. 'I'm not convinced.'

Daniel didn't answer. He drew in a long breath and fixed his gaze on the scratched surface of the table in front of him.

'You didn't kill Alison Fleet, Daniel. But for some reason you are very, very anxious to make us believe that you did. If that's not a game, I don't know what is.'

'I killed her.'

'And you can recall every last detail, can you? Where she was? What she said to you when she saw the knife? How it felt as the blade parted her soft flesh?' Her voice rose with every sentence until it echoed around the small room. 'You can remember what you did with that knife, can you? Where's the knife, Daniel? Where is it?'

'I don't know! I don't *know!*' His voice rose, then he fell silent. After a while he looked directly at her, and he said, 'I just know that I killed her. Now I can't remember anything. It happens sometimes. I forget things.'

'Like killing someone?' Charlie Button's expression was incredulous.

'Like *anything!* I have gaps. There are times when I don't know where I've been or what I've done. Usually it's only seconds or minutes, but recently it's got worse.'

'And you had one of these "gaps" on the night that Alison Fleet died?'

Daniel Kinder nodded miserably.

Marie frowned. 'So when you were "yourself" again, was there blood on you?'

'No, but I think I was wearing different clothes to the ones I put on that morning.'

Marie's frown deepened. 'And where are they now?'

Kinder shrugged hopelessly. 'I can't find them.'

How on earth did the psych department at the hospital let this go? Marie thought. If they weren't linked to dementia, serious memory lapses were generally the result of a trauma, or due to an underlying disease, like a tumour. Or stress, of course, and she'd seen that Daniel Kinder could become stressed to breaking point in the blink of an eye.

For some reason she didn't think he was faking this. She'd seen and heard it so many times before. "I can't remember" was a well-worn excuse, and she usually saw through it straight away. But Kinder was different somehow.

She sat back in her chair and looked at him earnestly. 'Know what I think?'

Kinder's eyes didn't leave hers, but he said nothing.

'I think you're scared about your memory loss. You've convinced yourself that you are a murderer's son, and you are trying to protect Skye Wynyard.' She intensified her stare. 'Protect her from what you believe you could do to her.'

Daniel's face became immobile, a mask devoid of emotion. He seemed to switch off completely. His back straightened, and in an arctic tone that could have frozen molten lava, he said, 'No comment.'

* * *

Skye Wynyard sank down onto the sofa and heaved a sigh of relief. The last of the police officers had left and she was thankfully alone. It would take all evening to put things straight again, although she had to admit that the search team had done their best not to cause too much disturbance. They had mostly concentrated on the attic, and frankly she was glad that they'd stripped it out. She never wanted to go up there again. Even seeing the closed door at the top of the stairs was giving her the heebie-jeebies.

Sergeant Marie Evans had rung her a while back, saying that the Thai Embassy had confirmed that Mrs Ruby Kinder had flown up to the north-eastern province of Loei, with the intention of joining a meditation group in the Phu Ruea mountains. Apparently she had then gone into the forest on a silent retreat at an undisclosed location. There was no way of contacting her, although the local police had been alerted and would make every effort to reach her.

Skye and Ruby got on well. The older woman was more like a friend than the mother of her boyfriend, and part of Skye was relieved that Ruby was not around to see the carnage that her only son had caused. *And* not around to feel the heartbreak that he was dishing out to those who loved him. Sergeant Evans had said that Daniel was back in custody and after he'd been interviewed, she would see if a visit could be arranged. She made no promises, and Skye had gathered from her words that Daniel was in deep shit.

She lay back on the sofa and tried to relax. She was exhausted, mentally and physically, but she still had the house to put to rights. She knew that Ruby would never blame her, but she still felt responsible, and she wished like hell that she'd never committed herself to helping Daniel feed his pet neurosis.

Skye stood up and went to the kitchen where she found the vacuum cleaner, dusters, polish and other assorted cleaning materials. With a determined intake of breath, she decided to get the house into some semblance of order.

She was just plugging in the hoover when she heard her phone ringing.

'Skye? Sorry to bother you, but are you okay? One of the porters here said there were police vans outside the house where you are staying.' The worried voice of her departmental manager was the last thing she had expected to hear.

'Yes, Lisa, I'm fine. It's all just a dreadful misunderstanding.' She wanted to blurt the whole thing out, but managed to rein herself in.

'Is this the personal problem that made you take leave at such short notice?' Lisa Hurley's voice was full of concern. 'It's so unlike you to ask for time off, I've been worrying about you ever since. If there's anything I can do, or if you need to offload? I've got an A-level in Active Listening!'

Skye smiled for the first time in days. 'How long have you got?'

'All night, if it helps.'

'Well, right now I have a very large house to clean. We've had policemen's size twelve boots tramping all over it. But maybe tomorrow?' Would it really hurt to talk to someone? She didn't think so. If someone was good enough to help her out, why should she say no?

'I've got a better idea. Tell me where you are and I'll come over with a bottle of Fitou, an M&S microwave meal, a can of Pledge and an industrial-sized packet of J-cloths. How does that sound?'

'Like the sound of a lifebelt landing next to a drowning woman.'

'Excellent. Give me your address and I'll be there within the hour. By the way, have the press caught on? Are you being staked out by reporters and cameras?'

'Not yet, but I'm sure it's imminent. See you later!'

Skye closed her phone and blew out air. She didn't have to tell Lisa everything, after all, and then she could get her opinion. Lisa's speciality was working with stressed-out staff and patients, so she could be a very useful person to talk to.

Skye felt a huge weight lift from her shoulders. Lisa Hurley was not only highly intelligent, she was also practical, and funny with it. Of all the people she knew, if she could have picked someone to unburden herself to, even though Lisa was technically her boss, it would have been her.

Skye picked up the hoover and switched it on. She no longer felt so alone.

CHAPTER EIGHT

It was evening by the time Jackman caught up with Marie, and her troubled face told him that Kinder's interview had been far from straightforward.

They sat in his office and he told her about the dead woman.

'The super is keeping everything quiet until we have the pathologist's report. Then we'll know what we're dealing with.'

'How is she managing that?' Marie looked tired and worried.

'Luckily there was a sweep of field workers in the Bracken Holme area scheduled for today. One of the other teams had a tip-off that a gang master had a new batch of illegal immigrants coming in. She's using that as a cover for the police presence out there. It seems to be working so far, but obviously she can't stretch it out for ever.' Jackman leaned back in his chair and raised his arms above his head to ease his aching shoulders. 'Because the place is so remote, and the body is down in the cellar, there's no tent or awning, so that helps to keep the profile low.'

'So much for the recent directive about transparency. Now diplomacy is the watch-word. And you think we have a second murder by the same killer?'

Jackman nodded. 'Jacobs said as much, off the record. Although . . .' His voice tailed off.

'Oh no. I sense a huge *but* about to descend on us!'

He gave her a weary smile, 'No, it's not that. I'm certain it's the same killer, but there wasn't that sense of the body being carefully "arranged" that we picked up on at Alison Fleet's crime scene. The girl today had just been dumped. End of story.'

'So you don't think she was killed in situ?'

'I very much doubt it. There was no sign of a struggle, no blood spatters. I'd say she was killed somewhere else and taken to the Drover's Arms because the killer knew it was abandoned.'

'And that it was miles from anywhere.'

'Exactly. The moment we get some info from Jacobs, we can get out there and start asking questions. What we don't want to do is start a panic. The moment someone says "serial killer," we will be at the centre of a maelstrom. And there's still an outside chance that we already have the killer lounging comfortably in our own custody suite.'

'Look out! There's a pig flying over!'

'Okay, okay. I know you think he's just deluded, but an old aunt of mine always used to say, "If you believe you can do it, then you *can*."'

'Her words of wisdom are duly noted, sir, but I still think he's caught up in this ridiculous illusion that he is Françoise Thayer's diabolical offspring and that if he's left alone with her, he'll probably slice and dice Skye Wynyard.' Marie yawned. 'Did the super say we can get an expert in?'

'In her own crusty way. I think she's on our side regarding that. But her budget requires her to make cuts somewhere else to cover the cost.'

'I'm not sure what's left to cut,' replied Marie gloomily. 'We're on an austerity programme already. Our staffing levels are rock bottom and our vehicles look like they came direct from the knacker's yard. Even our once splendid dog section is down to PC Nobby Clarke and a half-blind German shepherd called Itchy.'

'Nice, though.'

'Which one are you talking about?'

'Don't be silly.' Jackman threw her a withering look. 'Nobby Clarke, of course.'

Marie smiled. Then she looked at him with concern. 'Are you alright, sir? It couldn't have been very pleasant, seeing that dead girl.'

'Is it ever? But no, I'm fine. You never get used to it, but you find ways of getting by, don't you?'

It was Marie's turn to nod. 'You do, but maybe it's time you went home, had a long, hot shower and a very large Scotch, in whichever order you see fit.'

'Soon. I think I've got everything in place that I can. Someone is trawling through missing persons for any female who was reported missing around two to three weeks ago. Forensics promised to send us reports as and when they have them, and there's little more I can do tonight.' He scratched his head. 'Except maybe have another word with Daniel Kinder.'

'Well, good luck, sir. He well and truly clammed up when I told him why I think he's here.' She stood up. 'Still, it's worth another try. I'll join you, if you like? He's had a supper break and a strong coffee so he should be good to go again.'

* * *

But Daniel was far from good to go.

Marie watched his body language while Jackman questioned him, and he was not a happy bunny.

'My colleague here seemed to strike a nerve earlier on. Is she right about your concerns for Skye Wynyard's safety?'

Daniel's jaw was thrust forward and he didn't speak for some time. Then he said, 'No, the sergeant is *not* right. It was her ridiculing my belief that my biological mother was Françoise Thayer that upset me. I simply cannot understand why you can't appreciate the truth.' His eyes narrowed. 'I suggest you take a look at the Haines murder case, and the trial of Françoise Thayer, because there will

74

be strong similarities with the killing of Alison Fleet. And if I know that, then I had to be there, didn't I?'

Jackman was silent, but Marie snapped back, 'I thought you couldn't remember what happened. Your convenient memory loss.'

'Just check the old case. And that's all I'm saying tonight.' Daniel Kinder clasped his hands together in his lap, lowered his head and stared unblinking at his long, pale fingers.

Jackman glanced at the clock and abruptly stood up. 'Interview terminated at eight fifteen.'

Outside, he snorted angrily. 'I know how we can settle this rubbish once and for all. Tomorrow we contact the evidence storage facility and get hold of everything that pertains to Françoise Thayer. We'll access the database and check her DNA against Kinder's for a maternal match. Maybe he can't find the answers he needs to untangle his head, but I'm damn sure we can.'

* * *

PC Kevin Stoner was on his third day of sick leave and until now, he hadn't left the house. Working with Zane Prewett was pushing him to within touching distance of seriously screwed, and he was at a loss to know what to do. Pulling sickies wasn't the answer, but until he could get his head straight, it was all he could think of.

Even if it hadn't been his turn to pick up his nine-year-old niece from taekwondo, he would have had to go out. Over the last few hours he had developed an intense disliking for the person he had become. Two months of working with Prewett had turned him from a pretty good copper into a gold-plated loser.

He walked towards the footpath that led to the sports complex, and wondered what his colleagues were thinking about him. They probably considered him a right wimp. Not that anyone liked Prewett, not even the senior officers. DI Jackman had actually taken him aside a week or so ago and warned him off crewing with Zane Prewett.

Kevin pushed his hands deeper into his jeans pockets and sighed. Nothing in this world would make him happier than ditching that shit-bag, but it wasn't that easy.

Kevin knew things about Prewett. Bad things.

But then Prewett had made it his business to find out things about him too, and that was where the problem lay. From his first day as a probationer, Kevin had taken great care not to speak about his home life, and in particular about his father's vocation. And luckily for him, no one had ever asked if he had any family connection with the Right Reverend Michael Stoner, the county diocesan bishop. But then it wasn't that surprising. Half of his colleagues were philistines, and the other half only entered a church for a wedding or a funeral.

As the ugly cement block building grew closer, Kevin decided that after he'd delivered Sophie safely home, he would talk to his brother. He couldn't go on bottling this up forever, or he'd finish up in a small locked room, dribbling and singing nursery rhymes to himself. Ralph was coming up to thirty and had a good head on his shoulders, so Kevin's revelations would probably not surprise his older sibling.

The footpath ran in a straight line and passed a row of back garden fences before opening out onto the playing field area. The sports hall and gym were on the far side of the football pitch. He was early. He was always early. There was a bar and café inside the complex that made a wicked double espresso and Sophie knew that's where she would find him.

'Hello, Kevin.'

He wasn't sure which came first, the words or the flattened side of a hand powering into his solar plexus.

With a grunt of pain and exhaled air, he doubled over, clasping his ribcage.

'A word, my friend.'

Hardly knowing what was happening, Kevin was grabbed and thrust roughly through an open gate and into an overgrown jungle of a garden.

'What the f . . . ?' He gasped out, but a grip of steel had fastened itself around his wrists and as he heard the gate slammed shut, he found himself thrust downwards into the grass and mud. A knee found its way accurately into the well between his shoulder blades and a jab of pressure made him squeal in shock and pain.

'Now, much as I enjoy a bit of roughhouse fun, we need to talk.'

The pressure eased, but Kevin found himself choking with the damp soil and weeds that had been forced into his mouth when he hit the deck.

With a little murmur of exertion, his assailant suddenly yanked him back into a standing position and thrust a finger into his mouth to remove the garden rubbish that had lodged there.

Kevin coughed and spat out mud.

'In here. This place has been empty for months, but the shed will do nicely for our little heart-to-heart.'

It wasn't so much a shed, more of an aging summerhouse, rotting and dilapidated, but it did have some vaguely serviceable plastic garden chairs. And it was into one of these that Kevin was pushed.

'Sit, and stay there. I need you to listen.'

Zane Prewett stood over him, his eyes cold and pitiless. 'I thought we had an understanding, Kev, my boy? A friendly agreement?'

Kevin didn't feel like talking yet. Gritty soil still coated his tongue.

'See, it's not looking good on me, you swinging the lead like this. Because everyone knows that's what you're doing, and quite soon some nosey bit of brass is going to start asking questions, understand?'

Kevin gave an almost imperceptible nod of his head.

'I want you back, I want everything cosy, and I want to see you smiling.' Zane's own smile made Kevin feel sick to the stomach.

'I know where I am with my own little crewmate, and I don't like working with the spare dicks they keep giving me. They cramp my style, if you catch my drift?'

Oh yes, thought Kevin. I know exactly what you mean. Someone might just spot some of your dirty little deals, the ones I have to turn a blind eye to.

Zane drew up another chair and jammed it in front of him. He flopped down into it and they sat toe to toe. 'Obviously I need to make the situation a little clearer for you, and that's fine. We've got,' he glanced at the massive diver's watch that dwarfed his wrist, 'oh, another fifteen minutes before you have to pick up sweet little Sophie.'

Kevin felt a boiling anger rising inside, but he knew that he was powerless against Zane's size and his dirty way of fighting. He gritted his teeth and said nothing.

'Good, I see we understand each other. And I'd hate for anything to happen to such a pretty kid, so we'll leave that part of this conversation there, shall we?' Zane sat back and stared at him. 'But the rest still stands, young Kevin. You remain the loyal crewmate, my constant companion and trusty sidekick, and your father, bless his saintly soul, doesn't find out who you're fucking. Deal?'

Kevin wanted to die. This wasn't histrionics. It just seemed like a really good idea.

'And just in case all that is not enough . . .' Zane reached into his inside pocket and produced an envelope. 'It never ceases to amaze me what people will do for money. And some will even do it for nothing if you press the right buttons. Helping an upright police officer like myself in the execution of his duties, getting dirty coppers off the streets . . .' Zane chuckled. 'Oh, the public spirit rises and they are *so* happy to help.' He removed a wad of computer-printed photographs from the thick envelope and held the first one up for Kevin to see.

If he'd wanted to die before, then what he felt like now was indescribable.

Two young men executing a tonsil-destroying kiss. One was thrust back against a darkened wall, and the other had his hand reaching eagerly into the tight jeans.

Kevin closed his eyes, then blinding, white-hot rage burst from him. 'You bastard! Give me those!' He lunged forward, but Zane was already on his feet.

'Oh, don't worry, sweetie, these are all yours.' He flung them in the air, and they cascaded down onto the filthy floor of the summerhouse. 'The originals are perfectly safe, and copies are packed up ready to mail to the Right Reverend, *if*, and I repeat, *if* you are not back on shift tomorrow, bright and chirpy and fully recovered.' The eyes were little more than slits. 'Got it? Now, take your little fag-bucket and get your fucking act together!' He strode to the door, as Kevin threw himself to the floor, grabbing at the pictures.

'Nothing will happen, okay? Either to your pretty niece, or to your pious father's blood pressure, as long as you play ball with me. Although not literally, of course. *I'm* not like that.' He glanced down at the photographs and raised a sardonic eyebrow. 'Right little dark horse, aren't we?'

Then leaning back around the flaking wooden door frame, he grinned lasciviously, and blew Kevin a kiss.

* * *

It was edging towards ten o'clock when Lisa Hurley finally looked at her watch and gasped. 'Lord! I have to go. I'm in early tomorrow to take an induction course.'

Skye had known how late it was getting, but had chosen to ignore the fact. It just felt so good to have some company in the big house. She feigned shock at how the time had flown, and reluctantly went to get Lisa's jacket.

'I can't thank you enough,' she said, meaning it. 'From the moment when that knock on the door came, and I saw that the police were there, well . . .' She gave a little shake of her head. 'It was horrible. But talking to you has helped me get back to some normality. I really believe that Daniel and I can sort everything out now.'

Lisa took her jacket, and lightly touched Skye's arm. 'I'm sure you will. And I'm touched that you trusted me with your story. I know it can't have been easy for you.'

She smiled warmly. 'Skye, I'm always around if you need me.' She walked towards the door. 'And I'll cover your leave of absence from the department for as long as I can.' She opened the door and a flash made them both jump.

'Shit!' Lisa stepped back inside and pushed the door to. 'I do believe that's the first of many cameras that will get stuck in your face over the next few days. Sorry, Skye, but the media circus has just begun.' Lisa drew in a deep breath. 'Oh well, here goes. Lock the door, don't answer the bell and put the security alarm on immediately I've gone.' She paused. 'Will you be alright?'

'I was expecting it. I'll be fine. And tomorrow, I'm heading out of this mausoleum and back to my flat.'

'Smart girl. You take care.' Lisa stepped out into the humid evening air, and Skye saw her hurry across the drive with her head down. She locked the door behind her.

Skye switched off the electric doorbell, made sure all the windows were locked, and activated the alarm system. She hadn't needed Lisa to tell her that. She had said she was fine, but she wasn't. Her head was clearer and she felt much better about Daniel and his misguided crusade, but she still hated being alone in the house.

Skye went to her room and sat on the edge of the bed. She didn't even want to undress. As they cleaned the house, Lisa had talked easily to her, and Skye had found herself revealing more and more, until Lisa knew almost everything.

And it really had helped. Not once had Lisa ridiculed or put down some of the wilder aspects of Daniel's "mission," and she'd given Skye some serious food for thought when it came to looking at the situation from a psychological point of view. Lisa had done a course on genetic influences, with a special interest in adoption studies involving different natural and adoptive parental environments. It had also covered intelligence and how differently certain people reacted to being told that they were adopted. Skye understood that only too well, although she hadn't said so. She was adopted too, but she saw it in a completely different way from Daniel. He was obsessed with knowing about his biological parents, whereas she couldn't give a damn. As far as she was concerned, she was the luckiest kid alive. She had a wonderful loving family, and the reason why she had been rejected by her natural mother was irrelevant to her. Whatever it was, it would have involved something painful or unpleasant. Sod that for a game of soldiers!

Skye yawned, kicked off her shoes but kept her clothes on. She wrapped herself in the duvet, closed her eyes and tried to shut her ears to the repeated knocks on the door. She couldn't bring herself to switch off her bedside lamp.

* * *

Lisa Hurley sat in her car on the opposite side of the street to the Kinder house. Two or three men now hung around the door, huddled together and talking gruffly. Every now and then, one would hammer on the door for a while until he gave up and let one of the others try.

Lisa leaned back in the seat and watched them impassively. She would take bets that by tomorrow morning the neatly raked gravel drive would be heaving with reporters and media vans.

Then her gaze turned to the upstairs rooms of the house. She had followed the pattern made by the house lights as Skye moved from room to room, checking windows, closing curtains and extinguishing lamps. Now there was only one square of light left on the dark façade of the expensive property.

Lisa watched it for a very long time, before turning on the ignition and slowly pulling away.

* * *

Daniel dreamed about his mother. It wasn't a pleasant dream.

He had been walking along beside one of the long, straight waterways close to home. He had been holding Skye's hand, and they were walking towards a brightly coloured merry-go-round, the kind of gilded, decorated carousel that you still find all over Paris. He could hear the evocative sound of the mechanical organ, and Skye was asking if they could ride the painted horses.

As the smiling Skye tugged his hand and drew him towards the swirling carousel, he felt a terrible sense of foreboding, and his feet refused to move forward.

From somewhere behind them he could hear someone calling his name, but he was too scared to turn around. Now the music had turned into the sound of a howling wind, and whatever was behind him was pulling him back with enormous strength. He shrieked out to Skye to run, but her hand had already been torn from his and he saw that she was high above him, clinging to the back of a golden wooden stallion with blazing, blood-red eyes.

And then the horses were racing, galloping in a blur of colour, and taking Skye with them.

As the merry-go-round spun faster, it began to rise up and move away from him. He screamed out for Skye, but she was just a tiny toy figure on a toy horse that was disappearing into the thick white clouds that tossed and turned over the waterway.

"My boy."

The words filtered through the howling wind and Daniel's heart turned to ice. He tried to run, but he was held fast, attached to the horrible apparition that was materialising behind him. He realised that he was being held by a thick rope. He dared to turn, to see if he could free himself, and saw that it was not a rope at all, but a pulsating, slimy, purplish-blue umbilical cord.

"No!" he screamed. "Skye!"

"She has to go."

"No!" he cried again, but he was being drawn slowly backwards.

"Oh, my boy," she crooned.

The darkness was encroaching. He smelled the foul breath that fell across his shoulder. As he disappeared into the black abyss opening up beneath him, Daniel heard the words, "Come to Mummy."

CHAPTER NINE

Heavy grey clouds had accompanied Marie on her trip into work this morning. No magic moments to savour today, and frankly, that was fine because the big dark skies echoed her mood. It was one of those mornings, thankfully rarer now, when she missed Bill. Missed him so much her chest ached. Her husband had been killed almost ten years previously, and sometimes it still hurt like hell.

When she arrived at the station, she realised that she wasn't the only one who felt as though the end was nigh.

God knows what time Jackman had got in and surprisingly, both Max and Charlie were also at their desks.

'No one told me there was a pyjama party last night!' She unzipped her leather jacket and looked at her colleagues. 'I'd have brought the popcorn.'

'Couldn't sleep,' grumbled Max, shaking his head. 'And I *always* sleep. My gran says I could have slept through the Blitz.'

'I had a bad night too,' added Charlie.

'Yeah, but in your case it was brought on by eating that Ruby at midnight.'

Charlie sighed and gave Max a long-suffering look. 'It was closer to eleven actually, and it's not my fault that the only late night takeaway in my street happens to be Indian.'

Marie hung her jacket over the back of her chair and looked over to where Jackman was staring thoughtfully at the whiteboard. 'And you, sir? Bad dreams? A bad curry?' She grimaced. 'Or both?'

'Neither.' He turned to her with a tired smile. 'I settled for a Spanish omelette and air-fried chips, then spent most of the night in the company of the Blonde Butcher.'

'I agree there was nothing much on the telly, but I could think of better things to do.' Marie drew out her chair and sat down.

'She bothers me,' said Jackman.

'Not as much as she bothered George and Lydia Haines,' added Max grimly. He pushed his chair away from his desk and turned to Jackman. 'Why did she kill them, guv? It was long before my time, and I can only remember bits and pieces.'

'If you'd asked me that yesterday, I wouldn't have known.' Jackman walked over and sat on the edge of Marie's desk. 'But after my late night cramming session on the computer, I can tell you quite a bit about the thankfully departed Françoise Thayer.'

Marie scanned her mental databank but only came up with newspaper headlines containing words like *evil, vicious, cold-blooded, monstrous* and *heinous*, depending on whether they were tabloid or broadsheet.

'To begin with, and this is not widely known, she was suspected of killing at least five other people before the Haines. And as this was both unproven *and* took place in France, it didn't filter through the system at the time.'

'And she still managed to get a job as an au pair in the Lincolnshire countryside?' asked Charlie.

'She changed her name prior to coming to England. There was no way she could disguise the fact that she was French, so she took another French name and disappeared into our system.'

'The age-old story,' grumbled Max. 'But how come she turned psycho on her employers?'

'Over a power cut and a bacon sandwich.' Jackman threw Marie an enigmatic smile. 'The final straw is usually something quite insignificant, I know, but this really takes the biscuit — or the sandwich.'

'Tell us more.' Marie leaned forward and rested her elbows on her desk, suddenly very interested.

'Françoise Thayer was an obsessive personality. She was jealous, dominating and fancied the pants off the farm manager, a man named Ian Farrow.'

'He was in the frame for the murders, wasn't he?' asked Marie, as snippets of the old case filtered back into her memory.

'Yes. He was suspected of being in it with Thayer, but he was just another of her victims, even if she didn't kill him.'

'Did he feel the same about her? Fancy her, I mean?' Charlie asked.

'Not at all. But he was a gentle man, something of a loner, and she misread his friendly attitude towards her, which was nothing more than politeness to a fellow member of the Haines' staff.' Jackman pulled a face. 'She misread a lot actually. It had got around that he was a divorcee, which made him fair game, but what she didn't know was that the marriage had failed because of his homosexual tendencies.'

'Oops.' Max tried to stifle a smile.

'The flashpoint came when Thayer saw Lydia Haines walking across the yard to where Ian Farrow had a small barn conversion, and going inside. Thayer had been out on an errand in the town, and she was unaware that there had been a power cut affecting the whole of the farm estate. As Lydia used a solid-fuel Aga to cook on, and Farrow had been out in the fields all day, she had cooked him and several of the others, bacon sandwiches to tide them over until the power returned. Françoise Thayer believed that Lydia was entering Farrow's living quarters for an assignation, and her jealousy exploded. Even when she learned that the power had been down, she decided that Lydia had used it as an excuse to get into Farrow's bed.'

'And she killed both Lydia *and* her husband?'

'With nary a bat of her long eyelashes, she hacked them both to death.' Jackman stood up. 'And I think she would have killed Ian Farrow too, except that he went into the town that evening and got too drunk to drive home. He spent the night in his Toyota, parked close to the Shrimp Boat Inn.'

'And Dotty Daniel reckons Thayer's his ma?' Max drew in a disbelieving breath. 'If I thought something like that, I'd keep my trap well and truly shut.'

Marie became serious. 'Daniel is totally obsessed by the thought, and we need to convince him otherwise.'

'Unless he's right,' said Charlie — Saltern's own prophet of doom.

Jackman nodded. 'Exactly. So, one way or the other we need to know the truth. And as soon as the relevant departments have woken up, I want you three to get me everything you can from the Thayer trial — transcripts, evidence boxes, and most of all forensics reports, ones that mention DNA.' His voice had hardened. 'We need to present Kinder with solid evidence before we start trying to infiltrate his mind.'

Max nodded, then said, 'What about the time restraints on holding him?'

'Even if we have to bail him, Kinder won't be going far. He *wants* to be here, probably just as much as we love having him as a house guest.'

'And what about Alison Fleet and our Jane Doe?' Much as Marie wanted to get to the bottom of Daniel's sinister parentage, she didn't want their ongoing cases to suffer.

'I'll hold the reins on Operation Nightjar. The foot soldiers are doing everything possible, and until we get more forensic reports back, we'll be kicking our heels anyway.' Jackman had a slightly over-enthusiastic look in his eye and Marie hoped that Daniel Kinder's quest wasn't going to cloud the DI's usually sound judgement.

'Don't worry, guys, this is solid background work to do with the Fleet investigation. If anything happens that requires us to change priority, I'll be on it like a shot. So go to it.'

Marie watched him go into his office and close the door, then she turned back to her two detectives. 'Okay, gang, we're now the cold case squad. Let's make a plan, shall we?'

* * *

If the day had started gloomily, it got steadily worse, until by two o'clock, Marie was about ready to call HR and ask for an immediate transfer to a small Scottish island. Preferably one inhabited only by sheep.

She smashed the phone down in its cradle and glared at it murderously.

'I don't like that look.' Jackman had appeared beside her desk. 'It smacks of incipient insanity, or maybe the intent to murder.'

'I consider both suggestions to be high on the list of possibilities.' She looked up at him and threw her hands in the air. 'This is hopeless! The last five hours have been like a kid's pantomime! But distinctly *not* funny.'

'Thayer?'

'Yes, Françoise sodding Thayer.' She exhaled very loudly, then slouched back in her chair and said steadily, 'How long ago was this case? Twenty years? Not long in the grand scheme of things. I have a freezer that's older than that, but with all the technology that we now have at our fingertips, can we get the information that we require? Like hell we can!'

Jackman pulled a chair over from an empty desk and sat down next to her. 'Slowly, and from the top.'

Marie groaned. 'I don't think I have the energy, but the bottom line is this. The storage facility that held the evidence from the Thayer case suffered a serious fire some ten years back. Evidence boxes that were not completely destroyed were salvaged and moved out in a hurry and transferred to other temporary stores. As the case had been brought to a satisfactory conclusion and was already a decade old, they weren't given priority, and now . . .' She spread out her hands, palms up. 'They could be anywhere, or nowhere. There is no record that they were cremated, but there's no record of them in any other storage facility either. This trace is dead, guv, stone dead.'

The other two detectives ambled over to join them, and Max said, 'Not only that, things are also well cocked up by the fact that Thayer was suspected of murders in France.'

Charlie stared at his notes. 'Yeah, a lot of the information on her earlier life seems to have been transferred abroad.'

Max's mouth drooped. 'Right, and with our budget, try finding details that are not just held by another force, but another country. It's blinking ludicrous.'

'Damn it,' muttered Jackman. 'Not what I'd hoped for. And without a lot more sound evidence to link Daniel to the killer, the police budget that you fondly mentioned sure isn't going to extend to lengthy calls or trips abroad.' He bit on his lower lip. 'Dare I ask about DNA?'

'You can ask.' Marie scratched her head. 'But that was the reason I just used my phone as a therapeutic tool to express my anger.'

'Can I make a one-word suggestion?' Charlie offered.

All eyes turned to him, all clearly trying to guess what that word might be.

'Orac. If there's something lurking in our systems somewhere, she'll be the one to find it.'

Marie smiled broadly. 'Sometimes, Charlie Button, I really love you. Another hour pounding this keyboard would have put me in a straightjacket.' She stood up. 'I'll go see her.' She stopped and looked enquiringly across to Jackman. 'Or maybe it would sound better coming from you, sir?' But Jackman was already on his way back to his office. All she heard were the words, 'Very busy. You sort it.'

Max smirked at Jackman's retreating back. 'You know what I think?'

'Forget it, sunshine.' Marie threw him a dark look. 'Don't even go there.'

* * *

Orla Cracken, known to everyone from the chief constable down as Orac, didn't look up when Marie entered the IT unit. In fact for one creepy moment Marie envisioned Orac as a kind of robot, an integral part of the bank of computers, monitors and screens that surrounded her. She was as immobile as the keyboard in front of her, and in her ramrod straight position she looked more like an automaton than a human being.

Marie decided that Orac was the kind of woman who would still look striking in a duffel coat and fluffy slippers. She needed no props to make her stand out, but Marie had never seen her without those weird metallic lenses.

'We need your help,' said Marie quietly, not wishing to upset the strange calm of the room full of machines.

'Who doesn't?' came the terse reply.

It was true. All seemingly unsolvable problems ended up on Orac's desk. And nine times out of ten she would produce the answers. The trouble was she also had to help three other area forces. The Fenland Constabulary had very little that was special, and their budget was as tight as anyone's, but they did have Orac, and that was a valuable commodity indeed. Sadly, she was too valuable to keep to themselves.

'We've run into a barrier chasing down info from an old case. I'm hoping you can find something that we've missed.'

Orac turned round and gave Marie a shocked look. 'I sincerely hope I can, or I'm in the wrong job.' Her eyes flashed brightly like the shiny surface of a CD. 'Is it important? I'm up to my neck right now.'

'Jackman thinks it's very important.'

'But he didn't come himself?'

Marie said, 'You're not the only one up to your neck. We have two dead women and one mega-flaky suspect.'

'Ah yes, Mr Daniel Kinder, the one whose computer I swept yesterday.' She raised an eyebrow. 'And your boss didn't even grace my doorway with his presence, after I'd slaved all afternoon on his behalf. He sent a small, spotty boy to pick the data up.' She tilted her head to one side in an imitation of reproach. 'I'm beginning to think he's scared of me.'

'Jackman? Scared?' Even to herself, Marie's derision sounded unconvincing.

Orac smiled wickedly. 'Okay, Detective Sergeant. Whatever you say. So, you need an old case resurrected?'

Marie explained. She could see that Orac's mental data processor was ticking over, already formulating search programs. 'This sounds a little more interesting than chasing offshore accounts and bogus vehicle licence plates.' She turned back to her machines. 'Leave it with me. I'll ring when I have something for you.'

With a final glance in Orac's direction Marie left the room with the humming, whirring machines and their strange overlord.

As she strode up the stairs from the basement, she wondered why Orac had mentioned Jackman twice in that short conversation. She grinned as she tried to imagine Jackman and Orac sipping wine in some quiet bar. Maybe not. How about walking hand in hand by the river at sunset? Hell, no. That was even worse. And the thought of a romantic dinner in a small intimate restaurant finally made her snort with laughter. It would certainly be something of a turn up for the books. No one knew anything about Orac's private life. It had been intimated that she didn't have one and that the only hard thing she needed was a hard drive. A person as enigmatic as the IT boss was certain to give rise to speculation. She was a genius, that was clear, but the grapevine had whispered that she was ex-

MI5, and that she'd been used as a scapegoat in a major hacking scandal. That was why she had finished up in a two-bit, rural county police station, crunching numbers for provincial coppers. Someone else said that she had been put out to pasture, simply because she knew too much, but too much about what, they couldn't say.

Marie didn't believe any of the mess-room theories, but she had to wonder why such a techno-mastermind was working in a one-time wine cellar in Saltern nick.

'Just be grateful for small mercies,' she whispered to herself as she approached her floor. 'The woman is brilliant, and she's in *our* basement. And stop fantasising, it's bad for your blood pressure.'

Back at her desk the notion continued to plague her. She looked across to where Jackman was in deep conversation with a uniformed officer. It was hard to be objective when she knew him so well, but slowly the odd thought was becoming less of a joke. Maybe he was more Orac's type than she'd realised.

Marie tried not to stare at him. She decided that Orac would be unmoved by his good looks. It would be the mind that would concern Orac, and Jackman was well-endowed in that department. *And* he was clever enough to know when to temper his academic manner of speaking. He was able to adopt the street-level vernacular and the gallows humour when it was appropriate. Perhaps Orac had lifted her strange eyes from her smartphone or tablet and seen all this.

'I said, any luck?'

Marie's head snapped up and she saw an amused Max Cohen looking down at her. She hadn't even noticed him approach her desk.

'You were well away with the fairies, Sarge.'

'Oh, not really. Just mulling over one of the universe's multifaceted conundrums.'

'Right.' Max gave her a perplexed stare. 'Well, when you've worked it all out, do let me know. In the meantime, any luck with Orac?'

'She actually seemed mildly interested. Is that the kind of luck you're looking for?'

'Respect! I've seen disapproval, impassiveness, and buckets of irritation, but rarely interest. I'd say you've scored a hole in one.'

'In which case, whoopee,' said Marie flatly. 'She'll ring us and summon us back to her cave when she has some answers.'

'Great! Can *I* go?'

'No. Didn't you go before, to pick up the data from Kinder's computer?'

'No, the boss sent Charlie.'

'Ah, that explains it.'

'What?'

'Nothing. Go do some work.' Marie glanced up and saw Jackman beckoning to her.

She went into his office where he pointed to one of the chairs. 'I've had the prelim from the pathologist regarding Alison Fleet, and a few scribbled notes about Jane Doe. The most important point is that it appears that the same knife was used. Jane's poor condition has prohibited anything positive yet, but even the angle and depth of the stab wounds seems to indicate the same killer.' Jackman shook his head. 'Jacobs has pointed out that there are still considerable differences about the way the attacks were carried out, but he suggests that Jane Doe's death may have been a result of a bout of extreme anger on the part of her assailant, whereas Alison Fleet's was carefully considered and deliberate.'

Marie screwed up her forehead. 'But surely that indicates two killers? One organised, and one disorganised? And they are at opposite ends of the serial killer spectrum, aren't they? Two very different beasts?'

'If we were talking *serial*, yes, you're right, but what if the first death was not premeditated, and only after she was dead, did our man discover his true vocation?'

'Possible.' Marie mulled the idea over in her head. Very possible, actually. As Charlie had said, they had to start somewhere, and whereas these killers usually escalated up through cruelty, sadistic behaviour, sexual assault and rape to abduction and finally murder, there was always the odd chance of an accidental trigger sending the already twisted mind off the scale.

Jackman picked up a report. 'Jacobs says that whoever killed Alison Fleet was thorough to the point of retention. So far forensics have found no residual evidence left by the killer, no prints, blood, fluids, hair or fibre at the scene, and whereas that means we cannot place Daniel Kinder there, we can't place anyone else there either.'

'So we can't prove he *was* there, but we also can't prove he *wasn't*. Wonderful!'

'It is complex, that's for sure.' He ran his fingers through his hair. 'And there have been no matches via missing persons on our unknown woman either.'

'You said she was wearing designer clothes? She's obviously not a drop-out or a runaway, so why hasn't a woman like that been reported missing?'

'She could be a business woman? Someone who travels a lot? Single? No dependents? Maybe even no immediate family?'

'Maybe foreign?'

'Could be. And she could still be a runaway. Charity shops and places like the Salvation Army hand out donated clothing. Some of that is good quality. We need the full post-mortem to know the condition of her body prior to death to answer that one.'

'Or someone ringing in begging us to find their beloved daughter, or wife, or girlfriend.'

'You think we'll get that lucky?' asked Jackman grimly.

'Probably not, but let's not get too negative.'

'Excuse me, sir, but Superintendent Crooke asked me to give you a message.' Charlie leaned around Jackman's door. 'She said could you go up to her office immediately, and, quote, you are going to owe her big-time.' He turned to Marie, 'You too, Sarge.'

Marie nodded to Charlie, then raised an eyebrow at Jackman. 'The royal summons, no less. Better do as she says. Maybe that comment about luck was an omen.'

* * *

As they approached the superintendent's office they heard voices coming from inside the room, and Marie stopped in her tracks, one hand grasping Jackman's elbow and pulling him back.

'Wait!' she said urgently.

There was an odd intensity in her voice, and Jackman realised that her fingers were still tightly attached to his jacket sleeve. 'What's the matter?'

'That voice. I'd know it anywhere. It's Professor Guy Preston.'

Jackman thought hard. The name rang bells but no torrents of information flooded his brain. 'Well,' he said with a smile, 'It makes a change for you to know someone that I don't.'

Marie shook her head. 'This is incredible! I had no idea he was back in this area.'

'You've lost me. Who is Guy Preston?'

'He's a top psychologist, sir. Back when I was a baby tec, he helped us with the Austin enquiry . . . well, things went a bit pear-shaped at one point . . .' Her voice faded. 'Look, I'll tell you about it when we are alone. It's something I don't want anyone getting the wrong idea about, and it's not exactly common knowledge.'

'Now, I'm really interested,' whispered Jackman, 'but we'd better not keep the super waiting. Tell me later, and promise to leave nothing out.' He looked at her from beneath his eyebrows.

Marie ignored him and drew back her shoulders as they entered the office.

There, the penny dropped. Preston had written some very interesting papers that had been part of Jackman's reading assignments at Cambridge. He was a powerful man, an outspoken but respected psychologist, and Jackman wondered how the hell Ruth Crooke had managed to stretch the budget far enough to accommodate a man of his professional stature.

'I believe you two already know each other,' said the superintendent, glancing from Marie to the doctor.

Marie held out her hand. 'It's nice to see you again, Guy, and certainly something of a surprise.' She turned to Jackman and introduced him.

The handshake was firm, but not bone-crushing. Jackman saw a man in his late forties, his greying hair longer than average though neatly cut. A close, well-trimmed beard. The only thing that spoilt what Jackman thought of as the "Indiana Jones" good looks was an old jagged scar down the side of his face, one that even the beard could not disguise.

'DI Jackman, it's a pleasure to meet you — and Marie, I can't tell you how good it is to see you again. And you're a detective sergeant now? That's excellent news.'

I see, thought Jackman, first name terms, huh?

'Professor Preston is working at the old military hospital out at Frampton Shore. He has a key role in the new psychiatric secure unit that is being opened later this year.' The superintendent stretched those thin lips about as far as they would extend. 'And he's very kindly accepted my request to give us the benefit of his expertise.'

Preston raised his hands, palms up, 'It's no big deal. I'm at something of an impasse right now. The building work is at a critical stage. They're putting in the security systems. The place is off-limits to anyone except the security experts, construction workers and their entourage. It hardly seemed worth trekking back up to Northumberland, so . . .' He smiled. 'If I can help, that's great.'

Jackman was trying to bring to mind some of Preston's work. Bingo! Something clicked neatly into place. 'You wrote an important paper on female psychopaths: *When Conscience is Lacking*.'

'Good Lord! And here was me thinking only a handful of bored students ever saw that! Not that I think any of them ever bothered to read it.'

'I read it, and I did it voluntarily. It was a fascinating study.'

'Thank you.'

Jackman thought the man looked like someone who taught yoga or Tai Chi. He had a calmness about him, a good quality in a psychologist. His patients would trust him quite easily. He glanced across to Marie, and saw mingled emotions on her face. They puzzled Jackman.

'Superintendent Crooke has given me the bare bones of the case, but perhaps one of you could fill me in on the details?' Preston looked at Marie.

If Jackman hadn't known that Marie had been happily married for many years before her husband's death, he might have thought that there was history in those meaningful glances.

'No problem,' Jackman said quickly. 'Come down to the CID room with us. You can meet the rest of the team and . . .' He looked at Preston. 'I would really like your opinion on this strange, obsessive wall decoration done by the person we have in custody.' He held open the door, and the doctor and Marie walked through. Jackman turned back to Ruth Crooke. 'You were right, ma'am. I do owe you one.'

'You'd better believe it, Detective Inspector Jackman, and one day, I'll come a'calling, never fear.'

She gave him a small smile. It wasn't much, but it told him that she really was on his side, and sod the budget.

Downstairs, they gave Preston a quick tour of the department. While Max showed the psychologist their reconstruction of Daniel Kinder's wall-work, Jackman took Marie aside.

'So you've worked with Preston before?' he asked quietly.

'Well, as I said, I was only a lowly baby tec, but he was a massive help with a complex and very delicate investigation. I'd say he was instrumental in getting Terence Marcus Austin taken off the streets for life.'

'But if you were such a minion, how did you get on first name terms with the big cheese?' Jackman hoped his question didn't sound like some kind of jealousy.

'I saved his life.' She shook her head. 'Look, can we do this later?' She looked to where Preston stood staring at the board. 'You better go talk to him. And, sir, we are very lucky to have him. If anyone can understand Daniel, it will be Guy Preston. I've never met anyone who can find his way around a sick mind like that man.'

Jackman was still trying to get his head around her statement. Saved his life? He managed a nod and dragged himself back to the present. 'If his academic papers are anything to go by, I know exactly what you mean.'

'Can I meet the artist himself?' asked Preston, staring at the reconstruction.

'Of course.' Jackman beckoned towards his office. 'But first, a coffee, and we'll fill you in on what we know to date, okay?'

Preston smiled. 'Sounds good to me. Lead on.'

Half an hour later, Guy Preston sat back in his chair and let out a long sigh. 'I guess I need to see him before I pass any comment, but everything you've told me to date says that Daniel Kinder is just haunted, well, obsessed, by his own belief that he's a killer's son. I would be very doubtful that he's killed anyone.'

'That's our thoughts too, but we have to prove it. One mistake on our part could cost someone their life.' Jackman said grimly.

'And you your job, no doubt?'

'If I put a killer back out on the streets, then believe me, I'd be the first one to put my neck on the bloody block. And anyway,' he added almost to himself, 'I'd never be able to live with myself if I put innocents in danger.'

Marie smiled at Preston. 'My boss has a conscience.'

'Heavens! That's something of a rarity these days.'

Preston looked thoughtfully at him, and Jackman felt a creeping tendril of discomfort. He was being scrutinised by a leading psychologist, and Jackman couldn't help wondering what he saw. Jackman forced a smile and changed the subject. 'I'll ring the custody sergeant and have Kinder brought up to an interview room.'

The doctor stroked his chin thoughtfully. 'Excellent, but before we do, I think I should tell you that I know a fair bit about Françoise Thayer. I spent a lot of time researching her and a couple of other women killers with the intention of writing a book on them. It's actually very strange that Superintendent Crooke decided to rope me in on this.'

'So you probably know more about Thayer's mindset than anyone, and you're sitting right here in the boss's office!' Marie sounded amazed.

'More or less, but I suggest we don't tell Daniel.'

Jackman thought about that, then said, 'I see your point.' He looked at Marie, then back to Preston and explained about all the missing documentation on the murder trial and the loss of the evidence boxes.

The doctor's face turned from bland to dumbfounded. 'But that's a travesty! Thayer was one of the coldest and most manipulative, wicked killers this country has ever seen! And all the legal data on her has gone?'

'To all intents and purposes. Vanished into thin air,' said Marie.

'Could it have been a deliberate act?'

Marie shook her head. 'I can't see why. It's much more likely to be one damned great cock-up.' She scowled. 'And believe me, they do happen.' Her frown lifted. 'But we do have an ace computer boffin who is tracing everything that's been left floating in the ether regarding that old case. Between the two of you, we could find ourselves with a pretty comprehensive history.'

'Well, if it would help, I think I can probably lay my hands on some of my old research. As I said, it was something I tackled years ago, so it's not on my laptop, but the hard copy will all be filed away.' The psychologist passed a hand through his hair. 'Luckily my work and my case notes are already with me at my flat. It's only some of my personal belongings that are still at home in Northumbria.'

'Are you planning on moving here permanently when the new psychiatric unit opens?' asked Jackman.

'Oh yes. I have been given a purpose-built chalet in the grounds. All very Nordic and spacious, but until my contract starts, I've rented a flat in Hanson Park.'

'Very nice.'

'Too much like Stepford for me. I like my privacy, my own space, but it's somewhere to pitch up until my new home is finished.'

'And do you have family back up north?'

'Not really.' His face clouded over. 'My wife died last year, so there's not much to hold me there anymore. It was her home county, not mine.'

'I'm sorry to hear that,' said Jackman. 'And please forgive me. My policeman's curiosity got the better of my manners.' He lifted the phone, pressed the extension for the custody suite and spoke to the sergeant.

'Kinder will be in interview room three in ten minutes.'

As Marie and Preston talked about the new project at the secure unit, Jackman had an opportunity to take a closer look at their new colleague. It didn't take him long to realise that his face was not the only part of him that was scarred. There was an ugly mark on the back of his left hand. It could have been a burn, or maybe a badly healed puncture wound. Jackman wondered why Guy Preston had not had plastic surgery, especially to the side of his face. The scar was tethered and puckered, and Jackman couldn't see why it needed to be there. To afford a flat in Hanson Park, and to be senior enough in his profession to be asked to head up a new psychiatric unit, Preston would hardly be on the breadline, and even if he were, the injury was bad enough to warrant the NHS sorting it out for him. So why leave it?

Jackman tossed a few theories around in his head. Some women found scars attractive. They thought they made the man who bore them look virile, tough. Other women would think they were a sign of vulnerability, and that too could be a turn on. Or was it nothing to do with sexual attraction? Was Preston afraid of the knife? A friend of Jackman's father, an eminent thoracic surgeon, was terrified of operations. This fear almost cost him his life when an aneurism threatened to rupture. So what's Preston's story? he mused to himself, then glanced at his watch. 'Right, time to go. Mr Kinder awaits us.'

* * *

Daniel sat quietly, waiting for his next interview. The only other person in the room was a silent uniformed custody officer. He was glad that the woman had nothing to say to him, because he was suffering from the grand-daddy of all headaches.

In a matter of days Daniel's whole life had become a series of horrible contradictions. He badly wanted to be with Skye, but he also wanted her far away from him. He wanted to be safe in his own home, but he also craved the locks on his cell door. He longed for sleep, but feared it because of the accompanying dreams. Most of all, he wanted to know the truth about himself. But another part of him was terrified of finding out.

The room filled up with people.

Daniel watched as the senior officer removed a new tape from its sealed packaging and placed it into the machine. Then he listened as the detective inspector introduced himself and invited the others to do the same.

'Daniel, do you have any objection to Professor Guy Preston being present, and talking to you during this interview? He is a medical expert.'

Daniel looked directly at the bearded man and knew instantly what kind of medicine he practised, but he thought he should ask the question anyway. 'What is your field?'

'Guy Preston is a psychologist,' said the detective sergeant.

'And if you are happy to talk to me, I promise to tell you the truth, no matter what,' Preston said.

'Do you specialise?' asked Daniel calmly.

'I do. I'm a forensic psychologist and a behavioural investigative advisor. I work with the police on serious crimes.'

'Like murder?'

'Amongst other things.'

'Good.' Daniel felt something like relief course through him. 'If you deal with killers, then you'll understand that I'm not lying.'

Preston stared at Daniel thoughtfully. 'I meant what I said about telling the truth, Daniel. Are you prepared for that?'

'I am.' Daniel closed his eyes and felt the stinging behind the lids. 'I believe I am the son of Françoise Thayer. I believe I killed Alison Fleet. I want proof of that.'

'I'm not here to prove anything. That's down to the detectives, but I will listen to you and give them my informed opinion.'

Daniel knew that was the best he could ask for. This man reminded him of his child psychologist all those years ago. It was frightening to know that you might have to face your demons, but it was also reassuring to be able to voice your fears and not be ridiculed.

The man suddenly smiled at him, and once again he was a small boy, with empty spaces, gaps in his life. Gaps that scared him more than any bogeyman or vampire monster.

'Okay, Daniel. Let's start at the beginning.'

CHAPTER TEN

Charlie Button pushed his chair away from his computer and rubbed his eyes. 'What do you think of the shrink, Max?'

'Sorry, sunshine, but I have trouble with people who have more brain cells than my screen has pixels. I just googled him, and he's an academic with a capital "A." He's got degrees coming out of his ears and he's published more papers in learned professional journals than you've had hot dinners.' Max puffed out his cheeks. 'Still, if he can help us with Dippy Daniel, he's okay with me.'

'He's going to be the head honcho at the new secure unit at Frampton.' Charlie shivered. 'I wouldn't want to spend my whole life in a place like that, in the company of nutters.'

'You can talk!' laughed Max. 'You spend yours with rogues and villains!'

Charlie nodded. 'Yes, but you know where you are with criminals, don't you? But with flakes, well, there's no logic, is there?'

'There's logic, alright.' Max's face was serious. 'It's just twisted. It's *their* logic, and everything makes perfect sense to them. That's why they can do the things they do.' Max moved the cursor across his computer screen, then sat up straighter, staring at the document that he had just accessed. 'Well, well.'

Charlie looked up. 'Found something?'

'I'm not sure. I'm working on Alison Fleet's background, and I've just seen that she was married before, when she was young. Funny that her husband didn't tell us. It's a major thing, isn't it?'

'Maybe she never told him. Some people are very private about their past, and it could have been a bad marriage.'

'It would be a tough thing to keep schtum about. After all, there would be certificates and stuff like that to get around.' He shrugged. 'Still, it could be done I suppose. Maybe I should trace Alison Fleet's first husband and see what happened to their relationship.'

'Good idea. I'm still trying to trace Jane Doe, and I'm having no luck at all.'

Max thought about the decomposing body in the beer cellar of the Drover's Arms, and shivered. For some reason he desperately wanted her to have a name. He needed to see a picture of the real woman, the live, loving girl that she most likely had been, not that horrible disintegrating mess on the cellar floor. A name and a face would give his brain a proper picture to concentrate on, one that would allow the other nightmarish image to fade a little. He knew it would never disappear completely, but a human face, a girl with a proper name, would make it easier. 'Keep at it, my tenacious little friend. It's vital that we know who she is.'

'Easier said than done, but you're right. I've no doubt someone will be tearing their hair out wanting to know where she is.' He turned back to his screen and muttered, 'Okay, Button, try looking at it from a different angle. Let's forget about tracing the woman, and go back to her clothes.' His youthful face took on a determined expression. 'Don't you worry, Jane, we'll find your real name, I promise.'

* * *

Skye opened the flap of the cat carrier, stroked the silky head, then bundled the suspicious and now protesting animal into the box.

'Sorry, sweetie, but I can't leave you here alone and as I've no intention of commuting, you're coming with me.' She looked at the shopping bag filled with pet food, cat milk and treats, then at the vet bed and litter tray. 'I get the feeling that this will be something of a learning curve for both of us, Asti-cat.'

It wasn't a perfect solution. She wasn't sure that the small soft hunter would adjust to being a house cat, but it was worth a try. The less time Skye spent at Daniel's home the better. Her last night alone there had totally freaked her out. The media had hammered on her door and there were several anonymous telephone calls in the early hours. She had risen early, gathered up her uniforms, clothes and toiletries and, using a circuitous route, had driven back to her flat. Asti was her only problem, but as she didn't think she could face the barrage of press staked out on Daniel's doorstep, the cat would either have to go into a cattery, or try her luck as a flatmate in Skye's two bedroom ground-floor flat.

So here she was, at Daniel's place, hopefully for the last time until her lovely, mixed-up boyfriend was back with her again. Whenever that might be.

She had already cleared the fridge of anything perishable, and checked that the answer-phone was set. Now Skye walked around making sure that all the windows and doors were locked.

'Right, Cat-astrophe, are you ready for your first photo-shoot with Saltern's press?'

The cat let out a piteous yowl.

'I know exactly how you feel. But let's get this over, shall we?'

Skye set the alarm system and opened the front door.

She should have been used to the bright flashes by now, but she gave a grunt of anger, grasped the carrier tighter and pushed her way towards her car. Questions rained down on her and reporters pushed cameras into her face, but she remained tight-lipped, secretly hoping that she might run one or two of them over on her way out.

It was ironic. She'd always been so proud that Daniel was a journalist, and now here she was, fighting them off as if they were a swarm of malaria-infested mosquitoes.

She glanced into her rear-view mirror as she pulled out onto the road, and was disappointed to see no bodies strewn across the gravel. 'Don't worry, we'll get them next time,' she said to the cat. 'Now, hang onto your scratching post, we're taking the scenic route, just in case we're being tailed.'

The journey took twice as long as it should, and as she pulled into the parking area at the back of her flats, Skye was relieved to find it empty.

Tavernier Court was a sympathetic conversion of old, red brick railway buildings with beautiful grey slate tiles. The architect had retained as many of the original features as possible, without making the place look like a Thomas the Tank Engine theme park.

None of the flats had more than two bedrooms, which meant that it was a relatively quiet development with very few children, and that suited Skye. It wasn't that she didn't like children, but bored kids during school holidays could play havoc with shift work.

As she pulled in to her designated parking space, she felt a wave of relief. She loved her home. From the moment she had set foot in it, she had felt at peace. She felt safe there, something that she never felt in Daniel's expensive townhouse. Every day she offered up a little prayer of thanks to her grandmother for leaving her the money for the deposit. Her job alone would never have allowed her to buy a home in Tavernier Court. It was not big, but it was what estate agents always refer to as a "very desirable location."

She secured the car and walked to her front door. She unlocked it and carried the cat inside. After retrieving all her bags, she closed the door and opened the flap on the carrier.

'Welcome to your new home,' she said to Asti. The cat strode out, her tail flicking angrily.

'Well? What do you think?'

The cat stalked regally around, tentatively sniffing at the furniture. She didn't look very pleased with her unscheduled change of residence.

'Believe me, it's better than the Cats' Hotel, so if I were you, I'd start looking just a tad excited about your holiday destination.' She placed the plastic tray against the wall in the hallway, undid the sack of litter and poured it in. 'Now, first things first. Pin back your ears, because I'm going to explain the house rules.' She fixed the cat with a firm stare. 'Actually, there is only one rule.' She pointed to the tray. 'Got it, fur-face?'

Her mobile rang before she received an answer. Skye suddenly felt apprehensive. Coming back home, she had felt distanced from all her recent troubles for a moment. Now what? She looked at the display.

'Hello, Sergeant Evans. Is everything alright?'

Marie Evans' voice was calm. 'Yes, this is just an update and a call to check on how you are. We know the media are hounding you.'

'I'm back at my own house, Detective. I was going to ring you and give you my landline number. I don't think I'm cut out for dealing with paparazzi.'

'I'm glad to hear it. You'd have to be a psychopath to enjoy that kind of attention.' Sergeant Evans hesitated, then went on, 'There's no news from Thailand, I'm afraid. Finding Ruby Kinder is like looking for a needle in a haystack. The map they seem to be using is as useful as a blank sheet of paper.'

'I'm worried about the house,' said Skye. 'There are some beautiful things in it, and I'd hate there to be a break-in. I feel responsible.'

'It really isn't your problem, Skye, but I'll make sure that our beat bobbies keep an eye on it, now we know it's empty.'

'That would be great, thanks.' Skye exhaled. 'How is Daniel?'

'That brings me to my next point. He's fine . . . well, he seems okay at the moment. More relaxed and approachable.'

'Can I see him?'

'DI Jackman wondered if you would be able to come in early this evening, at around six, if that is convenient. There are some things we'd like to discuss with you, and someone we'd like you to meet. After we've spoken, you can see Daniel for a while.'

To her horror, Skye realised that part of her was afraid of seeing Daniel, scared to see him in a police station. It was just so *wrong*. Daniel was as much a killer as Scooby Doo was a pit bull. Yet she had to see him. She did want to see him, she needed to. She needed to hold him — though she couldn't imagine being able to do that. 'I'll be there, Sergeant. But who is the person you want me to meet?'

'A man called Guy Preston. He's a doctor, Skye. Daniel has spoken with him and I really think it's already making a difference.'

Skye closed her eyes. A psychiatrist. Next they would be pumping Daniel full of chemicals and turning him into a zombie with all the creative genius of a pumpkin.

'I think you'll like Professor Preston, Skye. He's a very eminent man in his field, and he has Daniel's best interests at heart, I promise you.'

I wonder, thought Skye. 'Is he a psychiatrist?'

'No, he's a forensic psychologist. Big difference. And he's good — you can take that from someone who knows.'

'Okay.' Skye knew Daniel needed help, and this man could be the answer to her prayers. Marie Evans was right, there was a big difference between the two. If a good psychologist saw Daniel's problems for what they really were, he might finally get his head sorted out, and be able to come home. 'Thank you, Sergeant Evans. I'll see you at six.'

Skye closed her phone, and it rang again immediately.

'Home yet?'

'Oh, Lisa, yes. Got back a few minutes ago. I was just settling the cat, and then I was going to text you.'

'I'm finishing early today so I thought I'd check you're okay before I go home.'

'I'm fine. Well, I am now I'm out of that house. I was well spooked last night.'

Skye watched Asti stalk across her lounge and take a swipe at a leaf of one of her houseplants. 'And thanks for all your help. I really appreciate it.'

'My pleasure. I love cleaning up after muddy-booted men who've just trashed a nice property. It's a hobby of mine.'

'In which case, you need to get out more,' laughed Skye. 'Or take up origami.'

'You sound brighter.'

'I'm going to see Daniel later.'

'Ah, that explains it. Well, I'd better let you get on, but anything you want, just ring. You've got my number.' Lisa paused. 'Even if it's late and you just want to talk after seeing your other half, I'm a night owl, so feel free to phone me.'

'I might just do that. And thanks again for yesterday. You really were a lifesaver.'

Skye went to the kitchen and found homes for Asti's cat food and other feline accoutrements. She glanced up at the kitchen clock, a shabby-chic copy of a rustic French café wall clock, and decided that she just about had time to get some shopping before going to the police station. Then she wondered if it was fair to walk out and leave the cat alone before it had settled in properly. She glanced through the door into the lounge, and saw Asti curled in a tight ball on her sofa.

'My fault, I guess. I should have told you the house rule about animals and furniture.' Skye picked up her bag and keys. 'But as you're obviously so comfortable, I'll just do the shopping. Okay with you?'

Asti yawned. Skye shook her head and headed for Tesco.

CHAPTER ELEVEN

After the interview with Daniel, Guy Preston said that he would go home to try to find his old research on Françoise Thayer, but he would definitely be back for the meeting with Daniel's girlfriend.

Marie found herself alone with Jackman in his office. She knew her boss would be eaten up with curiosity about her connection with Preston and decided she had better put him out of his misery. She dropped down into his visitor's chair and smiled wearily at him. 'It's okay, I won't make you beg. So, if you're sitting comfortably, I'll begin.'

Jackman settled himself in his captain's chair, and looked at her expectantly.

'Once upon a time, during a particularly fraught interview with the very dangerous Terence Marcus Austin, things went, as the saying goes, tits up.'

Marie began to describe what had happened. She was transported back to the small, stuffy room where she had sat with three others, and a man that she later found out was a deranged psychopath.

Guy Preston sat immediately opposite Austin, still only a suspect at that stage, and contemplated him.

Marie felt uneasy, and she had no idea why. All the other interviews had been like a game, in which Austin tried to outwit the psychologist.

But today Austin was in a very different place. He mumbled incoherently to himself, and seemed to be talking and listening intently to someone only he was aware of. No matter how much Preston cajoled and reasoned, Austin was having none of it.

Terence Austin was something of an enigma, far from what you would expect a murderer to be like. He was bright, intelligent and had a clean-cut appearance that would not have been out of place on an advertisement for men's shampoo. He had always seemed to look forward to his sessions with Professor Preston, but right now Marie was feeling alarmed.

'Maybe we should suspend this interview, Doctor?'

Two custody officers stood silently at the back of the room, and one of them cleared his throat. Marie took it as an assent to her suggestion, but Guy Preston slowly shook his head and in a calm voice said, 'I'm certain that Terence wants to talk. Don't you, Terence?'

Austin sat rocking backwards and forwards, the fingers of both hands lightly touching and forming an arch, but he said nothing.

'Well, even if you choose not to speak, your body language is telling me everything I need to know right now.' Preston began making notes in very small and very precise handwriting. 'You can be quite transparent when you behave like this. It's pretty much text-book behaviour.'

The doctor clearly wanted to make Austin angry, but she didn't know why. Was it to snap him out of his present state? To let Austin know that Preston was tired of his play-acting? She thought the doctor was treading on thin ice.

'I'm sorry.' The voice was soft and full of contrition. It came as a shock to Marie. She had been preparing herself for a full-blown explosion of rage.

Austin placed his hands gently on the table, one over the other. His head was slightly bowed, and he appeared to be praying, or seeking forgiveness.

Then Marie saw the glint in his eye.

The next few seconds were pandemonium. The events unfurled in a weird kind of slow motion.

Austin's hand was suddenly galvanised and he snatched Preston's pen. Before any of the officers present could move, he stabbed it viciously at the doctor's face. Preston, leaning forward over his notes, didn't see it coming. He turned fractionally, and that action possibly saved his eye, but he could do nothing to stop the pen digging into the soft tissue of his cheek, and ripping and tearing through the flesh, down to his jaw-line.

Marie screamed to the custody officers to call for help. One smacked his fist into the rubber panic button strip that circumnavigated the room, but the other remained rooted to the spot.

Austin used those valuable instants to plunge the pen downward and skewer Preston's left hand with his makeshift weapon.

Preston let out a cry of disbelief and excruciating pain, but Marie had seen that Austin wasn't finished yet. He wrenched the pen from Preston's bleeding hand and she knew he was about to strike at the psychologist's throat.

As Austin drew his arm back ready to thrust, Marie threw herself around the table, grabbed at his wrist and slammed into him. The weight of her body took him off balance and the pen was deflected. It slid across her ribs. As they hit the floor, the two officers went into action, following them down, wrenching Austin over onto his stomach and bringing his arms up behind him. As Marie rolled away she heard the reassuring sound of the ratchet on the handcuffs clicking into place around the attacker's wrists.

'The whole thing was over in seconds.' Marie looked at Jackman, and shook her head. 'I've been over and over it in my head, and I still wonder if I could have prevented him getting so badly injured.'

'Sounds like he provoked the attack,' answered Jackman. 'Why goad Austin?'

'Apparently it's pretty standard procedure. A good psychologist can take someone right to the very edge, and ninety-nine point nine times out of a hundred they bring them back safely with the result they need.'

'Well, it didn't work that time, did it? And you said he was good?'

'He is, sir. He's brilliant. And he didn't give up on Austin. He couldn't be directly involved again but he worked closely with his successor and ensured the correct outcome. Preston only misjudged Austin once, and in fact it was probably the only professional mistake he ever made. But it nearly cost him his life. That's why he never had plastic surgery. He uses those scars to remind him never to underestimate the people he works with.'

Jackman nodded. 'Ah, I did wonder about that.'

'And he never blamed Austin for what happened, only himself.'

'All the same, if it was me, I'd get those scars attended to. I wouldn't be able to forget something like that. I wouldn't need reminding.' He paused. 'That was a little like what happened to Fred Cox, wasn't it?'

'Similar. Just proves that you can't let your guard down for one second.' Marie remembered the incident. A detective had been injured during an interview when the man being questioned had smashed his mug on the table and thrust the broken shards into the detective's face. Luckily, DC Cox had good reflexes and had put his hands up to protect himself, but even so, he had needed an operation, thirty plus stitches and a month off work.

'But it would never have happened if some muppet hadn't given the prisoner his coffee in one of the canteen mugs.' The bad guys always got polystyrene or disposable beakers.

'No one could have predicted what Austin did to Preston. Until that point, Austin had always been remarkably unemotional, and sometimes really good-humoured. Most of the team, with the exception of Guy Preston, who always believed that Austin was the killer, were certain we'd got the wrong man. He was not the only suspect, and initially he seemed the least likely be a killer,' Marie said.

'And afterwards? How did Preston react to your preventing his throat from being perforated?'

Marie felt a wave of discomfort wash over her. 'In truth? It was weird. He knew he might have been killed and he was, well, deeply moved, I guess.' She drew her face into a frown. 'But it was me who found it most difficult. Terence Marcus Austin admitted that he had fully intended to pierce the carotid artery and he knew exactly where it was located, so his intention had been to kill. So I suppose my actions did save Guy Preston's life, but for some odd reason, I kind of felt resentment at Guy's puppy-dog gratitude. I felt an overwhelming responsibility to be nice to him. It was a difficult time.'

'I've heard this before. You would expect it to be the other way around, but often it isn't. I believe it comes from the fact that you've stopped a human life being taken, so you feel duty bound to continue to protect it.' He sat back in his chair and looked pensive. 'Did it cause any problems?'

Marie drew in a breath. 'It would have done, if my husband hadn't been so understanding. Guy seemed to need to talk about what had happened, and I was the natural one to talk to. A bond had formed between us, whether I liked it or not, and people did comment.' She raised her eyebrows. 'You know how a load of coppers can gossip.'

'Oh yes. I'm surprised you survived unscathed.'

'Oh, I had to point out one or two home truths, believe me.'

'So what happened? Where did Preston go?'

'He got involved in a new project. The Home Office were setting up a think tank studying the possibilities of profiling in the case of serious crimes. They offered him a two-year research grant. He moved away, and I can't say that I was upset by his decision. The last I heard he was up north working as an advisor to a specialist unit offering forensic psychological support to major crime enquiries.

Hell, I didn't even know he'd married, let alone lost his wife.'

Jackman tilted his head slightly to one side. 'Considering what you've just told me, will it be difficult for you to work with him again?'

Marie grinned and shook her head. 'Absolutely not, sir. It was a shock to see him again, but all this happened years ago, it's water under the bridge. He's a great guy, excuse the pun, and I have no doubt at all about his expertise.' She lost the smile. 'Don't hold that one slip-up against him, sir. He's what our Max would call the big kahuna. He'll get to the bottom of why Daniel Kinder is here and bleating about being a killer, I'm absolutely certain.'

Jackman leaned back and stretched. 'Then tonight's little tête-à-tête could be interesting.' He glanced at his watch. 'What time did we ask Skye Wynyard to get here?'

'Six, sir. Maybe we could grab something to eat before the evening session gets under way?'

Jackman agreed. 'Go see how Max and Charlie are doing, and if they are willing to stay on for a bit, get them to organise some food for the four of us, okay?' He pulled out his wallet, handed her thirty pounds and with a pained expression added, 'And if it could be anything other than pizza, I'd be forever grateful.'

Marie took it and nodded. 'I'll make your feelings known, guv. Oh, sir, I meant to ask, are you going to tell Kinder about the second dead woman?'

He frowned. 'We'll play that one by ear, shall we?'

As Marie approached her desk, the phone rang from an internal extension. She snapped out her name.

'I thought I'd ring you directly, Sergeant, rather than ring Jackman and be fobbed off — as usual.' Orac's voice crackled dryly from the receiver. 'I have some information that you might find interesting. Have you got ten minutes?'

'Absolutely. I'll be down right away.'

* * *

114

Orac's subterranean kingdom was lit only by the light of the display monitors. She sat in her usual place, staring at one of the active screens. Marie wasn't sure what she was seeing. It appeared to be one moving mass of figures and symbols.

'Although it has nothing to do with the film, it *is* a matrix.'

Orac turned to Marie and smiled. 'Do you know anything about linear combinations of quantum states?'

Marie smiled back. 'Ah, my best subject! How did you guess?'

Orac's smile broadened. Slightly. 'I'm studying advanced computer graphics and we use matrices to project a three-dimensional image onto a two-dimensional screen, which gives us a more realistic appearance of motion. The thing about this,' she pointed to the screen, 'is that it's highly addictive. The more you learn, the more you want to understand. Right now I'm well into numerical linear algebra.'

Since Marie could think of no answer to this, Orac turned back to her desk and picked up a hefty folder. 'This is everything I could find without breaking the law too badly. Luckily there was a fair bit of information still squirreled away in old files. Plus I'm trying to isolate possible relocation sites for the evidence boxes, and,' she handed Marie a slip of paper with a name and a number on it, 'I think this could be the best bit.'

'Peter Hodder?'

'He's the DI who led up the Haines double murder enquiry. He retired eons ago and his biological clock should have stopped a decade back, but I suspect he's a covert android. I've spoken to him and he's as switched on as the Blackpool Lights. If you want to know about Françoise Thayer, I suggest you take a short trip over the county line to Rutland and go see Peter Hodder.' She passed Marie the folder. 'He's a really sweet old guy, and was clearly badly affected by Thayer. It was his last case and I almost heard his teeth grind when I mentioned her name.' Orac blinked those odd eyes. 'But even so, he's willing to talk to you.'

'Thanks for that. I really appreciate it.' She looked back to the complex monitor screen. 'I'd better leave you to your algebra.'

Orac swung her chair back to face her screen. 'I hear you have a well-messed-up Jane Doe in the mortuary? Any luck with tracing her identity?'

'Sadly she's not quite presentable enough to circulate pictures — well, not without giving half the population nightmares.'

'If you let me have the forensic photos of the head, exact measurements of the skull and any confirmed details about her size, colouring etc., I'm trialling a new version of FADAR.'

'I'm sure I should know what you're talking about, er . . . ?'

'Facial Description And Recognition program. It's my own design, software that takes forensic facial reconstruction to a whole different level. It's a fusion of forensic science, anthropology, osteology and anatomy. Your boss would be *so* interested in this, given his academic background, if he *ever* found the time to venture down here.'

'I'm sure he would,' said Marie sincerely. 'But could you really give us an idea of what she looked like?'

'Simple. Get me that data, and she's all yours. Now would you like 2-D, or 3-D?'

'Whatever you think is best. I'll get onto that as soon as the forensic department opens tomorrow.'

'If you ring now there's a chance of getting it tonight. I think you'll find that that oddball Jacobs and one or two of his acolytes are working late this evening.'

'How the hell do you know that?'

Orac gave her a wicked half-smile. 'It's not too difficult to tap into the security camera system over at the mortuary and the forensic laboratories. I checked the car park just before your arrival and Jacobs and his little band are still slaving away.'

'Right.' Marie was already embarking on a fantasy about Orac being Big Brother. She pulled her phone from her pocket. 'In which case, I'll request it straightaway.'

Orac had been correct. Surprisingly, the pathologist who answered the phone said that he could retrieve the information quite easily and would email it directly to Orac.

'Nice one,' said Marie appreciatively to the IT wizard. 'It doesn't always come together as easily as that.'

'It does when you know exactly where everyone is.'

'I see your point. Well, thanks again. This is all a really great help.'

'No problem. I'll send you the reconstructed picture of your Jane Doe as soon as I have it.' Orac had already turned away and her eyes were fixed on the screen of moving figures. 'Come back anytime.'

Marie stopped outside the closed door and took a deep breath. Orac being nice? More than that, Orac being nice, helpful *and* friendly?

Marie shook her head in puzzlement, and with the heavy folder firmly under her arm, made her way back to the lifts.

CHAPTER TWELVE

'The preliminary forensic reports are in, Sarge,' Charlie said as soon as Marie entered the CID room. 'The guvnor has them now.'

'Great, and I have a whole load of info on the Haines murders, and an intro to the retired DI who arrested Françoise Thayer.'

'How's the custody clock on Kinder, Sarge?'

'We have until ten p.m. to either charge or release him,' Marie said. 'And it's still six of one, half a dozen of the other as to what we do with him. Let's pray that the forensics will help.'

Max grimaced. 'Anyone fancy a little flutter? Ten to one they find something that connects Dimbo Danny with Jane Doe. Any takers?' He waited for a moment. 'Thought not.'

Inside Jackman's office, Marie discovered that she had been right not to accept Max's wager.

'I'd get more bloody help from a horoscope reading!' He threw the forensic report across the desk. 'Jane Doe. No DNA, no blood other than hers, no scars, birthmarks or tattoos, and no fingerprints that tally with anything on our computer system. The only small ray of hope is that one of Jacob's greatest skills is pin-pointing time of death. He's certain, having taken into account the fluctuating temperatures in that cellar and the state of decomposition, along with the opinion of a consultant forensic entomologist, that she had been dead for around twenty-one days.'

'Well, that's somewhere to start, isn't it? And don't get too suicidal about identifying her, because I come bearing tidings of great joy.' Marie told him about Orac, and watched his face clear from outbreaks of thunder to bright sunny spells.

'Orac? Are we talking about the same person?'

'Could there possibly be more than one?' asked Marie with eyes wide.

'There has to be, if the one you spoke to is offering to help us out. Orac doesn't work like that. Perhaps there are two of them. Maybe she has an evil twin.'

'Let's not knock it, huh? A picture of Jane Doe is exactly what we need right now. And, sir?' She looked at him almost admonishingly. 'It really wouldn't hurt to go down and thank her if we get a successful identification.'

Jackman looked shifty. 'Mm, well . . . Let's see what she comes up with first.'

Marie placed Orac's files on his desk. 'She's already come up with all this on the Haines murder case, *and* made contact with the arresting DI.'

'Now you *are* freaking me out. What does she want, do you think?'

At a rough guess, thought Marie, the answer was Jackman. 'Pass, but there's a lot of useful stuff here. I suggest that as soon as we've spoken to Skye and Daniel, the boys and I get to work on this little lot. Then we can at least find out something concrete about Françoise Thayer and her natural-born son.'

Jackman nodded. 'I agree. Now let's go eat before Miss Wynyard gets here.'

* * *

Jackman had tried to keep the atmosphere relaxed. And it had worked, until he asked her how much time she had spent in Daniel's company on a certain few days three weeks previously.

'Something else has happened, hasn't it?' Skye's composure shattered. 'Oh no!'

Marie nodded slowly. 'It hasn't reached the press yet, and we would be grateful if you could keep it to yourself, but another body has been found.'

'And you suspect Daniel? That means you are taking this whole ridiculous scenario seriously!' Her voice dropped almost to a whisper. 'I thought you understood.'

'We *have* to take what Daniel tells us seriously, Skye. Supposing we ignored his statement and he turned out to be telling the truth.' Jackman kept his tone reasonable. 'And Daniel does know a lot about Alison Fleet.'

'Hardly surprising. He's spent the last decade studying murder.' Skye sighed. 'I think his mother knew Alison Fleet. I wouldn't even be surprised if Daniel hadn't visited the Fleets' house at some time with Ruby Kinder. Both women were heavily involved in charitable causes.'

Jackman sat up. 'You never mentioned that before.'

'So much was going on that I never even thought about it. It's just that when I was cleaning up the house after the scene-of-crime officers, I was dusting some picture frames and I saw a photograph of Daniel's mother and father at a charity race night, and Alison Fleet and her husband were at their table.'

'So, there *is* a connection between them,' breathed Marie.

'But it's something of a double-edged sword, isn't it?' added Jackman. 'The fact that they knew each other could indicate that Daniel had a motive to hurt her, and it could also be a simple explanation of how he knows the layout of Berrylands.'

Guy Preston, who had been listening intently, finally spoke. 'Let's go back to Daniel's whereabouts when the other woman died.' He smiled gently at Skye. 'Were you staying with Daniel on the dates mentioned?'

Skye leant forward and picked up her handbag from the floor. She removed a narrow pocket diary and began turning the pages. Then her shoulders sagged. 'No. I was at Sheffield Hallam University. It was a three-day career workshop for OTs. I stayed over with an old school friend who works at the uni.' She closed the diary and Jackman saw tears forming in her eyes. 'Does Daniel know about this other death?'

'Not yet. But we will need to know where he was, before our time for holding him in custody runs out.'

'He was at home alone, or at his office working.' Skye's voice was shaky. 'I rang him several times. You can check my mobile phone records, if it will help him.'

'That doesn't prove anything, I'm afraid. He could have been anywhere.'

'Sometimes I rang the house, I'm sure I did.'

Poor kid, thought Jackman, she's clutching at straws.

Preston sat forward. 'Skye, I'm very interested in what Daniel calls his "gaps." Have you ever witnessed Daniel having one of these memory lapses?'

'Yes, although they generally happen when he's alone. He goes off somewhere, then he can't recall where he's been. If you are around when it happens, he just seems to be distant, in a sort of dream state for a short period of time. It doesn't last long, but it *is* disturbing, believe me.'

'I do. I've seen it before, and unless I'm mistaken, it's not amnesia.'

Jackman listened with interest. 'So what is it?'

'It's a "fugue state," known as a dissociative fugue. The sufferer can very suddenly decide to make a trip away from home, and then have a complete inability to recall anything about it.'

'And what causes it?' asked Jackman.

'Severe stress, although there are a few medical causes, like epilepsy or complex partial seizures or substance abuse, but they are rare. It's generally stress-related.'

'Can you cure these fugues, Professor Preston?' asked Skye.

'Psychotherapy or hypnosis can be useful, but a psychiatrist needs to exclude the medical causes before any treatment is offered.'

'There's something else that you should know,' Skye said slowly. 'Daniel has no memory of anything prior to his fifth birthday. His whole early childhood is a total blank.'

There was a silence. Then Guy Preston asked, 'Do you know the reason for that?'

'His mother said he had an accident. Apparently he fell from a swing and sustained a head injury.' She looked at the doctor. 'She said that his "gaps" most likely stemmed from that.'

Preston drew in a deep breath. 'It's feasible, I suppose, if the damage was severe. But a fall from a child's swing? I'm not convinced it would cause fugues. They are much more related to stress.'

'And could he kill, during one of these episodes?' Jackman asked.

'People have been known to assume new identities while they are in these states, so the answer, I suppose, is possibly.' Guy bit his lip. 'If Daniel is suffering from a mental disorder, there could be a partial or complete breakdown of the control he would normally have over his thoughts, emotions and behaviour. In his "other" identity, he might have a very different set of values to the Daniel Kinder that you know.'

'A split personality?' asked Marie.

'No. Multiple personalities are quite different. The fugue state is simply a reaction to severe stress.'

'And if you were able to relieve that stress?' suggested Jackman.

'The fugues would most likely dissipate organically.'

'Which brings us firmly back to Françoise Thayer and the fact that our prisoner believes he is the murderer's son,' growled Marie.

Guy nodded. 'I agree. So why don't we sort out that little conundrum?'

'Ha!' Skye barked out a sharp, humourless laugh. 'I have been trying to do that for months! And Daniel has for years! It's not that simple.'

Marie leaned across and touched Skye's arm. 'Hey, listen. We have access to channels that you don't. We have a huge technological support system at our disposal, and we'll use it. We need those answers as badly as you and Daniel, because if he's not the killer, someone else is, and they are getting away with murder.'

'Absolutely,' said Jackman. 'Now, we are going to have a word with Daniel. We are not sure whether he will be charged or released, but either way, we'd like him to cooperate and work closely with Professor Preston here. We'd like you to be there too, as long as Daniel is in agreement. Would you do that?'

'Of course.' There was no hesitation. 'Right, the sergeant and I will go talk to him, and then you can see him for a while.' He stood up. 'Not alone of course, but I'm sure you can understand that.'

Skye simply said, 'Thank you.'

CHAPTER THIRTEEN

'Nice drum, huh?'

Kevin Stoner stared gloomily out of the car window at the big executive-style house. 'I suppose. If you like that kind of thing.'

Zane Prewett licked his lips. 'Oh, do cheer up, my little friend! Surely you'd like a swanky flash pad like that? I didn't see all of upstairs when we were here with the SOCOs, but I bet it's got a king-size water bed, and mirrors all around the master bedroom. I've already sussed the log cabin with the hot tub in the back garden, and a very useful games room, with a well-stocked bar no less.' He nudged Kevin. 'Think what you and some of your pretty little friends could get up to in a place like this.'

Kevin kept his eyes on the Kinder property, and tried to pretend that he was alone in the car.

'Oh well,' said Prewett. 'Even if your imagination has gone on strike, mine hasn't. And right now, I'm seeing some very juicy pussy getting naked in that tub.'

'Shut up, Prewett! I'm sick of listening to your foul mouth! So just give it a break, will you?' Kevin slumped back in his seat and gritted his teeth.

'Oooh, touchy, aren't we?' Prewett swung round and faced him. 'But I'd be a bit careful if I were you, Mary-

Jane. You're starting to piss me off with your holier-than-thou attitude, when I've got certain evidence to prove that you're nothing but a dirty little hypocrite. I mention "pussy" and its filth, but *you* can shag some fairy up against a wall and that's alright. Catch my drift?'

'But *I* don't think sex is everything, Zane. Not like you. It's just a small part of my life, and sadly for me, it just happens to be one you've found out about.'

'Yeah, bummer ain't it?'

Kevin knew he couldn't go on like this. If it was just down to him and Zane, maybe he'd actually take the bastard on. He'd throw up his hands and tell his father that he was being blackmailed because he was gay, then turn the tables on Prewett and cough up all the shady deals that he knew the bent copper was involved in. But when Prewett was threatening his young niece, Sophie . . . That was too much of a risk to take. Kevin knew that most bullies are cowards, but he had the feeling that Prewett really would carry out his threat, and no way would he put Sophie or any of his family in jeopardy. There had to be another way.

As Kevin drove slowly up the tree-lined street, he tried to think clearly. He edged the car out onto the river road and felt his tense neck muscles begin to relax. Maybe it was time to stop thinking like the bishop's son. He'd turned the other cheek far too often. Zane Prewett clearly deserved a different kind of treatment.

By the time they were back at the station, a tiny embryo of a plan had formed in his mind, and for the first time in months, PC Kevin Stoner felt almost happy.

* * *

As Jackman was about to enter the interview room, a civilian handed him a brown envelope. 'Just arrived, sir. From the Home Office pathologist.'

Jackman tore open the seal and quickly scanned the toxicology report. The attached note simply said, "Interesting," and was signed by Jacobs. 'What the hell . . . ?'

Marie looked at him and tilted her head.

'Alison Fleet had enough happy pills in her system to cheer up half the county.'

'Antidepressants?' Marie looked confused. 'But didn't Bruce Fleet say she wasn't on any medication?'

'Well, he actually said none that he knew of, which is a different thing I suppose. But all the same, it's odd. I'd always thought that her OTT exuberance was a natural thing. Perhaps she was just permanently high as a kite.'

'Then we need to speak to her GP.'

'Pop back and ask either Max or Charlie to get onto it straightaway.' He handed her the report. 'People don't take that kind of medication without good reason.'

'I wonder if it's connected to her first husband, the one that Bruce Fleet doesn't know about.'

'Doesn't know, or won't talk about.' Jackman said thoughtfully. 'I think we should go have another word with Mr Fleet. I can't believe he knew so little about his loving wife, can you?'

'Then let's get this interview over, and go pay him a call.'

As it turned out, the interview was far from the breakthrough that Jackman had expected.

Daniel Kinder had seemed subdued, almost depressed, and had meekly agreed to their suggestion of working with Dr Preston. His response was unenthusiastic, a sort of dreary acceptance of the way things would have to go.

Jackman had stared at Kinder while the doctor had explained certain things to him. He had seen no sign of the fiery young journalist of the recent past, no spark of anger and not even any joy at being told he could see Skye.

After an hour Jackman brought the interview to a halt, and asked Preston and Marie to join him in his office.

'We simply don't have enough solid evidence to hold him.' He knew his voice betrayed his exasperation. He looked at Guy Preston. 'What do you think about him, honestly?'

The psychologist drew in a long breath, then let out a low whistle. 'I think he has serious problems, but deep down, I don't think he killed Alison Fleet.'

'Or the other woman?'

'I don't think he killed anyone.'

They had told Daniel about their mystery woman, their Jane Doe, and he had responded with a shrug. He had said, in a voice that sounded hopeless, 'I can't tell you that I didn't kill her, because I don't know. I'm afraid it's down to you to prove it, one way or the other.' He had then added, 'It shouldn't be too difficult, surely? I thought that with the advanced technology there is these days, you could tell where anyone was at any given time.'

'We don't live in a sodding episode of CSI,' Marie had flung back. 'Get real, Daniel, this is the fens, not Miami, and right now we have a police budget that wouldn't oil a surfboard for a year.'

Daniel Kinder had shrugged again.

Jackman sighed. 'Well, I have to decide what to do by ten o'clock. And I still don't feel happy about letting him go.'

'Me neither,' said Marie. 'Although I no longer believe that he's here to try and find an exposé for one of his articles.'

'If he is, he's putting on a great show of being a sandwich short of a picnic.' He gave the doctor an apologetic smile. 'Sorry. Not exactly the most scientific way of putting it.'

Preston smiled back. 'Oh, I don't think he's shamming. Not for one moment. But I'd stake my reputation on the fact that he's not a serial killer.' He looked at Jackman, his face now serious. 'If you suspect that you really do have a serial killer on your patch, it's not Kinder. They don't just emerge fully-formed. That kind of killer evolves over a long period of time. It takes years of gradual change until they reach what I call the initial killing stage. He doesn't fit the pattern.'

'But you're not saying that Daniel Kinder couldn't possibly kill, just that he's not a serial killer.'

'Exactly. Although I find it hard to believe that he has it in him to kill at all. Maybe if he's sick, as we said before, or if he is driven by his belief that he has Françoise Thayer's blood running through his veins, then perhaps he is . . .' He shook his head. 'But I'm not convinced.'

A knock on the door interrupted them, and an excited Max appeared. 'I think you'll want to see this, sir.' He smiled and handed Jackman a printout on photographic paper. 'Jane has a face!'

Jackman stared at the image, and a fair-haired, very attractive woman looked back at him. She had grey-blue eyes, straight shoulder-length hair, high cheek-bones, and a full, well-shaped mouth with straight white teeth. Somehow he felt that she looked very English — not blonde enough to be Scandinavian, not angular enough to be Germanic, she just seemed fair and soft, the typical "English rose" type. 'Hello, Jane,' he whispered, then offered the picture to the others.

'Wow!' said Marie.

'Oh Lord! It's hard to match this beauty to your forensic photo on the whiteboard in the murder room,' said Preston.

'And Orac actually produced that in just a few hours?' Jackman asked Marie.

'Less than that. I really do think thanks are in order.'

'Mm, of course. Really wonderful work.' He saw Marie's narrowed eyes, and quickly looked away. 'I think we should show this to Daniel, don't you?'

They all hurried back down to the interview room. Charlie and a uniformed officer were watching while Daniel and Skye Wynyard talked.

'This woman,' said Jackman bluntly, and laid the photo on the table where they both could see it. 'Do you recognise her?'

To his surprise, there were two sharp intakes of breath.

'Jules! It's Julia Hope,' said Skye, clearly shocked.

'And you, Daniel? Do you know her too?'

He shook his head. 'Not really . . . I mean I don't actually know her, but I'm sure she was in a group of nurses that I interviewed for the newspaper article on the NHS.' He gnawed on his bottom lip. 'I don't think I spoke to her personally, but I do recognise her. Is she . . . is she the woman . . . ?'

'The woman who you may, or may not, have killed? The one whose death it is up to us to sort out? Yes, Daniel, that's her.' He turned to Skye. 'But you do know her?'

'Yes. She works on the orthopaedic ward, but she's been off on holiday for a couple of weeks.'

'Some holiday,' growled Marie. 'She's been lying dead and unidentified for three weeks! Didn't anyone think to check on why she didn't go back to work?'

'I . . . I don't know,' stammered Skye. 'It's not my department. She's a nurse, not an occupational therapist.' She stared wide-eyed at Marie. 'You're sure she is dead? The photo is slightly . . . well, not quite like her somehow.'

'Because it's a reconstruction, isn't it?' Daniel's voice was flat. 'From her dead body.'

Skye pushed it gingerly away from her.

'Precisely,' said Jackman, seeing again the rotting corpse on the cellar room floor.

'So what can you tell us about her, Skye? Is she married? Single? Does she have family?' Marie asked.

'She's not married, I know that, but I don't know much else, other than that she lives with her sister, Anna, somewhere in Saltern town.'

'So why didn't this sister report her missing?'

'Anna's an army medic. She could be away somewhere. Jules did mention her being in Afghanistan, although that was a while back.' Skye looked askance at the picture. 'She was really beautiful.'

Not when I saw her last, thought Jackman. 'And how about you, Daniel? Have you seen her since the hospital interview for which the entire hospital nursing staff loves you so much?'

Daniel looked at him from under tired, drooping eyelids. 'How the hell would I know? I'm the freak with the memory loss, remember?'

'Are you? Are you really? I wonder.'

CHAPTER FOURTEEN

'A vague connection between the two victims and Daniel Kinder isn't enough to hold him, Jackman.' Superintendent Ruth Crooke chewed on the end of her pen. 'Frankly, in Alison Fleet's case, *you* have closer links than he does. You'll have to let him go.'

Jackman knew it was useless to argue. She was right. There was no evidence, not one shred. The CPS wouldn't even laugh them out of court, because it wouldn't get that far. 'Easier said than done, ma'am.' Having a "first" was usually a nice thing, especially as you got older, but this was the first time that Jackman had had a murder suspect who actually wanted to stay in custody, and he knew Kinder would take the news of his imminent departure badly. It was all a matter of *how* badly.

'And I want you to make sure that he receives psychiatric help, and he goes nowhere we don't know about until *we* say so, right?'

Jackman nodded. 'I don't think he'll stray far. And Guy Preston is going to do a full evaluation on him. Meanwhile we are collating all we now know about Françoise Thayer. We need to put that side of the investigation to bed, and as speedily as possible. If there is another killer out there, we have to forget about Daniel and move on, fast.'

'I'm glad you said that, Jackman, because we need to move at the bloody speed of light on this. Now we have a name for Jane Doe — and by the way, the sister flies in later tonight to identify her formally — I have to make a televised statement to the press.' She tightened her already tightest of lips, 'You have until the morning to work out what the hell I am going to say to them.'

Jackman stood up. He felt an enormous weight on his shoulders, and he was still unhappy about releasing Daniel. 'Then I'd better get moving, ma'am. I have a reluctant free man to prise from his cell.'

* * *

It was not until after eleven o'clock that Daniel Kinder was finally ready to leave the station. Although perhaps "ready" was not a good description. Kicking and screaming was closer to the truth.

Marie had been pretty certain that without Skye Wynyard's endless patience and gentle cajoling, they would have had to use physical force to evict him. Even then, he had utterly refused to go home or, because of his fear of hurting her, stay with Skye. Finally they reached a compromise — well, Skye did. Daniel would stay at Skye's flat, where his precious cat was already in residence, and Skye would crash out at a friend's place for the night. They would reconvene the next morning and in the cold light of day, try to find their way to a satisfactory solution. And only then did Daniel finally acquiesce. No one could do anything further for him, and other than walk the streets, Skye had come up with the only sensible alternative.

And now the murder room was quiet. Only Marie and Jackman remained.

'Have we just let a killer loose?' he asked softly.

'Whatever, we had little choice, did we? And we'll be watching him like a hawk. Wherever he goes and whatever he does, he'll have company.'

'Why don't I feel consoled by that?'

'Because we both know that even if he's not a killer, he's a loose cannon, and completely unstable.' Marie sighed. 'I've never seen anyone so volatile, so changeable in his moods. If I didn't know otherwise, I'd think he was on drugs.'

'But he's as clean as you and I,' murmured Jackman, '. . . which points directly to a psychological disorder. A fact that unsurprisingly does nothing to calm my jangling nerves.'

Marie yawned. 'Time to get some rest.' She picked up the fat folder that Orac had provided. 'Mind if I take this home for a little light bedtime reading?'

'Be my guest. Only promise to leave the light on, and don't ring me at two in the morning because you've scared yourself half to death. Bedtime reading and Françoise Thayer do not go together, believe me. I've been there. She was a cold-blooded, inhuman savage, and if Orac has discovered more about her than I gleaned from the Internet, then be warned.'

Before she could answer him, the desk phone rang. Jackman groaned, made a face, and picked it up.

'DI Jackman here.'

Marie could faintly hear a woman's voice speaking rapidly, then Jackman hit the loudspeaker button and a vaguely familiar voice filled the room.

'I'm so very sorry, but I didn't know who to turn to. It's so unlike him. I'm sure he's at home, but he's just not answering my calls. Inspector, I'm scared something has happened to him. He's been acting so strangely since Alison died.'

On the crackly line, Marie couldn't put a name to the voice. She shot Jackman an enquiring glance and he scribbled a name on a notepad: *Lucy Richards, Bruce Fleet's sister.* Marie immediately recalled the worried face of the woman who had been with Fleet when they had broken the news of Alison's murder.

'Most likely he's just gone out for the evening, or maybe he's had a few drinks too many and passed out.' Jackman's voice was steady. 'What makes you so sure he's at home?'

'For one thing, the police only allowed him back into Berrylands this afternoon. It's his first night back there and he's been dreading it. I wouldn't worry so much, but his car is in the driveway and my brother never walks anywhere if he can help it.'

'How do you know about his car?'

'Because my husband drove out there. He knocked, but couldn't get an answer.' The woman's voice became shaky. 'He's not too pleased at my ringing you, Inspector Jackman, but I have a very bad feeling about Bruce.'

'Okay. I would normally send a crew out, but I'm just about to leave here, so if it helps to put your mind at rest, I'll go myself.' He raised a long-suffering eyebrow at Marie. 'I'll ring you when I have some news.'

He replaced the receiver.

'You didn't have to do that, sir. A squad car could go just as easily.'

Jackman shrugged. 'Maybe her bad feeling has rubbed off on me. Anyway, we wanted a word with Bruce Fleet about all those missing details of his late wife's life. It's a valid excuse to bang on his door. And if I catch him half-drunk or just very tired, maybe he'll speak a little more freely.'

'I'll come with you, as long as you drop me back here or home afterwards.'

Jackman glanced up at the wall clock. 'It's almost midnight. You go get some sleep.'

'Rubbish, sir. Dawn Haven Marsh is pretty remote. If something is wrong out there, you might need your trusty sidekick. And if Fleet is just pissed, then we can be home and tucked up in our beds in an hour or so.'

Jackman pulled his car keys from his jacket pocket. 'Why is it so difficult to argue with you, Marie?'

She grinned smugly. 'Because I'm always right, sir.'

* * *

Marie loved driving over the fens at night. There was a surreal quality to the lonely, often misty roads, and all sense of perspective disappeared. For a while the road would lead one way, then it would veer off in a completely different direction, and if you didn't know the narrow, winding, reed-edged lanes, or have a damned good sense of direction, you could become hopelessly lost.

It took twenty minutes to reach Berrylands but they felt as if they had been driving for hours.

'Shame we don't still have a uniform on watch.'

'Little point once the place had been thoroughly gone over by forensics. It is the husband's home, and the SOCO team wouldn't have handed over the scene unless they were certain it was clean.'

Berrylands was silent. An upstairs light glowed in the landing area, and another seemed to have been left on somewhere on the ground floor, but there was no sign of life.

'She was right about the car.' Jackman looked at the big Toyota Land Cruiser. 'Still, let's do this the sensible way.' He pulled out his phone, scrolled down to the name Bruce Fleet and hit the green call button.

Marie smiled to herself. One of Jackman's little habits was to log everyone remotely connected to a current case into his phone contacts, deleting them only after the case was closed. As he waited for an answer, Marie walked up to the door, rang the bell and rapped her knuckles against the polished wood. Around her were all the signs of the recent police activity — trampled flower beds, muddy patches across the lawn and dried dirty footprints across the tiles in the open porch. She abruptly forgot about broken flower petals and stiffened when she heard a faint sound within. She moved closer to the door, pushed open the letter box and knelt down to listen.

The tinny sound of a repeated track of music was coming from somewhere inside the house: Fleet's mobile. 'Sir, his phone is ringing. I can hear it.'

Jackman hurried to her side. 'Let's check round the back, and if we have no luck, we're going to have to force an entry.'

'I'm with you on that, sir.' Marie moved swiftly to the path that ran around the property. 'That bad feeling Lucy Richards was talking about has just made its way into my veins too, and I don't like it.'

* * *

Skye sat in her car and stared at the dark, blank windows of her friend's flat. She had left a brief message on Isabel's voice mail saying that she was on her way, but it hadn't dawned on her until she had parked up, that Isabel was away visiting her mother in Cardiff. And to her dismay, her friend had not left the spare key in its usual hiding place. It was something that Isabel and Skye always did, certainly not a habit that her new friends in the police force would advise. *Just in case*, they always said, and now, the one time Skye had need of it, Isabel had forgotten to leave it out.

Skye flopped back in the driver's seat and felt sick and tired. Her time in the police station with Daniel had been harrowing, and seeing him in such a strange emotional state had wiped her out. And now, instead of creeping into a soft, warm bed, she had nowhere to go.

She pulled out her phone and clicked on her contact names. It was midnight, and there were very few friends living locally that she felt she could ring at this hour. Penny had a new baby. Richard had a new girlfriend, and Paul and Andrea were going through a far from amicable split in their stormy relationship. Gina? Well, maybe. She was not exactly a close buddy, but she was a nice, genuine work colleague and she wouldn't like the thought of Skye being homeless for the night. It was worth a try.

After the phone had rung for a time, Skye cancelled the call before it went to answer-phone. There was no point in leaving a message.

She let out an exasperated sigh. She did still have the keys to Daniel's house, but she'd rather sleep in the car than go back there. Part of her said, just go home. Tell Daniel exactly what has happened and *make* him understand that he's being ridiculous by thinking that he's going to hurt you. And another part said that Daniel was too fragile to even try to reason with. Forget it. Either find another friend, or find somewhere to park and bed down on the back seat. Not that she was sure if she could fit into the back seat of the little Kia without getting cramp in the first ten minutes. She went back to the list of names on her phone, and finally saw a glimmer of hope. She tapped in the number and after only three rings, her call was answered.

She blurted out what had happened, and relief coursed through her as the voice on the other end said, 'Good Lord, girl! Get yourself around here right now. The guest room is all made up and you're welcome. Very welcome.'

Skye smiled to herself, the load lifting from her tired mind as she turned on the ignition. Why on earth hadn't she thought of Lisa Hurley before? Her boss had been so kind in helping her clear up Daniel's house. She should have been the first person to ask. With a little laugh, Skye accelerated away from Isabel's darkened home and towards a safe haven for the night.

* * *

Marie ran around the side of the farmhouse. Immediately the back garden flooded with light from the security system. She found herself in a beautifully designed patio area of flagstones and raised flower beds full of bright colours. One side of the garden had a long Victorian-style loggia which was covered in a cascade of clematis and roses. But Marie knew that this was not the time to wax lyrical about the Fleets' garden.

'You check the French windows!' called out Jackman as he ran past her. 'I'll get the back door.'

She grabbed the brass handles and turned. 'Locked, sir.'

'Same here, damn it.' Jackman sounded edgy.

'There's another door further along.' Marie went around Jackman and approached a smaller door. It had etched glass panels in the top half, and she could see that it opened directly into a utility room that housed a washing machine and a large tumble-dryer. She twisted the handle, and it opened inwards. 'Okay, we're in,' she whispered, 'as long as the internal door isn't locked.'

It wasn't, and soon she and Jackman were systematically checking the rooms. 'Downstairs all clear.'

They approached the wide staircase, and Marie felt her heart begin to pump harder. Over the years she had found some very unpleasant things during house searches. The only thing she never found was nothing at all.

But Berrylands turned out to be the exception. The bedrooms were empty, and nothing seemed to be out of place, as far as she could tell. There was a sense of disorder and intrusion, left over from the search for evidence following Alison Fleet's murder, but nothing else. They double-checked all the rooms, and Jackman even climbed the loft ladder and looked around the attic. Then they went back downstairs.

For some reason they both made for the kitchen.

Marie stood where she had been when the brutalised body of Alison Fleet was lying on the quarry-tile floor, and took a deep breath.

Something was wrong.

'You feel it too?' Jackman asked softly.

Marie nodded. Bruce Fleet's car keys lay on the scrubbed pine table. 'Keys,' she muttered.

'Car keys.' Her head snapped up. 'Okay, so Bruce's car is out front, but didn't Alison have a car too? Where is it?'

Jackman straightened. 'There's a garage block on the other side of the property.' He moved quickly towards the back door and unlocked it. 'Come on!'

Together they ran out and around the house to a big gravelled area for turning and parking vehicles, but even before they reached the garage, they could hear a familiar, low, rumbling noise inside.

Tiny tendrils of exhaust fumes were seeping from beneath the doors.

'Oh shit!' exclaimed Jackman, yanking on the heavy wooden door. 'It's locked on the inside!'

'Personnel door!' Marie dashed around the side of the building. 'At least that will be easier to break down.'

Luckily the upper half of the smaller door was glass, and it yielded immediately to Jackman's elbow.

Marie slipped her hand over the remaining shards, and deftly turned the key.

'Cover your mouth and nose. This stuff is dangerous even in small doses.' Jackman pulled his jacket up to his face. 'Breathe in as little as you can. You get to the car and switch off the ignition. I'll try to unlock the main doors and let in as much air as possible.'

Marie knew they were too late. Bruce Fleet had been out of reach for hours. She also knew that they could be risking their own health for a dead man, but they had to do it. 'Hell, I didn't think this could happen these days, not with catalytic converters?'

'Look at the car.'

As Marie pulled her own jacket tightly across the lower part of her face, she saw the old Morris Minor Traveller. Alison Fleet's idea of a run-around was a classic museum piece. 'Oh bloody great!' She glanced at Jackman. 'Let's go.'

They both heaved in a lungful of air, and ran into the garage.

Bruce Fleet had done a thorough job. Not only had he locked the garage doors, he had also locked himself inside the old car. But it *was* an old car, and Marie immediately saw the hosepipe running through the back window and into the Morris's interior. Grabbing a garden spade from a collection of tools hanging on one wall, she forced it into the gap, and levered it upward. The winding mechanism snapped, the window crashed down, and she had immediate access to the door lock.

Already her lungs were burning, but she leant over the driver's seat, turned off the engine, then felt for a pulse in the man's neck.

'Dead?' asked Jackman, mumbling through tightly closed lips.

She nodded, moderately sure that she was right, but she nonetheless leaned down Bruce Fleet's side and pulled on the door release.

Jackman had opened both big doors and air was now rushing in, but still they dared not breathe. Together they hauled the heavy body from the car and dragged him outside, where they fell in a heap on the gravel, coughing, choking and gasping for air.

After a few moments, Jackman checked the man's vital signs again, then pulled his phone from his pocket and rang the incident in.

'It's too late for him, but I'm afraid we need to be checked over.'

'I thought we breathed in carbon monoxide all the time, one way or another?' Marie thought of heavy smokers and poorly ventilated rooms.

'And every time you do, you diminish the number of red blood cells carrying oxygen to your body.' He smiled at her. 'Don't worry the medics are on their way and they'll give us some oxygen. Are you feeling okay?'

'Bit of a headache, but other than that I'm fine. How about you?'

'The same. I think we'll live.' He gazed down at the crimson-faced dead man. 'Unlike Bruce Fleet. We are looking at a lot of questions here, aren't we? Was it just grief, do you think?'

Marie raised her eyebrows. 'Or guilt?' She leaned forward to look closer at something sticking out of Fleet's breast pocket. 'Well, I'll be . . .' She pulled on a glove and carefully removed the folded sheet of paper. 'He made it almost impossible to rescue him, but it looks like he's been kind enough to leave us a note.' She unfolded it. 'I need some light.'

Jackman pulled a small Maglite from his pocket and shone the beam onto the white paper.

Marie read aloud:

"I am sorry. Sorry to have to choose an easy death, rather than live out an agonising life. Sorry for everything that happened. Sorry for my friends. If they loved me, this will cause them pain. If they didn't really love me, it will still be shocking. And finally, sorry to the one who finds me, but at least asphyxiation is gentler on the eye than death inflicted by the blade. BSF"

Jackman let out a low whistle. 'Contrite and poetic, I'm sure, but no mention of his beloved wife.'

'Was he ill? An agonising life usually means that someone can't bear the pain any longer.'

'He looked fit as a fiddle. Maybe he's talking about the agony of losing Alison?'

'Or the agony of screwing up his life in some way?'

'Or living with the fact that he's a killer. Maybe the reference to the blade means something, and "I'm sorry for what happened." That's a bit ambiguous, isn't it?'

They stared at the note, half hoping that everything would miraculously become crystal clear. It didn't. Marie carefully folded it again and slipped it back into the man's pocket. 'Forensics will want this left in situ.' She sat back on her heels and wished the headache would go away.

'I suppose it really is suicide?'

Marie didn't laugh at this. Jackman would have seen some very strange things in his time on the force, and she herself had seen murder take on a variety of forms. It was possible that it was murder disguised as suicide.

'Gut says suicide.'

He kicked aimlessly at the gravel. 'I agree, but where this case is concerned, I won't be a hundred per cent convinced about anything until Jacobs confirms it.'

'Well, first thing tomorrow I'm going to ask Max to find out everything he can about Bruce Fleet. He's been working on Alison Fleet, and there are a lot of mysteries attached to that lady. Maybe they spill over into her husband's life.'

Jackman sat down on the ground next to her. 'And I'm going to have to talk to Lucy Richards. I promised I would, and I can't do it over the phone. It wouldn't be fair.'

Marie reached out and gently touched his arm. 'If this gas is as wicked as you reckon, you need some oxygen and some rest before you go racing off breaking the sad news to relatives. Let uniform handle it for you. They'll send someone to the house, and they *are* very good at it.' She looked at his worried face and admired his sense of responsibility. Jackman liked things done properly, and as he had promised Lucy that he would update her on her brother's welfare, then naturally he would be the one to go and break the news. End of.

'No, I'll go. A lungful of oxygen will soon sort me out.' His head fell forward and his voice dropped almost to a whisper. 'This case is going to hell in a handcart, isn't it?'

Marie sighed. 'It is a tad confusing, but I'm certain more information about the Fleets' background and private life will answer a lot of questions. Max and Charlie are well underway with their enquiries, so it shouldn't take long.'

Jackman smiled wearily. 'Always the glass half full, aren't you, Marie?'

She grinned. 'Someone has to be.' She looked up. 'And I do believe I hear the sound of an oxygen cylinder winging its way across the fens.'

Blues and twos in the distance lifted her spirits. She'd had enough of Berrylands. She had only been here twice, and on both occasions she had been presented with a dead body. Suddenly her quiet little home in Church Mews seemed very attractive indeed.

CHAPTER FIFTEEN

With his cat clasped tightly in his arms, Daniel wandered around Skye's flat, talking constantly. He couldn't bear the silence. He had tried the television, but every channel seemed to carry something more inane than the last.

'I wish she had locked me in,' he murmured to the cat. He had tried to find a way to ask Skye, to beg her to lock the doors and windows, and take the keys with her. But he'd seen her face, pale and gaunt with worry, and he knew he couldn't inflict further anguish on her. The idea would have sounded insane to her, and would probably have confirmed the fears that were no doubt incubating in her mind.

He went into the bathroom and searched through the cupboard for something to make him sleep, but there was nothing. Skye had no problem sleeping. As he already knew, Skye was one of those healthy people who kept little more than paracetamol in her medicine cabinet.

Daniel walked back to the bedroom and pulled back the duvet. He bent down and sniffed gently at the pillow. It smelled of her fragrance, something sweet and flowery, summery, just like her. Tears welled up in his eyes. He wanted her here with him. He was desperate to hold her close, to dive into those blue, blue eyes, nestle in that fresh-smelling hair and kiss her clear, pale skin. He wanted to move on top of her, enter her and lose himself in her. It was the only time he ever felt peace, and the terrible thoughts and ideas stayed away. It was the only time he was truly happy.

How could he even think he would hurt her? He would *never* hurt her. The Daniel that lay crying into her pillow could never hurt Skye Wynyard. The problem lay with the other Daniel, the one who woke up and didn't know where he'd been, who had precious minutes and hours stolen from him. The one whose head hurt so much that it felt like exploding. What of him?

Daniel curled up into the foetal position and, still crying, placed his thumb in his mouth and sucked.

* * *

PC Kevin Stoner dressed quickly, then ran down the stairs and into the hall. He paused for a moment to make a swift appraisal of his appearance in the full-length mirror. Black jeans, black T-shirt and a plain black hoodie. Perfect. He looked like any other bored and unidentifiable youth roaming the streets after dark. Only he wasn't bored, and he wasn't intending to aimlessly roam anywhere. Kevin's nocturnal activities had a very definite purpose.

He checked his watch, then walked into the kitchen where he poured himself a shot of vodka. The alcohol jolted through his head like a firework exploding in his sinuses. This wasn't his usual way of hitting the town, but tonight's entertainment was about as far from his normal hedonistic routine as it got.

He walked into the lounge and sat down. On the leather sofa beside him was a small Nike sports bag. He'd checked the contents three times already, and his fingers played anxiously with the zipper. Everything's there, he told himself. His face grew hard, his eyes narrowed and his lips tightened. His plan would work, and he would be able to get his life back on track again. In future he would have to be a damned sight more courageous than he'd been in the past. That would mean discovering just how much forgiveness his father had in his puritanical heart, but it would have to be done. Nothing like this was ever going to happen to him again. No one would ever make him feel dirty or weak, and no one would ever threaten his family. After tonight, his life would take on a very different aspect.

He looked again at his watch. Timing was crucial, but the second hand dragged terribly slowly around the face of his watch. He couldn't be early. Taking a deep breath, Kevin stood and picked up the holdall. There was no going back now. He was committed to his assignment, and he'd see it through to the end. With an unaccustomed prayer, he found his house keys and strode through the front door.

He didn't dare take his car, but he was fit and knew exactly how long it would take him to walk to Riverside Crescent. As he marched along he went over what he was going to do. He believed he had made provision for any unexpected hiccups.

As he went he began to relax, and he even afforded himself a little smile. This whole thing was only possible because Zane Prewett was such a nasty piece of work. His mission tonight would succeed because Kevin was a conscientious and observant policeman, and his partner a lying shit. And because he was a lying shit *and* a bully, Prewett would never expect his meek and terrified little nancy boy of a crewmate to lift a finger against him.

Kevin's smile widened. Oh, Zane, how wrong could you be!

As he turned the corner into Riverside Crescent, Kevin saw a police patrol car move slowly away from him. He took it as a good omen. Even the boys in blue were working to schedule. As it disappeared he stayed close to the road's neatly clipped hedges and then slipped silently into the garden of the Kinder house. There were two points where he could safely approach the property without activating the security lights, and he moved cat-like, between shrubs, trees and flower beds, until he reached the side door to the integral garage. In his pocket was a key and a sheet of paper, courtesy, albeit without his knowledge, of PC Zane Prewett. He slipped the key into the lock, moved quickly inside, then hurried through to the hall and looked for the security alarm keypad. He took a torch from his bag and punched in the numbers written on the paper, then waited nervously. There was a double beeping sound, and to his relief, he saw a green light flash up on the display. Stage one completed.

With adrenalin pumping through his veins, he began to experience the kind of buzz that villains must get when they turn over a big job. However, most of them wouldn't be doing it with help from Old Bill. And most of them wouldn't be lucky enough to be walking in with a spare key. Zane was certainly thorough when he handed over such sensitive information to his criminal friends.

Kevin made his way into the lounge, and was delighted to see that it had been cleaned and tidied since they had removed Daniel Kinder's weird art mural from the attic. It would help his plan no end. The gods really were on his side tonight.

He placed his bag on the floor and knelt down. He had decided to use his torch only if it was really necessary, and his eyes were already becoming accustomed to the dark. A street light outside shed a weak unreal glow into the room.

He first took out an evidence bag and, with gloved fingertips, shook out a ten-pound note. It was folded in a very particular way: two edges to the centre, and then in half. He looked around and decided that the best place to leave it was between a rather nice writing desk and a small display cabinet housing photographs and the kind of odd mementos that people bring back from their holidays. The banknote wasn't obvious, but it wouldn't take too much finding. It was a bit of a gamble using money, but with the exception of Prewett, Kevin would vouch for the honesty of all the other coppers at Saltern nick.

That done, he took another smaller evidence bag and shook out a dark strand of hair and let it fall near the ten-pound note. It might get picked up, or it might not. If it did, well, all the better.

He glanced down at the luminous dial of his watch. He needed to get out as soon as possible. His guests would be arriving within the next fifteen minutes, and he would like to be a little way away when they did. From the bag he removed a large soft duster, and even though he'd used gloves, he carefully cleaned everything he'd touched. He wanted to be sure that the room's next occupants would have pristine surfaces to handle.

He moved swiftly back to the hall, punched in the alarm security number and made his way back to the garage. In seconds, he was outside, panting in relief.

One last, very important thing to do. From his bag of tricks, Kevin removed a third evidence bag, and took out a small, slim cell phone. He moved into the bushes, and dropped it, not too carefully, into a clump of those flowering plants that his mother loved so much, a cluster of pansies. How apt, he thought cheerfully.

Kevin then retraced his footsteps back along Riverside Crescent to where it met a long, straight road on the corner of which was a bus shelter covered in graffiti. It was far too late for a bus, but it was a great place to loiter unnoticed and watch the big house in the crescent.

He'd been there only a moment when he saw a figure walking very deliberately towards the Kinder house. Something about the dark figure made him stiffen. It didn't look like the person he was expecting, and if it wasn't, who the hell was it?

The man moved silently into the garden and disappeared. Then Kevin heard a vehicle approaching and breathed a sigh of relief. His mystery man had been the outrider, the scout, and the rest of the posse were bringing up the rear. And they were right on time. The whole thing was working to perfection. A second man arrived, slipped into the garden, near where Kevin had entered, and three minutes later a dark van with the registration plate covered, drove into the driveway. It moved slowly round to the garage area, out of sight of any late night passers-by.

Kevin waited for exactly ten minutes, then took a brand new pay-as-you-go mobile from his pocket and dialled 999.

And now it was time to go.

Kevin jogged home the scenic route, using the back lanes and the river footpath. He wanted to be off the main road when his compatriots came bombing along towards the Kinder place. He stood by the river for a few moments and tried to still his racing pulse. The water flowed dark and deep, and helped to calm him. He stared into the inky darkness and decided that it had all gone rather well. And now here he was, strolling home in the moonlight with a smile on his face. It was done. Now it was down to his fellow officers to be thorough, and Zane Prewett to be where he'd said he would be tonight.

By the time he was home, Kevin Stoner felt as if he had managed to set in motion a massive chain of events, one that would send Zane Prewett on a very different path to his own. And tonight, for the first time in a long while, Kevin thought his nightmare might just be over.

* * *

As Kevin still buzzed with leftover adrenalin, Sue Bannister was feeling a buzz of a different nature.

Her husband was working a night shift at the hospital, and had left the house in a blaze of fury. Nothing new there. But the quarrels were becoming too frequent, and Sue was at her wits' end.

She knew he was having an affair with one of the nurses. He had no idea that she was aware of it, but then he was a bloke, wasn't he? She also knew that the fights and the quarrels were because he felt guilty. She was pretty sure that he still loved her, but — well, he was a bloke, wasn't he?

Sue had made herself a gin and tonic. It wasn't a large one, she didn't want to get tipsy, but it had given her the courage to make the call. He had listened to her, in a way her husband never did. He had been really interested in how she felt, but then he was always like that, kind and interested. And tonight, for the first time, he had offered to come over.

Sue wriggled a little on the bed. She had never done anything like this before. She looked down at her clothes. They were pretty, almost sexy but not too provocative. She shouldn't appear too eager.

She took another sip of her drink. He had asked her several times what time her husband got home, and whether he ever left work early. She had assured him that he was *never* early, more often very late, and that was probably because he and his cheap little nurse had shifts that allowed them to have a quick shag before he came home for breakfast.

This thought pumped anger and hurt through Sue's veins, and made her even more ready for her visitor. At the very least, she could offload, pour out her heart to him, and know that someone was actually listening. At best, well, Sue glanced at the clean and tidy bed. After all, *she* hadn't started this and, as the proverb said, what was good for the goose . . .

She swallowed the rest of her drink, checked the time and went downstairs. The back door was unlocked. She had told him, casually, to use the back door, that everyone did, and maybe it was best that no one saw him on the front doorstep late at night. In her street, curtains twitched no matter what the hour.

As she reached the bottom step, she heard a slight noise. He hadn't let her down! Sue patted her skirt, glanced in the hall mirror, and gave a nervous little smile. She took a deep breath and walked into the kitchen.

* * *

The man who stood opposite her, just a few inches away, looked as if he had just stepped from a hospital.

From head to toe he was clad in operating greens, from the pull-on cap covering his hair to the protective slip-ons over his shoes. He wore a face mask.

Sue tried to assimilate what she was seeing in front of her. But the information failed to compute. Useless information jumped into her brain. 'Eye-rest' green, they called it, opposite to red on the colour wheel. It was used on the walls, for theatre linen, and the staff wore it. Blood stains on green are far less garish than scarlet splashes on bleached white.

Sue opened her mouth to speak, but his hands took hold of her and spun her around. He clamped a gloved hand over her mouth.

If this was supposed to be a sex game, if she had accidentally given him a very wrong impression of what she needed from him, she had to stop him. Now.

But how could she? The hand was crushing her lips into her teeth. She couldn't even swallow properly, let alone breathe. Her free arm flapped feebly like a bird with a broken wing, as useful as tissue paper. Blind panic overcame her confusion. This was no game.

And then he hit her. Hard, on the back of her head.

CHAPTER SIXTEEN

Kevin timed his entrance to the station perfectly. He made sure that he was wearing the long face that had become his trademark over the past few months.

Men and women officers, shortly about to stand down from the night shift, were scurrying around with big smiles on their faces, exchanging excited high fives.

'What's happening?' Kevin asked a young PC called Gus Bannon.

'Hey, your shift missed out on a blinder last night! Drew Wilson and his crew only tried to do over the Kinder house! But we had an anonymous tip-off, and we managed to nick most of them.' He allowed a small frown to cloud his delight. 'Shame that two of them legged it, but four, including Drew himself, are downstairs in the slammer.'

'Really?' Kevin tried to look surprised and impressed. 'We've been trying to get something on that shower for months, but they were always a step ahead of us.'

'I know, but something went badly wrong last night. You should have seen the star-burst when we turned up. Villains scattering in every direction. Blinding!'

Kevin clapped him on the shoulder. 'Good collar, mate. Well done.'

He made his way towards the locker room. He knew that Zane would be there already. Kevin opened the door and looked around. The room was empty apart from Prewett, sitting white-faced on one of the wooden benches. Kevin slipped his miserable face back into place, though his heart was singing.

'I've just heard about last night's shout at the Kinder house.' He kept his tone flat, then looked quizzically at Zane Prewett and dropped his voice to a low whisper. 'I thought Drew Wilson was one of your "mates." So what happened?'

Zane jumped up from his seat and started pacing the room. 'Fuck knows! But if Wilson decides this cock-up has anything to do with me, then I'm dead meat.'

Kevin fervently hoped that would be the case. He said, 'But you did send him the info on the place. I saw you clocking the alarm system code *and* you made me cover for you when you buggered off out to get the back door key copied.'

'Yeah, *and* I texted him and told him to abort when we let that nutter Daniel Kinder out! Why the hell he went ahead, I have no fucking idea.'

Kevin stared at Zane. 'Are you sure he got your message?'

'He acknowledged it like he always does.' Zane groaned noisily. 'Then the stupid bastard goes out there anyway.' He turned his pasty face towards Kevin. 'And that's not the worst of it. My fucking phone's gone missing.'

Kevin feigned shock. 'Bloody hell, Zane! If anyone finds that, you really are in deep shit.' He paused for a moment then asked, 'Do you think Drew Wilson will try to drop you in it?'

'What do you think, numb-nuts?' Zane's face became a mask of anger. 'I bet you're loving this, aren't you?'

Kevin was elated. He wanted to yell out that he was happier than he'd ever been in his life. He said, seriously, 'You are a bent copper, Zane, and you mix with low life. Even you must have realised that that sort of game can't go on for ever. You've been swimming with piranhas, and now they've been reeled in they are going to strip the flesh from your bones.'

Zane swung round and grabbed Kevin by the lapels, backing him into one of the lockers. 'Well, even if they do, you, my little faggot, will keep your mouth shut!'

Kevin smelled Zane's sour breath and saw anger and fear in the eyes that were just inches from his.

'What I said before still holds good, so remember it well, or your precious little Sophie will be the first to realise that you don't cross Zane Prewett! You suffer, Kevin.' He grimaced. 'There's a lot you can do to a pretty young thing like that — life-changing things.' He pushed Kevin roughly to the floor. 'And that's without those lovely pictures that are all ready to go to Daddy, though I doubt he'll want them for the family album.'

Kevin struggled up. 'Oh, don't worry about me. You know you've got me exactly where you want me. I won't be talking to anyone. This almighty mess is totally down to you, Zane. You've done this all on your own.' He straightened his jacket. 'You should thank your lucky stars that this didn't happen on our watch. Can you imagine what sort of fiasco that would have been, if you'd been sent to round them up? Drew Wilson would have lynched you! Now I suggest we get outside and try to act normally.' He moved towards the door and couldn't resist adding, 'Even if you are shitting yourself.'

* * *

By ten in the morning, Skye was beginning to wish that the police had kept Daniel locked up. He had rung her mobile at eight thirty and had told her, his voice trembling, that his mother's house had been broken into. Her first thought was that she had not locked up properly, or had forgotten the alarm, but she knew that hadn't been the case. It wasn't her house and she had been extra-careful.

'The police are in there with their forensic zombies stomping all over the place again. Twice in a matter of days! My mother will go berserk.' He had sounded like a child on the verge of a tantrum.

'Daniel, your mother is thousands of miles away in the jungle communing with fern plants and dragonflies. And I'm sure we can tidy it up again,' and she had stressed the word *again*, 'before her return.' Not something she relished after her "cleanathon" with Lisa. The Thai police were trying to locate Ruby Kinder, and the moment they did, she would be on the first available flight home. 'Did they take anything of value? Was anything damaged?'

'Nothing. Well, there would have been, but someone called the police. They caught them before they could drive away in their van with half of mother's house on board.'

'Thank God for that,' said Skye. Things were bad enough in the Kinder house, without thieves making off with their precious belongings. 'And how are you, sweetheart? Did you get any sleep?'

Daniel made a strange snorting noise. He said, 'I don't know. I thought I did sleep, and the police said they called here to tell me about the robbery, but . . .' his voice faltered. 'I didn't hear them.'

'Then you slept really well, didn't you?'

'You don't understand, Skye! I don't think I was here.'

He didn't say anything further. He didn't have to. Skye felt a headache forming behind her tired eyes. She wanted to cry, but asked calmly, 'Where were you when you woke up?'

'Here, in bed. But when I got up, there was . . . there was dirt on my trainers.' His voice was now trembling again.

'Stay there,' she said. 'I'm coming home.'

* * *

153

The team, with Guy Preston, sat in Jackman's office. They were on their second round of coffee. They had begun with the attempted burglary on Daniel Kinder's house.

'If it hadn't been for that anonymous tip-off, it would have been the perfect screw,' said Marie. 'The press had given up camping on the doorstep, the mother's abroad, Daniel was still supposedly in custody, and with Skye moved out, they had an empty drum to turn over. Hell, even the cat had gone AWOL.'

Jackman frowned. 'Convenient, that anonymous call, wasn't it? Gave our lads exactly the right amount of time to get there and catch them with stolen stuff in the van *and* all of them with their hands still in the till, so to speak.'

'If it was a neighbour you'd have thought they'd have given their name, wouldn't you?' said Charlie. 'No reason not to.'

'A mate of mine who went out there last night reckons it was Daniel Kinder who rang 999.' Max rubbed at his chin.

'Daniel?'

'He's pretty sure he caught sight of him when the balloon went up. Not in the house, but out near the road. And when they went round to Skye Wynyard's place to tell him about the attempted theft, he either wasn't there or he didn't answer the door. They couldn't get hold of him till early this morning.'

'So what did he say to them?' asked Jackman.

'Said he'd taken something to make him sleep. Reckons he was dead to the world.'

Jackman let out a worried snort. 'Hell! That man is still giving me grave cause for concern. But we need to get on. We have to discuss the Fleets, our second victim, Julia Hope, *and* we still need to find out all we can about Françoise Thayer.'

Jackman drew thick, heavy circles on his notepad, trying to clear his overladen brain. 'Right, let's list what we have, then we'll decide how to proceed.' He looked at Max and Charlie. 'Kick us off with what you know about the Fleets.'

Max nodded towards Charlie, 'After you, mate.'

Charlie looked at his notebook. 'One, they were in big financial trouble. The Fleets' brewery was going down the pan fast, and somehow Bruce Fleet had managed to conceal the debts from everyone. Two, Alison Fleet's GP never prescribed antidepressants, but large quantities were found hidden in her shoes in the bottom of her wardrobe at Berrylands.'

'Were there any labels on the containers?' asked Guy Preston.

'No. They were loose in polythene bags, no packaging on them.' Charlie flipped over a page. 'But forensics identified them as something called clomipramine hydrochloride, and it appeared that she'd been taking them for some time.'

'That's a tricyclic anti-depressant,' said Preston. 'It's widely used for depressive illness and a myriad of other problems. But if her GP didn't give them to her, who did?'

Charlie went back to his notebook. 'The GP firmly stated that Alison Fleet had no major health problems and he had never had to refer her to any kind of hospital consultant in the fifteen years that she had been on his books.'

'Then it sounds like she was self-medicating via the bloody Internet.' Preston's voice was tinged with anger. 'It's so damned dangerous. Some people never learn until it's too late, then we have to pick up the pieces.'

Max leaned forward. 'I don't know how she got the pills, Prof, but I think I know why she was trying to keep her head above water.' He ran a hand through his thick, dark hair. 'We've had some of our guys check out her accounts, the charity accounts in particular, and they are a complete mess. Money has been transferred back and forth between different funds, and massive amounts are missing. It looks like she was trying to cook the books, big-style.'

'To bail out hubby?' asked Marie.

'Maybe,' Max frowned, 'but there are no withdrawals with corresponding payments into the brewery or Fleet's personal account.'

Charlie joined in, 'And she wasn't squirreling it away for a rainy day either. Her own funds were at rock bottom, and she didn't hold any offshore stuff either.'

'Which brings us to her first husband,' Max continued. 'His name is Skinner, Ray Skinner, and he showed up on Alison Fleet's iPad. We believe that she has been in contact with him recently, but he's not been easy to pin down.'

'Do we know why they split up?' asked Jackman.

'They were very young when they married, and there were hints about domestic violence, but there's nothing on record to say that she ever filed against him. It's mainly speculation from the few bits of information that we managed to dredge up, but we've nothing concrete.'

'So why see him now?' mused Marie.

'Why indeed? He sounds like he should have been a part of her life that she'd rather forget.'

'Perhaps he wouldn't let her,' said Charlie. 'Blackmail could be the answer to the cash-flow problem.'

Jackman nodded. 'Then keep looking for him. He could also be the reason she hit the pill bottle.'

He was about to continue when the phone rang. He spoke for a few moments and replaced the receiver. 'Well, one thing has been clarified. That was the lab. Bruce Fleet's suicide was exactly that: a suicide. His prints are all over the hosepipe and car body near the exhaust pipe. He locked both the car and the garage doors from the inside, and he definitely wrote the note. Fingerprints are all we have so far, as the other tests will take time, but they have confirmed that death was caused by chemical asphyxiation and preliminary investigations suggest that it was by his own hand.' He grimaced. 'At least we don't have a third murder victim on our hands.'

'We just need to prove that he isn't a dead murderer,' Charlie added dourly. 'Bruce Fleet could have been at his wits' end with his business going under. Then he finds that his wife is haemorrhaging money to a previous husband that he knew nothing about, and he totally loses it.'

'You're forgetting his alibi, Charlie-boy.' Max chipped in. 'He was miles away, talking to a load of brewery bigwigs.'

'Then use the same scenario, but Bruce pays someone to do the dirty work for him, and as you just said, the grieving husband has a smashing alibi.' Charlie sat back, looking smug.

'And our dead nurse, Julia Hope? The same knife was used. As yet we have found no connection between her and the Fleets, so why kill her?'

Charlie shrugged. 'Yeah, well, I haven't got that far.'

Jackman leaned back and stretched. 'We know very little so far about Julia Hope. We don't even know *where* she was killed, let alone why.'

'I've asked uniform to check the hospital CCTV from the last time she worked. They are going to try to build up a picture of her movements from when she was last seen, to when we know she died,' said Marie. 'Plus they are speaking to all her work colleagues and friends to try to find the last person to have contact with her.'

Preston looked thoughtful. 'Could the hospital be the common denominator between the two victims? Provided of course that there *is* a common denominator?'

Max joined in. 'Well, Julia was a nurse, and Alison was taking big doses of prescription meds. Is there any chance that there was some kind of illegal drug dealing going on at the hospital?'

Jackman grunted. 'I can't say that had occurred to me.'

'It's possible.' Marie looked at Jackman. 'Worth a few discreet enquiries, guv?'

He nodded slowly. 'I'd say so, but only *very* discreet ones. If the staff are prepared to give one of our constables a dose of laxatives simply because he was doing his duty, then God help anyone who accuses them of drug dealing!' He paused, and then said, 'And we are still left with trying to discover whether Daniel Kinder is a murderer's son with a hereditary penchant for killing.'

'Or a pillock with soup for brains,' finished off Max.

'Nicely put, Max. Although I think his problems go considerably deeper than your, er, assessment.' Guy Preston gave the young detective a patient smile.

'Sorry, Prof. But that's what it boils down to, isn't it? Either he's a dangerous killer, or barking enough to muck up a serious murder investigation.'

'Well if you put it like that, I have to agree.' After a few moments' silence, Preston pulled a laptop from its leather case. 'By the way, I've scanned a lot of my early research on Françoise Thayer. Maybe one of you guys could print off copies for everyone? They are saved in a folder under her name.'

'No problem.' Charlie took the laptop and headed for the door. 'Back in five.'

'And I've been getting into the stuff that Orac accessed. You were right, boss. It makes grim reading.' Marie pulled a face. 'I tried to concentrate on her personal life, especially anything about her conceiving a child.'

'It was a boy, and he was taken into care, right?' added Preston.

'Right. For his own safety, he was given a new identity and scrupulously monitored both physically and mentally throughout his early school years. Now, at this stage in the game, unless Orac can work some more magic, he's untraceable.' Marie gave a little shrug. 'We have no date of birth because she never registered him. The child's age matches Daniel Kinder's, but then it probably matches a lot of others too.'

'I don't know if your research mentions it, but the boy was very badly treated,' added Preston. 'Physical abuse, mental torture, and probably a lot more. When he was finally got away from her, he was a mess.'

'Was there ever a name for him?' asked Jackman.

'No. He was referred to as Boy Six throughout all the reports.'

'Why six?' Max looked puzzled.

'I never found out, although it was suggested that he went into care on the sixth of the month. It was probably something as mundane as that.'

Marie thumbed through Orac's folder. 'It says the same here, and adds that Boy Six was so severely traumatised that it was considered improbable that he would ever be able to recall the things that happened to him in his early life.'

'Oh shit,' murmured Max. 'Just like Dan the Man.'

Before anyone could answer him, Charlie Button pushed the door open and passed around copies of Guy Preston's research notes on Françoise Thayer.

Marie was still looking at Orac's file. She looked at Jackman and said, 'What's quite chilling is the fact that Thayer may have killed up to seven other people. The French police still have open cases that are attributed to her, but remain unproven. And all of them were vicious, brutal attacks involving weapons with sharp blades. It seems that she had a thing about knives, razors, axes, anything that could inflict the maximum amount of damage to her victim.'

'And cause the maximum amount of blood loss,' Preston added. 'You'll see from my notes that I was certain that she suffered from something called hematomania, which is a morbid fascination with blood.'

Charlie's eyes widened. 'What? Like Dracula?'

Preston let out a short laugh. 'You're closer than you think, Charlie-boy. People suffering from this disorder are your real-life vampires, only not all of them actually drink it.'

Jackman nodded. 'I've heard of it. Isn't it similar to hematolagnia?'

Now Preston widened his eyes. 'Forgive me for saying so, but not too many DIs are familiar with a psychological term like that one.'

Jackman shrugged and went on. 'A blood fetish is a term used to describe the belief within a society or culture that blood as a material substance possesses powerful or magical properties. As I recall, translated, it means "bloodlust" and it's generally a sexual thing, involving sadomasochistic play and blood-sports.'

'You're correct. Even in its sexual form, it's very dangerous, not just because of the permanent injury and scarring that it causes, but because of illnesses transmitted though the blood.'

'This is gross.' Max sounded sickened.

'Believe me,' said Preston grimly, 'It was a very good thing that the media played down Françoise Thayer's case. If the public had known what she really got up to, they would have all hidden at home behind locked doors until she was captured. Things would have come to a standstill.'

'Orac's documents say that the Home Office pathologist believed that she had a very specific method of killing. She would first cut her victims so that they bled profusely, but were not initially in mortal danger. She then proceeded to inflict deeper lacerations, all producing copious quantities of blood, until she finally either finished them off, or watched as they bled to death.' Marie swallowed. 'As you say, "Blonde Butcher" was something of an understatement.' She read on. '"And the pooling blood was disturbed."' She looked at Preston. 'What the hell does that mean?'

'She placed her hands, palms down into the warm blood, and slowly moved them in a circular motion. It was something she took delight in demonstrating, miming of course, to anyone who was sick enough to engage with her.' Preston puffed out his cheeks, 'She didn't drink, or bathe in it. For Thayer, it was that first touch, the feel of freshly let lifeblood on her hands. I think it was her sole means of gratification.'

'Sick bitch,' growled Max.

'Ditto,' agreed Charlie.

'Well, edifying as all this is, it still doesn't get us any closer to knowing about Daniel's parentage, does it?' sighed Marie.

'No, but I have an idea.' Jackman scratched his head thoughtfully. 'As Orac has been kind enough to make contact with the detective who headed up the original enquiry, it wouldn't hurt to go have a word with him. I may be greatly mistaken, but there's an outside chance he's kept something, some small item that never made it into an evidence bag.'

'A memento?' Charlie looked sceptical. 'Why?'

'It often happens. It's usually when a case is never solved and the detective finds that he can't let go.'

'Keepsakes, mementos, trophies, souvenirs, tokens. They are all very powerful, as you know, DI Jackman, if you've studied sociology.' Preston looked at him with undisguised new interest.

Charlie sniffed. 'Well, I knew serial killers liked trophies, but I'd never thought of a copper collecting stuff from dead people.'

'It's not stuff from dead people, Charlie,' said Jackman tolerantly. 'It's just something from a case that they can't ever forget, a case that probably stole months, maybe years of their lives. It could have been the final straw, the case that wrecked their marriage or sent them screaming to the bottle. It's deeply personal, Charlie. It was *their* case.'

'I'll go,' said Marie. 'I'll give him a bell, and if he can see me, I'll leave straightaway. If I go on the bike, I can be back by the afternoon meeting, hopefully with some answers.' She looked at Jackman. 'And I know what you're looking for, guv. Don't worry.'

Jackman smiled and nodded. 'No speeding, now.'

Marie threw him a look that said, 'Yeah, right,' placed the paperwork on his desk and left the room. Jackman noticed the looks on the faces of the three others. He was thinking of DNA.

If the old detective had taken something, it could have belonged to the killer herself, and there was an outside chance that with their new technology, forensics could retrieve something. It was a long shot, but even with Orac and her superhuman skills, it could take weeks to track down those missing evidence boxes, only to find that they had been reduced to a small pile of ashes in a burnt-out building. It was certainly worth a try to get the mystery of Daniel Kinder off his back.

'So she's still riding motorbikes, is she?'

Preston's voice brought Jackman back to earth.

'Oh yes, like the wind,' said Max. He gave an exaggerated shiver. 'You wouldn't get me on one of those things for all the tea in China.'

Jackman listened to the three men talking about the dangers of motorbike riding, and he felt a sudden irritation. Actually, the irritation was all for Preston and his casual comment about Marie. Its implication was that they were bosom buddies. And for some reason, Jackman didn't like that.

He scratched his head and wondered why it should bother him. After all, he and Marie were not an item, and he certainly did not harbour thoughts in that direction, but they *did* have a relationship. He was unable to describe it, but it was a powerful connection, and he knew that if he asked her, Marie would say she felt it too. They were partners, and he knew that he would lay down his life for her if it ever became necessary. It was a bond built on mutual respect, and he admired her deeply. It was something he had never come across before in a working CID team. From the things that Marie had told him about her previous senior officers, he was pretty sure that she had never experienced it before either. He decided that it gave him a certain right to express his opinion when it came to people who impinged on her life. And Preston's comment about her riding a bike had sounded almost disparaging, as if Preston was entitled to say what was best for her.

'Tell the professor about what sarge did after her husband died.' Charlie was looking at Max, an awed expression on his boyish face.

Jackman tensed. He thought about pulling the plug on the conversation, but it really wasn't down to him. What Marie had done was something that he believed to be deeply personal, and that had taken great courage.

'Did you know Bill Evans raced a vintage motorbike, Prof?' Max asked.

Guy Preston shook his head. 'I knew they went to race meetings, but I didn't know he competed.'

'Bill was a top motorcycle cop and a vintage bike racer in his spare time until ten years ago, when he crashed and burned.'

Jackman winced. Bad choice of words, Max, he thought.

Max pulled a face. 'The sarge told us he was on an old Vincent Black Shadow, his pride and joy. The track was greasy and he took a rear wheel blow-out. He was killed outright.'

Preston blenched. 'Was Marie there? Did she see it happen?'

Jackman took up the story, anxious to end it.

'It happened right in front of her. But what Charlie was talking about was what Marie did afterwards.' Jackman took a deep breath. He was still moved by what she had done. 'She retrieved his shattered bike and rebuilt it. Then, on the first anniversary of his death, she took it to the same track, and raced it in his name. She didn't win, but that wasn't the idea. She completed the course and took third place on the podium, which was more than she had hoped for, but she went home content. She had given him closure in the best way she could.'

The bike, as far as Jackman knew, was still in her garage, now wrapped up and protected from all harm. Marie now rode a Kawasaki Ninja ZX-6R that was probably already on the road and heading towards Rutland.

'But we digress. We still have two dead women, and we are a long way from giving either of them closure.'

CHAPTER SEVENTEEN

Skye watched Daniel as he sat on the floor cradling the cat. His shoulders were hunched and his knees were drawn up to his chest. Skye felt her world begin to disintegrate.

Daniel needed help, and if he didn't get it soon, he'd finish up being sectioned. How could he have gone from being an intelligent young man with a brilliant future to . . . this? He had become an unreachable and tragic stranger. She could only guess that his long-time obsession with a sick killer had been somehow exacerbated by the death of Alison Fleet, and it was too much for his mind to cope with.

But what should she do? It was all very well to say that they'd work with the police shrink — and she was mightily relieved that Daniel had gone along with that suggestion — but it would be an hour a day, if they were lucky. Then, when the novelty had worn off, it would be an hour a week, then once a month.

She sank down onto the floor next to him and hugged him. They must have stayed that way, without speaking, for a very long time, because when the doorbell rang and she moved to get up, her arms and legs were stiff.

Daniel seemed not to have heard the bell. Indeed he hardly seemed to notice that her warm embrace had slipped away. Skye felt a pang of fear as she went to answer the door. What would it be this time? Whose sombre face would she find on her doorstep? What awful news would she hear? Skye wondered if she could take much more.

'I'm so sorry to intrude.' Lisa Hurley looked eaten up with concern. 'But you left your phone at my place when you hurried off earlier.'

Skye stared at the dark red mobile phone in the outstretched hand, and almost laughed out loud. The person at the door was just a friend with a bit of lost property. She smiled, but felt tears escaping from the corners of her eyes. 'Thank you so much. I didn't even know I'd left it.'

Lisa Hurley looked on the verge of tears herself. 'Skye, you need some help. You can't deal with all this alone. You're making yourself ill.'

Skye bit back the tears, drew in a shaky breath, then beckoned Lisa inside.

They walked slowly down the hall and halted in the doorway to the lounge. Skye pointed to the still form sitting on the floor, like a stone Buddha. 'Look at him. Look at my Daniel, Lisa. I love him, but I just don't know what to do anymore. I don't know how to help him.'

Lisa Hurley stared at Daniel, then turned away and went to Skye's kitchen. Without a word she filled the kettle and turned it on, then took three mugs from the dresser. 'How long has he been like that?'

Skye, grateful to be doing something mundane, opened a new jar of coffee. 'An hour? When I got back he was edgy, nervy. He kept pacing up and down and fretting that he'd had another of those episodes where he doesn't know where he's been. Then he just sank down onto the floor and withdrew.'

'He needs medication. Some serious medication by the look of it, and he shouldn't be on his own.' Lisa narrowed her eyes. 'Who has he been referred to?'

'Professor Guy Preston. He's a psychologist working with the police. We are supposed to be seeing him this afternoon.'

'Where?'

'At his home.'

'That's not right, surely?' Lisa frowned. 'He should be seeing Daniel in a clinic.'

Skye sighed and placed a spoonful of coffee in each mug. 'He's seeing us privately. It's a condition of Daniel being released. And as far as I can make out, this Guy Preston is going to be taking over the new psychiatric unit out at Frampton Shore, but it's not finished yet, that's why he's offered to see us at his place. He's a top man by all accounts.'

'You've spoken to him?'

'Yes. I liked him, he was really supportive,' Skye swallowed. 'I trust him. I really believe that he can help Daniel.' She pushed the mugs closer to the boiling kettle. 'But most of all, he's on our side. He doesn't think that Daniel killed anyone, and he's told the police so.'

Lisa leaned back against the workbench. 'That's great, but he really needs to see him when he's like this.' She looked straight at Skye. 'I hate to say this, but he's in a bad way, and at this stage he needs more than just your love and support. He needs professional medical help.'

'Then I'll explain just how bad things are to Guy Preston when we see him this afternoon. Maybe he'll have Daniel admitted to hospital.'

'It would be the best thing. But right now, we need to try to talk to Dan.' Lisa poured water, milk and sugar into the mugs. 'He will have to be a damn sight more responsive if he's going to have a productive session with a psychologist.'

Skye led the way back to the lounge, then abruptly stopped. The cat wound itself around her legs.

'Daniel?' Slopping coffee, she put the mug down on the table and ran to check the bedroom and bathroom. 'He's gone!' she called to Lisa.

Lisa raced to the open back door and looked outside. 'He's out here!' she shouted back.

Skye ran to Lisa's side and saw Daniel half walking, half running down the back alleyway.

'Daniel! Come back!'

Together they ran after him, and for a moment, Skye thought he would come back to her. He paused, turned and looked at her with the saddest expression. Then he said, 'Don't come near me, Skye! Get away from me!' And then he ran.

They chased after him, but when he vaulted a fence and disappeared into the maze of old railway buildings, Skye knew they wouldn't catch him. She felt Lisa's hand on her shoulder as they both gasped for breath.

'There's a police car out in front of your house,' she panted. 'We should have called them first instead of chasing him ourselves. I'll go tell them what has happened. You go home and ring Professor Preston, okay?'

For a moment Skye looked longingly in the direction Daniel had taken, then she nodded, turned around and trudged back to the house.

* * *

Marie decided that Orac had been right about retired DI Peter Hodder. He *was* a sweet old guy. He made tea in a proper tea pot and carefully strained the leaves through a silver strainer.

Hodder lived in a warden-controlled apartment in a converted mansion. The grounds were spectacular, if somewhat overgrown, and although the old house looked cold and austere from the outside, the apartments were surprisingly welcoming, spacious and clean. Hodder's retained some of the original features, including a long casement window that looked out over the gardens, a cast-iron surrounded fireplace and heavily ornate ceiling coving.

'So is this the new detective sergeant's uniform these days?' Hodder's eyes twinkled at Marie's motorcycling leathers and heavy protective boots.

'Not exactly.' Marie grinned at him. He made a refreshing change from some of the hard-baked, embittered and overweight retired detectives that she'd met in the past, and from his steady hand and focussed gaze she was certain that he hadn't had recourse to the bottle either.

She accepted the tea and sipped it gratefully. 'I'm sorry that I'm not here to talk to you about a more cheerful subject, but we are hoping that you may be able to help us.'

The old man eased himself down into a soft reclining leather chair and adjusted the position. 'This cost a fortune, my dear, but goodness me, it's worth it! After Lord knows how long on the beat, and years chasing rogues, the old joints need all the help they can get.' He settled back and folded his hands in his lap. 'But it's not chairs you want to talk about, is it? It's that she-devil, Françoise Thayer.'

''Fraid so.' Marie set her cup down. 'We've had two murders on our patch and a young man has confessed to them both. The problem is that there is no supporting evidence to say he did kill the women. He only thinks he's the killer because he believes that he's Thayer's son.'

'Oh, he does, does he?' The old man's rheumy eyes widened. 'Not something I'd be happy to admit to.' He gave a mirthless laugh. 'I read about one woman in the newspaper, but there's another?'

'Yes. We kept it quiet until we had her identity, but it will be on tonight's news. She was a nurse at the local hospital.'

'And were both women brutally stabbed?'

'Savage attacks, both of them.' She paused. 'There was a lot of blood.'

Peter Hodder looked at her thoughtfully. 'So you know about Thayer's little penchant for sanguineous liquid?'

'Yes, we do.'

'And you are making comparisons with the new cases and her slayings?'

'We have to. We don't want to, but because of things that our suspect has said we can't ignore the possibility.' Marie picked up her cup, and then told him about the missing evidence boxes and trial transcripts. 'It's hard to find parallels when your original records have most likely gone up in smoke.'

'Damn near impossible, I'd say.' Hodder sipped his own tea. 'But how can I help? It's been years, and my memory is not what I'd call one hundred per cent reliable anymore.'

'It was your last major case, sir. I suspect that you can remember every detail, in glorious Technicolour, but that's not exactly what we're looking for.' Marie licked her lips and wondered how to phrase her request without upsetting the old boy. 'We desperately need to prove whether our suspect is or isn't a blood relative of Françoise Thayer. If the evidence boxes had been available we could have done a DNA test on something of hers and settled it.'

'But they aren't. And now you are wondering if I might just have a tiny keepsake?' His face darkened. 'Believe me, Sergeant Evans, I needed nothing to remind me of her. I have my nightmares and they will never let me forget that evil mocking smile.' He sat back, all trace of anger gone. 'I believe that the word "evil" is grossly over-used, but it's completely apt where Françoise Thayer is concerned. She was the only woman — no, the only *person*, that I have ever encountered who was utterly soulless and beyond help, from either man or God. She affected the lives of every single one of the officers who worked on that case. I am certain that even though she is dead and gone, none of them sleep soundly because of her.' He blinked. 'So I'm sorry, Sergeant, but I was never even slightly tempted to secure a token of any kind, let alone one that might still contain some precious DNA.'

Marie nodded. There it was.

'However, I do still have my pocket-books.'

Marie stiffened.

Peter Hodder smiled. 'I dug them out them immediately after I spoke to that wonderful scary woman from your IT department.' The sad smile widened. 'Luckily I was always very good about keeping accurate records, very fastidious. You won't get DNA, but you will be able to relive the horrors of my nightmare with me, as the case unfolded.'

Marie's spirits lifted. This was better than she'd hoped for. She had done a check on DI Peter Hodder, and his record was exemplary. He was a real intuitive policeman with a nose for the truth. It was no surprise that he'd been methodical and thorough. 'You're a hero, sir. And I'll make sure that you get them back as soon as we've finished with them.'

'Frankly, my dear, I think it's time they moved on to pastures new. Use them, and I hope they are of some help to you, then place them in an evidence box, seal the lid, and cross your fingers that lightning strikes twice and a second secure evidence store burns to the ground.'

'We really appreciate your help. It is a confusing case and it's difficult to separate head and heart when it comes to our self-confessed young suspect.'

'When fused, head and heart make up something called gut. Listen to what your gut tells you, Sergeant Evans, because it's rarely wrong.'

'I think he's psychologically disturbed, but not a natural killer.' She gave a thoughtful sigh. 'I'm just not certain that his unhealthy obsession and his apparent memory losses haven't pushed him into dangerous waters.'

'Then keep him close, my dear. I couldn't bear the thought of Françoise Thayer reaching back from the past to damage more innocent lives.' He replaced his cup in its saucer and looked at her. 'If the boy does turn out to be her son, would you let me know?'

Marie stood up. 'It's the least I can do, sir.' She picked up the package of notebooks. 'Thank you again.'

He walked with her to her motorbike. He stroked the shiny vivid green paintwork and murmured, 'Beautiful. Really beautiful.'

Marie nodded and understood immediately that there had been a beloved bike in the old man's youth. She smiled at him. 'What was it?'

'A 350cc 1957 Matchless G3L, closely followed by a 1960s 600cc Triton.'

'You were a café racer!' Marie laughed out loud. 'The Ace Café?'

Hodder nodded and smiled warmly, and in that smile Marie saw an echo of the daring young man who had tried to coax the elusive "ton" from his bike as he raced from café to café.

'Don't tell a soul, but I still renew my membership in the '59 Club.'

'Good for you! Once a biker, always a biker.' She pulled on her helmet. 'Thanks again. We appreciate it.'

'Stay safe,' he said as she flicked on the electric ignition, 'and remember, trust your gut, and keep him close.'

CHAPTER EIGHTEEN

'I'm always sorry to find someone butchered in a kitchen.'

Jackman looked at the pathologist, and wondered what kind of man he was. He stared with undisguised distaste and said, 'I'm not exactly keen on finding people butchered in *any* place.'

'Mm, but in the kitchen it plays havoc with the tile grout. I often wonder how people manage to get rid of it.' Jacobs seemed truly bemused by the homeowner's predicament. 'Carpet can be ripped up and replaced, but lovely expensive tiles like these, I mean they are top quality stone-effect porcelain. It's such a shame.'

Jackman didn't answer. He couldn't.

In front of them was a pretty woman in her thirties. Just a short while ago she must have been going about her daily life, feeling safe in her own home. Now she lay on what Jackman had just been informed was her porcelain tiled floor, her head caved in and slashed to ribbons by a sharp knife.

'As there is no weapon here, and the wounds appear to be consistent with the other two deaths, I suspect we have a third murder by the same hand, Inspector.' Jacobs seemed to have managed to drag his thoughts away from the possibility of steam cleaning grouting, and back to the victim. 'But this is much more like the way he killed Alison Fleet than his manic attack on Julia.'

Jackman saw the same clean cuts in the woman's clothing. This time the skin beneath was creamy white, not slightly bronzed like Alison, and not decaying like Julia. This woman's skin was reminiscent of pale Victorian porcelain. Jackman sighed.

He stared for a long while at Sue Bannister, and had the same feeling he had had with Alison Fleet, that something was not right. There was that odd "arranged" aspect to the scene. What had Marie called it? Stage-managed. It was a display. He wished that Marie was with him, but the call had come in only a short while after she had left for Rutland and he had not told her about it. Jackman knew that Marie was an awesome rider, but he still thought it prudent not to fill her mind with the news of another violent death when she had a long trip ahead of her.

Charlie Button stood in the doorway, looking green. Jackman knew that the kid was doing his best to observe dispassionately what he saw, but, as Max would have said, he was making a right dog's dinner of it.

Charlie hated the cloying metallic smell of congealing blood, but more than that, Jackman was aware that he also hated the injustice of it. The mere fact that someone had stolen a life that wasn't his to steal made Charlie Button sick to his stomach. It also made him angry, totally determined to catching and seeing the offender punished.

Jackman smiled sadly. One day Charlie would make a very good detective, but he had to learn how to deal with things like this. Not that it was easy. Of the four of them on the team, Jackman believed that only Marie had achieved a healthy, professional attitude towards death. She was by no means a hard woman, but somehow she had found a way to compartmentalise what she saw and what she felt. He thought about Max, and how he had cried because he couldn't look death in the face.

And what of himself? Jackman smiled inwardly. His way was to escape. When faced with the carnage that was such a part of his chosen career, he allowed his mind to slip back to his mother's stables. He smelled fresh, warm hay and the heady, cloying stink of horse manure, and loved both. He heard the noise of the horses shuffling around and felt the smoothness of their coats beneath his hand. When sadness and chaos surrounded him, the stables reminded him that there were places in the world where there was peace. Where words were spoken softly and with kindness.

'Have you spoken to the husband, Charlie?'

'The doctor's still with him, guv. Poor guy's totally hysterical.'

'He found her?'

'Yes, sir. He was late home from work apparently. Got the shock of his life.'

'Stay here, Charlie. Talk to him as soon as he calms down. I need to get back and set a few things in motion.'

'HOLMES?'

Jackman nodded. He'd always thought the acronym for the Home Office Large and Major Enquiry System was rather contrived, but the system was a lifesaver for managing a case of this nature and magnitude. And now they had HOLMES 2, which made it considerably easier for an SIO to control a serious crime investigation like a serial murder. Because, like it or not, Jackman now knew that this was what they had. The new HOLMES 2 system could handle massive sophisticated searches using cross-force information from multiple sources.

The only problem was that the HOLMES operator worked from the subterranean area where Orac ruled. There was no escaping it, Jackman would have to go down there in person. He tried to fathom out why that woman reduced him to a quivering wreck whenever they met. As usual he came up with very little, other than the fact that Orac was so different from the people he normally dealt with that he had no idea how to treat her. She was like some exotic, multi-coloured bird in a cage full of sparrows. The last time they had needed to speak, Jackman had been almost incapable of stringing a sensible sentence together.

Charlie broke his reverie. 'Should we pull in Daniel Kinder, guv?'

'It was the first thing I did when we took the shout. He might have a perfectly good alibi, and I hope he has, but right now, he's still the main suspect.' He nodded to Charlie. 'I'll see you back at the station when you've spoken to the husband.'

As Jackman started his vehicle, his mobile rang. He touched the answer and loudspeaker buttons, and Max's anxious voice filled the car. 'The unit outside Skye Wynyard's house say that Kinder's done a runner. He had another of those weird fugue things, and now he's disappeared.'

'Shit! How the hell did he get past them?'

'He legged it out the back, sir.' Max sounded well pissed off. 'As usual, it all comes down to bleeding funds. There are several rear and side routes out of Tavernier Court, and they don't have the manpower to cover them all.'

'Why does that not surprise me?' muttered Jackman.

'I've put out an all cars call to apprehend him, guv, and uniform are checking any places that he is known to frequent.' He paused, then said, 'Maybe we should go public? Get his face out there to the masses and ask for their help.'

'And have a witch-hunt along with mass hysteria on our hands? Not yet, Max. There are no two words more threatening and terrifying to the public than "serial killer." And if you suspect him to be on your own doorstep, then you can multiply the fear factor by a hundred. Just keep looking for him while I think this through.'

He hung up and felt his chest tighten. Jesus! If they'd let Kinder go, and he'd killed again on the very night he was freed, they would all be looking for new jobs, and he, as SIO, would be hung out to dry. A picture of the stricken faces of his father and mother loomed, to be quickly replaced with that of Sue Bannister lying in a thick pool of blood on her expensive porcelain tiles.

His eyes narrowed. Concentrate! No matter how hard he tried, Jackman just couldn't see Kinder as a serial killer. Even the psychologist had said as much. No, they certainly needed to bring Kinder back in, but they must spread their net wider, and somehow catch whoever was doing this. No one was going to hang his team out to dry, not while he was still around.

Jackman jammed his foot down and set off. He needed to get back to base and take hold of this case by the scruff of its neck, before it destroyed them all.

* * *

Lisa Hurley stared anxiously at Skye. 'I hate to leave you like this, but I need to get back to work.'

'You go. You've been brilliant, but there's nothing we can do until they find him.'

'You can have a key to my place. Use it as your own. When I finish work, maybe we can sort out some kind of plan.'

Skye shook her head. 'Thank you, but I need to be here, in case he comes home.'

Lisa frowned. 'I'm not sure that's a good idea. I'm not saying that he'd do anything to hurt you, but,' she paused, 'he's certainly not himself, is he?'

Skye hung her head. She could hardly disagree with that, could she? 'Alright, I'll wait until this evening, then I'll go to your place — if you're sure that's okay?'

Lisa reached into her bag, removed a set of keys and unhooked one from the ring. 'Spare front door. Keep it until this is over.' She touched Skye lightly on the arm. 'I'll see you later.' At the door she halted. 'Ring me if he turns up or if the police find him, won't you? Use the direct line to my office.'

Skye nodded. Then she said, 'Wait, Lisa. Maybe you should have a key for here too? With all this going on, I think I'd feel safer knowing that someone I trust was holding a spare key for me. If you don't mind, that is?'

Lisa smiled. 'Of course I will. It makes sense.'

Skye went into the kitchen and pulled open a small drawer in one of the units. After sifting through various odd keys she located a key fob shaped like a crescent moon with two shiny keys attached. She took it back to Lisa. 'The front one is silver, and the bronzy one is for the kitchen.'

Lisa put them in her bag, then checked her watch. 'Gosh! Must fly. Ring me!'

Skye nodded as the door closed behind the tall, efficient woman who had suddenly transformed from boss into guardian angel.

She walked back into the kitchen and decided that what she needed was coffee. Her head felt as if it had been caught in a tornado. Things were happening all around her and she had no control over any of them. As the kettle boiled she heard her mobile ringing.

'Skye, so sorry to bother you, but I was worried about you. The police have been to my unit again, and they say Daniel is missing.'

'Mark?' Skye tried to push away her disappointment that it wasn't Daniel. 'Yes. He was here last night, but he left this morning, and I've no idea where he went.'

Dan's friend, Mark Dunand, sounded as fraught as she was feeling. 'What the hell's going on? Why do they think Dan's mixed up in a murder? He wouldn't hurt a fly!'

'*We* know that, Mark, but the police don't, and no wonder. Dan's been acting like a complete fruitcake. I'm worried sick about him.'

'Me too.' His voice became calm and he said, 'I was wondering if you have half an hour to spare? I think we should put our heads together about Daniel. If he's in deep shit, and I suspect he is, then I'd like to help.'

'It doesn't get any deeper, Mark, believe me.'

'Meet me at Jonny's Wine Bar at three? This place is heaving with packers. We've had a big delivery in from Columbia and they'll be working here for hours getting the orders out. I think a quiet corner at Jonny's might be better than being overheard by this load of eavesdroppers.'

'I would, but I really need to wait here in case Daniel returns. You couldn't come to my place, could you?'

There was a short pause, then Mark agreed. 'Right. Give me an hour, and I'll be with you.'

* * *

Marie hurried through the foyer doors, where she almost collided with Guy Preston, who was just leaving.

'Daniel's disappeared,' he said breathlessly. 'I'm going to see how Skye Wynyard is holding up.' He looked at Marie, an uneasy expression on his face. 'I suspect the poor kid's almost at breaking point, and I want her to know that we are there for her.'

Marie's eyes fixed him with a shrewd stare. 'And?'

'And what?'

'There's something else, isn't there, Guy?'

'It's not for me to say, Marie. Your boss is in his office. He'll fill you in.'

She'd only been gone a few hours! What the hell could have happened in that time? 'Okay, I'll go see him.' She began to move away.

'Marie?'

She turned back.

'I didn't realise that your husband had died. I mentioned him to your team and they told me what happened. I'm really sorry. He was a very special man, wasn't he? And a great copper.'

'I thought so.' No matter how much time went by, she still found it hard to think of Bill as gone forever. She hated to hear people use the word, *was*. 'Thank you, Guy. And I'm sorry for you too. You lost your wife, so you know how it feels.'

Guy nodded. 'Sometimes it's almost too overpowering to think about, isn't it?' He shrugged, as if to pull himself together. 'Actually I was wondering if, well . . . maybe we could have a drink and catch up? It's clear that a lot's happened since we worked together last and I thought perhaps . . .'

Warning bells began to chime. Guy was a lovely man and undeniably attractive despite the scar, but she didn't want to get close again, not like before. She gave him a smile, the warmest she could muster right then and said, 'Maybe when the case is over? Right now I need every scrap of attention focussed on catching our killer. Is that okay?' By the time the case *was* over, she'd have thought up another, more permanent excuse.

'Oh, of course! I didn't mean now. I'd just like to know how you're doing, that's all. So, raincheck, huh?'

'Raincheck, and if *you're* not going to tell me what's going on around here, I'm going to find the man who can.' Marie widened the smile and hurried away from Preston. 'Catch you later.'

As she moved towards the staircase Marie felt his eyes still on her. She didn't want to turn round. Didn't want to see those pleading eyes.

* * *

Relief spread all over Jackman's face when Marie came into his office. All his life he'd preferred flying solo, but since he'd teamed up with "Super Mario," he felt somehow lacking when she wasn't around. And on a case like this, her input was priceless.

'There's been another one,' he said without preamble.

'Shit!'

'Shit is a pretty good word. Describes both the situation and exactly where we'll land if we don't come up with some answers pretty soon.'

'And Daniel's gone missing too?'

He groaned. 'Tell me about it.'

'I leave you alone for four hours and look what happens!' Marie flopped into a chair. 'You'd better fill me in.'

Jackman gave her a swift précis of what had happened to Sue Bannister, then shook his head. 'We *have* to get Daniel back here, and fast. I've got every available man, woman and dog out there looking for him,' he bit his lip, 'but even so, I still don't think it's him, do you?'

'I don't know, sir, I really don't. One moment I'm convinced he's just screwed up and the next I get the shivers thinking about what he might be capable of.' She sat up straight. 'But whatever we think, we need to get him back and into a nice secure little cell, and then we can make up our minds about him.'

Jackman was about to reply when Max knocked quickly on the door and almost fell into the office. 'Sir! I think you should get downstairs! There's a situation.'

Max turned tail and ran.

Jackman and Marie stared at each other and hurried after him.

'Situation?' asked Marie, taking the stairs two at a time.

'Don't like the sound of that!' Jackman's heart was pounding. Would it concern Daniel again?

They rushed along the corridor after Max, and as they approached the main hall they could hear shouting.

'What the . . . ?' Marie threw open the big doors and looked at the debacle taking place on the chequered black and white floor.

'Zane Prewett, I'm arresting you on suspicion of burglary at the Kinder premises in Riverside Crescent, Saltern-Le-Fen.'

Jackman's mouth dropped open. Prewett was spread-eagled on the floor with three uniformed officers trying to restrain him. A string of swearwords flooded from his twisted mouth as he heaved and fought to get up.

'And Stoner, you're staying too. We have reason to believe that you are involved.' The sergeant's voice boomed around the hall and echoed up to the floors above.

'Kevin Stoner?' breathed Marie, looking at the pale, shocked face of the younger policeman. 'Oh no! Surely not?'

'He's Zane's crewmate. They'll have to assume they're in it together, whatever *it* is. Although,' Jackman puffed out his cheeks in exasperation, 'I've been telling the silly sod for ages to dump that piece of garbage. Now look what's happened.'

Letting out a stream of curses, Zane Prewett was half-carried, half-dragged down towards the custody suite.

Jackman walked over to the sergeant. 'What was all that about, John?'

The big man made no attempt to cover his anger. 'It's been a damn long time coming, Inspector Jackman, but finally that slimy shit has slipped up. Our lads found a mobile phone belonging to Prewett in the garden of the Kinder house when we apprehended the Drew Wilson gang.'

'Couldn't he have dropped it when the house was originally searched by your guys?' asked Marie.

'He could have, but he didn't.' There was grim smugness in the sergeant's smile. 'It had been used since the house search, and used to text Drew Wilson and tell him that the house was empty and the job was on.'

'The bastard!'

'Exactly, Sergeant Evans. It had his prints all over it, *and* one of the SOCO team found a ten-pound note on the floor of the lounge. It was folded in exactly the same way that Zane always folds the bank notes in his pocket, and with his dabs on it too.'

'Surely *that* could have been there since the search?'

'It could have been, but Skye Wynyard and a friend cleaned the house from top to bottom after our guys left.' He raised his eyebrows. 'And on top of that, our dear friend Drew Wilson is, as we speak, furnishing one of our teams with times, dates and *all sorts* of information about ten other lucrative jobs that had come his way over the last two years, via PC Zane bloody Prewett. I'm afraid he's toast.'

Jackman whistled. 'I wouldn't like to be in his shoes in the coming months.'

'Whatever happens, the shit-bag deserves it. There is nothing worse than a bent copper,' growled the sergeant. 'But right now I need to get him charged and sent to another station. He can't stay here.'

'And Kevin Stoner?'

'He will have to be relieved of his duties of course,' The sergeant lowered his voice. 'I think he's just been dragged into something he couldn't find his way out of. Prewett is a nasty piece of work. I wouldn't put it past him to threaten the boy with something.' He scratched his neck. 'I needed Prewett to think I was arresting Kevin too, but it hopefully won't come to that. We'll talk to him. Obviously we need to do this by the book — we can't afford not to — then we'll take it from there.'

Jackman nodded. 'I like Stoner. I'd hate to see him end up on a charge of perverting the course of justice. And I agree with you that if he guessed there were dirty dealings afoot and turned a blind eye, I'm pretty sure he didn't do it lightly. He has the makings of an excellent police officer, and it would be a sin to lose him because of his rotten crewmate. I'd check out the threat aspect, if I were you.'

'I will, don't worry.' The sergeant turned and walked off towards the stairs.

'Well, I'll be blowed,' muttered Max. 'So there was something corrupt within these walls after all. I wonder if Dan Kinder was hunting for dirt on Zane?'

Marie and Jackman shook their heads in unison. 'Very doubtful, my friend. Daniel's problems go deeper than Zane Prewett feeding the local criminals inside info for their next burglary.'

'Ooh, but I'd love to sit in on the interview.' Max gave a wicked grin. 'I'd like to see him try to squirm out of this lot. He's been nicely sewn up, if I'm not mistaken.'

'Sewn up?' asked Marie.

'Two cock-ups on one job, Sarge? Remember, this is a bloke who has obviously been operating successfully for years. Drop a note *and* lose your phone? Now that is sloppy. And sorry, he's a first-class prick, but Zane's not sloppy.'

Marie tilted her head to one side. 'I see your point.'

Jackman did too, but decided that he had to leave this particular enquiry to others. There would be a lot of officers ready and only too willing to get their talons into Zane Prewett, and he had a killer on his mind. And with a third victim, it was a serial killer too. *And* his kill cycle was accelerating.

CHAPTER NINETEEN

Skye stepped back and Mark came in. He hugged her quickly and murmured, 'I'm so sorry.'

She smiled wanly. 'I don't know what to say.'

He unzipped his jacket and followed her through to the lounge. 'God, this is a right mess, isn't it? What on earth has happened to him?'

'I wish I knew.' Skye turned towards the kitchen. 'Would you like a drink? Tea? Coffee?'

'Have you got anything stronger? My head's a shed.'

'I've only got wine, I'm afraid. Neither Daniel nor I drink much.'

'Wine's fine, thanks. Right now I'd drink anything that had alcohol in it.' Mark dropped his skinny frame down onto the sofa and ran a hand through his mop of unruly hair. 'It only really sank in when the police came back and ransacked Dan's office a second time.'

Skye went to the kitchen to find a glass, and called back. 'I'm still trying to get my head around it, and I don't think I'm making a very good job of it.' The last thing she felt like was wine, so she switched on the kettle to make herself an instant coffee. 'Is Fitou alright? It's already opened, but it's still okay.'

'Perfect.' Mark was behind her, leaning against the door frame. 'As I said, I'd probably drink meths if you offered it.'

Skye poured hot water into her mug and opened the sugar canister.

'Not joining me?'

'I have to keep focussed and ready to drive if Daniel calls and needs me.'

'I don't think one small snifter would push you over the limit.' Mark accepted the glass that she offered him. 'You look strung out.'

She picked up her coffee and moved past him into the lounge. 'Caffeine will do fine thanks. Wine in the daytime makes me lethargic.'

They sat down and Skye wondered what to say to Mark. She had no answers about Daniel's strange behaviour, and she was tired of churning over different hypotheses. In fact, she suddenly resented Mark's presence and wished that she had put him off.

'Can I ask a personal question?' Mark had half emptied his glass in a single gulp.

Skye looked at him and hoped that her thoughts didn't show on her face.

'You don't think . . . ? I mean, in your heart of hearts, is there any chance——?'

She interrupted him, speaking sharply. 'How long have you known Daniel?'

'I've known him for ten years, maybe more.'

'Then there's your answer. You said yourself he wouldn't hurt a fly. He's just in very bad place right now and the timing of these recent murders really stinks. They have tipped him over the edge.' She looked at Mark reproachfully. 'Don't *you* start doubting him too!'

Mark threw back another slug of wine. 'I'm not, I just needed to know if you had any doubts. After all, you are the closest to him by far. If he's really lost it, then I wondered just how serious you thought it could be.' He placed the glass on a coffee table and looked at her intently. 'So, I suppose the best thing we can do is to help find him.'

Skye nibbled on her bottom lip. 'Half the Fenland Constabulary are out there trying to do just that. I've racked my brains to try to think of somewhere he might go, somewhere special, somewhere that means something to him, but everywhere I've thought of has been checked and double-checked. And if he's had one of his memory-loss episodes, he could be absolutely anywhere.'

'That makes me feel pretty useless.' Mark sighed, then stood up and began to pace the floor. 'You're right, he's my friend, and I should be doing something positive, not making up ridiculous scenarios. I need to *do* something practical.'

Skye felt a small rush of sympathy. 'I know exactly how you feel, but I don't know what to tell you. Until he's found, or he comes home, there's very little we *can* do.'

Mark flopped back onto the sofa. 'Ever since you came asking about Dan and his recent assignments, something's been bothering me.' He leant back into the soft cushions. 'One of my packers seemed very interested in Daniel. Every time he came in to work, this guy was there, asking him questions. It got so that I had to ask him to leave Dan alone.'

Skye sat up. 'Who is he?'

'He's been with me for about six months. Good solid worker, never lets us down, even when a shipment comes in early, or really late.'

'So why the interest in Dan?'

'He said he's a fan of Daniel's work, and Carla, my manager, believes him. She said he can quote some of Dan's pieces verbatim.'

'That's a bit extreme, isn't it? Even I can't do that.'

'Me neither. But I suspect he has something verging on OCD. He's methodical to the nth degree, and when he's picking out orders, he's meticulous. Carla reckons he's never made a mistake, and that is rare, believe me.'

'What's he called? What's he like?'

'His name is Nick Brewer, and he's twenty-four, maybe twenty-five. He's not a local, but he's British. He's very intelligent. Carla asked him why the hell he was doing a packer's job when he had qualifications coming out of his ears.'

'What did he say?'

'Beggars can't be choosers these days. If you want to work, you take whatever is on offer.'

'Well, we know that to be true. Perhaps that's why he likes Daniel. Dan researches everything so thoroughly, and he always has an informed and original viewpoint.' Skye sipped her drink. 'Maybe it's not so strange. Dan does have a good few fans — you should see his Facebook page.'

'I have. But there's an intensity about Nick that I find unsettling. Carla feels it too.'

'And do you think Dan noticed it?'

Mark shrugged. 'Dan was always polite to him, and thinking about it, maybe Dan encouraged him to talk.'

'Dan loves people. He's curious about their emotions and their strange situations. That's how he manages to write so well. He listens to what people have to say, because he's honestly interested in them.'

'So maybe Nick told him something that he was curious about?'

'Maybe, but I don't see how this fan could be connected to Dan's obsession with a murderer, do you?'

Mark shrugged again. 'Okay, so I'm clutching at straws. I'm just trying to find some clue that might help.' He looked at Skye. 'Do you reckon I should have a word with Nick?'

Before Skye could answer, her doorbell buzzed. She jumped up and ran to the door, with Mark trailing behind her.

'Professor Preston!' Her hopes rose. 'Any news?'

His face told her everything.

'No, but in the light of Daniel's recent disappearance, I was worried about you.' He looked across to where Mark stood silently in the lounge doorway. 'Oh, I'm sorry. I should have phoned first. Is it a bad time?'

Skye shook her head and introduced Mark to the psychologist. 'We feel so helpless. We were trying to formulate some sort of plan to help find Daniel.'

'To be honest, the best thing you can do is to wait here. I have a feeling he'll be home soon.' Guy Preston gave her a sad smile. 'This is the hardest part, isn't it? Just hanging on in there.'

Skye decided that she liked the doctor. He seemed compassionate without being cloying. 'Could you explain to Mark about the gaps in Daniel's memory, the fugues that you told us about? I was going to tell him about them but you'll do it so much better than me.'

Preston nodded and proceeded to describe what can happen when stress steals the memory away.

'Shit,' muttered Mark. 'You know, he had a weird turn once at the office. Carla, that's one of my employees, she found him on the roof. He didn't seem to know why he was there. He tried to cover it up afterwards but it was clear that something was wrong. Is that the same sort of thing?'

Preston said, 'It's the start. But they can intensify considerably.'

'And you believe that's why Dan disappeared from here earlier?'

'I do. And I would suggest that the trigger was the burglary at his house. That's enough to upset anyone, let alone someone as fragile as Daniel. His mind can't cope. It shuts down, and a different Daniel comes along and takes him away from whatever it is he can't deal with.'

Skye felt a black cloud descending over her. 'And this other Daniel could do terrible things, couldn't he?' She felt Mark's arm go around her.

'He could, I can't deny it, but let's not go there yet. I'm certain that Daniel is not responsible for anything more than believing a lie, and scaring the life out of himself — and all of us.'

'God, I hope you're right, Professor, I really do.' Skye leaned back against Mark, and burst into tears.

* * *

Daniel saw a hazy figure close beside him, and instinctively drew away. A searing pain tore through his left arm and he cried out.

'Hey, back with us at last. We'd almost given up on you.'

Daniel squinted, trying to make some sense of the shadowy form kneeling next to him.

'Thought you were a goner, mate.'

'Where am I?' Daniel heard himself speak and almost laughed. He hadn't thought people really said that. 'Sorry, but who are . . . ?'

'The bloke that saved your life, I guess.' The voice was young, with a hint of a city accent. 'The only thing that I'm not sure about is whether you're going to love me or hate me for it.'

Daniel struggled to sit up, then noticed the dressing on his arm. It was bulky but already stained with seeping blood. 'What the hell happened to me?' There was panic in his voice.

'Whoa! Cool it! And keep that arm elevated. It's taken ages to get the bleeding under control. You need to go to hospital, but considering the situation, we thought we'd give you the chance to decide for yourself.'

The boy — Daniel was sure it was a boy — gave a little laugh.

'If you survived, that is.'

Daniel lay back. 'Survived what?' He looked around. The place was in shadow, there was a pervasive smell of damp, and in the background he heard a gentle trickle of running water. 'And where are we?'

'Close to the river. One of the big houses along the bank has this old boathouse. It's never used, so we come here sometimes.'

'We?'

'Ellie and me. She's my friend.'

Daniel looked round, but saw no one else. 'Tell me what happened. Please.' He stared at his arm, 'And what the hell I've done to myself.'

'You've slashed your arm, just above the wrist. Ellie and I found you. As the whole town is crawling with police, and you clearly picked a bad day to try to kill yourself, we thought . . .'

'Kill myself?'

The boy stared at him through the gloom. 'Oh shit. Don't tell me it was some kind of bizarre accident?'

Daniel's head was spinning. He didn't know. All he did know was that his arm hurt like hell. He croaked, 'Please just tell me.'

The boy passed him a small bottle of water and he drank from it gratefully.

'You were on the path along the riverbank, beneath the iron bridge. Ellie and I heard you cry out, and we found you clutching your arm. It was horrible — blood was spurting everywhere. Then there was a splash, so we reckoned you'd thrown the knife, or whatever you'd used to hurt yourself, into the water. Then you gave a groan and went down like a sack of spuds.'

'But . . . . ?' He pointed to the stained dressing.

'Sorry. You'll find a twenty pound note missing from your wallet. This bloke I know has got a bad leg. He gets medical stuff from a clinic, and he'll sell it if you pay him enough.' He shrugged. 'I reckoned you could afford it.'

'And you stopped the bleeding? How?'

'I haven't always been on the streets, you know.'

Daniel's head began to ache. What on earth had he done this time?

'Look, I'm sorry if we've cocked up, mate.' The boy shook his head. 'We just thought that all the questions at the hospital . . . and then they'd call the rozzers . . . well, we didn't think you'd want all that.'

'It's not your fault. God, you've saved my life! I'm not going to blame you for anything. And you were right. I really don't need any questions from the police right now.' He looked at the boy. 'What's your name?'

'Tez.'

'Where's Ellie?'

'She comes and goes,' he said. 'She'll be back sometime.' He paused, a hint of sadness in his voice. 'Or maybe she won't. She didn't like all the blood.'

'How did you get me here?'

'It's only a few yards, and you'd come round enough for me to help you walk. Ellie went and saw about the bandages, and I did what I could to stop you bleeding to death.'

'You did a good job, Tez. Thank you.'

'The hospital would have done a better one.'

'If you hadn't found me, no hospital in the world could have done a good job. I'd have bled to death.' A tiny part of the old Daniel sparked to life. Tez's story could have the makings of a gritty and emotional article. Already he saw the youth as a sort of urban Robin Hood, a street crusader. He eased himself up, careful not to move his arm too much. 'You're not like the other street kids.'

'You're right there, mate.' He gave a little laugh. 'For one thing, I don't do drugs.'

'So why the streets?'

'Let's not get into that, alright?' Tez stood up. 'Right now, you need to tell me what you want to do. I'll help you, but I don't have all day. If I don't get to the spot where I kip, some other bastard'll nick it. It's the warmest place in town so it took a bit of fighting for.'

'You've done enough, and I'm really grateful.'

Daniel had no idea what he was going to do. It was the middle of the afternoon and his clothes were covered in blood. He couldn't walk anywhere like this. And then there was the overriding question. Why was he in this state? Why was he bleeding like a stuck pig? Had he injured himself? Or had someone else done this to him? The last thing he remembered was Skye holding him and the cat, tightly, in a safe and warm cocoon. How much time had passed since then?

As he considered all this, he felt an odd sort of calm. Yes, his mind was in turmoil, but in a frightened, almost normal kind of way. He was sick to his stomach, but he felt that *anyone* who found themselves in such a strange situation would be nauseous. Until now, he had been disturbed, even he was able to see that. Years ago he had written an article on self-harm, and he remembered something a teenager who cut herself had said: *It's the only time when I'm in control. It silences the inner scream, and afterwards, for a while, I feel good.*

He was right-handed, and it was his left arm that had been cut. Maybe that's what he'd done? Or maybe not. How could he tell? Daniel sighed. Enough was enough. His life had spiralled out of control, and right now the only place he could think of going was to Guy Preston's house. He must beg Preston to get him to a place of safety.

A place of safety. It sounded so good. Somewhere away from harm —from harming others. And if he was really lucky, he might find some answers.

He touched his pocket. His phone was still there, and also his wallet. Tez was certainly not your average street kid. He eased the wallet out and flipped it open, one-handed. Laying it on his legs, he removed five notes and held them out to Tez. 'It's nowhere near enough, and I

192

dare say if anyone else had found me, this would be up someone's nose by now. Take it, please.'

Tez didn't reach for it. 'There's a hundred quid there, isn't there?'

Daniel nodded.

'No thanks. Give me a twenty and I'll take it. More than that could mean trouble for me out here.'

To the twenty pound note, Daniel added his business card. 'If I can help you in any way, I will. And if I ever get myself sorted out, I'll come and find you, Tez. You shouldn't be here.'

Tez tucked the money away. 'Hasn't it dawned on you that some of us are here because it's infinitely better than where we came from?'

Dan tilted his head to one side. 'But it doesn't have to be better than where you could go, does it?'

Tez gave a little humourless laugh. 'Dreams, mate. It doesn't do to have dreams. Day to day, that's how we cope.' He moved closer. 'We need to get moving. Think you can stand?'

'I can stand, but I'm not sure where the hell I'm going to go.' He looked down at his bloodstained shirt. 'Will you sell me your hoodie?'

'You can have it. The Sally Army will sort me out something to replace it.'

Dan took another note from his wallet. 'Go to a charity shop and buy something warm. And this is purely a transaction, not charity, if that's what's worrying you.'

'It's not that. I've seen kids stuck with a knife for less. It doesn't do to carry money on the streets.'

'Then spend it. A coat and a meal for you and Ellie should take care of that.' He thrust the note at Tez, who reluctantly took it and peeled off his jacket.

'One last favour?'

'If it doesn't take too long,'

'Just go to the address I'll give you. If we are close to the iron bridge it's only a five minute walk. Could you tell me if there are any police watching the place?'

Tez looked closely at him. 'Are you the reason that Saltern is infested with the Old Bill right now?'

'I suspect I might be, but I'm not sticking around to find out.' He gave Tez his address in Riverside Crescent, and as the boy loped off, Dan slipped his good arm into the sleeve of the hoodie, draped the other side over his shoulder and zipped it up. It wasn't perfect, but it covered most of the bloodstains.

If there was no one watching his house, he'd go there, check his wound to see just how serious it was, clean up, get some fresh clothes and then re-evaluate his situation. He still considered Guy Preston to be his best bet, but he desperately wanted to let Skye know that he was safe. Well, more or less safe, but she mustn't see him like this. Whatever he did, he would have to clean himself up first.

He leaned back against the boathouse wall. His mind was clear. His only worry was how long would it stay that way.

CHAPTER TWENTY

Kevin Stoner sat in an empty office and waited for the inspector. The room was at the top of the stairs that led down to the custody suite. Through the slightly open door, Kevin could hear his ex-crewmate down below, howling fit to kill. His threats and obscenities resounded throughout the station.

'*Ex-crewmate.*' The words had the most exquisite ring to them. Kevin didn't care that he was in line for the grilling of his life. He knew precisely what he was going to say, and he prayed that it would clear him of any involvement in Zane Prewett's crimes. What was coming could go two ways. He would either be thrown to the wolves, or his previous good conduct record would save him. Either way, it would mean an end to his association with Prewett.

The door opened and the chief inspector strode into the room with his sergeant. Kevin jumped up and stood to attention as Sergeant John Cadman closed the door behind them.

'What the blazes is going on, Stoner? Did you know about any of this? Because if you did, then whoever your father is, bishop or not, I'm going to hang you out to dry!'

Kevin took a deep breath, and clasping his hands tightly together behind his back, said, 'Sir, I admit that I suspected that PC Prewett was conducting himself improperly, but when I challenged him I was subjected to serious threats to both myself and my family.'

Inspector Jim Gilbert slumped into his chair and expelled air loudly. 'Oh great! Just what we need. Explain, Stoner. Every single damned detail.'

Kevin nodded. 'Of course, sir, but before I do, there is something that you really should know, and I need to ask for your help.' He hesitated, then added, 'It's a very delicate matter.'

The inspector flashed a worried glance at the sergeant and narrowed his eyes. 'I'm hardly going to say yes until I know what the devil you're talking about, am I? Not that I consider you to be in any position to be asking for favours.'

Kevin, still bolt upright even though he wanted to roll up into a tiny ball, told the two policemen about the photographs that Zane had had taken of him *in flagrante delicto*. He worded it carefully, exactly as he had rehearsed, and finished with a humble apology. 'I would never do anything to bring shame on the Fenland Constabulary, sir. This was a private, intimate moment and Prewett paid someone to spy on me with a surveillance camera. I am both humiliated and deeply distressed by this, sir. Should those photographs fall into the hands of the media, you know the furore they would cause, and not just to me, my family, and the police force, but to the other person in the pictures as well.'

The inspector's eyes narrowed to tiny slits. 'Do we happen to know said "other person," Stoner?'

'Yes, sir,' said Kevin slowly and clearly. 'He's the son of a senior officer.'

Inspector Gilbert gritted his teeth and let out a string of expletives. Then he turned to John Cadman and said, 'Sergeant, I want you to take one trusted officer and go immediately to Prewett's home and retrieve those photographs. I also want cameras, his computer hard drive and any other external hard drives, memory sticks or removable storage devices, anything that can store pictures. Bring them to me here. Do it now, before any other team conducts a full search of Prewett's property.'

The sergeant gave a curt nod and made for the door. 'On my way, sir.'

'Oh, and John, when you get back, get someone we trust to check that he hasn't stored those pictures online. If he has we will need to gain access via the company who provides the service.' He grunted, 'Frankly, I doubt Prewett was savvy enough to encrypt them and upload them to a dark web host site, but you never know. We'll just have to hope he's not that bright.'

Cadman hurried off and Inspector Gilbert looked suddenly weary, as if the life had gone out of him. He shook his head. 'Sit down, Kevin. You mentioned a threat to your family. I'm guessing that you are not just talking about those photographs being sent to your father?'

'No, sir. Although Zane was going to Dad first.' Kevin sat with his back still straight. He didn't dare to relax a single muscle until this was over. 'I have a young niece, sir. My brother's girl. Her name is Sophie and she's only nine years old. Zane threatened to hurt her, and from the things he said, I believed he really intended to harm her if I said anything.' He hung his head. 'I was terrified. And as I had no actual proof of any of his illegal activities, I couldn't say anything, and I also couldn't risk anything happening to my brother's girl.' Kevin looked up at his commanding officer. 'I'm sorry, sir. I've let everyone down. Even DI Jackman noticed something was wrong and warned me to get away from Prewett. I wanted to tell him everything, but I kept thinking of the things Zane said he would do to Sophie. *Life-changing things*' were the exact words he used.'

'And do you swear that you had no involvement with any of his deals with Drew Wilson, or any other criminal for that matter?'

'I swear, sir.'

The inspector leaned back in his chair and folded his hands in his lap. 'I accept that, Kevin. Prior to teaming you up with Prewett — and ironically the reason for that was to try to make him step up and toe the line — you had an unblemished record. There will be an investigation, of course, and you will be required to answer a lot of questions, but I'm hopeful that your future career will not be tarnished.'

Kevin swallowed. 'Thank you, sir.' He hesitated, desperately wanting to ask about the photos.

'And I suggest you forget that those pictures were ever taken. We have enough problems right now with a triple killer loose in Saltern, so we damn well can't afford any further scandal. By the end of the day, all trace of them will have disappeared, and I very much doubt that Prewett will mention them, considering that he was using them to blackmail a fellow officer.' He gave a snort of disgust. 'Hell, we knew he was a troublemaker, but none of us suspected he was bent.' Kevin saw contrition in his face. 'I'm sorry that you were ever crewed with Prewett. It was done with the best of intentions, but it put you in an impossible situation. I apologise.'

This was better than Kevin had dared to hope. 'There's nothing to apologise for, sir. I should have had the courage to come to you long before this, so it's entirely my fault.'

The inspector stared at him. 'Does your father know about your sexuality?'

Kevin swallowed noisily. 'No, sir. He would be devastated.'

'I beg to differ.' Gilbert gave him a sad smile. 'He might not have chosen that particular path for you, but I suggest that you credit him with a little more understanding.

He could be aware of it already, but waiting for you to take him into your confidence.' The inspector gave him a look that was almost fatherly. 'I also suggest that you tell him very soon. No one can blackmail you for something everyone knows about. And this *is* the twenty-first century, Kevin. People are more liberal than twenty years ago.'

Kevin nodded. 'I will, sir. I've had enough of secrets.'

'I have to suspend you, you do realise that?'

'Absolutely, sir, and I'll do whatever is expected of me.' Kevin stood up, removed his warrant card from his pocket and placed it on the inspector's desk. 'Is that all, sir?'

'For now. Get yourself home, come out to your father, and remember what I said about those photos. Not a word to a soul. Forget them. They never existed.'

Tears were creeping into his eyes as he left the room. Even if he got away with this — and it was by no means certain that he would — Zane Prewett had damaged him. He would never forget those damned photographs as long as he lived.

* * *

Reluctantly, Jackman took the lift down to the basement. He was still trying to work through his irrational fear of Orac. Okay, perhaps fear was not the right word, but he certainly found their meetings disturbing. Marie seemed quite at ease with her, and from the amount of info that Orac had produced, she and Marie seemed to have struck up a pretty good working relationship.

It had to be the eyes. Or was it her extraordinary self-confidence?

As the lift slowed down, Jackman's pulse speeded up. Perhaps it was neither. Orac was a one off. She was like no one he had ever come across in his entire life, even at university. He shook his head, tried to quell what felt suspiciously like excitement, and walked towards the door of the IT room.

He pushed it open, only to find an empty workstation. For a moment he wasn't certain if he was relieved or disappointed.

'Can I help you, sir?'

A woman came out of an adjoining office. Her long dark hair was caught back behind her ears with a wide scarlet hair band and she looked to Jackman just like a latter-day Alice in Wonderland. 'Er, yes, thank you, I'm looking for the HOLMES operator.'

'Oh, good. I thought you might be looking for Orac. She's taken a few hours off.' She stuck out her hand. 'I'm Sylvia Sherwood. HOLMES is my baby.'

Jackman smiled. He'd been granted a reprieve. 'Brilliant. I'm DI Jackman, and I need your help. We now have three murder victims on this patch, and we suspect a serial killer, which is, of course, your domain.' He pointed to the fat folder he was carrying. 'This is what we have to date.'

'I've been expecting you actually. So it's three deaths now, is it?' The IT officer's face became immediately serious. 'Okay, I'll get onto it immediately. The system is considerably faster than it used to be. I'll link up and get the searches underway and keep you updated as we go, DI Jackman.'

He handed her the folder and turned to go. 'Oh, and when you see Orac, would you tell her I called by to thank her for all the information she sourced for us? It's much appreciated.'

The woman gave him an amused smile and said, 'I'll be *sure* to pass on the message, sir. She will appreciate your thoughtfulness, I know.'

As the lift doors sighed shut, a bemused Jackman thought he heard a muffled laugh emanating from the computer room. He frowned, then to his horror realised that his irrational fear of being in the same room as Orac had spread around the station. Oh, just great!

* * *

Marie looked up from Peter Hodder's notebook, and stared blankly at the wall. She had seen some terrible things in her time, but they paled into insignificance compared with what this man had had to deal with.

She sat back, amazed that he had dealt with it all with such dignity. Without Peter Hodder and his calm, diligent perseverance and methodical detective work, Françoise Thayer might have gone on killing for years.

She shivered as she closed the first book. There were several more but she wasn't sure she could cope with them all in one sitting.

'Sarge?' Max flopped down in a chair opposite her. 'Got a minute?'

'As many as you want, my friend. If I read much more about Françoise Thayer, I'll finish up as a head-case myself.'

'I've been trying to make sense of Alison Fleet's early life, and although I haven't tracked down her first husband, I've had a long talk to her sister-in-law, Lucy Richards, and I think I'm beginning to piece things together.' Max scratched his head.

'Let's have it then,' said Marie.

'Bruce Fleet's business was on the verge of total collapse, a far worse scenario than anyone originally thought. Without telling his wife, he had mortgaged their house to the hilt, and the bank was calling it in. What he didn't know was that Alison had noticed money disappearing from their account and suspected him of having an affair.' Max raised his eyebrows. 'She told Lucy of her suspicions, and Lucy convinced her that there was no way Bruce would be unfaithful, he loved Alison to pieces. So there had to be another reason.'

'So, was that why she started taking antidepressants?'

'Hold on, Sarge, I'm coming to that.' Max sat back and continued, 'Alison intimated to Lucy that something terrible had happened while she was married to Ray Skinner. I haven't discovered what exactly, and she never gave Lucy any details, but it had to be something pretty epic, because she's kept in touch with Skinner ever since. And I think that's where her money was going.'

Marie frowned. 'Bruce Fleet never knew? Surely his sister would have told him?'

Max shook his head. 'Lucy and Alison were like this.' He crossed his fingers. 'Really tight.'

Marie puffed out her cheeks. 'What could be important enough to keep in touch with an allegedly abusive ex when you are happily remarried?'

'Pass, but whatever happened, it sent Alison off the rails for a time. Lucy said that Alison admitted to needing mother's little helpers, but Lucy had no idea where they came from or what had caused the breakdown. And . . ,' Max paused dramatically, 'after the *event*, whatever it was, Alison spent time in Saltern General Hospital.'

'Another connection to that damned hospital,' said Marie, biting her bottom lip. 'But I thought we'd checked there when we were trying to find out where her medication came from?'

'We did, but she was admitted under the name of Alison *Skinner*, wasn't she? I have requested her notes, but it was a long while ago and prior to the computerisation of the records. The medical records officer said she'd do her best to locate them but frankly, Sarge, she sounded dead iffy about finding them.'

'The more you hear about the Fleets' problems, the more you can understand Bruce Fleet topping himself.' Marie sighed. Her head was beginning to ache. Every little snippet of information that they dug up seemed to lead to further mysteries, and it was easy to get side-tracked. 'Well, at least we know now that Alison was taking drugs to help her cope with something, even if we don't know what the problem was or where she got them from.'

'Well, I guess it rules out her being drugged by her killer.' Max sniffed. 'Where she got them from? My money's on Ray Skinner. I reckon she kept in touch because he was her dealer.'

Marie nodded. 'And maybe he was her killer too.'

'Maybe.'

'We need to find him, Max.'

'I've put all the details onto QUEST and marked him as "of interest" to us.'

'Good.' Marie knew that the search technique linked to automatic fingerprint recognition and also to the DNA database. 'Where and when was he last seen?'

'One week before Alison's death, in Peterborough Market. And that coincides with the last entry on Alison's tablet. We tried to contact him from her phone, but his number was unobtainable, and since then, zilch. He's dropped off the radar.'

'Either because he's a killer or because he's a drug dealer.'

'Or both.' Max pulled a face.

'Right. Well, we'd better tell the DI about this. He'll want to give Ray Skinner's name to the HOLMES operator. HOLMES might pick up a connection between Skinner and our other two victims.'

'Now that would be very nice, wouldn't it?' Max gave her a grim smile. 'But going on present form, I get the feeling that lady luck isn't going to be that generous.'

'Oh, thee of little faith.' Charlie Button placed a hand on Max's shoulder and grinned at him. 'You can forget QUEST. Guess who's just found Mr Ray Skinner?'

Max raised his eyebrows. 'Well, looking at that self-satisfied grin, I'd guess it's you, you smug little git.' He punched Charlie's arm. 'Okay, how did you manage it?'

'I decided to take a different tack.' Charlie pulled up another chair. 'We are all so used to dealing with scumbags that we believed he was hiding because he was a villain, either threatening Alison or supplying her with drugs. So . . . ,' he paused, 'I began to wonder if he was just an ordinary nice guy. And if he was, why had she been keeping in touch with him without telling Bruce Fleet?'

Marie leaned forward. 'But what about the alleged domestic violence?'

'It wasn't him, Sarge. It was Alison who dished out the right-handers.'

'What? Alison Fleet? Faithful wife and charity worker?' Marie's eyes were wide.

'It wasn't her fault, Sarge.' Charlie looked down at a sheaf of notes. 'And Ray Skinner is well cut up about her death. But he is coming in to see us and I'm sure that now he knows that Bruce is dead, he'll drag all the secrets out of the cupboard and fill in the details. The crux of it all is that Alison and Ray had a baby. It was conceived before they married, when she was little more than a kid herself, and she couldn't cope. She suffered terrible post-natal depression, and it ended with some kind of situation that made Ray fear for the baby's safety.'

Marie drew in a long breath. 'They split, and *he* kept the kid. That's why Alison never lost contact with him, and her missing money went to supporting her child.'

'Ah, and she never fessed up to her new husband,' added Max.

'More or less. Alison was in a very bad place for quite some time,' said Charlie. 'Apparently it was messy, but that's the bottom line.'

'So she spent the rest of her life trying to make up for what she'd done as a youngster.' Marie nodded. 'Makes some kind of sense now. So when is Skinner coming in, Charlie?'

'First thing tomorrow.' Charlie pulled a sheet of paper from the sheaf. 'By the way, Sarge, he's devastated to know that she was still self-medicating. He thought she was off the tablets donkey's years ago.'

'So he has no idea where she got them from?'

'None whatsoever.'

'Well, good work, Charlie. How did you track him down?'

'Worked out their ages when they married, then used Facebook and a couple of other networking sites to find an old school friend of Ray's who had kept in touch.' He pulled a face. 'Not exactly expert police detecting, more like something from CBeebies actually.'

'But it worked, mate,' said Max cheerfully. 'Who needs Orac and HOLMES 2, when you've got Charlie Button and social media?'

Marie laughed. It took away the horrors of what she had been reading in Peter Hodder's old notebook. But not for long. Finding Ray Skinner was a good thing, but it didn't help with finding their killer, or Daniel Kinder.

Her amusement faded. They were no further forward. 'Okay guys, time to press on. We have three dead women, and we're as much in the dark as we were on day one.'

As the two younger detectives returned to their desks, Marie's phone rang.

'It's Guy. I just thought I'd report that I've seen Skye Wynyard.'

'How's she holding up?'

'Frustrated, scared, but pretty well, all things considered. I wasn't able to have an in-depth talk as she had one of Daniel's friends with her.'

Marie thought that Preston sounded mildly irritated.

'So I've come home,' he continued. 'I don't think for one moment that Daniel will turn up for his appointment, but just in case he has a moment of lucidity, or maybe nowhere else to go, I thought I should be here for him.'

'Good idea, Guy. I'll ring you if any of our officers pick him up in the meantime.'

'Thanks, and while I'm twiddling my thumbs here, I'll get on with his profile.' He paused, and then added, 'Marie? I'm sorry if you misunderstood me earlier. I was only suggesting a drink to catch up. After all, it's been years since we worked together, but now I'm thinking that maybe it didn't come over quite like that.'

Marie gritted her teeth, but said, 'Oh come on, Guy, we've known each other for long enough, haven't we? Of course I didn't get the wrong impression. When this is over, a drink would be lovely.'

She had told Jackman that she had no problem working with this man, but was that true? Even after such a long time, Guy Preston still had the power to affect her, and she wasn't sure that she liked it. Last time she had had Bill to pour out her heart to, but now there was no one, other than Jackman. He was certainly sympathetic and a damned good listener, but considering the severity of the case they were working on, she wasn't sure that it was appropriate to start bleating about her personal problems.

Marie said, 'Sorry, but I have to go, Guy.' She hung up and let out a loud, exasperated sigh. Everything was irritating her. She was certain it was because as soon as they had let Daniel Kinder out, another dead woman had turned up. He might have had nothing to do with it, but it certainly didn't look good, and when the press got hold of it, God help the Fenland Constabulary.

CHAPTER TWENTY-ONE

Daniel was scared. Tez had assured him that the back of his house was clear of blue uniforms, but when he had crept along the alley that backed onto his property, he had found a white squad car blocking the exit. For one moment he had been overwhelmed by an urge to run up to it and throw himself into the arms of the waiting coppers, but something had stopped him.

And now he was cowering in a musty-smelling shed in one of his neighbours' back gardens. He knew that it had already been searched, as muddy chevrons still marked the wooden flooring where damp boots had trodden.

Only a matter of hours ago he had been begging the police to keep him locked up, and now he was avoiding them. His arm hurt, it felt like hot coals were being pressed against his torn skin, and he was so tired that all he wanted was to lie down on the wet floor and go to sleep. But he couldn't even do that. He dreaded sleep and all that came with it.

He drew the smelly jacket closer around him and tried to think straight. After a few minutes he gave up. Pain and confusion were making logical thought impossible. What had happened to his arm? Why was he cut so badly? He stared at the damp and bloody dressing wrapped around his forearm and tried to remember. But he had no memory of what had happened, although he was certain that he had not injured himself — well, not deliberately.

He leaned back against the wooden slats of the shed and felt tears welling up behind his tired eyelids. He should get his arm treated before it got infected, if it wasn't already.

With an effort that felt almost superhuman, he struggled to his feet. There was only one place he could think of to go. It wasn't too far away and hopefully he wouldn't be recognised in Tez's old jacket. Daniel gave a bitter little laugh. One thing was for sure, he resembled a down-and-out far more than the up-and-coming young journalist of just a week ago.

Daniel slipped out of the back gate and stumbled off in the direction of the only person who could help him.

* * *

It was a second or two before Guy Preston recognised the bedraggled figure leaning heavily against his doorframe.

'I didn't know where else to go.'

The voice was broken, sending anguish and pain into the surrounding air. Guy knew that the young man was close to meltdown.

He held both arms out wide in welcome. 'Come in, come in, Daniel.' Then he looked closer at the sagging figure. 'What on earth has happened to you?'

Daniel pushed himself from the doorframe and moved inside. 'I wish I knew.'

Guy led him to the kitchen and pulled out a chair. Daniel dropped into it gratefully, and Guy eased the filthy jacket away from Daniel's left arm. 'Can I take a look at that for you?'

'I thought you healed minds?'

'I trained as a medical doctor before I decided to study psychology.' He smiled at Daniel, trying not to look as though he was analysing him. He carefully removed the stinking jacket and let it fall to the floor. 'Not your usual style, Daniel.'

'A friend gave it to me. I could hardly roam the streets looking like a hit-and-run victim.'

'And you have no idea how this happened?'

Daniel didn't answer.

'One of your "gaps," I presume?'

Daniel nodded silently.

Guy looked at the blood-soaked bandage with something like confusion. 'Well, if the person who dressed this was the "friend" who owned that salubrious jacket, he must be quite something. This has been applied with considerable care, unlike his choice of outdoor attire.'

'Sorry but the Salvation Army handout store isn't exactly Armani.'

Guy tried to gauge the extent of the injury before removing the bandages. There had clearly been considerable bleeding but it seemed to have stopped now. 'I think the best thing we can do is get you into the shower and cleaned up, and then I'll deal with your wound.' He moved towards the door. 'Come on, I'll get you some fresh clothes and some towels.'

In the bathroom Daniel stripped down to his boxer shorts and held his arm over the bath for Guy to remove the dressings. It was the first time Daniel had seen the wound, and the moment the pressure was taken away, fresh blood began to ooze from the gaping, ragged gash in Daniel's arm.

'Right. Shower as quickly as you can. Irrigate it thoroughly. I'm going to need to stitch that.' Guy opened a cabinet and took out a box with a red cross on the lid. 'Luckily I keep a few sutures and needles in case of emergency.' He turned to the door. 'Shout when you're decent and I'll try to put you back together again.'

'I wish you could do that for my head.'

'It's not impossible, Daniel. Give me time and I'll try, I promise.'

As Guy moved towards the door, Daniel said, 'Professor Preston? Please don't call the police just yet. I know you have to, but can you give me a few moments to talk to you first?'

Guy nodded. 'No problem.'

Outside the door, Guy exhaled. In a strange kind of way Daniel's injury was a blessing. If he could help him now, Daniel would trust him more. And if he were to give a correct evaluation of his state of mind, he *had* to gain his trust.

Guy went into his bedroom. From his wardrobe he removed a plastic container that held an assortment of sterile dressings and plasters. It was going to hurt like hell, but the best he could offer Daniel was a couple of paracetamol and tell him to grit his teeth. It was either that or take him to A&E. Guy was certain which option Daniel would choose.

'Ready!' Daniel called out from the bathroom.

'On my way!' he called back, and picked up the box. 'Let's get you fixed.'

It took some twenty minutes to suture the wound and redress it. And after checking that Daniel was up to date with his tetanus jabs, there was little more that Guy could do.

'You want to talk?'

Daniel looked down at his arm and said, 'If I agreed to go into a psychiatric hospital, would *you* be able to look after me?'

Guy bit on his bottom lip. 'I have no connection with Saltern hospital, so if you went there, I'm afraid your care would be entirely up to the hospital psych team. However, I do know a smaller private hospital up on the edge of the Wolds. It's called Banner House and the director is a friend of mine. I'm sure he would allow me to work with him on your case.'

Daniel looked hopefully at him. 'I have money. And I know I need help.'

'I'm not being patronising, Daniel, but that last statement is the biggest step in the whole process.' Guy sat back and told Daniel something about his friend's hospital and the kind of treatments that they found effective. 'I'm not going to bullshit you that it will be easy, because it won't, but by accepting treatment, you are already on the road to getting your life back.'

'That's all I want.' Daniel looked hopefully at him, 'My life back.' He paused. 'I can't continue like this for much longer. I don't even know who I am anymore.'

'I do need to let the police know where you are, you do understand that, don't you? They have half the Fenland Constabulary combing the streets looking for you.'

'I did notice,' said Daniel with the hint of a smile, then added, 'There is one thing that I do know, Professor Preston. And that is, I *am* her son. Françoise Thayer's life-blood runs in my veins.'

'Is blood something you think about often?'

Daniel frowned, his eyes narrowed, then he whispered, 'I dream about it.'

'Do you? Can you tell me about your dreams?'

Guy sat and listened as Daniel described the horrors of his blood-filled nights, and he began to feel uneasy. Could Daniel be affected by hematomania too? Surely that was too much of a coincidence? And this new injury? Was it possible that he had inflicted such serious damage on himself? In which case, could Daniel have been right about Françoise Thayer all along? Guy swallowed and tried to keep his expression bland. Was he really sitting here talking to the infamous murderer's son?

His mind a jumble of thoughts, Guy tried to decide what to do. Finally he said, 'You sit there and relax. I'm going to phone my friend about getting you admitted. I think we need to do a lot of talking, Dan, and I've got all the time in the world for you, okay?'

Daniel nodded. 'And the police?'

'They can wait a little longer.'

Guy went into the room that he was using as a temporary office and closed the door. His head was spinning. Never once had he believed Daniel's story — until now. Excitement coursed through him. Thayer's son? Now wouldn't that be something! Shaking his head, he picked up the phone and dialled his colleague's number.

Three minutes later he went back to Daniel. 'All arranged. As soon as the police have spoken to you — as long as they don't decide to hold you again — I'll take you straight to Banner House and we'll get your treatment underway. Okay?'

Daniel gave a slow nod. 'I'm ready.' Then he asked, 'Are the police coming?'

Guy sat down opposite him. 'I thought we'd talk first. They'll be here like greased lightning when I let them know you are with me. Let me just tell you what I think about your condition, then I'll make that call.' He leant closer to Daniel. 'This is how I see it . . .'

* * *

'Forensic reports.'

Marie looked up as Jackman stopped at her desk.

'Very interesting forensic reports actually.' Jackman placed two printouts in front of her. 'We may not have anything specific to tie a killer to our three victims, but we now have something concrete that links the three women.'

Marie looked at the papers. 'Toxicology reports.' She scanned them, then let out a gasp, 'They *all* had antidepressants in their systems. And it's the same drug, Clomipramine hydrochloride.'

'If we can trace where they got those drugs, we'll be hot on the heels of our killer, I'm sure of it.'

'It has to be the hospital.' On her fingers, Marie counted off the various connections. 'One, Sue Bannister's husband worked there. Two, Julia Hope was a nurse there. And three, Alison Fleet did regular charity work there, oh yes, and she had been a patient there years ago, although I realise that last one is a bit tenuous.'

'Well, if you're going down the hospital route, don't forget our other line of enquiry. Daniel Kinder is their shining Sir Galahad, and his girlfriend, Skye Wynyard, is an occupational therapist.'

Marie was just about to reply when Max called across the office, 'Boss! Your desk phone is ringing.'

Jackman hurried to his office and disappeared inside, leaving Marie pondering about the antidepressants. She knew that there was a very good reason why Alison had been self-medicating, but what about the others? What dark secrets had driven Sue and Julia to acquire little help-ers that didn't come from their GP or a respectable consultant? She opened the file on Julia Hope. Good family, no money worries or apparent debts, generally had excellent health and was known to be highly gregarious, something of a party animal. She was very popular and no one that they had spoken to knew of any serious problems in her life.

Marie grunted, closed the file and opened the one on Sue Bannister. Again, nothing leapt out at her.

'Marie! My office.' Marie dropped her file and went to Jackman's office.

He had just replaced the telephone. 'That was the Thai Police. They have located Daniel's mother.'

'About bloody time! Where is she?'

'They are bringing her in from some godforsaken spot in the forest to somewhere with fairly good network coverage. They think she'll be with them in a couple of hours and then they are going to set up a Skype video call.'

Marie gave a little whoop of relief. 'Brilliant! At last we may get some answers about Daniel's background.'

'Let's hope so. The Thai officials have booked Ruby Kinder onto an AirAsia flight from Chiang Mai to Bangkok where she can get the first available flight home. Perhaps she will be able to talk some sense into her son.'

'How long will all that take?'

Jackman pulled a face. 'Well, it's a couple of hours' flight down from the north to Bangkok, then, depending on the departure time of the flight home, I reckon another twelve hours plus to London Heathrow.'

'So we're talking about tomorrow lunchtime, if we're lucky,' mused Marie.

Jackman nodded. 'Will you give Skye a ring and tell her about Daniel's mother? And tell her that we'll explain about the break-in and assure her that Skye is in no way to blame.'

'I'm on it, sir.'

Marie walked back to her desk and rang Skye Wynyard.

She answered at the first ring and straightaway asked if she could come to the station and be there for the video link. Marie agreed, and hung up. Her phone rang again immediately.

'He's with me, Marie. Daniel Kinder is safe with me.'

Marie exhaled air in an exhilarated little whoop. 'Thank God for that, Guy. Is he alright?'

'He's injured himself, and he doesn't know how he did it.' Guy paused. 'Nasty gash across his left forearm. I had to suture it for him, but there's more good news. He's agreed to go into Banner House Psychiatric Unit voluntarily.'

'Has he indeed?' Marie felt doubly relieved. Assuming he wasn't their killer, the combination of seeing his mother again, getting some professional help, and having regular visits from Skye in a safe environment could really put Daniel back on the road to recovery. 'That's excellent news. Although we will have to interview him regarding the third death — if you think he's fit enough, that is?'

There was a short silence. 'He's very fragile. He swings from being sensible and aware, to being severely neurotic in a matter of moments, but he knows that he can't go on like this, and he does want answers.'

'Then we'll pick him up.'

'I was wondering if you'd like me to bring him in? Hopefully I can keep him on a stable enough level for you to talk to him. He could freak and run again if he sees blue lights outside the flat.'

Marie frowned. 'Are you happy with that? Bringing him in alone?

'I wouldn't have suggested it if I didn't think it was for the best,' said Guy, then added, 'But thank you for thinking about my safety. I know why you are saying it, but Daniel is a very different animal to Terence Austin. I'll be fine.'

Marie clamped her teeth together in irritation. She hadn't been thinking about Austin at all, just that she didn't want to lose Daniel Kinder again. A squad car and two officers might have been a safer bet. 'Okay, Guy, if you honestly think it's the best option. When are you leaving?'

'Five minutes. So we'll see you in fifteen.'

* * *

Evening was approaching, and as Kevin Stoner was clearing out his locker, DC Max Cohen sauntered into the changing room.

'They're moving him out, mate. Saw the custody sergeant saying a fond farewell.' Max grinned at Kevin. 'You can breathe again.'

Kevin returned the smile, more faintly. 'Maybe we can *all* breathe again.'

Max flopped down on one of the locker room benches and stared at Kevin. 'I don't know how you did it, but you made a bloody good job of it.'

Kevin tensed. 'What do you mean?'

Max's grin widened. 'Hey! Don't be coy! The whole station should be thanking you for getting rid of that piece of shite. You're a hero, mate!'

'I don't know what you're talking about, Cohen. And I'd be grateful if you kept your mistaken ideas to yourself.' Stoner was beginning to panic.

'Calm down, mate. This is between you and me. I know you're going to have to stick to whatever your story is, for the sake of keeping the gold braid happy, but I'm just saying, respect, man.' He stood up. 'That's all, and you can sleep easy, I won't be sharing my views on your part in Zane Prewett's timely exit from Saltern. You've done us all a favour.' Max clapped a hand on Kevin's shoulder as he left. 'As I said, man. Respect.'

Alone in the locker room, Kevin sat down heavily on the bench. If one of the detectives had been able to see straight through him, surely his bosses would too? He knew he had Inspector Jim Gilbert on his side, but even Gilbert was answerable to the higher-ups. And then another thought entered his aching head. What if Prewett put two and two together and realised what he had done? Would he and his family ever be free of Zane's threats?

Before he could formulate an answer, the door opened again. This time it was Sergeant Cadman. 'Ah, glad I caught you before you left, Stoner.'

Kevin began to stand up, but the sergeant waved him back, and sat down on a bench opposite him. 'I thought you'd like to know that Prewett has been taken to Lincoln.' He paused briefly, then went on, 'And I've just got back from Prewett's flat. We found everything we needed, if you understand what I'm saying.'

Kevin nodded, and relief flooded through him. This was the reason he'd been hanging around for the last few hours. He had not wanted to leave the station without knowing that the sergeant's unofficial task had been completed successfully. 'Thank you, sir. I can't tell you how much I appreciate it.'

'I'm sure, son. I reckon your life has been hell for the last few months, hasn't it?'

He gulped back a sob. 'Pretty much, skipper.'

Cadman sighed and shook his head. 'I just wish you'd come to me and told me what was happening. Hindsight's a wonderful thing, but I should have realised that something was going on. Like most of the others, I thought he was just a cocky, lazy bastard. It never occurred to me that he was as rotten as he was, and the devastating effect it was having on you.'

'It's my own fault, skip. I just didn't have the balls to stand up to him.' He swallowed. 'To tell the truth, this has hit me hard. It's made me doubt my ability to be a good copper. In fact, I'm not sure if maybe I shouldn't rethink my choice of career.'

'Rubbish! You're a good lad with a bright future. When someone threatens those you love, common sense and clear thinking go out the window. If the threat had been directly to you, you'd have handled it quite differently, but Zane made you scared for your little niece, didn't he? He was very clever, Kevin, but it's all over now, apart from the legal stuff. And although that won't be nice at all, I'm willing to gamble that Prewett will be going down for a long time.'

'I'm sure he'll invent a way to try to involve me.'

'Maybe he will, but no one will believe a word he says. He messed up, and he only has himself to blame.' Cadman nodded. 'And between you and me, he has no alibi at all for the evening of the break-in. He won't walk out of this one, I promise you.' The sergeant stood up. 'Now you get on home. And forget all about giving up policing. Once this is over, we'll get you teamed up with a bloody good partner, and Zane Prewett will fade away like a bad smell.' He halted in the doorway, 'Or maybe you'd like to think about doing your exams to get into CID? I know for a fact that DI Jackman would support that decision.' Cadman raised his eyebrows, 'Think about it?'

Kevin nodded. 'I will, skipper.'

Alone again, Kevin leaned back against the locker doors. He had thought about giving up policing not because of the damage that Zane had done to him, but the devious way he had handled it. If he was capable of setting up such a calculated and underhand scheme for dumping a fellow officer in the shit, maybe he was no better than Zane. But then he thought about Sophie. He had no doubt at all that Zane, or one of his cronies, would have actually inflicted "life-changing" harm to the child. And the thought of that made his skin crawl.

Kevin sighed aloud. Well, he'd done it now. He'd just have to live with it. And he knew one thing about Zane Prewett that the others didn't. The reason why Kevin had been able to set him up so confidently was because he knew exactly where Zane had been at the time of the break-in. Sergeant Cadman had said that he had no alibi, and he hadn't. Well, not one he could use, because he had taken great delight in bragging to Kevin that he was shagging the wife of one of the uniformed inspectors.

Kevin smiled. He'd seen the message arranging their next liaison when he'd taken Zane's phone and sent that text to Drew Wilson telling him that the Kinder house would be empty.

Kevin gathered up his things. Sometimes he wished that his father had chosen a different profession. Something like a bookie, or a tree-surgeon, anything that would have freed Kevin from his awful sense of right and wrong. His father had brought him up knowing all about sin. And Kevin knew that he had sinned.

CHAPTER TWENTY-TWO

'Where the hell is Guy Preston? They should have been here half an hour ago. Try ringing his mobile again, Marie.' Jackman was pacing up and down his office.

'I just did, and he's not picking up. Something's wrong, guv.'

'Isn't it just,' growled Jackman. 'Wouldn't it be nice if something went right with this case?'

'I *knew* I should have sent a car.' Marie looked thoroughly miserable.

Jackman stopped pacing. 'It's not your fault. His justification would have convinced me too.'

'I had a gut feeling, and I allowed Preston to persuade me. There's no excuse, I was a prat.'

Jackman looked at the wall clock. The video link with Thailand had been pushed back an hour, as Ruby Kinder's trip from the forest had taken longer than expected. It was now scheduled for thirty minutes' time. He began pacing again. Uniform had ascertained that Guy Preston's car was not outside his address and a neighbour had seen Preston and a younger man drive off almost three-quarters of an hour ago. It was only a ten-minute drive, so where the hell were they?

A knock on the door, and a familiar figure entered.

'Guy!' Marie stood up. 'Thank God! We thought something had happened to you, but . . .'

'Where's Daniel Kinder?' said Jackman.

'I lost him.' Guy Preston looked ruefully at Marie. 'I'm so sorry. I should have let you deal with it.'

'But how did it happen?' Marie asked. 'You left home together, didn't you?'

Jackman suddenly realised that Preston was not his usual immaculate self. His jacket sleeves were smeared with dirt, his trousers were dusty, and his loafers were caked with mud.

'Oh, we left okay. Then he said he felt sick.' Guy looked furious with himself. 'And as he'd just had his arm stitched up with no anaesthetic other than a couple of paracetamol, I believed him. I stopped. He got out the passenger side. I turned off the engine, and fool that I am, left the keys in the ignition and went round to help him.' His anger grew. 'He took me off guard and pushed me down a bank on the side of the Sluice road. By the time I clambered back up, he'd driven off.' He heaved a sigh. 'I've just walked here from the Blackland Sluice gates.'

Marie pulled a face. 'And I'm guessing that your phone is in the car.'

'Got it in one.'

'So much for Daniel being stable,' said Marie.

'Actually I think he was very stable,' Guy said. 'Calculating and totally in control is how I'd describe him.'

Jackman chewed on the inside of his cheek. 'So you think he planned the whole thing?'

'I'd say so.' Preston sank down into a chair. 'He must have realised that you would find him if he went to A&E, so he used me to patch him up, then when he was ready, he took off — with my car. Oh yes, and with some of my clothes as well.'

'We'd better get a shout out to traffic to stop the car,' said Marie, opening her notebook. 'What make of vehicle is it? And the licence number?'

'I've already spoken to the desk sergeant on my way in.' Guy shrugged. 'He's dealt with that side of it.'

'Good,' murmured Jackman. 'They'll soon track him.'

'I hope so.' Guy suddenly looked exhausted. 'Do you know, I was certain that we were getting somewhere. He seemed so different, so honest. We talked for ages. And, strangely, he had two opportunities to make a run for it. Twice I went into my office to make phone calls, and on both occasions my car keys were sitting on the hall table. It would have been much easier to sneak out quietly, but he didn't.'

Marie looked at him. 'If you spoke for ages, maybe something came up in the latter part of the conversation that spooked him?'

Guy looked at her thoughtfully. 'I really don't think so, but . . .' He shrugged. 'If there was a trigger, then I don't know what it was. He had me completely fooled.' Guy rubbed at the muscles at the back of his neck. 'How could I have been so trusting? No — worse than that — how could I have been so smug, so blindly assured of my own capabilities?'

'Don't beat yourself up, Guy,' said Jackman. 'Even if he is screwed up, Daniel's still an intelligent and likeable young man and none of us know whether we're Arthur or Martha when we talk to him. One minute, I'm convinced he's a sad kid with an unhealthy obsession with his mystery parentage and the next, I'm certain he's our killer.'

'Fine, but I'm the bloody psychologist,' muttered Guy. 'And if *I* can't understand Daniel's thought processes, then I'm not doing my job very well, am I?'

Thankfully Marie's mobile rang before Jackman had to find something else to say.

'Skye? What's the matter?' Marie listened, then said, 'Don't worry. I'll get one of our officers to pick you up. We'll see you shortly.'

Jackman gave her an enquiring look.

'Her car's got a flat tyre, and she's desperate to see Ruby on the link-up.' She looked at him evenly, 'And if Daniel's on the loose and has some plan in his twisted little head, I think she'll be safer here with us, don't you?'

'Absolutely. Organise a car right away.' As Marie left, Jackman looked at Guy Preston. 'And I'll get Max to run you home so that you can get cleaned up. By the way, you said that Daniel had on some of your clothes?'

'His own were covered in blood. He's now wearing a pair of designer jeans, a pale blue Ralph Lauren polo shirt and a light grey bomber jacket.'

'He was covered in blood?'

'From the wound in his arm.'

'Are his old clothes still at your place?'

'In my bath. I was going to dispose of them when I got back.'

'Then Max must bag them up and bring them straight back here. There's a chance there's more than just his blood on them. We need them for forensic services.'

Guy nodded. 'Ah, I see. I didn't think of that. Yes, I'll show Max where they are. Luckily only Daniel handled them, so they won't be contaminated.'

'Did you want to be here for the video link? Only it's getting a bit tight for time.'

Guy Preston shook his head. 'I've had enough excitement for one day. You can tell me all tomorrow, DI Jackman. I think a long hot shower is on the cards when I get home.'

'We'll let you know the moment your car turns up, and if it doesn't, I'll pick you up myself in the morning on my way in.'

'Much appreciated.' Guy brushed ineffectually at his dirty jacket. 'Once again, I'm sorry about what happened. It's entirely my fault that Daniel's not downstairs in an interview room. I should have listened to Marie.'

'Forget it.' Jackman forced a smile, though he privately agreed with Preston. 'Marie is *always* right. Sickening, isn't it?'

Guy Preston was looking anxious. 'DI Jackman? I have to say that I'm really not sure about Daniel Kinder anymore. That gash on his arm for a start. Was it an accident? Did someone do it to him in self-defence? Or was it self-inflicted? The main thing is the way he drew me in. If he could deceive me so skilfully, Inspector, he could deceive anyone.'

As Guy Preston walked away, Jackman stared after him and thought about Marie and her odd connection to the psychologist.

Even though she had told him what had happened during the Terence Marcus Austin case, Jackman still felt vaguely uncomfortable about them working together. It was hard to believe that the little secretive glances the doctor kept giving her didn't reveal his hopes for a relationship. Marie had said that that wasn't the case, but he wondered if she was right, though she seemed to be handling it well. She was friendly, but treated him like just another colleague. She was managing to keep Preston and their past history at arms' length, but she did it kindly, and that couldn't be easy.

His lips pursed in concentration. Why was he thinking about this for goodness sake? He was in the middle of a triple murder enquiry, and he was a detective inspector, not Marie Evans' nanny! So what if Preston did have the hots for her? It was none of his business. Marie was a very attractive woman and Preston could hardly be blamed for fancying her. With a grunt, Jackman picked up the forensic reports that lay in front of him and forced himself to concentrate on his work. As he began to read, he was transported into a kind of dream.

He was seated on Glory and riding at a gallop across the damp sand at his old home. And beside him, on her gleaming black and green Kawasaki, was Marie. Her chestnut hair, whipped by the wind, was as soft and shiny as Glory's flowing mane.

Suddenly Jackman understood something that had never occurred to him before. They came from totally different backgrounds and had followed very different paths to get to where they were now, but they were so alike that it took his breath away. Marie had once described to him the pure exhilaration of riding her bike at breakneck speed on an empty road. And he knew precisely what she was talking about. He too had experienced every racing heartbeat and every tremor of that exhilarating pleasure when riding Glory along the beach. He closed his eyes and breathed deeply. Come on, Jackman! Anyone would think he was jealous of Guy Preston. No, he was simply dog-tired and his concentration had gone up the pole. He shook himself. The pressure of this terrible case was getting to him. He didn't indulge in fantastic thoughts mid-investigation. In fact, he didn't indulge in them at all.

He took up the toxicology report and began to read it out loud in an effort to bring his errant mind back into focus. After a time, it began to work.

* * *

Ruby Kinder's face was narrow, weathered and full of concern. Marie looked at the slightly fuzzy video picture and decided that if Ruby had been searching for a cure for her grief, she hadn't found it.

The video connection was a little jerky and didn't quite sync with the sound, but as long as they gave each other time to speak, it was manageable.

As tactfully as he could, Jackman had explained the situation regarding her son. Ruby had expressed total disbelief.

'But he's never shown the slightest interest in his biological parents!' she burst out.

'Because he didn't want to hurt her, or his father,' whispered Skye from behind Jackman's shoulder. 'He loves them and felt that to keep on to them about his real mother was a betrayal of everything the Kinders had done for him.'

Jackman relayed what Skye had said.

'Oh, Daniel, if only you'd talked to *me*! I could have saved you all this . . . I know *everything* about his early years, DI Jackman.' She paused and cleared her throat. 'They would never have let Sam and I adopt him if we hadn't been made fully aware of his traumatic history.'

Jackman leaned forward. 'Traumatic?'

Ruby sighed. 'We were advised by the psychologists never to talk to him about his past, as it could cause massive problems in later life. He was monitored carefully for many, many years.'

Marie sensed Jackman's tension as he fought the urge to hurry the woman.

'Daniel's mother was a drug addict, DI Jackman. Somehow, despite social services' constant intervention, she managed to hold on to her three children.'

'He has siblings?' Marie asked.

There was a long silence, then Ruby said, '*Had* siblings. No one realised how close to breaking point Daniel's mother was, then one night she drove her three boys into a nearby wood, attached a hose to the exhaust pipe and sealed the four of them inside the car.'

Marie gasped. She immediately recalled the smell of exhaust fumes inside Bruce Fleet's locked garage.

'It happened in Derbyshire. You probably heard about the case. Her name was Lucy Carrick. She killed herself and Daniel's two brothers. Dan was the only survivor. A man searching for a lost dog smashed a window and dragged him out.'

'Oh my God!' Skye was unsuccessfully fighting back her tears. 'My poor Daniel!'

Ruby kept on talking. Perhaps she felt that if she stopped, she might never find the strength to start again. 'Apparently he was desperately ill for some time afterwards. They suspected both cardiac and brain damage, as the carbon monoxide had caused blood damage, and the lack of oxygen could have allowed his main organs to fail. But he pulled through, although we were told that the effects of prolonged inhalation of carbon monoxide could lead to severe memory loss. They said he could also suffer with depression, visual disturbances, lack of concentration, confusion and a multitude of other things.'

'But even so, Daniel made it into a career that requires intelligence, concentration, a good memory and the ability to understand others. And he succeeded,' Jackman stated.

Ruby Kinder rubbed her eyes wearily. 'Yes, he did, thank the Lord. But his early years with us were fraught with anxiety, and the doctors were absolutely right about some of his problems.'

'His memory loss?'

'He has no recall whatsoever of his first five years, but we considered that a blessing. It was the small, almost inconsequential blanks that were the most disturbing.'

'Why?' asked Marie.

'Because things happened during those missing moments, and Daniel didn't remember a thing about them.'

'What kind of things?' asked Jackman, sending a worried glance in Marie's direction.

'Temper tantrums, lashing out, angry outbursts, and sometimes just wandering off with no recollection of how he got to where he ended up.'

Marie whispered, 'Guy Preston should be here. He needs to hear this.'

'Don't worry, it's being taped. We'll go over it with him.' Jackman turned back to Ruby Kinder. 'Did you know that these incidences of memory loss were still happening?'

'No, Inspector Jackman, I didn't. And I cannot imagine why he has a fixation on that terrible woman, Françoise Thayer. I've never once heard him mention her.'

'And you don't make a habit of visiting the attic room in your house?'

Ruby Kinder looked completely baffled. 'No. Why should I? Daniel said he keeps all his old research papers for his articles up there in case he needs them again, and old computers and printers, stuff like that. He said it's a bit of a dumping ground and he keeps it locked because he's researching other people's personal lives.' She frowned. 'Why?'

When Jackman explained, Ruby's face disintegrated into confusion and pain. She pulled herself together and asked, 'And now you say he's missing?'

'I'm afraid so. We have officers all over the town and the adjacent countryside looking for him. He was seen just a matter of hours ago, so we'll find him, never fear.'

'Then I need to tell you that there's a chance that some of his horrific childhood has seeped back into his memory.' Ruby now looked composed, almost hard. 'The doctors said there was a tiny possibility that it might, but it seems he is misunderstanding what he remembers. He was terribly ill-treated by his mother's druggy "friends." I cannot even describe the state that child was in when Sam and I saw him in the hospital. You would need to talk to someone with more experience than I, but I suspect that he's remembering his real mother and some of the terrible things he saw happen. He's a clever and inquisitive young man, DI Jackman, and I think he chanced on the story about Thayer in his research and made a terrible and incorrect connection with the murderess. Don't you?'

Jackman's breath caught in his chest, then he exhaled. 'You could be right, Mrs Kinder.'

'Then he's horrifically wrong about his birth mother! He'll be in hell, Inspector! You *have* to find him, and for God's sake, tell him the truth!'

Jackman struggled to reassure her, but Marie sensed the desperation underlying his words. He went on to tell her about the attempted break-in at her house.

'I'm not worried about the house. I just want to see my boy safe.' Ruby Kinder paused and said, 'Is Skye Wynyard there with you?'

'She is. Would you like to talk to her?'

'Oh yes, please. She loves my son, Inspector. This must be agony for her too.'

Feeling like an eavesdropper, Marie listened to the conversation, hearing the affection in their voices as they spoke.

Skye asked, 'That scar on Dan's head, did he really fall off a swing?'

'Oh yes, that was true. To this day I can still hear his scream. I went cold. And I felt so guilty. He'd suffered so much already, all I wanted to do was love and protect him, and he almost died falling from a swing.' She smiled wanly. 'Skye, I have to go now. I daren't be late for my flight out of Chiang Mai. Take care, darling, I'll see you as soon as I'm home.'

Jackman closed the video connection and they sat in silence. All Marie could see was three young children in a car full of deadly fumes. And she knew that Jackman was imagining the same thing.

Then Jackman yawned loudly. 'What are we going to do about Skye?'

Marie stretched. 'It's getting late. I thought maybe I'd send out for something to eat. She could stay and eat with us. I don't like the thought of her going home when Daniel is still roaming free.'

'Me neither. Though we can't force her to stay if she doesn't want to.'

'I'll go ask her.' Marie stood up. 'By the way, any luck getting hold of Guy Preston?'

'Yes. He's still pretty angry with himself about what happened. And now he's kicking himself for not staying for the Skype call.' Jackman fiddled with a fountain pen on his desk. 'He reckons that Ruby could be right about her son. Childhood memories flashing through his mind could have led to him creating a hybrid "mother," part real, and part Françoise Thayer. And Guy says that bothers him a lot.'

'It bothers me too. Along with the fact that Guy's car has not been seen, even though we're checking every CCTV camera in the whole of Saltern. It looks like Daniel Kinder just drove straight into a black hole.' Marie felt in her pocket for some money. 'What do you fancy eating?'

'A deliciously cooked pan-fried sea-bass with olive crushed potatoes and a sauce vierge. Or no, perhaps slices of prime tournedos steak on a bed of truffle oil mash, served with a wild mushroom sauce and a Stilton crouton . . .'

'I'll put it to the team,' Marie replied with a straight face, 'Though I suspect that the flame-grilled Whopper with fries and coleslaw will get more votes.'

'Philistines!'

Skye was talking on her mobile phone when Marie found her.

'That was Dan's friend, Mark Dunand. He's going to pick me up after he's seen tonight's freight consignment in safely. He's offered to drive me around some of Dan's old haunts, just to see if we can find him. I don't hold out much hope, but it's better than doing nothing.'

'Then you'll have time to eat? I'm afraid it's only a junk food takeaway.'

Skye nodded eagerly. 'I haven't eaten since I don't know when. That would be great, thanks.'

Marie took Skye with her into the CID room and asked Charlie to go and fetch the burgers. As soon as he'd gone Skye said, 'I don't know if this is relevant, but Mark told me about one of his packers who seemed a bit over-interested in Daniel. Do you think it could be something to make enquiries about?'

Marie looked at her. 'What form did this interest take?'

'Mark said he could quote Dan's articles almost word for word, and he was always hanging around Dan when he was in his office.'

'Do you have his name?'

Skye fumbled around in her shoulder-bag. 'I wrote it down, Sergeant.' She produced a yellow post-it note and handed it to Marie. 'Nick Brewer. He's apparently highly intelligent. Far too well qualified to be a packer but Carla, Mark's manager, said that he was taking on any work he could in order to feed himself.'

'I can't think that it's anything more than a crush, or a bit of hero-worship. I'm sure Daniel's inundated with messages and comments about his journalistic articles, isn't he?'

'Oh yes, he has a massive following.'

For some reason, Marie was not concerned in the slightest about this Nick Brewer's apparent fixation on Daniel. On the other hand, Mark Dunand *did* interest her. For one thing, she had not met or spoken to him and she liked to be able to put a face to a name. 'Have you known Mark for long?'

'About three years, I guess, but Dan has known him since they were teenagers.'

'Does Mark know about Daniel's, er . . .' Marie tried to find the right description, 'obsession with Françoise Thayer?'

'Oh no,' said Skye. 'I'm the only one that Dan has ever confided in about the attic room.' Her face fell. 'And now I seem to have told the world.'

Marie reached across and squeezed Skye's arm gently. 'You've done all the right things for Daniel, Skye. You love him, and you are only trying to make things right for him. You have nothing to reproach yourself for.'

'I feel that I've made things worse.'

'None of this is your fault. And you now know that it's not Daniel's fault either, not really.' The vision of the three children in a locked gas-filled car came to her with a jolt.

'He's suffered so much. It's no wonder he's as disturbed as he is.'

'And the worst thing by far, is that he's got it all wrong,' said Skye miserably.

'Not entirely.' Marie sighed. 'In fact he was absolutely right, wasn't he? His mother really was a murderer. But she wasn't Françoise Thayer. Lucy Carrick wasn't a ruthless, brutal killer with a morbid bloodlust. She was a drug-addicted girl who couldn't cope anymore.'

'The wrong woman, but still a killer.' It was Skye's turn to sigh. 'What a mess.'

Marie nodded, then said, 'Are you comfortable being out with Mark tonight? We do have an awful lot of officers out there, searching really hard.'

'I'm fine with it. As I said, doing nothing and not knowing where Dan's gone is driving me mad.'

'Skye, if you should find him, promise me that you won't go near him. I know it might sound silly, but ring us immediately. I'm not saying that you are in any danger, but we've lost him once, and we can't have that happen again. You need professionals with you to bring him in safely. Okay?'

'I understand. Although nothing will ever convince me that Dan would hurt me.'

Marie gave her a worried smile. 'I hope you're right.'

* * *

Daniel sat in the darkness and listened to the silence.

For the first time in weeks his mind was not bombarding him with lies or confusing him with muddled thoughts. He felt completely clear-headed and very, very peaceful.

The only words that he heard now were Guy Preston's. They had finally stilled the inner turmoil. He knew that he had done the right thing by going to see the psychologist, not just get his wound attended to, but for what Preston had said.

He smiled a little ruefully. He was sorry that he'd had to push the doctor down that bank, but he'd known that it wouldn't hurt him. It had been a gentle gradient and the ground was soft after the early rain. He was sure that the only thing damaged was the man's dignity, and maybe his expensive suede shoes.

It hadn't been premeditated. It had been completely spontaneous, triggered by what the doctor had told him about his condition. He just needed some time to himself before he went to the police. Now he knew the truth and a weight had lifted from him.

Daniel closed his eyes and felt the welcome darkness seep in. He had somewhere to go and someone special to see, but it could wait a little longer. For a few minutes he would just enjoy the peace, the darkness and the silence.

The corners of his lips lifted into a slow smile.

CHAPTER TWENTY-THREE

Lisa Hurley sat in the driver's seat of her car and watched the small house in Tavernier's Court. It was certainly a pleasant location. The warm red brick of the old railway buildings drew you back to a time when you might see billowy clouds of steam and hear the stokers shovelling coal.

But Lisa felt far from mellow. Her back was straight, her shoulders tight as titanium rods, and her eyes were sore from staring into the darkness.

The night was cool with a chilly wind coming in off the North Sea and her windscreen was soon speckled with fine misty rain.

She had been sitting there for almost an hour. He would come, she was certain of it. And she knew it would be soon. She glanced down at her watch, then stretched and took from her pocket the key fob with the silver moon.

Lisa stepped from the car and locked it. Then she walked away from the house until she reached a narrow walkway that led to the garages. Skye's little Kia was still parked in her numbered space close to the property. Skye herself had left some time earlier, in a squad car driven by a police officer.

After a careful look round, Lisa stepped down the concrete path. Before she reached the garage block, she veered off onto another path that ran along the back gardens. She counted the houses, then unlatched the correct gate and entered the little patio garden. Easy to maintain, she thought as she walked quietly towards the darkened house. Lots of pretty stone paving, coloured gravel and neatly-walled raised beds, just right for a hard-working career girl like Skye. Lisa almost whispered the name out loud, and she shivered as she did.

The key turned easily in the lock, and she reminded herself not to jump if Daniel's cat suddenly wound itself around her legs. It wouldn't do to scream and draw attention to the house. Not yet.

Lisa closed the door and placed the key into the inside lock, but left it unturned, just as she had seen Skye do. Locking doors was never a priority when you came from a rural background.

On her earlier visit Lisa had carefully taken note of the layout of the small property, and now she was able to move easily through it in the dark. As she had expected, as soon as she entered the lounge, the cat stalked towards her, yowling as it sashayed across the floor. 'Hello, you,' she whispered, then stooped, gathering the animal up and clasping it tightly to her. 'Sorry, chum, but we can't have you roaming free. A feline welcoming committee is the last thing I need.' She pushed the cat into the dining room and closed the door.

She then hurried up the stairs and paused on the landing. Through the long window a street light gave enough brightness for her to see her wristwatch clearly. She gritted her teeth. It was time.

She moved into Skye's bedroom and pulled the curtains, taking care to see that they met tightly. Then, with a sharp intake of breath, she switched on the bedside lamp.

From there, she hurried to the en suite shower room, and after ensuring that the blind was pulled right down, put that light on as well. The bright cluster of tiny halogen ceiling lamps made her squint. Then she leaned into the shower cubicle and switched on Skye's waterproof radio, a plastic piece of fun, shaped like a dolphin. Tinny music echoed round the small room as Lisa turned on the water. After carefully placing a thick towelling bath sheet close to the door of the shower, she stepped back into the bedroom and pulled the door half closed. In just a few steps she was back out on the landing and moving quickly down to the guest room. It was diagonally opposite Skye's, and if she left it ajar, Lisa could just make out a view of the staircase and Skye's slightly open door.

Okay, she thought, as she eased herself back against the wall to begin her vigil. Let's see what's really in that twisted mind of yours, shall we?

She knew that there would be soft footsteps padding up the stairs. She had been certain that they would pause outside the door, and someone would grip the handle and move stealthily inside the room. But what she hadn't planned for was the fact that the sheer terror of hearing them would turn her blood to water. She had not counted on heart-juddering, gut-loosening *fear*.

It was only the knowledge of what he might be there for that steadied her tremors and rallied her courage. This would be positive proof that Skye really was in as much danger as Lisa believed she was.

She tried to remain detached. She pretended that she was doing nothing more than watching a scary movie.

But Lisa was totally unprepared for who she saw walking up Skye's stairs.

Through the narrow gap, Lisa saw a tall figure moving towards the landing. She had expected a man in jeans, trainers and a hooded sweater. Instead, this figure was wearing a familiar green V-neck tunic and matching trousers. His hair was covered by a scrub tie cap and his face was obscured by a surgical mask.

As her confused brain tried to process this unexpected sight, Lisa suddenly noticed that whoever this was held a wicked-looking long-bladed knife in his gloved right hand.

What had she got herself into?

After Skye had told her that Daniel was still missing, Lisa had been afraid that her friend could be in danger from him if one of his strange fugue states took him over. But she couldn't possibly have imagined what was happening now.

As the man slipped into the bedroom, Lisa knew she had to act fast. She pulled her mobile phone from her pocket. She had switched it off when she entered Skye's flat, and it played an infuriating little tune when you activated it. But she had no choice. She jabbed her finger on the power button and prayed that the noise from the shower would cover it up.

Lisa gave him enough time to get right into the bedroom, then she tiptoed out of the guest room, and after taking a deep breath, crept towards the open door.

If she could just get downstairs and outside, she could lock him in, giving her enough time to dial 999 and either hide, or make it to her car.

She glanced into Skye's room and saw him standing with his back to her, outside the shower room. His head was tilted as he listened, and she saw his fingers tense and tighten on the handle of the knife. She only had seconds before he realised that Skye was not there, and with a silent prayer on her lips, Lisa hurled herself past the doorway and down the stairs. As she ran, she hit 999 on her phone. It was the best she could do.

Halfway across the lounge, she knew she wasn't going to make it.

Behind her the soft-soled shoes slapped on the stair treads. They were travelling much faster than she had expected. For a moment she felt as though she were in one of those nightmares where you try to get away from something but are unable to move. She made it to the kitchen, hearing a distant voice asking which emergency service she required. 'Police!' she screamed. 'Tavernie—'

The phone flew from her grasp and she heard the crunch as he ground it into the floor . . .

It was an odd feeling. Not pain, well, not immediately. Just cold. She thought of the word "rending" as it cut through the flesh across her neck and shoulder.

This had been meant for Skye.

Utter white-hot rage filled Lisa Hurley, and with a superhuman effort she spun round and threw herself at her attacker.

For a moment he was taken by surprise and reeled backwards, almost losing his grip on the knife. Lisa grabbed at the nearest thing available, which happened to be a cast-iron skillet, sitting on the hob. She swung it with all her failing strength.

A loud grunt told her that she had caught him a glancing blow, and she prayed that it would be enough to allow her to get out of the house. But then the pain of her own injury hit her. Searing, burning pain blasted through her shoulder, and she crawled towards the back door.

Dragging it open, she let out a howl of agony and desperation. Her car seemed as far away as the North Pole and a sickening wave of dizziness told her that she would not remain conscious for long. The second stab of the bloodied blade caught her somewhere in the back of her ribcage.

The last thing that Lisa Hurley saw before darkness carried her away was the retreating green-clad figure running across the garden and disappearing through the gate and into the night.

CHAPTER TWENTY-FOUR

'Knife attack in Tavernier Court, guv!' Charlie almost fell over his own feet as he rushed around the desks in the CID room. 'It's Skye Wynyard's home.'

Jackman jumped up from his perch on the edge of Marie's desk. 'Skye's place? But isn't she here with us?'

'Yes, sir. She's downstairs in the foyer waiting for her lift to arrive. But it's not Skye, sir. It's an older woman, name of Lisa Hurley. She had a Saltern hospital ID card on her.'

'That bloody hospital again!' Marie let out a curse as she grabbed her jacket from the back of her chair. 'Is she badly injured?'

'She's being taken to ITU, sir. Sergeant Masters thought you would want to attend.'

'Dead right I do.' Jackman pulled his car keys from his pocket. 'Charlie, make sure that Skye Wynyard stays put. No wandering the streets looking for Daniel and she's to tell whoever was giving her a lift to go home, understand? I want her here.' His eyes swung to Marie. 'Let's go.'

As they screamed into the hospital car park, a trolley surrounded by paramedics was being pulled from the back of an ambulance. Hurrying after the group, Marie tried to pick up what they were saying. Amidst the medical jargon, she understood that their patient was still alive.

'Will she make it?' Jackman called out, flashing his warrant card at one of the doctors.

The doctor didn't take his eyes off Lisa as he merely said, 'We're trying.' Then he called out, 'Resus! Now!'

Jackman and Marie watched through an open doorway. The team worked frantically, until someone said, 'She's stable.'

'Good work everyone. Is theatre ready to take her?'

'Five minutes, sir.'

'Excellent.' The doctor peeled off his gloves and blood-soaked apron and threw them into a yellow bin. Eyebrows raised, he walked over to Jackman and Marie. 'Close call. She needs surgery on both sites. The shoulder and neck injury is the shallowest, we think it's mainly soft tissue damage, but the second stab wound is much deeper and gave us a bit of a scare.' He pushed his dark hair back from his forehead. 'The knife managed to penetrate the deep muscle layer of the back, slip through the ribcage, and lacerate one of the lower bronco-pulmonary segments of her right lung. Hopefully the surgeons can remove the damaged part without adversely affecting the other segments.' He took a deep breath. 'She also has bleeding into the cavity below the lung.' He pointed to the base of his own ribcage by way of explanation. 'Here. It's what's called the pleural recess. It's the space the lung expands into during inspiration.'

'But she'll survive?' asked Jackman urgently.

'We have every reason to believe that she will.' He paused. 'Unless there is more internal damage than we could see.'

'Can we talk to her, Doctor? Is she conscious?'

'I'm afraid not, Inspector. You'll have to wait until she's out of theatre.'

Jackman let out low groan of exasperation. 'Just so long as everyone is aware that this was attempted murder, and we think she will have seen her attacker. It's vital we speak to her as soon as we can. Do you understand, Doctor?'

'Absolutely.'

'We'll have officers here around the clock. I'm sorry if it's an inconvenience, but that's the way it is.' His face darkened. 'The last time our presence was required in this hospital there was considerable bad feeling against our officers. Some of the nurses went out of their way to obstruct them. I sincerely hope that we won't meet that kind of attitude again.'

'I was informed about that.' The doctor looked embarrassed. 'I apologise. I assure you that this time you'll receive all the assistance you need. Serious warnings have been issued, Inspector. It won't happen again.'

They stood back as Lisa Hurley, festooned with drips, drains and an assortment of monitors, was made ready for theatre.

Marie looked at her white face and wondered what on earth she had been doing at Skye Wynyard's home, and how she had come to be stabbed so viciously.

'You will need this.' The doctor handed her a neck chain with a badge and pass on it. 'She's one of ours, Sergeant. This is her identification. She's the administrative head of the occupational therapy department.' He gave a little shrug. 'It's tough when you have to work on a colleague. Affects us all.'

Marie nodded. It was the same when a fellow officer was injured. 'So she is Skye's boss.' She looked at Jackman. 'Curiouser and curiouser.'

'Skye.' It was little more than a sigh, but everyone turned to look at the woman on the bed.

'Just relax, Lisa. We've got you safe now. You're on the way to theatre. You're going to be fine.' The doctor held her hand.

'Skye? Where is Skye?'

Marie and Jackman moved to her bedside. 'We are the police, Lisa. And Skye's okay. We have her safely at the police station.'

'Keep her there! He was trying to kill *her*, only he found me . . .' The voice began to fade.

'Who was it, Lisa? Who hurt you?' Jackman said.

'Take care of Skye. Take ca . . .'

Marie leaned closer. What were those last three words? Could she have heard correctly? 'Hang on in there, Lisa. And don't worry about Skye. She's safe.'

The bed was rushed away with its entourage of attendants.

Jackman and Marie turned to go. 'What did she say?' asked Jackman.

Marie frowned. 'I'm not sure. It doesn't make too much sense, but I'll tell you what I think when we're outside. If I'm right, I don't think this is the kind of news that Lisa would want spread around the hospital.'

Jackman nodded. 'Then wait till we get to the car. Right now I need to organise a round-the-clock watch on Lisa Hurley, then we have to get back to the station. Forensics are going to have to go over that house in Tavernier Court with a fine-toothed comb. If it's the same killer, then he wasn't allowed to finish the job, so ten to one he'll have left trace evidence.'

While Jackman was making his calls, Marie took the opportunity to ring Charlie and ask him how Skye was.

Charlie's voice was hesitant. 'I've been trying to get hold of the boss, Sarge. But his phone has been tied up and yours was switched off. Skye had gone by the time I got down to reception. Daniel's friend must have already collected her.'

'Oh shit! Listen, Charlie. Lisa Hurley was not the intended victim of that knife attack, Skye Wynyard was.'

'Hell! Well, I've already asked uniform to put out an "all cars," Sarge. We need to notify her of what has happened at her house before she walks in on a major crime scene.'

'Isn't she answering her mobile?'

'No, Sarge. It's switched off.'

'So her voicemail won't be activated, damn.' She thought for a second or two. 'Try a text. She'll pick it up when she switches her phone back on. Then go and tell uniform that finding her is now a priority. Someone is out there with a sharp knife and he is hunting for Skye. Got it?' She thought for a moment. 'What about this friend of hers, this Mark Dunand? Do we have a mobile number for him?'

'I know we have his business number, Sarge, but I'm not sure about a mobile. I'll update uniform about the girl, then check it out.'

As Charlie hung up, Marie looked anxiously at Jackman. 'So much for promising Lisa that Skye was safe.'

Jackman closed his phone and the colour drained from his face. 'Please don't tell me she's left the station?'

Marie nodded grimly. 'Could this get any worse?'

'Not much.'

As they hurried across the car park, he asked, 'What was it that Lisa said?'

'I think . . ,' said Marie slowly, 'I think she said, "Take care of my daughter."'

'But surely Skye said that her parents were in France somewhere, renovating a holiday cottage?'

'That's right, in the Dordogne. But earlier, when we were talking about why Daniel was so obsessed with knowing about his birth mother, she told me that she was adopted too, but she had no desire to find her own mother. As far as she was concerned, whoever gave her up did her a favour. She had a happy childhood, a good education and parents who loved her.'

Jackman unlocked the car and threw open the door. 'Maybe pain and all the drugs made Lisa confused. She might well have a daughter and she's just mixed them up.'

242

'And you believe that, do you?' Marie fastened the seat belt.

'Well, you clearly don't.' He turned to her and gave her a hopeless half-grin. 'Of course I don't believe it. I'm clutching at bloody straws, aren't I?' He switched on the ignition and drove towards the exit.

Marie flipped open her phone and called Charlie. 'Any luck?'

There was a long silence, and Marie began to feel nervous. Then Charlie said, 'I'm sorry, Sarge, but it's worse than I thought.'

'Is that possible?'

'Oh yes. I've been speaking to the desk sergeant and apparently while Skye was waiting in the foyer, she had a phone call and left immediately after it. A short while later the bloke who was supposed to be giving her a lift turned up. Well upset, he was. The sergeant thinks he's a bit keen on Skye from the way he carried on.'

Marie gritted her teeth. 'So as *we* didn't ring her, Dunand didn't ring her, and her boss certainly didn't ring her, it had to be Daniel, didn't it?'

'Or maybe the prof?' said Charlie. 'He's been trying to keep an eye on her while Daniel's on the run, hasn't he?'

'Mm, he has.' Marie thought hard. 'Listen, Charlie, we are on our way back to the station. Go make sure that uniform know how urgent it is that we find Skye, and we'll see you in ten.' She closed her phone and explained to Jackman what had happened. 'Shall I ring Guy Preston?'

Jackman nodded. 'I don't think for one minute it was him, but it's worth asking.'

Guy answered after two rings. 'Sorry, Marie, but no, it wasn't me.' He sounded agitated. 'Oh Lord, so do we believe that she went to meet Daniel?'

'It looks that way. But listen, Guy, if you should happen to hear from them, and it *is* possible that they'll come to you, ring me immediately, won't you?'

He gave a remorseful little laugh. 'Oh, I won't get caught out like that again, Marie! If they turn up here, I'll lock them in if I have to, and if either of them contact me, I'll be on to you like a shot.'

Marie thanked him, ended the call and stared at her phone. 'Guy never called her. So she has to be with Daniel.' Jackman's face was set hard and he didn't take his eyes from the road. 'She trusts him. Even after everything that has happened. She believes in him and trusts that he is not the murderer.'

'And you, Marie?' he said, without turning his head. 'What do you believe?'

She closed her eyes for a second. 'I never thought he was a killer, but things are escalating out of control, and now that we know about what happened to him as a child, well . . .' She gave a small shrug. 'You can't afford to put your trust in someone as badly damaged as Daniel is.' She heard again the words of the old retired detective, Peter Hodder: "Keep him close." She shivered in the warm evening. 'We really need to find him.'

Jackman brought the car to a halt in the police station car park. 'At least if Skye and Daniel are together, Skye will tell him what Ruby Kinder told us about his real mother. If anyone can convince Daniel that he's been living under a terrible illusion, it will be Skye. There is something about that girl, and she really loves him. She's the right person to break the news.'

Marie wasn't convinced. 'As long as he believes what she's telling him. It's a bit like telling a little kid there's no Father Christmas. He might think we've set her up and it's all lies. We have no idea how he'll react to such momentous news.'

'True.' Jackman removed the keys from the ignition. 'But right now we'd do better to just concentrate on finding them. And maybe we should bring in Daniel's friend, Mark Dunand? He and Skye were about to drive out and check some old haunts of his and Daniel's. Maybe he knows of places we don't.'

Marie flung open the car door. 'Good idea. If Max hasn't thrown in the towel for the night, I'll get him to go pick up Dunand.' She hurried beside her boss as he moved quickly towards the back door of the station. 'Have you met this Dunand guy?'

Jackman held the door back for her. 'No. I think Charlie saw him when they went to search Daniel's office. Why?'

'I like to put faces to names, and I like to get a feel for people. You can't do that when you've never looked into their eyes.'

'Then all the more reason to take a look at him.'

Marie and Jackman entered the CID room and Charlie moved towards them. 'I found a mobile number, Sarge. But Dunand said he's going out to look for Skye himself.'

'I hope you told him to do nothing of the bloody sort,' spat out Jackman.

'I did, guv. I said the last thing we needed was a maverick out on the streets, and that we needed him to work with us, but he more or less told me to get lost.' Charlie looked aggrieved. 'He was quite aggressive. He said he had a hell of a lot more chance of finding her than we did, then he switched his phone off.'

Marie pulled a face. 'Did he specifically say he was going to look for *Skye*? Not Daniel? Or both of them? Just Skye?'

Charlie stared at her. 'Just Skye. He never mentioned Daniel's name once.'

'But he's *Daniel's* friend,' mused Max. 'If he was so worried about his mate, you'd have thought he'd be eager to find him, not just Skye.'

Jackman frowned. 'This is worrying,' he murmured. 'I think we need to pull out all we know about Mark Dunand.' He looked from Max to Charlie. 'Go to it you two, and check carefully whether he has any connection with Saltern hospital.'

'Sir?' Marie looked pensively at her boss. 'Dunand imports exotic foliage from abroad, in particular from Columbia.'

There was a short silence while she waited for the penny to drop.

Max's eyes widened. 'Ah, you're thinking about Columbia's other big export — drugs.'

'It's probably nothing,' said Marie, 'but it's worth checking whether he's been in any trouble with us in the past.'

'The drugs our victims took were prescription drugs, not heroin or cocaine,' added Jackman. 'But drugs are drugs, and dealers don't just stick with one product. There's an awful lot of "on demand" dealers out there — put in your order, and as long as you've got the cash, they'll get it for you.' Jackman punched a clenched fist into the palm of his other hand. 'The more I think about it the more I think that we need him here. You guys start digging up everything you can.' He turned to Marie, 'You ring the HOLMES operator and get her to feed Dunand's name in, and I'll get uniform to try to track him down and bring him in.'

Marie moved swiftly to her desk and picked up the phone, as the other two detectives hurried back to their computers and began their searches.

As she replaced the receiver, a thought occurred to her. Guy Preston had met Mark Dunand when he called in on Skye, and as he was a psychologist, maybe he had a take on the man.

Marie picked up her phone again, then hesitated. Perhaps she should run it by Jackman first? She frowned. There was absolutely no reason to do that. Jackman would tell her to go ahead. He wasn't her guardian. No, the reason that she didn't want to ring Guy was simply because she didn't want him to get the wrong idea. She had phoned him several times this evening, and she was keen not to give him any encouragement.

Her hand rested on the telephone. Sod it! The case came first. She lifted the receiver and punched in Guy's home number.

'Sorry, I know its late, Guy, but we need your input on something.' She spoke in a clipped, official tone and emphasised the "we."

'For you, anything. How can I help?'

'Mark Dunand? You met him. We need your first impressions.'

'Well, I only saw him briefly. If I'd known you would be asking questions about him, I'd have taken more notice.' Guy's voice had lost its flippancy.

'It's your job to assess people, Guy. After all the years you've spent analysing minds, I bet you do it automatically.'

There was a short laugh. 'I suppose so. Let me see . . .' He hesitated. 'I didn't care for him overmuch, but that's just a personal feeling, not a professional opinion. He seemed rather "attached" to Skye, a sentiment she clearly didn't share. In fact I got the strong impression she wanted him gone.' Again he paused. 'He was pretty strung out, tense and jumpy. He has a strange habit of pulling out his fingers to make them click. It was irritating in the extreme. And he watched Skye a little too much to be just a mate of her boyfriend, if you get what I'm saying.'

'I do, and it doesn't make me feel too comfortable.'

'Why do you want to know about Dunand?' asked Guy.

Marie wondered how much to say to Preston, but saw no reason not to tell him everything. 'Someone made an attempt on Skye's life tonight, only they got the wrong woman. And Mark Dunand is out there somewhere in the town, hunting for Skye.'

'Good Lord! That's terrible! And is this other poor woman dead?'

'No, thank heavens, but she's in theatre right now, and although the doctors are hoping for a good result, she may be bleeding internally.'

'Then let's hope she saw her assailant and can give you a description when she comes out of the anaesthetic,' said Guy. 'Are you thinking it might be Mark Dunand?'

'We're not sure about anything, but we certainly need to find him and talk to him.'

'I'd offer to grab a cab and come in and assist, but I've had a couple of large brandies. I'm not sure I'd be too much help. Frankly, Marie, that run-in with Daniel Kinder really shook me up. I wouldn't say this to anyone else, but when I saw him coming for me, all I could see was Terence Marcus Austin's face. I was absolutely petrified, and I really thought I'd got on top of all that.'

Marie visualised him touching the jagged scar on the side of his face. 'I'm not surprised, Guy. If you've been in a situation where your life is threatened, and then something else threatening happens, it sets off all the old fears.'

'Thank God someone understands.' Guy hesitated for quite a long while, and Marie sensed that he was about to tell her something else. A wave of compassion swept over her. She knew she needed to keep him at arm's length, but she still felt for him. The man spent his whole life trying to help messed-up people. Sometimes he must need someone to listen to *him* once in a while. 'What's wrong, Guy?' she asked gently.

'Oh, it's nothing to do with the past. I've been thinking about my conversation with Daniel. You asked me if I might have mentioned something that caused him to suddenly run off like that. I said no, but now I'm not quite so sure.'

'Go on.'

'The thing is . . . I discovered that he has a morbid fascination with blood.'

'Daniel?' Marie's voice rose. 'Oh God! Surely you don't mean that horrible fetish that Françoise Thayer had?'

'No, not exactly like that, but he said that he dreams about feeling blood on his hands, and sometimes he's almost drowning in it.' Guy sounded uncomfortable. 'I just hope that in some way, and completely unintentionally, I didn't reinforce his belief that he is a murderer's son.'

Marie felt her skin turn cold. 'Is there a chance that you did?'

'I never said as much, but I admit that I was making comparisons in my mind.'

'But he's not a mind reader, Guy. Did you actually say anything to reinforce his stupid theory?'

His silence was response enough, but then he said, 'I don't know. As I said, not in actual words, but my body language, or maybe what I *didn't* say could have led him to another of his wild conclusions. So I guess the answer to your question is, I might have done.'

Marie hung up and hurried to Jackman's office to relay everything that Preston had said. 'What worries me is the fact that if Daniel is not with Skye he won't know what his mother has told us.'

Jackman bit on his thumbnail. 'Which means that he still believes he's a killer's offspring, and he could be under the impression that his psychologist agrees with him!' He let out a low groan. 'Call Preston in. We need to know *exactly* what he did or didn't say.' Jackman grimaced. 'Damn! I forgot. He hasn't got a car, has he?'

'And he's had a few drinks, guv. Daniel attacking him, albeit only a hearty shove, brought back bad memories of the time he was injured.'

'As long as he's not totally rat-arsed, get someone to pick him up. I want to know what he thinks Daniel's state of mind was when he stole his car.' He looked at Marie sombrely. 'I'm afraid there's a damned good chance that it *was* Daniel who attacked Lisa Hurley. I've just been told that there was a key left in the back door, and Daniel has a key to Skye's place.'

'Oh shit!'

'Precisely. Come to think of it, it would be quicker if you and I called in on Guy Preston. Give him a ring and tell him to expect us. There's nothing else we can do until the officers on the streets locate our missing trio. And,' he pulled a face, 'so far that doesn't look too promising. I've just had an update from Inspector Jim Gilbert. They've checked and rechecked Daniel's home and all the neighbouring properties and outbuildings, plus in Mark Dunand's absence, they got hold of his chief packer, a woman called Carla, and unlocked Daniel's office at Emerald Exotics. They are running out of places to search.'

Marie nodded, and flipped open her mobile.

'Right, let's go grill the shrink. I'll get my jacket.'

As she walked back to the CID room, Max hurried past her and knocked on Jackman's door. 'Lisa Hurley is out of theatre,' Max called over his shoulder. 'The crew at the hospital want the boss to be there when the doctors bring her round.'

'Too right.' She turned back and re-entered the office.

'I'll go to the hospital. Marie, you go see Guy. We'll meet back here in an hour.' Jackman's face clouded over, and when Max was out of earshot, he added, 'Are you okay doing that? I don't want to put you in a difficult situation with your old "friend."'

'I can handle him, guv. What's important right now is the investigation.'

'Okay. One hour.'

CHAPTER TWENTY-FIVE

Marie arrived in the parking area outside the doctor's residence in less than five minutes. As she lifted off her helmet, she looked at her surroundings. The only word she could think of at that moment was "posh." The gardens were clearly tended by professional gardeners and not the residents, and she was certain there would be no peeling paintwork or rusty railings in Hanson Park.

Preston's voice sounded thick and slightly slow when he answered her ring. 'Ground floor. It's the garden flat towards the back of the property.' Marie wondered whether he had been sleeping or had hit the brandy bottle again.

It was evident that the present occupier wasn't intending to stay in the luxury apartment. Through an open bedroom door, Marie saw suitcases, sports bags, boxes and cartons piled in a heap.

'Through here. The main room is relatively tidy.' Guy opened a door to a large airy open plan lounge diner.

The room *was* tidy, although Marie thought "bare" was more apt. The kitchen looked almost untouched. Guy was clearly not into home-cooked gourmet meals.

He looked at her apologetically. 'Bit basic, I know, but there seemed little point in unpacking too much when I'll be moving out in a few weeks.' He raised an eyebrow. 'I thought DI Jackman was coming with you.'

'Our injured woman has made it out of surgery and he wanted to be there when she wakes up.'

'Of course, of course,' Guy nodded, and, glass in hand, turned towards the kitchen. 'Want a drink?'

'No thanks. My bike cost well over nine grand. I want to keep my licence so I can carry on riding it.'

'Point taken. How about a coffee?'

'That would be great. It's been so busy that I can't remember the last drink we had. I'm spitting feathers.'

'Black with one, isn't it?'

That was exactly right, but it irritated Marie that he had remembered correctly after so long. 'Oh, I've upped the sugar intake since then. Make it two, please.'

While Guy prepared the drinks, Marie looked around and wondered what this particular "place to pitch up in" was costing him. Still, she had to admit that it was very nice. The lounge, furnished only with two large leather recliners and a matching sofa, extended into a spacious conservatory, and then out to an immaculate patio garden. It was so quiet that it was hard to believe you were in a block of apartments.

Along the full length of one wall were stacked plastic boxes containing books. Marie looked at the titles and saw that they were all academic or reference books, mainly relating to forensic psychology or murder. 'I'd worry if I didn't know you better,' said Marie, picking up a thick tome entitled, *In the Mind of the Predator.* 'Not a single Mills and Boon.'

'I haven't got round to unpacking those yet.' Guy grinned as he handed her a mug of coffee. 'But from your last call, I don't think you're here to start a book club. Come and sit down.'

He motioned her to one of the armchairs, while he took the other.

'We need to know exactly what kind of mood Daniel Kinder was in just before he nicked your car and left you on your back in the mud.' Marie gave up trying to keep it light. 'The thing is, Guy, we have no idea where Skye Wynyard is, and we are very concerned for her safety.'

'From Daniel? Or from this Dunand chap?'

'Who knows? Skye is convinced that Daniel won't hurt her, but we're not so sure anymore.'

Guy placed his mug on the floor and leaned back. 'This is my fault, isn't it? If only I'd listened to you when I had Daniel here under my own roof, none of this would be happening.'

'Forget it. Both Jackman and I agreed that we would have done the same thing if we'd been in your shoes.' It wasn't quite the truth, but they needed to move on. 'So how did he seem to you? And what did you actually say to him?'

They talked for about a quarter of an hour. At the end of it, Marie decided that Guy was reading far too much into what Daniel *might* have picked up from him. Daniel was flaky. He could have kicked off at the slightest thing.

'Well, from what you've told me, I really don't think you said anything that could have fed his delusions.' Marie felt a resurgence of compassion. 'And he scared you, didn't he? I'm sure that's why you are feeling so shaky.'

Guy stared at his scarred hand and nodded. 'When he went to push me, I froze. I knew it was only Daniel, and reason told me that he wasn't going to hurt me, but hell, Marie, it could have been Paddington Bear coming for me and I'd still have freaked out.'

Before she could reply, his mobile rang. He looked at the display. 'It's one of the directors of the new Frampton Unit. God knows what he wants at this hour, but I'd better take it.'

'Go ahead.'

Guy went out into the conservatory and Marie heard him speaking about some financial issue. She glanced at her watch. As soon as he was off the phone she'd make her escape. She smiled to herself. She hadn't wanted to come here alone, but she thought she'd handled it rather well. Perhaps she was being a little hard on Guy Preston. After all, they did share a traumatic experience. Perhaps they just handled things in different ways. And *she* hadn't been injured like Guy. She saw again the bleeding wound in his shocked face, and his hand skewered by Terence Marcus Austin's makeshift weapon. She smiled at Guy Preston's tall figure standing staring out into the dark garden and decided it was time to stop being a hard-arsed bitch and cut the man some slack.

* * *

Kevin Stoner poured a large splash of vodka into a shot glass. He felt drained. A great shadowy weight had lifted like a black shroud from his shoulders. Finally he had found the courage to open his heart to his father, and the bishop had suddenly been transformed into . . . his dad! They had talked together for over an hour.

His inspector had been right. His father had known that he was gay, but had respected his son's privacy. If Kevin wanted him to know about his sexuality, then he'd tell him in his own good time.

Kevin had told his father as much as he dared about the reason for his suspension. His father had offered his unconditional support. The photographs were not mentioned. When Kevin left his parents' home with a spring in his step, he had cursed himself for not coming out a very long while ago.

Kevin took his drink through to the lounge and flopped down onto the sofa. He picked up the remote to his sound system and took a sip of vodka. Music flooded the room and relief coursed through him. He raised his glass and said, 'Bon Voyage, Zane. Enjoy your new life inside.' He let out a long, contented sigh. His only problem now was the fact that he'd been suspended, just as they had the biggest case that Saltern-Le-Fen had ever seen.

He stood up, ambled to the kitchen and poured himself another shot. Tomorrow he would talk to his boss. He needed to know how long the process would take.

He'd only been home a few hours but with Zane gone, he was already dying to get back into the thick of things. The Daniel Kinder case was huge, and he wanted to be part of it.

Kevin sat down again, sipped his drink, and then a sudden thought struck him. A fragment of conversation from earlier that day came back to him. Just before leaving the station he had heard one of his colleagues talking to his crewmate about Drew Wilson and the foiled burglary. Wilson had apparently stated that they had sent a lookout in first to make sure that everything was on track, the scout had signalled them by mobile phone, and the rest of the gang had brought the lorry in.

Kevin blinked. But that wasn't right, was it? As he had hidden in the bus shelter waiting to blow the whistle on them, he had seen *two* men go into the grounds of the Kinder property. He closed his eyes and thought hard. He had wondered about it at the time, but then the truck had pulled in and the robbery was about to get underway, and he had forgotten all about it. And that wasn't all. He had also heard that one of the police squad who went in after Drew Wilson had believed that it was Daniel Kinder who made the anonymous call. And why? Because he was certain he had seen Kinder slip out of the gardens as they arrived.

Kevin tried to sort out his thoughts with another slug of vodka.

So had he seen Daniel Kinder that night? It was possible. The figure had the right height, the right build. If he had, then Kinder had not been asleep at Skye's place at all. He had been out on the streets, and hence had no alibi for the time when Sue Bannister was murdered. 'Oh fuck,' he murmured softly. How was he going to let CID know about that vital piece of evidence without dropping himself straight in the shit?

Kevin stood up and began to pace. As he did, another thought hit him. If it *was* Daniel that he saw, where had he been when the gang arrived? And how had he managed to avoid them and then escape unnoticed? When Kevin had seen the man enter, he was heading in the direction of the path that led to the back garden. He frowned. Maybe he had been in that covered spa area where the hot tub was housed. It was a chalet-style wooden structure with a bar, pool table and comfortable seating. And it wasn't on Zane Prewett's list of rooms that contained valuables, so it wouldn't have been of interest to Drew Wilson's gang.

Kevin's copper's brain accelerated into top gear. So why was Daniel Kinder going there? To hide a murder weapon? To conceal bloodstained clothes?

Kevin slowly sat back down and drew in a deep, shaky breath. He needed to share this information with the detectives, but how the hell could he do it without losing the job that he was already only hanging onto by the skin of his teeth?

He could think of only one thing to do, and that was to go and check out the chalet himself. That way he'd know for sure whether it was worth risking his career.

Kevin stood up. Time to put his dark clothes back on. He wasn't happy about it, but if it meant catching a killer, then he had no choice.

* * *

As Marie waited for Guy to finish his call, she checked out the apartment. Apart from what she had already seen, there appeared to be two double bedrooms off the wide hallway, probably both with en suite showers, a bathroom, and a small office. The door to this stood open, showing a desk with a computer, printer, and more packing boxes.

Marie wished that Guy would hurry up. Impatiently she stood up, picked up the empty coffee mugs and took them into the kitchen. She really didn't have time for this.

She located the dishwasher and popped the two mugs inside. She gave a little smile when she saw it filled with coffee mugs. Guy *really* wasn't into cooking.

Glancing at her watch, she decided that she couldn't wait for Guy to finish his call. She would just grab her helmet and wave to him, saying she'd ring him when they heard something.

As she moved out of the kitchen she saw Guy putting his phone back in his pocket. There was a preoccupied look on his face, and she wondered if all was well with his new project.

'Sorry that took so long. The finance director of Frampton has no regard for what time it is. I guessed from your pacing that you need to be getting away.'

'I do.' Marie took up her crash helmet and slipped it over her arm. 'And I'm sure you have nothing to worry about regarding what Daniel might have assumed.'

Guy nodded and turned towards her. 'I do appreciate you coming here. I don't think anyone else would have understood why I was so freaked out by Daniel shoving me down a bank.' He paused, then added, 'But then I always could talk to you.'

Marie turned to go. 'No problem. Look, I'll ring you if we find Daniel or Skye. And you *must* ring me if you hear from them, okay?'

'I will. I promise.' He walked past her to the door. 'I'll let you out. I need to buzz you through the front security door.' He lightly touched her arm, and the hand lingered just a little too long. 'And thanks for understanding.' He looked at her with an odd bleakness, then moved towards the security keypad. As he did, Marie leaned forward and pecked his cheek with a fleeting kiss. 'You have to let the past go, Guy. You're an unbelievably brilliant psychologist, but don't they say, "Physician, heal thyself?" When this is over, take your new position at Frampton and build a new life. Move on from Terence Marcus Austin.' She paused, silently adding, *and from me.*

CHAPTER TWENTY-SIX

Jackman stood in the doorway to the recovery suite, fretting. It was taking much longer than he had anticipated to bring Lisa Hurley round. Twice, the doctor had come out to him and apologised for the delay. Lisa was out of the woods, but she hadn't taken the anaesthetic well and needed considerably more aftercare than they had expected.

At last, as midnight approached, a thin-faced nurse beckoned to him.

'You can come in now, Inspector. Just a few minutes to begin with. She needs rest, then she'll be able to talk to you properly.'

Jackman breathed a sigh of relief and hurried forward. What he wanted from her would not take long. Someone else could sit with her and get the finer details. He only had three important questions. He sat down by the bed, close to her side.

'Do you know who did this to you, Lisa?'

The woman swallowed painfully. 'No. He wore those things.' She pointed to one of the theatre assistants who stood a little way away talking animatedly to a nurse. 'Scrubs. Hospital greens, with a face mask.'

Jackman's face creased into a confused frown. So was the hospital really at the heart of all this? 'Was there anything else you noticed about him? Height or build? Eye colour? A particular cologne?'

'I was running for my life, Inspector. I didn't stop to take notes.' She attempted a smile, then sighed and said, 'I was certain that it was going to be Daniel. Skye had said he was going into fugue states, and that he was worried he might be violent. Then *I* saw him in some kind of stupor myself, and I was convinced that she was in danger. I was terrified for her.'

'So you tried to trap him?'

'She rang me and told me you were about to come and collect her, as you'd arranged a video call to Ruby Kinder. So I knew that she would be out of the house, but Daniel didn't. I tried to make it look as if she was at home and in the shower. And then I waited.'

'And Skye is your natural daughter?'

Lisa's eyes opened wide. 'How did you know that?' Her eyes darted around the room.

'Hush, it's okay. No one else knows. You told us yourself, just before they took you to theatre. They'd given you morphine for the pain, so I guess that's what did it.'

'Oh no! I don't believe it. But you can't tell her, please, Inspector! Don't tell Skye. She mustn't find out, it would ruin everything.'

Jackman glanced around too, hoping her outburst hadn't attracted attention. 'That's not our business, Lisa. I won't be saying anything.' Not that I could anyway, she's bloody well missing, he thought morosely.

The nurse gave Jackman a warning look and held up three fingers. Three minutes.

'Lisa? Did your attacker have a dressing on his forearm, or a recently stitched wound?'

Lisa frowned. 'No. I didn't see much, but I would have noticed that because the tunic top had short sleeves.'

So it wasn't Daniel, thought Jackman. And if it wasn't, who was it? He closed his eyes and tried to think. They needed to find Mark Dunand. And with Skye still missing, Jackman's fears were mounting by the second.

'You get some rest, Lisa. We'll talk again, but right now I need to get back.'

She sank back into her pillows. 'One thing, Inspector.' Her voice was soft, almost a whisper. 'I tried to hit him with a cast-iron frying pan. I think I only winded him, but it must have hurt.'

'Where did you hit him?'

'I aimed for his head, but he moved and I'm not sure where I made contact.'

Jackman gave her a reassuring smile. 'We'll get him, Lisa. And we'll have police officers here with you constantly, so don't worry. Just get well.'

'Don't worry about me. You concentrate on keeping Skye safe.' She closed her eyes.

Jackman leaned forward, squeezed her hand and moved away from the bed. After a few words with the two constables who were going to keep watch, he hurried from the recovery ward and out into the night. He found Marie's number on his phone and breathed a sigh of relief when she answered almost immediately. He told her briefly what Lisa had said, then asked her how long she would be.

'I'm just leaving Guy's place now. I'll be back to base in ten.' She paused, and added, 'And just to let you know, I'm certain Guy never said anything to upset Daniel, okay?'

'Okay, Marie. See you soon.'

Jackman flipped his phone shut, and as he ran towards his car he prayed that they would find Mark Dunand before Dunand found Skye.

* * *

Once again Kevin Stoner stood in the graffiti-covered bus shelter and watched the Kinder house. This time a squad car was parked out front, although the occupants seemed happy to remain inside it.

He was in no rush. He knew that he had only one stab at this, and he couldn't afford to get caught. If he found anything incriminating, then he would decide on the proper course of action to take. As he prepared for his late night sortie, he was confident that he would find a murder weapon, bloodstained clothing, or maybe even Daniel Kinder himself.

Kevin decided that the crew in the car were there for the long haul. And as he knew there would be officers patrolling the river walk along the back of the properties, he needed to find an alternative way in.

He stared at the front gardens and devised a plan. There were only two things that could cock his idea up, and there was little he could do about dogs loose in the gardens or concealed sensor lights. He had not heard barking either tonight or on his previous visit, and no surrounding lights had gone on when Drew Wilson and his gang had arrived. So, he'd better get on with it.

A slight bend in the road concealed his dark figure from the police car, and in a few seconds he was safely hidden in a small area of conifers in the front garden of a house three down from Daniel's.

Luck stayed with him as he moved over low walls and through shrubbery, until he was in the garden next door. Between this and the Kinder place was a sturdy wooden fence. He surmised that it was about five feet high, as he could just see over it and get a fairly good idea of the layout in front of him.

Kevin tested the strength of the wood, and was grateful that the residents had paid for quality. He was slim, but years of swimming had given him considerable upper body strength. He breathed in, flexed his arms, grasped the top of the fence and pulled himself up and over in one fluid movement.

He landed almost silently in a bed of ground cover plants, and without glancing round, sprinted across a few yards of neglected flowerbed and into a thick cluster of trees. There he sank down on one knee and did a quick recce.

The house was in total darkness but in the garden, filtered light from the street lamps lit up some areas while others were pools of black. Kevin followed the black areas around the house and out of sight of the road.

He was moderately certain that there would be no one stationed on watch in the back garden. There would certainly be two cars observing both the entrance and the exit to the river walk, and officers would patrol the lane every so often, but the river formed a barrier between the walk and the rest of the town.

A weak moon, shrouded in thin wispy cloud helped him make his way across the garden, and in moments he was on the patio outside the timber chalet that housed the hot tub.

Kevin slipped into a narrow space between a brick-built barbecue and a high, open-fronted log store and took stock. The hot tub area was like a three-sided chalet, the front being a run of folding doors that could be pushed right back to open the tub to the garden. In front of the doors was a spacious decking area and adjoining that, the patio where he now was. The chalet itself was attached to the house and from his hiding place, and in the strengthening moonlight, Kevin could vaguely make out two doors at the back of the long, spacious room. He also saw a bar, a pool table, bar stools, several reclining sun-loungers, large potted palms, and another wooden cabin close to one side of the tub, something that he supposed was a sauna.

For one horrible moment he had a mental picture of Zane Prewett and some big-breasted women cavorting in the steamy water. He watched the room for some ten minutes, but heard nothing and saw no movement inside. There was a small personnel door in the side of the chalet. It might be unlocked, people got blasé about things like that. Hoping that he wouldn't have to force the lock, he crept from his hideout and across the wide expanse of decking.

He stopped at the door and tentatively grasped the handle. It turned easily, and Kevin Stoner stole silently inside.

CHAPTER TWENTY-SEVEN

Jackman entered the CID room and was immediately set upon by Charlie Button and Max Cohen.

'It's coming together, sir. We've made a few finds regarding the dead women.' Charlie's expression was wide-eyed and eager, despite the midnight hour.

'Yeah.' Max didn't look quite so awake, but his brain clearly was. 'Sue Bannister's old man was having an affair with a young nurse, and Sue found out.'

Charlie took over. 'She was absolutely gutted but couldn't face seeing the family GP. A friend of hers has told us that she confessed to "seeking help elsewhere," as the friend put it.'

'And did this friend know where she obtained that help?'

'No, but she told her friend that the man who helped her was, and I quote, "An angel in her time of need."' Max pulled a face. 'And it looks like he turned out to be a bloody angel of death.'

'*If* it was the man who killed her,' corrected Jackman. 'We don't know that for sure yet.'

'I think we do, sir,' added Charlie. 'Because our party animal, the ever-smiling nurse, Julia Hope, was also having difficulties that she didn't want to share with her doctor.'

He threw Jackman a doom-laden look, 'and she too found herself an angel, one with a pocket full of helpful little pills.'

'Who told you this?'

'Her sister.' Charlie held up an email printout. 'Anna never said anything before because she didn't know about it. She'd had some problem with her email server, then found herself in the back of beyond for a couple of weeks. When she sorted it out and found this in her inbox she contacted us. Julia sent it a little while ago but Anna never saw it. It admits that she was fighting a serious form of depression and she was too scared and embarrassed to seek professional help. She told Anna that "A wonderful friend was helping her, someone she trusted totally."'

'Big mistake,' muttered Max. 'But add these to the fact that Alison Fleet's drug source was strictly non-kosher, and we know that they all approached someone who was apparently above-board and trustworthy.'

Jackman closed his eyes and thought. 'So, why kill them? If they were a source of income, why shoot the goose that lays the golden egg?'

Max scowled. 'Mm, that's the downside of it all. I'm buggered if I can think why he'd top them.'

'Maybe we should hit the CCTV? See if we can pick up one of the women meeting up with a man.' Charlie didn't sound too convinced by his own suggestion.

'I think they would have taken care to be discreet, don't you?' said Jackman.

'I've asked a snout of mine to see if any of the local pushers deals specifically with those particular happy pills,' said Max. 'But frankly none of the low-life dealers around this town could be described as "angels." This bloke sounds like some super-smooth conman with a silver tongue and a direct pipeline to a drug supply.' He flopped down onto a chair. 'Where's the sarge, guv? Still with the shrink?'

'On her way back.' Jackman headed for his office. 'Tell her to see me immediately she gets in, and I think it's time you two called it a day. You're out on your feet.'

'How can we go home when everything is hanging in the balance, and the balloon could go up at any moment?' Charlie asked.

'Yeah, we have a missing killer, or perhaps just a missing lunatic, we're not too sure about that yet, his missing girlfriend, and now his bleeding best mate has gone missing, possibly hunting for the missing killer's missing girl!' Max rolled his eyes and spun two fingers either side of his temples. 'And you expect us to walk out on all this fun, guv?'

'Alright. One more hour. Then no matter who's missing, it's home, okay?'

Before the two young men could answer, a uniformed officer entered the office carrying a memo. 'We've located Professor Preston's missing vehicle, sir.' He handed Jackman the note and left.

'In a car park. Brilliant.' He took his phone from a pocket and punched in Guy Preston's number. Preston took a while to answer and was stifling a yawn as he spoke.

'Sorry, it's late, Guy, but I thought you should know that we've found your car.'

Guy apologised. 'Sorry, Inspector, I'd just dozed off. But that's great news. Where was it?'

'He'd left it in the best place to hide a car.' He paused. 'In a customer car park. It wasn't until the night security man did a walk round that it was noticed. It's not damaged, but we'll need to bring it in and give it the once-over before you can collect it.'

'Of course,' said Guy. 'And thanks for letting me know. He paused, then said. 'I suppose I couldn't have a quick word with Marie, could I? I found a bracelet on the floor after she left. The clasp had broken. I guess it has to be hers.'

'She's not back yet. But she does wear a bracelet. Shall I get her to ring you when she gets in?'

'But she left over twenty minutes ago,' said Guy quietly. 'And she said she was going directly back to HQ.' His voice rose. 'You don't think she's come off that awful bike of hers, do you?'

'Don't let her hear you call it that! And have you ever seen Marie ride?'

'Not recently.'

'I thought not.'

'Even a good rider can have a bad day,' said Guy nervously.

'Okay, I'll give you that, Doc, but with Marie the odds are different. I can only think that something has happened that she's needed to deal with. I wouldn't worry. I'm sure she'll be here soon.'

'Well, thank you again for letting me know about the car, and,' he paused, 'You would let me know if, er, well, if anything has happened to Marie?'

'Of course.' Jackman's reply was clipped. No matter how well Marie was dealing with Preston's crush on her, the man was obviously still attached to her.

He hung up. The sooner this case was over the better. Marie wasn't complaining, but it couldn't have been pleasant having Dr Labrador-eyes drooling after her. Though he wasn't too sure why, Guy Preston's fawning devotion was really starting to piss him off.

'Sir!' The uniformed officer who had just told them about Preston's car burst back into the office. 'A member of the public has reported seeing a motorcycle in the water close to the Blackland Sluice gate.'

Jackman went cold. 'What kind of bike? Did they say?'

'Just that it was a green one, sir.'

The coldness went to the marrow of his bones and he felt as if his heart had frozen. Please God, no. Not this, not now. Jackman swallowed. 'Who is handling the shout?'

'Two crews are out there already,' said the constable. 'And a fire crew has been dispatched to winch it out.'

Jackman thought out loud. 'There are no houses along that stretch, just the pumping station and a few moorings. What about the water company's CCTV?'

'Our officers have already contacted the waterways authority about that. Someone will check as soon as we can get hold of them.' The young officer stared at Jackman. 'Are you okay, sir? You're white as a ghost.'

'I'm fine,' said Jackman brusquely. But he was far from fine. In fact he felt as if his world was slowly falling into tiny ragged little pieces. 'I need to go.'

'The crew down there says there's a good chance that it's just the bike, sir. Trumpton reckons that there's no way for a body to get out of the sluice unless the gates are opened wide, and they won't be doing that until the water has been thoroughly checked. And there's no floater in the pool either.'

Jackman felt sick. Pictures of Marie face down in the oily black waters ran through his mind, and his stomach churned.

'I'll go, guv.' Max was suddenly at his side. 'I know the sarge's bike well enough, and I'll keep you informed of everything that happens.'

'Thanks, Max, but I want to go.'

'I'm sure you do, but you should be here, all things considered.' His face was lined with worry. 'And for some reason, I don't think she's in the water. I know that stretch of road and there is absolutely no reason for an experienced rider like the sarge to finish up in the drink, no reason at all. This stinks, guv.'

Jackman knew Max was right, but if Marie was hurt, he wanted to be with her, simple.

'I know what you're thinking, guv, but I'm dead certain that someone wants you wasting your time, pacing up and down the towpath and tearing your hair out, while they get on with whatever it is they are planning.'

Jackman exhaled loudly. 'Okay, but ring me if there's the slightest hint that she could be there, alright?'

Max nodded and moved towards the door. 'And if it's all a hoax, like I think it is, I'll get back here faster than bleeding Usain Bolt.'

Jackman decided it was time to call Superintendent Crooke. Things were escalating and she needed to be told. He sat in his office and stared blankly at the wall as he waited for her to answer. If Marie was not in the water, where the hell was she?

Jackman explained everything to a bleary Ruth Crooke. After a string of expletives, she told him to stay at the station unless anything critical occurred, and she'd be with him in twenty minutes.

As he lowered the phone back into its cradle, Jackman was suddenly overwhelmed by a feeling of discomfort. Something he'd heard over the last few hours didn't ring true, but he had no idea what it was that jarred so badly.

'Guvnor?' Charlie looked around his door. He never looked smart, but tonight he looked like he'd been dragged through a hedge backwards. 'Any news about the sarge?' he asked hopefully, while trying to tuck his shirt into his trousers.

'Nothing, Charlie. Max will contact us from the crash scene when he knows something.'

'It's not a crash scene,' said Charlie stoically. 'I'm with Max on this one. If it is her bike in the sluice, then someone dumped it there purely to keep us busy.'

'And what does that leave us with?'

'Clearly the sarge has been taken. We need to try to pinpoint exactly where and when she went off the radar. Maybe then we can find who her abductor might be.'

Jackman looked at the young detective in amazement. Charlie Button was no whiz kid, and he was not always the sharpest knife in the drawer, but just sometimes he had such belief in his own conclusions that he carried you along with him. 'Sit.' Jackman indicated a chair, then pulled a sheet of printer paper from the tray beneath the computer and passed it across to Charlie. 'Right. I spoke to her,' he pulled out his phone and checked the log, 'at exactly 23.16 hours. She said that she was just about to leave Guy Preston's flat in Hanson Park.' He watched as Charlie scribbled the time down. 'Then I spoke to Preston, and he said that she had been gone for over twenty minutes. Hang on, let me get it exact.' Once again he checked his calls log. 'Twenty-five minutes later at 23.41 hours.' He frowned. 'Her usual route, assuming that was the one she took, would have been to leave Hanson Park, go along Park Villas, and take the main drag, Saltern High Road, down towards the Blackland Sluice, then cut off round the back doubles to the nick.'

'Ten minutes max.' Charlie raised an eyebrow. 'Probably less, knowing the sarge's disregard for speed restrictions, and there's no traffic to speak of at this time of night.'

'So someone intercepted her between Hanson Park and a point close to the sluice towpath, where they dumped her bike.'

Charlie looked up. 'How would they do that exactly?' His brow creased with thought. 'How would you stop a speeding motorcycle? *And* make the rider get off and leave the bike?'

'Wave her down, I guess? Stage some sort of incident? Like an accident or a collapse. Marie would always try to help a person in distress.'

'Yes, she would, and she'd also stop if she saw someone she knew, like a person we are looking for.'

'Someone like Daniel Kinder.' Jackman knew that if she had spotted Kinder, Marie would have given chase. That was a certainty. He remembered Daniel shouting at Marie, asking why she didn't believe him. Daniel really didn't like Marie at all. He let out a low whistle. 'That's a distinct possibility.'

'How about I take a couple of uniforms and go out to Hanson Park? Maybe someone saw her leave and noticed which route she took? That would give us something definite, wouldn't it, guv?'

'You won't be too popular with the residents, dragging them from their slumbers, but you're right. Go see what you can find, Charlie.' He watched as the young man jumped up. 'And try not to ruffle too many feathers. We don't want any complaints if we can avoid them.'

'I'll be all charm and diplomacy, guv.' He stopped at the door. 'Should I call on the shrink? Just to double-check exactly when the sarge left?'

Jackman deliberated for a moment, then said, 'No, don't worry him. My phone log tells us quite enough. Let him get some sleep.'

'Okay, guv.'

As Charlie left, Jackman's mobile rang. He looked at the display and saw the name Skye Wynyard. He stabbed at the green button. 'Skye! Thank heavens! Are you alright?'

'I'm fine, Inspector, and I've heard from Daniel. He sounded so much more like his old self. He said that Guy Preston has really helped him. I'm so relieved, DI Jackman, I can't tell you!'

'Skye, we need to talk to him urgently. Did he say where he was?'

'No. But we spoke for ages, and I told him that his mother had been in touch.' She paused. 'I didn't want to tell him everything over the phone, but I said that I had really good news for him. With his record for disappearing, I thought I'd better keep him onside.'

'I agree,' said Jackman. 'But where are you? We need you back here.'

'I know. And I'll be back shortly, I promise.'

Jackman didn't like the fact that she'd sidestepped his first question. 'Skye? Listen, whatever you do, do *not* approach Daniel. Or Mark either. No matter what you think. I want you to come back here immediately, do you understand? You might not be safe.' Jackman waited for her reply, then realised she had gone.

He quickly rang her back, but it went straight to voicemail. He reiterated that he wanted her back immediately and prayed that she would react to his message. After a moment or two he jammed the phone back in his pocket. 'Damn! And double damn!' He left his office and ran down the stairs to the duty sergeant's office. In a few minutes the sergeant had contacted the crew outside the Kinder house and had been told that all was quiet, no one in, no one out.

'Quiet as the grave, sir,' said the sergeant, 'but if anything happens, I'll get hold of you immediately.'

As he trudged back up the stairs, Jackman tried to take solace from the fact that Skye was safe right now, but all he kept thinking was, how long for? And was Marie safe? Jackman felt as if someone had reached into his chest and squeezed every atom of air from his lungs. Wherever Marie was, she was far from safe, and if they didn't find her soon . . .

* * *

Kevin Stoner crept silently around the chalet room. He worked systematically, carefully lifting the thick cushions from the cane furniture and checking beneath the seats. He then moved on to the bar area. He opened the fridge, pulled bottles away from the back of the shelves and delved into a cupboard unit that was stacked with drinking glasses, jars of olives, boxes of foil-wrapped snacks and some very wizened lemons. He worked slowly and methodically, but found nothing.

Kevin stood up and stretched, suddenly feeling very glad that he'd decided to check the place out personally before getting the heavy mob in. It looked very much as though his theory had been a load of cobblers, and he might have just saved his own job by not going off half-cocked.

He stared at the hot tub. A thick turquoise-coloured thermal blanket was pulled across the surface of the water to keep the temperature up and any debris and dirt out. He knelt down and eased it back. There was a slightly unpleasant damp smell from beneath. The tub had not been in use for some while. He took his torch and shone it downwards, fearing that he would find something nasty floating in the stale water. But nothing nestled in the depths of the Kinder family jacuzzi.

With a soft sigh he straightened up and moved on to check the collection of planters that decorated the pool room. Taking care not to be seen, he lifted the plants out one by one, and made sure that nothing was concealed in the base of the pots.

As he replaced the last spiky-leafed, cactus-like plant back in its container, Kevin decided that his great idea was fast becoming a load of nothing. Still, he had yet to check out the sauna, and also the two doors that he guessed led into the house itself. Rubbing dirt from his hands, he made his way across to the sauna. He opened the door slowly, hoping that there was no light inside that came on when the door was used. Luckily it remained dark and he was able to slip into the small space without drawing attention to the chalet.

Inside it smelled pleasantly of some kind of Scandinavian wood. Aspen maybe? Or perhaps it was spruce. It was a traditional layout, with the walls panelled with the pale wood, and there were upper and lower slatted benches with movable backrests. On one wall there was a stove laden with coal, a wooden protective rail around it.

All very nice, if you could afford it, thought Kevin, as he looked beneath one of the benches. With a sigh, he slipped back out into the pool room and looked around miserably. There were only the two doors left to check, and as he didn't think it worthwhile trying to get into the main house, his sortie was just about over.

The door to the right had a glass panel in it, and carefully using his mini flashlight, Kevin saw that it did lead into the back hall of the house. He could see a security panel on the hall wall, and even though he had memorised the number from his earlier visit, he had no inclination to go inside. According to his boss, the house had been checked and rechecked when they first started the hunt for Daniel Kinder.

And that left the last door. Kevin frowned in the darkness. Whatever it was, it must have been checked out. But what was it? He thought about the layout of the house and couldn't fathom out why it was there. Surely this part of the wall backed onto the dining room? And there was no door in there. He knew that for a fact.

Kevin grasped the handle and turned. Nothing happened. It neither opened, nor set off the alarm. His frown deepened and his curiosity took over.

In the darkness, Kevin Stoner made a swift decision. He needed to know what lay behind the door, even if he woke half the neighbourhood, although hopefully if the alarm was activated, it would only bleep and he would have enough time to punch in the security number. He felt in his pocket and removed a small key-ring with several picks and skeleton keys on it. He was far from adept, but it was an art that had intrigued him since he was a kid. That and the fact that his first boyfriend had been a would-be escapologist, something that Kevin had found both hysterically funny and hugely erotic. Dominic's wild attempts at being a bound and chained Houdini often turned out to be more like bondage than escapology, but he did teach Kevin a lot about locks.

After about three minutes he heard a sharp click, and the handle finally turned. Kevin opened the door.

There was no alarm. And there was no room on the other side of the door, just a steep flight of stone steps. Of course! Kevin hit the side of his head with the flat of his hand. A house like this, with a hot tub and a sauna, would have a boiler room. His mood lifted. And what better place to conceal something!

Kevin went through the door and closed it behind him, then moved carefully down the stairs. After some six or seven steps, they turned sharply to the left, and after going down another short flight, Kevin found himself in a smallish cellar beneath the chalet room. At least he was now safe to use his torch.

He swung the narrow beam around and saw that he had been right. This place contained all the equipment for running the pool room. He stood for a while and tried to get his bearings. It obviously wasn't the main cellar — that would most certainly have been checked by the search team, but there was a good chance that they had missed this extra ante-chamber.

He thought carefully. They would have accessed the main cellar from the door close to the kitchen, gone down and thoroughly searched it. Then, if they had checked the chalet and seen the door there, they might well have assumed that it led directly down an area that had already been cleared. So this could be virgin territory! Kevin bit his lip and wondered if he dare look for an electric light switch.

Why not? No one could see a light down here, even the door at the top of the stairs was a solid one, and he had been careful to close it. He moved the flashlight around the walls but couldn't locate a switch.

He cursed out loud. Searching through all the boxes and shelves would take forever with his piddling little Maglite. He needed something far more powerful. Surely there had to be some form of lighting? He shone the beam upwards and saw the long flat white cover to a fluorescent strip. Feeling encouraged, Kevin moved back towards the bottom of the stairs, and squinted into the shadows. Yes! In a dark recess, he saw the plastic plate of a light switch. Brilliant! He moved quickly towards it, reached out his hand, then lurched forward down an unseen and very steep stone step.

With a cry that echoed around the small room, Kevin plunged head first into the solid exterior wall. His whole world became one fiery explosion of light, and then blackness followed, as he crashed heavily to the ground.

CHAPTER TWENTY-EIGHT

Jackman was sitting opposite Ruth Crooke. Neither spoke. He'd told her all he knew, and was beginning to feel terror mounting inside him. Looking at her pale face, he was sure she was feeling just as bad.

When his phone rang, he grabbed at it. 'Jackman!'

'It's me, sir. Charlie. I've spoken to some of the residents and got an exact time for when the bike left Hansen Park.'

'And it ties with our estimation of her movements?'

'Pretty much, give or take a minute or so. Several people heard her leave the parking area, and they were preparing to meet up in the morning to complain to Dr Preston about the noise.'

Jackman's eyes narrowed. 'What noise?'

'She revved up like a boy racer apparently.'

'Did anyone actually see her ride out?'

'Yes, sir. The last person I spoke to said that the rider had a full-face dark-visored helmet and a distinctive black, green and white sectioned leather jacket.'

Jackman's mind upped a gear. 'Charlie, go back to that particular witness and ask if they noticed the rider's boots or trousers. Do it now, and don't hang up.'

'Roger, sir.'

Jackman heard the young man's fast breathing as he hurried back along the road.

After a few long minutes, Charlie was back on the phone. 'No boots, sir, and she thought the rider was wearing jeans or dark trousers, not leathers.'

Jackman's chest was tight with anxiety. 'Thank them and get back here as quickly as you can, but make sure that a crew stays in the vicinity. Out of sight, but close, in case they're needed. Okay?'

He hung up, but before he could update Ruth Crooke, his phone rang again. This time Max's voice echoed down the line. 'Boss? I'm on my way back. It's the sarge's bike right enough, but there's no one in the water. And,' Max went on, 'I got the fire crew boys to check the bike over for me, and it wasn't driven into the sluice, it was pushed in. The gears were in neutral, and the ignition wasn't switched on.'

Jackman told him to hurry back, closed his phone, then turned to the superintendent. 'How long have you known Marie?'

'Years, why?'

'Have you ever heard her rev her bike and scream off like a hell raiser?'

'Never.'

'And if you were asked to describe what she looked like when she was about to ride off, what would you say?'

'That the rider was tall, slim and wearing full leathers that matched the bike colours of black and green, a full-face matching helmet, and customised racing boots.'

Jackman agreed. 'The boots stand out because of the added lime-green plastics. They would have reflected in the street lamps, and she had co-ordinating leather trousers, but the witness didn't see either. I don't think Marie ever left Hanson Park. I think she was snatched before she even got to her bike.'

'Then take your two boys and plenty of back-up and go tear Hanson Park to pieces.' Ruth's face was a mask of concern. 'Marie is in grave danger, isn't she?'

Jackman stood up and pulled his stab-proof vest from the back of his door. 'I rather think she is, ma'am.'

'I'll get an armed squad together.' Following him from the office, she suddenly took hold of his arm. 'You know where she is, don't you? I can see it in your face.'

Jackman clamped his jaw. 'I don't know for certain, ma'am, but I've got a damned good idea.'

* * *

Marie lay on Guy's king-size bed. She could hear him moving about in one of the other rooms. The panic at being unable to move a muscle was still threatening to overwhelm her, but Guy had told her that the paralysis was temporary, and for some reason she believed him. Maybe for her sanity's sake she had to.

Marie went over everything that had happened, from the moment that she realised that a thin hypodermic needle was piercing her skin.

She had just hung up after speaking to Jackman when Guy had leaned across to open the door for her. There had been the oddest expression on his face, and she had known that something was terribly wrong.

Numbness and dizziness had been almost instantaneous. Movement had become difficult, then impossible, and she felt him gather her unresponsive body into her arms and let her slide gently to the hall floor. To her horror, he had then held her eyelids open.

'Sorry, Marie, but you're such a canny detective it wouldn't have been long before you put two and two together.'

The words had come to her from a great distance, but quickly faded as a rushing noise filled her ears and shock and disbelief gave way to terror. Her body was paralysed, but she was fully aware of everything around her. Marie had always had a morbid fear of going into the operating theatre and being unable to tell them that she was still awake. Now her nightmare had become real.

She had been certain that she would die without being able to lift a finger to save herself. Then she had heard his voice.

'Listen to me, Marie. Nothing's going to happen to you. I know it's terrifying, but it's just a means to an end, I promise.' Guy had sounded calm, reasonable and oddly gentle. 'I'll reverse the effect, but only when I know you are properly secured.'

Guy dragged her away from the front door and along the hallway. He then let her go, opened a door and pulled her into the master bedroom, where she was now. Then he told her he had to go out.

'The drug isn't meant to stop your lungs functioning or your heart beating while I'm away. Believe me, it's not fatal. It's just taken care of your voluntary movement without you losing consciousness, okay? You're not going to die, Marie. The only problem you'll have is if anything happens to me, because if I leave you too long, your diaphragm could stop working, and that would not be a good idea.'

He was quiet while he heaved her unresponsive body up onto the bed. 'Sorry about this.' Panting from the exertion, he began to peel off her leather jacket. 'I have a couple of small jobs to do, and then we'll talk.' He stood up and looked at her forlornly, 'Because we really need to talk, Marie.'

He pushed his arm into her jacket and smiled. 'I'm glad you're not one of those skinny women. This is a bit snug, but not impossible to get on.' He adjusted the jacket and then said, 'Now, you relax. I won't be long.'

As soon as she heard the loud revving of her precious Kawasaki, she had known what he was doing. She silently cursed him to hell.

For half an hour she had remained motionless on the large bed, fighting to calm the jumble of manic thoughts in her head. Over and over she had told herself that she wasn't going to die. He'd promised her that much. She must try to think of a way out of her desperate situation.

Was this just some awful mad escalation of his feelings for her? Or was Guy the killer? What had he meant by saying that it wouldn't take her long to put two and two together? But surely Guy Preston couldn't be their cold-blooded murderer? She'd seen him in action and he was full of compassion, dedication and understanding. A serial killer couldn't do that, could he? Maybe he was protecting someone? But who? And if so, why on earth do this horrible thing to her?

Who was she trying to kid? If Guy was capable of imprisoning her in her own body — a person he was supposed to care deeply about — then what might he do to a stranger? Panic threatened to overwhelm her again, but she realised she couldn't afford to let that happen. She fought to regain some sort of calm. Trying to clear her mind, she thought about Jackman. If she could have smiled, she would have. Her boss was the most honest man she'd ever met, and other than her husband, the most sincere and genuine copper that she'd ever worked with. Despite his Oxbridge education and privileged background, he had never made her feel inferior. Just the opposite. He made her feel valued, like the true professional that she was. And that was a scarce commodity in the Fenland Constabulary. She knew she wasn't in love with him or anything like that. She was still in love with Bill, and she suspected that that would never change. But of all the people in the world who might be able to help her, she knew it would be Jackman. He *would* find her. Somehow he'd figure out that Preston was behind her disappearance. She just hoped that he'd do it soon.

Marie sent Jackman a mute cry for help. Time was not on her side, because even if the drug didn't kill her, she believed that after their *talk*, Guy Preston would.

Imprisoned in her unresponsive body, she had heard him talking to Jackman on the phone. He had put the call on loudspeaker, and she had had to suffer hearing Jackman's voice, unable to scream out to him to help her.

Marie felt anger begin to burn inside her rigid body, the heat almost intense enough to melt her frozen limbs. She began to wish she had allowed Terence Marcus Austin to finish what he had started. She bitterly regretted saving Preston's life, because he had mutated into something worse than any of his psychotic patients. She kept her rage burning. It might be the thing that would bring her through.

* * *

'I'm sorry that took so long.' Guy Preston walked into the room and placed a tray of what looked like syringes on the dressing table. 'Time to get you sorted out.'

Preston worked quickly and expertly. He secured her arms and legs to the bed with thick, soft restraints, and placed a wider strap around her waist. Then he filled a syringe and slid it into her arm. 'This will feel really scary, but try to relax. It will pass quickly.'

As soon as the needle was pulled from her arm her heart began to race. It was almost as terrifying as being paralysed.

'Keep calm.'

Guy's voice did nothing to soothe her. She was going to die, and the bastard didn't care. Whatever he had given her, it was making her chest heave and her heart thunder like a runaway train. She knew her body could not endure this kind of pressure for long. She'd never thought much about dying, until Bill was killed. Then she'd thought about it a lot. But she also thought about life. She needed to live, so that this monster, this heartless killer who had haunted her in the guise of a devoted friend, was removed from society forever.

'Calm down! I told you, it will pass.' There was a long pause and then he gripped the side of her wrist and took her pulse. 'This reversal inhibitor is new. It's fast, but not exactly stable.' He stepped back. 'You will probably experience muscle cramps and nausea for a while, but your blood pressure is going down.'

And he was right. Marie still felt as if there were a hammer drill at work inside her ribcage, but it was less frightening now. She drew in a ragged breath and tried to open her mouth.

His fingers covered her lips. 'Don't try to talk yet. Just maintain your breathing and try to relax.'

'How dare you! You bastard!' she croaked. Her jaw felt as if it would snap and her aching facial muscles screamed at her.

'It's all right. I'm not surprised at your anger.' For a moment the wounded puppy-dog look was back. 'I only did it because I didn't want to hurt you. I couldn't bring myself to hit you.'

'But you could do this,' she rasped. 'I wish you *had* hit me. I could understand that, but to do something as horrible, as outrageous . . .' She spat out, 'It's abuse, Guy. A filthy violation.'

'I'm sorry you feel like that. I thought you'd understand, maybe even . . . ?'

'What? Even be grateful? You sick son of a . . . !' She fought at her restraints but her stiff muscles cramped. She screamed, 'Have you any idea what it's like to be trapped in your own body, to be completely and utterly defenceless?' Tears welled up in her sore eyes and she struggled again.

'Please don't do that. I'm sorry about those too.' He pointed to the ties. 'We used to use them for electroshock therapy. They are meant to prevent the patient getting injured during the seizures.' He smiled regretfully at her. 'But in this case they are for my safety, not yours.'

'Too bloody right!'

Guy Preston gazed down at her. Then he sat on the edge of the bed, close beside her. He gave a pitiful whimper and said, 'Help me, Marie. I don't know what to do.'

Marie's anger gave way to bewilderment. She had to be careful. Whatever she said to him could exacerbate his psychosis. Tension came from him in waves, like static electricity.

She looked up at him. Now it was up to her to be the counsellor, and she would have to be as good as Professor Guy Preston had once been. Well, she had two points in her favour. The first was that she was still alive. He hadn't killed her. And second, he had asked for her help.

Marie forced a smile to lips still partly numb. 'Do you want to talk, Guy? It doesn't look like I'm going anywhere right now.'

Guy Preston placed his hand over hers. Marie saw an immense sadness in his scarred but still handsome face.

Guy stared pensively down at the puckered skin of the old wound on the back of his hand. 'I noticed it shortly after Terence Marcus Austin tried to kill me.' He looked at her for a moment and went on. 'I cannot tell you how many times I wished that you had *not* saved me. I should have died, Marie. He should have been allowed to push that pen right into my carotid artery.'

His hand began to gently stroke hers.

'It began when I saw his eyes. For years, I had been looking into murderers' eyes, but Terence Austin was different.' He sighed. 'I've seen emptiness, black holes where a soul should have been. I've seen callous indifference, and sometimes pure evil. I've talked to prisoners who have told me that murder means nothing to them. It's easy, they told me. But Austin's eyes held something that in all my years studying murder and murderers, I'd never seen before. It was a *connection*. That's the only way I can describe it, a connection between him and death. He existed only for that single moment. He was totally in control over life and death and all that mattered to him was that, the point of death. That was the reason why he continued to kill.'

Marie had also been close enough to look into Terence Austin's eyes, but all she had seen was a calculating predator. She stole a glance at Guy's tormented face and decided not to share her thoughts. Instead she said, 'I don't understand what you mean.'

Guy frowned. 'It *is* complex, especially for the layperson.' The frown gave way to a patient smile. 'Let me try to explain. We all have higher mental processes, in other words, our feelings of empathy. We identify with others and experience their emotions — anger, terror or joy — as if we ourselves were experiencing those feelings. And the most extreme experience is that of death. Do you see?'

Marie struggled, but said, 'Like getting involved in a scary film?'

'Yes, the fascination with death and dying in movies or documentaries. It's curiously compelling, and could be said to be a perfectly natural part of human behaviour. If we are honest with ourselves we all rubberneck at accident scenes, don't we? We visit concentration camps, ground zero, or queue for hours to see the cadavers in "Body Worlds."' Guy began to pace the room, gesticulating. 'We all have this fascination. Throughout history we have been fearful of death, and yet are drawn to it. Particularly to the moment when the soul leaves the body.'

'The point of death?'

Guy sighed. 'Precisely. I have studied this morbid subject in great depth, but never, never have I come closer to an understanding of it than when I looked into Austin's eyes. For a second I saw his total identification with the point of death, his *connection*, while his normal mechanisms became pathological and all human emotion was gone. It was a unique, life-changing moment.'

Marie didn't want to hear any more, but she did need to buy time. Somehow she had to keep him engaged. 'Did you ever visit Austin after he was incarcerated?' Her voice was still hoarse and her throat felt blocked and sore.

Guy nodded. 'Many times. I had a bond with you, but I had a stronger one with Austin.' He gave her an almost apologetic smile. 'He hated you, you know.'

Not as much as I hated him, thought Marie grimly.

'Because you denied him.'

'Didn't I just,' she said huskily, then gave a yelp of pain as a muscle spasm gripped her calf.

Guy massaged her leg until the pain subsided. 'Better?'

She nodded. 'Thank you.'

Suddenly it all seemed completely surreal and she wanted to roar with laughter. But Marie knew she had to keep her head. As they had been talking, she had noticed that amidst the used equipment on the tray on the dressing table, there remained a single large syringe, still full.

Guy continued. 'I talked to Austin at great length about what I had seen in him. After that he began to confide in me.' He tilted his head. 'It was Austin who suggested I study Françoise Thayer. He told me that she had what he called "the true affinity." That she was like him.'

Marie nodded, although her frustration was mounting. Why couldn't this *professional* see that Austin had been playing with him? He had been filling Guy's head with apparently deep insights into death, but all the time he'd just been doing what serial killers always did, feeding his own sick ego.

'I had no idea how much he affected you, Guy,' she said. 'I'm truly sorry.'

'I would like to say that it wasn't your fault, but actually I suppose it was.' He looked at her oddly. 'I was almost disappointed when he didn't kill me. That one look was so powerful that it sealed my fate for ever. And I had to see it again.'

'I don't know what to say.' How true, she thought.

'You and I, we used to talk about what happened in that room, and I always wanted to ask if maybe, just maybe, you'd seen it too.'

'I'm a police officer, Guy. I saw a bad situation flaring up. I acted instinctively in order to protect you. I never saw what you saw.'

Guy stood up. Then to her surprise he plumped up the pillow next to her head, and lay down beside her. He slipped his hand through hers and let out a contented little noise. 'Please don't think that I didn't appreciate what you did, because there were times, days when I was busy and work was full on, when I almost forgot about Terence Marcus Austin. I was almost free of what had happened. I still functioned, and oddly enough, I functioned very well.'

He moved closer. Marie tried not to jerk away.

'But you know what obsession is like, don't you? One tiny reminder, one sniff of the bottle or hit of the drug, and you're back with it. The thing was, I never saw that look again. No matter how many murderers I saw, they simply didn't have it.'

So you went looking for it.

Marie suddenly realised. Not only did he want to see it in others, Guy wanted to feel it in himself, to *be* it. He'd lived alongside death and the dealers of death all his working life, but he'd been an outsider. He could never truly empathise, only guess, and that wasn't good enough for him. And after witnessing Terence Marcus Austin's mind at work, Guy wanted to really understand. To live it.

'And did you ever find what you were looking for?' she said.

'No.'

So that, she quickly realised, was the root cause of his overwhelming sadness. He had killed for nothing. There was nothing there. It would have been like successfully breaking into the Bank of England's vaults, and finding them empty.

'The first one, that nurse, Julia Hope, was an accident.'

His voice was flat and unemotional again, but the confession was like a death knell for Marie. He was hardly going to let her go now.

'I'd been seeing her privately for over a month. She was showing signs of serious psychotic illness and I wanted her to be admitted for evaluation. I knew it would be upsetting for her, but I was sure she'd be able to handle the truth.' He sighed. 'But she didn't. I tried to calm her down, but she went completely berserk and came at me. I pushed her away and she fell and hit her head.'

'But she didn't die then, did she?'

He smiled and squeezed her hand affectionately. 'See, you always did understand me, Marie. No, you're quite right, she didn't die then. But when I saw all the blood, I realised that I'd been given a chance to feel what Austin felt, and I wondered if just maybe . . .'

She felt him shiver.

'When she was finally dead I realised that I'd gone about it all wrong. Terence Austin had been as serene as a boat becalmed when he attacked me. I had been close to frenzy.' He gave a little laugh. 'And after I got rid of her in that abandoned pub, I knew that I had no option but to try again. The bridge had been crossed. I had nothing to lose and I needed to find that missing rapture.'

'So you made it appear as if we had a serial killer on our patch.' Asking him that question, Marie felt almost paranoid herself, because Guy *was* a serial killer. He just didn't see himself as one.

'Exactly! And strangely, just then I had a plethora of flaky women needing my very private expertise, my ever-open door, my sensitive listening manner, and of course, my inexhaustible supply of under-the-counter antidepressants.'

'How wonderful to have such a wide choice of suitable victims,' muttered Marie. 'And as you'd studied murderers for most of your life, Françoise Thayer in particular, you dressed up the crime scenes. You staged them just for us. Am I right?'

Guy suddenly raised himself, leaning on one elbow. He turned to her, his face only inches from hers. His expression was now alight with enthusiasm. 'Can you imagine my surprise when Ruth Crooke asked me to help out as a consultant?' He laughed. 'It was too ridiculous! She wanted *my* expert opinion on my own murders. And when she told me that there was a deluded young man roaming around insisting that he was the birth son of Françoise Thayer and he believed that he was the killer! Well . . .' He shook his head. 'It was like a macabre Whitehall farce.' He became suddenly serious. 'But of course, by that time I'd found that *you* were the detective sergeant on the case. That's when it all went wrong, Marie. And now I don't know what to do.' He looked at her thoughtfully and ran the back of his hand along her cheek. 'With you.'

* * *

Jackman, Max and Charlie stood silently in the shadows and waited.

Back in the super's office, when Ruth Crooke had asked if he knew where Marie was, he had heard again Guy Preston's voice on the phone. The man was making very sure that Jackman believed Marie had left. Suddenly everything the psychologist had said sounded false. The bracelet, the chance of an accident on her bike, all intended to mislead him.

Preston had a fixation with Marie. He'd had it for years. Jackman bit on his bottom lip. Had Preston finally taken that fascination a step further? Or had he done something even worse?

* * *

They were gathered in the communal gardens outside the apartment block in Hanson Gardens. A uniformed team were with them, and two vans carrying the armed unit were quietly discharging their occupants in a service road at the back of the flats.

Their concern for Marie's safety made each one of them want to kick the door down, rush in and free her, but experience told them that the situation called for the utmost caution. For one thing, they didn't know what they would find. One wrong move and this would be Marie's last case, if it wasn't already. They were all painfully aware that they might find a body in that apartment, not a prisoner.

'Do we know the exact location of Preston's flat?' asked Max softly.

Charlie leaned forward and unfolded a printout, a floorplan of the building. 'It's the garden flat. Last door along the corridor. And it has one exit, a French window that opens out to the rear.'

'Uniform has that covered.' Jackman's mouth was dry. Everything seemed to be taking an age. And they didn't have much time. Every second counted.

'Ready when you are, Inspector.' The uniformed team leader touched his arm lightly. 'The armed officers are all in place.'

Jackman searched the shadows. The men in black were there, unseen, their rifles all directed at Preston's apartment windows.

Three men with thick body armour, helmets and cradled guns moved up alongside him.

Jackman swallowed, and then he stepped forward.

'Okay, with me.'

CHAPTER TWENTY-NINE

Guy Preston was now sitting at the bottom of the bed. He looked tired and haggard. 'I'm guessing it won't be too long before your inspector arrives on his white charger.'

'I don't think so. He has no idea you are involved.' Marie tried to sound convincing. 'He values your opinion. He's read your papers, your theses, and he admires your work. He will no more believe that you are implicated than I did.'

'Until you saw the knife in my dishwasher.'

Of course! She wanted to laugh out loud. Sure she'd seen it, but it hadn't even registered. It should have. A man who did no cooking would not need a very professional chef's filleting knife. She tried to sound calm when she said, 'Do you know, Guy? It never crossed my mind.'

'Don't lie to me, Marie. You were edgy, couldn't wait to get away. And it all happened after you put those mugs in the dishwasher.'

'Wrong, Guy. I just wanted to be back out hunting for Daniel and Skye. I'm not good at kicking my heels when there's work to be done.'

Guy rubbed at his eyes. 'Well, I'm sure you'd have made the connection before the night was over. I knew I wouldn't fool you for long. So I guess it's time.'

Marie looked across at the tray where the syringe lay. 'Is that for me? Or you?'

He drew in a long breath. 'It won't hurt, and it will be very quick. This is my last chance, I know it. And this time I know it will work. When I kill you, I'll finally find what Terence Austin knew. After all these years of groping in the dark, I'll truly understand.' His stare intensified. 'We are very close, and I'm sure that is important. I've always cared about you, Marie. All the time I was up north, I never forgot you. Even when I married Sara,' he shrugged, 'and I did that for her intellect and her fine academic brain. But we never had the deep attachment that I've always felt for you.'

'How did she die?' Marie wondered if she should have asked that question.

'As I said, I married her for her brain.' He gave a bitter bark of a laugh. 'And she developed early onset dementia. Karma, eh?'

'And did you kill her too?'

'I considered it. As much for her sake as for mine, but she beat me to it. She walked out in front of a tractor pulling a trailer-load of sugar beet.'

'That's horrible.'

'Worse for the tractor driver. Poor man. I counselled him for months after the incident.'

Marie felt like Alice in Wonderland, chatting amicably to the Mad Hatter — a triple murderer who cared deeply about people.

'But time is passing. I need to make a final decision and get on with it. I don't want my choices made for me by the remarkably intelligent DI Rowan Jackman.' Guy stood up and went to the bedside table. He returned to the bed carrying the tray, and sat back down. 'You do believe that I never planned this, Marie?'

'I know you didn't, but it doesn't have to be this way.'

Guy laughed softly. 'I think it does.'

Time was running out, and Marie knew that she had not done enough to save herself.

Jackman! Where are you?

Marie said, 'Can I ask a question?'

Eyes on the syringe, he nodded.

'Do you love me?'

Guy nodded slowly.

'Then let me live. Let me retain a memory of you as the good man, the friend, the doctor that tried to help so many people.'

'You denied Terence Marcus Austin, and now you want to deny me?'

Something snapped inside Marie. 'Oh hell! Then kill me if you must, but I'm telling you right now, you will be disappointed yet again, because you will *never* feel what Terence Austin did. Never! Because no matter what you've done, you are not a natural-born killer, and Austin was. He was an animal, a slayer of children and adults alike. He was as cold as death itself. He had no heart, Guy, and you do, because *you* have the capacity to love. There will be no eureka moment, no mystical, magical connection, because it doesn't exist! If I could, I'd tell you to run, get away before Jackman realises what's happening,' she said almost wistfully. 'But I can't. I can't allow you to put more lives at risk. You asked for my help, and now I'm giving it to you. I'm sorry, Guy, but you either kill me, or you ring Jackman, and we wait together until he gets here.'

He stood up stiffly, with the syringe in his hand, and moved towards her.

For some reason Marie didn't feel afraid. She felt calm acceptance drift over her like a fen mist. Maybe this was her time. At least she would be with Bill. She looked into Guy Preston's eyes and saw the terrible suffering and the damage that his work with one evil killer had caused. Marie smiled at him, the kind of smile you only offer to a dear friend. 'It's alright, Guy. I trust you to make the right decision.'

'I will, Marie. Because there is another way.' He leant over and kissed her gently on the lips, then stepped back and plunged the needle deep into his thigh.

'No!' screamed Marie. 'No! Not like this! Guy!'

He looked at her serenely as he depressed the plunger fully. 'You win, Marie. Jackman said that you were always right.'

CHAPTER THIRTY

Jackman was in front of the team that swarmed into the Hanson Park apartment block. He was no hero, but tonight was different. Marie needed him. He would not fail her.

As the heavy enforcer swung away from the shattered door, he leapt through, shouting her name. And just before the alarm shrieked around the building, he heard her calling his name.

With Max and Charlie at his heels, he ran towards the sound of her voice.

The scene in the master bedroom was like something from a fairy tale. The beautiful woman lay stretched out on the bed, with the dead lover on the floor beside her.

But Jackman saw only one thing. Marie. And she was alive.

'Fucking hell!' said Max, breaking the spell.

'Get the medics in here!' yelled Jackman, as rushed to her side. 'And get someone to deactivate that bloody alarm!'

'He's dead,' whispered Marie hoarsely, staring at the still form of Guy Preston. She looked up at Jackman with watery eyes. 'It was him all along. Can you believe that?'

Jackman began to untie her. 'I thought we were going to be too late.' He looked at her, adrenalin still coursing through him. 'He was going to kill you, wasn't he? I should have worked it out sooner. I should have realised! I'm so sorry, Marie.'

'Actually, guv, I'm getting a bit fed up with people apologising to me. For the past hour I've been having an eminent doctor telling me how sorry he was that he was going to have to murder me. And that's after he apologised for pumping me full of some paralysing drug because he was too fond of me to bang me on the bloody head!'

Jackman undid the last restraint and Marie struggled to sit up.

'All in all, it's been a piss-poor evening.' Marie looked at him furiously and then burst into tears.

Jackman sat down beside her and took her in his arms. 'Hey, you're safe now. But we need to get you to hospital. Do you know what drugs he gave you?'

She shook her head, wiped her eyes, then pointed to the tray at the bottom of the bed. 'I think the used syringes are on there, with the phials.' She exhaled loudly, then turned to him, her mouth slightly open as a thought suddenly occurred to her. 'Jackman! My bike! He rode off on it. Where is it?'

'Er, well, you know what you said about it being a piss-poor evening . . . ?'

Max joined in. 'It just got worse, Sarge. Your bike's in the Blackland Sluice. No, I lie. Actually it's lying on the bank in a pool of river sludge.'

Marie glared down at Preston.

Charlie grinned. 'I don't think it would be in very good taste if you kicked his body, Sarge.' The grin widened. 'But that's just my opinion.'

* * *

In the ambulance, Marie sat on the edge of the stretcher. 'I'm fine, guv. Cancel sending me to hospital. I just want to get away from here.'

Jackman looked at the paramedics. 'How is she?'

'Her vital signs are remarkably good, Inspector.' The green-clad paramedic looked mildly surprised. 'But we're not qualified to assess the side effects or late-presenting reactions of specific drugs. I'd definitely advise a full check-up at A&E.'

'You heard the man.'

'Preston promised that there would be no side effects, guv. Just some nausea and a few cramps. And you know what? I believe him.' She gave him a pathetic look. 'Please?'

'You shouldn't be on your own at home. Not after everything that you've been through.'

Marie sensed that he was softening. 'Look, I'm hardly going to be able to switch off after all this, am I? Take me back to the nick. If I start to feel bad, then I promise I'll go straight to the hospital.'

Jackman gave the medic a hopeless grimace. 'I've tried arguing with her before, you know. I've never won yet.'

'You could pull rank, *Detective Inspector*,' said the man pointedly.

'I could, but I don't have a death wish.'

'Well, we can't make her go.' The paramedic turned to Marie. 'But I have to make sure you understand that this is against medical advice. And you need to sign a disclaimer.'

'Don't worry. If things go tits up, I won't sue,' said Marie dryly, standing up. 'And thank you for checking me out.'

After signing the form, she walked to Jackman's car, one hand on his shoulder. 'You'll need to debrief me, guv. And I'd rather it was sooner than later.'

'Let's get back and get some strong coffee down you, and then we'll take it from there, shall we?'

* * *

Kevin sat up groggily. At first he was disorientated, unable to understand what had happened or where he was. His head throbbed and he fought back an urge to vomit.

Slowly it came back to him. He was in the Kinder house. And he shouldn't be.

He gingerly touched his forehead and felt the lump. He winced with pain and closed his eyes until it had passed. He thought about his instructions for head injury. Had he been unconscious for long? Had he been sick? Was he bleeding? He didn't think so, but some light would help. He felt around for his flashlight, but couldn't locate it. Then he remembered why he was where he was. He'd seen a wall switch.

Kevin pushed himself up against the wall, and ran his hand along it. Doing this made him dizzy, but after a minute or two he found the switch and the small cellar was suffused with light. He winced and closed his eyes. When he opened them, he finally got a clear picture of where he was.

He climbed up the step that had caused him to fall, and looked around. There were shelves full of boxes and plastic containers of pool chemicals and cleaners, and a mass of other unwanted items. Folding chairs for the patio leaned against a pile of sacks of barbecue briquettes. Coloured umbrellas, a set of boules and some croquet mallets were heaped together in one corner. Everything was covered in dust and dirt.

Kevin sank down onto a low barrel-shaped garden table and tried to work out what to do next. He felt terrible. His neck was stiff from the whiplash when his head hit the wall. His teeth ached where they had crashed together, and his head ached horribly. But he had come to do a job, and it would be stupid to bugger off now, when this was the only place left to search.

With a low groan, he stood up and reluctantly began to tour the room.

He was halfway round when he saw the blood. It wasn't much, just a smear. He touched his forehead, then looked at his fingers. They were dry. The skin was inflamed and swollen, but it had not broken.

He moved closer to the streak of dark, reddish-brown blood staining the lid of a cardboard box. Without thinking, he reached into his jeans pocket and withdrew a pair of protective gloves. He pulled them on, then carefully opened the box.

The metallic stink of old blood hit him immediately. The box, which had once contained packets of crisps, was jammed with bloodied clothing. He lifted a piece of fabric between his thumb and forefinger and saw that it was a red checked shirt. Beneath it nestled a pair of stained stone-coloured chinos, a black T-shirt and some other items.

Kevin took a deep breath. Now what the hell was he supposed to do? Part of him had doubted that it would ever come to this, and now it had, he felt a cold emptiness. He wouldn't get away with another anonymous call, and this was vital evidence.

With a sigh, he decided there was only one person that he could think of who might be able to help him. He carefully replaced the lid of the box, then sat back on the old table and pulled his phone from his pocket. He switched it on, leaned back against the wall of the cellar and watched as it began to search for a signal. Kevin moved slightly — a water pipe was pushing uncomfortably into his shoulder blade — then he sat bolt upright and listened.

Voices? He tilted his head to one side, then moved his ear closer to the pipe.

Through the thundering of his headache, he heard whispered voices echoing from somewhere upstairs, and to his dismay, Kevin realised that he was not alone in the house. If this was another team of police officers, he was well in the shit, but if it happened to be the owner of those bloodstained clothes, then he could be in for something far nastier.

Bitterly regretting that he'd ever left home in the first place, he decided to make his way back out into the garden and see if the crew on watch were doing a routine walk around the premises. Then, whatever happened, he'd scarper back to the safety of the bus shelter and make his call.

His head thumped with every step, but soon he was back out on the patio and breathing in fresh night air. All around him was calm. There were no lights on in the house and no policemen trampled through the undergrowth of the neglected garden. He edged around the side of the building and saw the police car, still stationary and still containing two bored officers.

So who was in the house?

He stared up at the dark windows and shivered. He wouldn't wait to get back out onto the road to make his call, but he would get far enough away from the house so as not to be heard talking.

Forgetting his pain, Kevin ran back into the shrubs, vaulted over the boundary fence, and dropped down into a crouching position. He opened his phone and to his relief saw that he had a strong signal. 'Come on! Come on! Pick up!' he whispered. Adding to himself, *Because for some reason, I'm scared. I'm really scared.*

* * *

As Jackman drove back to the station, he saw that Marie was beginning to relax. She was the toughest woman he knew, and already she was starting to show signs of the old Marie.

Max and Charlie sat in the back, and their constant banter and gallows humour helped to ease the tension.

Jackman was just telling them about his call from Skye, when Max's mobile gave out his latest ringtone — a police siren.

'I wish you'd change that,' muttered Jackman. 'We hear enough of them as it is.'

'I preferred the reggae version of *Any Old Iron*,' added Marie.

Whoever was calling Max took some while to get their message across, and after a few grunts and murmurs of agreement, Max finally said, 'Right, mate, now listen, you hang on in there. I'm with the guvnor right now, and we'll be with you in five, okay?' Max shut off his phone and touched Jackman's shoulder. 'Guv? We need to get to the Kinder house. Someone is inside, but there are no lights on, and they are there without the knowledge of the crews on observation outside.'

Jackman immediately slowed down. 'Who was that on the phone?'

Max drew in a quick breath then said, 'PC Kevin Stoner, sir. He was following up a hunch, even though he's suspended at present.'

'What the hell is he thinking? Bloody idiot!'

'He's a good bloke, sir. He'll explain when we get there.'

'Why not just get the crew outside to go in and do a recce? For heaven's sake, it's most likely Daniel. And I have feeling that Skye will have already told him that he's no murderer, so he's probably just gone home to try to get his head back together.' Jackman's words had no conviction in them. 'No lights on? And getting in without the police officers seeing him? Very iffy.'

'It's complicated,' said Max. 'But if the sarge is up for it, Kevin trusts you, and he's sure something is wrong.'

Jackman glanced at Marie.

'Let's go,' she said instantly. 'I could do with something to take my mind off recent events. Just do it.'

Jackman swung the car into a U-turn and accelerated back down the main road towards the river. 'Okay, Max. I gather you'd like a softly-softly approach?'

'Kevin Stoner will be in big trouble if the whole station knows what he's been up to. He's been hiding in a neighbour's garden, but he's going to make his way to a bus shelter at the road junction. He'll meet us there.'

'Okay. We'll hear what he has to say, then alert the officers on observation and we'll go check the house.' He looked at Marie. 'I'm still not too sure about you. Those medics wanted you hospitalised, not out searching for intruders.'

Marie gave him a smug smile. 'Remember what you said about never winning an argument with me?'

'Yes, but . . .'

'I'd forget it, guv,' said Max from the back. 'I suspect you're on a loser.'

'He's right. Just drive,' chipped in Marie. 'I've also got an odd feeling about this.'

They parked in the main road and walked to where Kevin waited in the shadows.

'This had better be good, Stoner,' growled Jackman. 'What the hell are you doing here? And how did you get that damned great bump on your head?'

'The head's nothing, sir. You see, when I was at home, I got to thinking about what some of the guys said about Daniel Kinder. That maybe he was on scene when they raided the house to catch Drew Wilson and his gang.' The words tumbled from the young officer's mouth. 'Then I wondered, if they were right, what was he doing there? After all, he was supposed to have taken sleeping pills at Skye Wynyard's place and been out of it, wasn't he?'

Max nodded. 'That's what he told the officers who called to tell him about the break-in.'

'So either he lied, or he was having one of his turns,' added Charlie.

'And if he lied, why? What was he up to here?' Marie stared down the road towards the Kinder property.

'That's what I thought, Sarge,' said Kevin. 'And although I know the house would have been searched when you were looking for Kinder, I thought I'd sneak over and take a really good look in the outbuildings and see if he'd been hiding something.'

'Like what?' Jackman asked.

Kevin stared earnestly at him. 'What would a possible killer hide? I reckoned either a weapon or bloodstained clothing.'

'But he's *not* the killer,' said Jackman softly. 'Only you wouldn't know that, Stoner. We have our killer. He was . . .'

he hesitated, 'He was discovered and apprehended a few hours ago by Sergeant Evans here. That's why I'm not rushing into that house with all guns blazing. Daniel's not our murderer.'

Kevin's mouth dropped open in astonishment. 'But . . . but I found bloodstained clothes, sir. There's a whole box of them, in a small cellar beneath the hot-tub room.' He heaved in a breath. 'And I heard whispering echoing down the water-pipe system from upstairs. Someone is definitely in there, sir. And on reflection, I think the alarm system is turned off.'

'Then we'd better check it out.' Jackman looked thoughtfully at the young constable. 'Go home, Stoner. You're in enough trouble. I'll tell the crew outside that we've had a call from someone about seeing a possible intruder.' He sighed. 'But you and I need to have a long talk at a later date, young man. And by the way, get that head looked at. You could have a concussion. Now go.'

Kevin Stoner threw him a relieved smile. 'Thank you, sir. I can't tell you how much I appreci—'

Jackman cut him off. 'Sod off, Stoner. We've got work to do.'

Kevin Stoner turned, and with a nod of silent thanks to Max, hurried away into the night.

* * *

Daniel sat on the floor of the attic and stared silently at the long-bladed kitchen knife that was laid across his lap.

Across from him, sitting cross-legged and leaning against the far wall, was Skye. She had no idea of how long they had been there, but it seemed a very long time.

They had made their way into the house by going across neighbour's gardens and slipping in the unwatched back door. The ascent up the stairs to the attic room in the pitch-black darkness had made Skye's heart race, but they hadn't dared to put a light on or use a torch for fear of attracting the attention of the occupants of the police car.

Daniel had not spoken since they'd arrived at his home, and Skye knew that she needed to be cleverer than she had ever been, in order to keep her darling, damaged Daniel from doing something that he would bitterly regret.

Somehow she found the courage to speak, and prayed that she had chosen the right words. 'I've spoken to Ruby. She is on her way home to be with you, Daniel, but she has told me something very important, and she wants me to explain it to you.'

His silence could have meant anything, so she pressed on. 'She knows all about your birth mother, Daniel, and it isn't Françoise Thayer.'

In the shadowy gloom of the attic room, she saw Daniel flinch. Then she heard him give a throaty chuckle, and it made her shiver.

'They've told you to say that, haven't they? The police: they've told you to convince me that it's all in my head.' Again that sinister laugh, then he said, 'I knew they would. They are *so* predictable.'

'The only person who has asked me to talk to you is Ruby. And she wouldn't lie to you.' Skye took a harder tone. 'The police told me to stay well away from you, Daniel. They don't want me talking to you at all.'

'Maybe they are right.' His finger slid slowly along the blade of the knife. 'Maybe you should have listened to them, Skye.'

'You have to know the truth. And I want to be the one to tell you about your childhood,' she drew in a long breath, 'because it isn't very pleasant.'

'You're wasting your time, my darling.' Daniel let out a long sigh. 'Because Guy Preston told me everything I need to know. I have the same condition as her, as my mother, Françoise Thayer. And it runs in the blood.' He gave a sharp bark of laughter, 'Quite literally.' His voice dropped to little more than a whisper. 'And I also have the same propensity to kill. He said he will try to help me, but we all know it's too late. It certainly is for those three women, and maybe for you.'

'Françoise Thayer is not your mother!' Skye shouted at him. Your mother's name was Lucy Carrick and she was a murderer too, if you must know. She killed your two brothers and tried to kill you too!'

There, it was finally out. No kind and careful consideration as she had planned, the information was simply screamed at him. And now she was in full flow, she couldn't stop, 'That's why you have gaps in your memory. That's why you are a mess, Daniel. She locked you in car full of carbon monoxide! You nearly died, and afterwards you were sick for years. Ask Ruby! Ask her! She'll tell you the whole sad story.'

Skye suddenly felt as if all the air had gone from her body, as if she had nothing left to give.

'You're lying. You have to be.' Daniel gripped the knife with both hands and rocked back and forth. 'You *have* to be.'

Skye wanted to shake him, and she wanted to hug him too, but most of all she wanted to cry. And so she did. She didn't know what he was going to do, and at that point, she didn't really care. It was out of her hands.

* * *

Jackman gave the observation crew the briefest of reasons why a whole team of detectives had turned up on their patch for a simple intruder query. But to his relief they didn't question it. They hadn't been told to stand down yet, so as far as they were concerned, there was still a serial killer loose. Half the Fenland Constabulary could have arrived and it wouldn't have worried them.

'You have a key?' asked Jackman.

'Yes, sir. We've been doing a check every couple of hours. And this is the security alarm code.' He handed Jackman a sheet of paper.

'Right, so you two cover the back. One of you take the rear kitchen door, and the other take the garden room. The four of us will go in from the front. And eyes peeled, lads.'

Stoner had been right. The alarm had been deactivated. And that worried Jackman. One look at his team told him that they had all come to the same conclusion: someone had been, or still was, in the Kinder house.

They slipped silently through the house, entering room after room, and whispering, 'clear,' as they left the empty rooms.

As they completed their check of the bedrooms, Marie took his arm and murmured, 'It all started up there, didn't it?' She pointed to the stairs to the attic.

'And will it all finish there, do you think?'

'One way to find out, I guess.' Marie stepped forward onto the first stair, but Jackman held her back.

'Not this time.' He moved around her and headed up towards the attic room.

The door was not locked. It opened easily and swung back with barely a sound.

In the pale moonlight that shone through the dormer window, they saw Daniel Kinder sitting with his back against the wall that had once been decorated like a shrine to Françoise Thayer. Skye lay still in his embrace.

Her arms were wrapped around him and her head nestled into his shoulder. A wicked long-bladed knife lay in front of them, and Jackman noted a disturbing dark patch of something wet spreading across the floor.

'Hello,' Daniel's voice was soft. He smiled wanly at them, 'Skye has just been telling me a story.'

'And it's a true story, Daniel. I heard what Ruby told her.' Jackman tried to keep his voice steady although he didn't like the strange distant quality of Daniel's voice.

'It's alright, Inspector.' Skye sat up, but didn't for one second release her hold on Daniel. 'Daniel knows everything now. He's just trying to take it all in. It's been a terrible shock, and his arm seems to be bleeding. I think we might need some medical attention for him.' Without changing her tone of voice, she threw an anxious look at Marie, 'But there is something you really need to know about Guy Preston.'

Marie swallowed hard, and her expression said that there was little that she didn't know about that man. 'Preston is dead, Skye. And he was responsible for the deaths of those three women.'

Daniel gave a shudder. 'Then I didn't hurt them?' His voice rose higher, 'But Guy told me . . .' His voice tailed off into silence.

'Guy Preston was setting you up to take the blame, Daniel,' Jackman said gently. 'You never hurt anyone.'

'I believed him.' Daniel suddenly let out a sob, then his whole body began to shake and tears cascaded down his face. 'I believed him.'

'A common mistake, so it seems,' muttered Marie. 'And I can say that from being in the unenviable position of being the next victim on his list.'

Jackman instructed Max to get the medics, then slipped on some gloves and knelt down and retrieved the knife. He still didn't totally trust Daniel Kinder around sharp objects.

CHAPTER THIRTY-ONE

Marie had made a list of people to contact. She liked things tidy and made a point of spending the last few days on an investigation cleaning up loose ends.

She skimmed the list. Only three names were left. She ran a line through the name Mark Dunand. She had seen him a few days before and had satisfied herself on the few small questions that hung over his head. She had already ascertained that his importing business was clean, no drugs, nothing illegal at all, and his interest in Skye had been, as she'd thought, unrequited love. My best friend's girlfriend, and all that jazz.

'Who's next?' She picked up the phone and dialled the next number. Peter Hodder answered after two rings.

'I promised to tell you if Daniel Kinder really was Thayer's son, sir, and I'm delighted to tell you that he is not.' She gave the retired officer the bare bones of the story.

He gave a shaky little laugh. 'I always hoped that her death would mean that the world was a safer place, Marie, but she still managed to taint that boy's life, even from her grave.'

'So I assume that you've not changed your mind about having your old notebooks back?'

'Absolutely not! I've felt so much better, just knowing that they have gone from my life. I'll never be free of her, but she's moved a little further away.'

They talked for a while, mainly about motorcycles, then he wished her well and they said goodbye.

Marie turned her attention to the copy of *Motorcycle News* that lay on her desk. She had sold the damaged Kawasaki to a young rookie copper who wanted to rebuild it, and she'd thrown her racing leathers in for good measure. Every time she looked at that black and green jacket, she saw Guy Preston's unhinged expression as he pulled it on.

So, it would seem it was time for something completely different. She stared, almost lustfully, at the picture of the electric blue and black Suzuki V-Strom 650. Now that was very nice, but there was also the scarlet and black Suzuki Gladius. She skimmed the spec, but veered off when she saw the description of the blood-red coachwork. She'd seen enough blood recently. She touched the glossy picture of the blue bike. 'Looks like it could be you, my beauty.'

'You sound scarily like Gollum, my precious.' Max looked over her shoulder and frowned at the shiny motorcycle. 'Ever thought of a nice safe car?'

'Piss off, Cohen.' She grinned at him. 'Time enough for one of those when I'm old and wrinkly.' She drew a line through the name Peter Hodder, then looked again at her list. The final name was Orac.

The IT genius had pulled out all the stops to help them, and Marie doubted that many people actually bothered to go thank her. Marie smiled to herself and took a small carefully wrapped box from her desk drawer. She stood up and glanced across to where Jackman's office door was firmly closed. She knew that he was expecting a visit from Lisa Hurley and had asked not to be disturbed for a while. Typical! Again he had managed to avoid a trip to Orac's underworld lair.

She found Orac in her usual place, wired in to her computer.

'Please don't be offended, but I wanted to say thank you. Your work was invaluable to the investigation.' She placed the silver-wrapped box on the woman's desk.

Orac looked up at her, those strange eyes glinting metallically in the glare from her monitor. Without a word, she opened the gift and stared at the ultra-modern hand-crafted earrings.

'Sit down, if you've got a few minutes to spare?' Orac said.

Marie sat.

Without taking her eyes from the earrings, Orac said, 'I've found your missing evidence boxes from the Françoise Thayer case.'

Marie's eyes widened. 'Really? Where are they?'

Orac glanced at her watch. 'On the A17, probably somewhere near King's Lynn. Traffic allowing, they should be with you in an hour and a half. They were in Norfolk, in a storage facility used for old closed cases.' She gave Marie a rare smile. 'Not that I think you'll need them now.'

'Certainly not for what I originally wanted them for, but they should definitely be kept somewhere safe. Documents and evidence as sensitive as that should never have gone missing.'

'Do you think you'll ever read the case notes?'

'I've read Peter Hodder's notebooks, Orac. They were enough for me.' She shivered.

Orac nodded. 'I have to admit that even I was shaken by some of the things I discovered.' She lightly touched the surface of one of the earrings. '*And* they brought back some very bad memories.'

Marie looked at her enquiringly. This was too weird for words. Orac had proper conversations with *no one.*

'In another life,' she stared at Marie. '. . . I had dealings with some ruthless people. I've seen men, deliberately and without conscience, take lives and torture people.

However, they did it for what they believed in, for the causes or the organisations that they were deeply committed to. But Françoise Thayer did it with a smile, and warmed her hands in their innocent blood. It's inconceivable.'

'It is,' Marie agreed, then chanced her arm and asked, 'What did you do, in this other life?'

'Things I'd prefer to forget.'

Marie decided that she had probably pushed it far enough, maybe too far, but Orac suddenly said, 'I was brought in from the field when one of those zealous men that I was talking about, blinded me with a purpose-designed stiletto driven directly into my left eye. A centimetre deeper and it would have pierced my brain.' She tilted her head forward, and pulling down the bottom lid, manoeuvred the contact lens down into the lower part of her eye, carefully removed it and then looked up at Marie.

Marie sat in stunned silence. Orac's left iris and cornea was almost totally black, giving it the cold, dead appearance of a shark's eye.

'Full thickness corneal laceration, Sergeant. Not pretty. So, I know for sure that there are some very unpleasant people out there.' Orac gave a cold laugh. 'But not you, DS Marie Evans, you are at the opposite end of the spectrum. This is a first.' She gestured to her gift. 'And they are beautiful, thank you.'

Marie stood up. 'They are from Jackman, too, but he's with someone in his office at the moment and . . .' suddenly she didn't want to make any more feeble excuses for him, so she just shrugged and pulled a face.

Orac let out an unheard of laugh. 'Oh Marie! Jackman-baiting is *such* fun.' She deftly slipped the contact lens back in. 'Before you go, two things: One, I only tease people I like; and two, tell no one about what happened to me,' she paused, 'or I'll have to kill you.' She turned back to her computer and once again, thousands of numbers began streaming down the screen.

* * *

Jackman leaned back in his captain's chair and savoured a few moments of comparative peace. His office door was closed, and for once no one was demanding anything of him. He stared at the gemstone globe that sat on his desk. It was not only beautiful but tactile, and he gently ran his fingertips over it, wondering at the patience of the craftsmen who'd constructed it. Each country was accurately cut to shape from stones like jasper, agate, jade and tiger eye. The oceans were mother of pearl and the lines of longitude and latitude were made of twisted gilded wire. It stood on a brass stand and took pride of place to the right of his reclaimed prize of a desk.

He pushed it, and gently made the world spin. If only everything were that easy.

As Jackman watched the Pacific Ocean, as it smoothly passed out of sight and the Americas appeared, there was a knock on his door.

'Someone to see you, guv.' Max stood back and held the door open for Lisa Hurley to enter.

Jackman jumped up, welcomed her and pulled out a chair. She eased herself carefully into the seat and grimaced.

'Still sore?' Jackman asked.

'Pretty uncomfortable, but all things considered, it's a drop in the ocean, isn't it?'

'It was far more than that, Lisa. He nearly killed you.'

'I'm trying not to think about the "what ifs" or maybes right now. I consider myself lucky beyond belief.' She looked at him with a curious smile. 'Rather like your sergeant, Marie Evans, I understand?'

Jackman nodded. 'Yes, maybe you two should start a survivor's club?'

Lisa smiled and nodded, 'Maybe we should.' Then her expression became serious. 'I came here to thank you for the care and concern you showed to Skye, and to respect-fully ask that the knowledge that you have about her being my natural child remains between us. She is very happy with her family, and with Daniel, and it was never my intention for her to find out about me.'

'You can rest assured,' Jackman leaned forward, elbows on the table, 'Marie and I will tell no one. You were her direct boss at the hospital and a caring friend. It ends there.'

Lisa looked close to tears. 'At least for once I was able to help her when she needed it. She is such a beautiful girl and I'm so proud of her.' She took a tissue from her pocket and dabbed at her eyes.

'Is it a coincidence that you both work in the same field of medical care?' asked Jackman. 'It's been intriguing me since we found out about you.'

'Oh no, I was in business management, working for a big private health care company. When I finally traced Skye, and discovered what she was training for, I transferred to a post in hospital administration. When Skye finally settled at Saltern General, I moved into a new post there; as manager in charge of staffing in the Physiotherapy and OT departments.' She smiled at him. 'And it was the best thing I ever did. I never wanted to give my baby up, but I was in a desperate situation and I had little or no choice if I wanted to put my child first. But I never forgot her.'

'Did *you* name her Skye?'

Lisa nodded. 'I have never seen a tiny child with such a sunny disposition, or such intensely blue eyes. And, the Isle of Skye was my grandparents' home. It just seemed fitting.'

'And what now?'

'I think it is time to move on. I've been offered a post down south, and I think I'll accept. I cannot afford for Skye to become suspicious about my concern for her. My mind is now at peace regarding her safety and her wellbeing. She has a family that loves her and I've no doubt that in time Daniel will make enough of a recovery to enjoy life again, like he did before. I really hope that the two of them will stay together.'

'They are very well-suited, and the prognosis for that young man is apparently excellent. His mother, Ruby Kinder is home now, with no more plans to run off to foreign climes, so with her and Skye as support, he has the best chance, I'd say.'

'Can I ask one last question, Inspector?' Lisa shifted uncomfortably in her seat. 'Did Guy Preston have any connection to our hospital? I've never seen him there and I work quite closely with the psych department.'

Jackman gave a little shake of his head. 'No, he was affiliated to several private hospitals and clinics. Obtaining drugs was easy for him. And when he chose his last two victims; it would appear that they had both asked for total discretion, for personal reasons they wanted to be seen off the record. We believe he even used a different name with them. He groomed them carefully, so that in the end they trusted him implicitly.'

'And then he killed them.' Lisa looked up angrily. 'How could he do that? He was a doctor! What happened to *First, do no harm*?'

Jackman bit at his bottom lip. 'Marie assures me that he *was* a good doctor once, Lisa. He was one of the best. He helped a lot of damaged people to get their lives back.' He told her about the way that a murderer had attacked Preston in the interview room.

'The mind has incredible strength, but on the other hand, it is as fragile as a butterfly wing.' Lisa stretched. 'I suppose if you work in that sort of environment and something happens to you, well, none of us know how it could affect us or what we are capable of, do we?' She rubbed gently at her injured shoulder. 'And talking of mental breakdowns, when I saw Daniel with Skye just before he ran away, I knew he was very ill. I went home and looked up all I could about fugues. For a long time there, that poor boy must have been in hell.'

'Apparently,' Jackman indicated the report lying on his desk, 'his life would have been chaos. At some points, reality would have had no meaning at all, then at others, he would seem to be his normal self.' He looked up at Lisa. 'And in his *other state*, he self-harmed. Not deep razor slashes or anything serious, except of course the last time. Generally it was just some sort of bloodletting. There were several sets of clothes found hidden in his cellar, all had his own blood on them, some quite old.'

'Wouldn't he have realised that he was doing it, when he was himself again?' asked Lisa.'

'Daniel says he noticed the wounds, but had no idea how he had got them. And it added to his anxiety about the gaps in his memory. Strangely, he was able to look and behave in an unremarkable manner, even when his mind was confused and distressed. It's the nature of the beast. But he is finally getting the best treatment, and now he knows that all of these horrible episodes were caused by the damage from the carbon monoxide, he has answers based on fact, so he can move forward.'

'As I hope we all can, Inspector.' Lisa stood up. 'And thank you again for your discretion regarding Skye. I've never believed in hiding the truth when it comes to parentage, and poor Daniel's case would bear testament to that, but just sometimes things are best left undisturbed. If Skye ever felt the need to trace her birth mother, then that would be different, but as things are . . .'

'Ignorance is bliss.'

Lisa nodded, 'Indeed, Inspector Jackman, indeed.'

THE END

ALSO BY JOY ELLIS

JACKMAN & EVANS
Book 1: *The Murderer's Son*
Book 2: *Their Lost Daughters*
Book 3: *The Fourth Friend*
Book 4: *The Guilty Ones*
Book 5: *The Stolen Boys*

NIKKI GALENA SERIES
Book 1: *Crime on the Fens*
Book 2: *Shadow over the Fens*
Book 3: *Hunted on the Fens*
Book 4: *Killer on the Fens*
Book 5: *Stalker on the Fens*
Book 6: *Captive on the Fens*
Book 7: *Buried on the Fens*
Book 8: *Thieves on the Fens*
Book 9: *Fire on the Fens*
Book 10: *Darkness on the Fens*

DETECTIVE MATT BALLARD
Book 1: *Beware the Past*
Book 2: *Five Bloody Hearts*

STANDALONES
Beware the Past

Join our mailing list to be the first to hear about
Joy Ellis's next mystery, coming soon!

www.joffebooks.com

Thank you for reading this book. If you enjoyed it
please leave feedback on Amazon or Goodreads, and if
there is anything we missed or you have a question about
then please get in touch. The author and publishing team
appreciate your feedback and time reading this book.